Ali Harris is a magazine journalist and has written for publications such as *Red, ELLE, Stylist, Cosmopolitan* and *Company* and was deputy features editor at *Glamour* before leaving to write books and have babies. She lives in Cambridge with her husband and their three children.

Also by the author

Miracle on Regent Street
Written in the Stars

A Vintage Christmas
(eBook short story)

First published in Great Britain by Simon & Schuster UK Ltd, 2012
A CBS COMPANY
This paperback edition, 2018

13 5 7 9 10 8 6 4 2

Simon & Schuster UK Ltd
1st Floor
222 Gray's Inn Road
London WC1X 8HB

www.simonandschuster.co.uk

Simon & Schuster Australia, Sydney
Simon & Schuster India, New Delhi

A CIP catalogue record for this book
is available from the British Library

ISBN 978-1-4711-7859-7
eBook 978-0-85720-294-9

Typeset by M Rules
Printed and bound by CPI Group (UK) Ltd, Croydon, CR0 4YY

Simon & Schuster UK Ltd are committed to sourcing paper
that is made from wood grown in sustainable forests and supports the Forest
Stewardship Council, the leading international forest certification organisation.
Our books displaying the FSC logo are printed on FSC certified paper.

The First Last Kiss

ALI HARRIS

**SIMON &
SCHUSTER**

London · New York · Sydney · Toronto · New Delhi

A CBS COMPANY

Give me a thousand kisses, then a hundred.
Then, another thousand, and a second hundred.
Then, yet another thousand, and a hundred.
Then, when we have counted up many thousands,
Let us shake the abacus, so that no one may know the number,
And become jealous when they see
How many kisses we have shared.

Catullus 5

To anyone who has ever loved, lost and loved again

There's no sweeter way to be woken than with a kiss. Sadly this morning – the last I'll spend in this house – I'm woken not by the soft graze of a lover's lips against mine, but by the prickly claws of the fat, purring cat lying on my chest.

'Morning Harry,' I murmur, tickling him under his chin and pondering that this morning, there is no man with a six-pack between my sheets, just the two-pack of Jammie Dodgers I munched my way through last night. 'It's the big day today, fella,' I say. Harry looks startled and licks his paws frantically. He has been anxious with all the comings and goings of the last few days.

'Aww, don't be silly, I'm not going anywhere without you and your sister.' I kiss him on the nose and lift him off the mattress and swing my legs onto the floor full of boxes. Once again, I can't help but think how quickly a life can be packed up. It makes everything feel so transitory. All this stuff we place so much importance on to make us feel at home, surrounding ourselves with comforting memory-triggers when really, most stuff is disposable. Actually, having a clear-out has been surprisingly cathartic.

I take a deep breath and try to work out what I should do first. It's too cold to have a shower as the heating hasn't come on yet. And besides, I'm gagging for a cuppa. I've some final bits of packing to do before the removal van arrives. Part of me is resentful that I'm doing this alone but I also know that today has to go like clockwork which, as any woman knows, means doing it myself. I balk a little and then smile as I realize just how much I sound like my mother. My teenage self would be *horrified*.

Outside, everything is shrouded in a sea of subterranean black. I shiver and throw my dressing gown on over my T-shirt and leggings, slip into my Ugg boots, blanching at the sight in the

full-length mirror that's propped up against a wall, waiting to be
bubble-wrapped. What a mess. My eyes are puffy and swollen, my
skin is grey and sallow with lack of sleep and to top it all my face
has broken out in some sort of rash.

I pause in the doorway and then turn back and extract the DVD
which I was watching last night from the TV in the corner of my
bedroom. I slip it under my arm, grab the half-eaten packet of
biscuits and go downstairs. I found the DVD yesterday afternoon
on top of an open box marked 'storage' and couldn't resist. I've
seen it plenty of times before, but not for a long time. It was 'our
film'. And everyone knows that you shouldn't open up old wounds
at times like this.

I pace up and down the lounge clutching my mug of tea, trying
not to look at the TV flickering in the lounge. It's paused on the
opening credits and I'm desperately fighting the urge to press play.
I've got too much to do to be distracted.

I clearly remember moving into this house. It feels like yesterday
and a lifetime ago. It was meant to be a Forever House (damn you,
Kirstie Allsopp, for giving me such high expectations), somewhere
to plant roots. Tucked away on a cute little street, just off the
bustling Broadway in Leigh-on-Sea with its eclectic little shops
and cafés, it had gorgeous views of the sea from the balcony just
off the master bedroom. But the house itself had been terribly
neglected. It was the definition of 'a project'; perfect for a young
married couple – and one I was eager to take on. It had always been
our dream to live somewhere like this and I loved every moment
spent making it feel like home, painting the bedroom duck-egg
blue and putting over the fireplace the canvas of a photo I took of
pebbles on Leigh beach. Weeks went by ripping up carpets, sand-
ing and varnishing the floorboards, exposing the original fireplaces,
painting the walls bright, life-affirming colours while Take That
blared loudly on the iPod to keep me company. And then, every
day at dusk, no matter what the weather was like, I'd go for a walk

with him, down to The Green that overlooked the sea and we'd sit on our bench and mull over the day we'd spent apart. We'd talk about the past and dream about the future. It was the happiest I felt every single day.

I walk over to the DVD player. *Don't go there again, Molly*, my 'sensible voice' says. Just one more time won't hurt. I clutch my cup of tea tightly as I press play. This is the very last time I'm going to watch it. Then I'll hide it back behind all the other soppy romcoms that occupy the shelves of my lounge. Or at least used to. I look at the now bare room that's devoid of all the personal touches – the vast array of photos, the abundance of scatter cushions and candles, the cat basket, the knick-knacks and memories that have made it home for so long – then I look back at the TV.

The sound is low but the rousing chords of the film's opening song perforate the silence. I press the volume button and rest the remote on the arm of the sofa. I close my eyes as the goosebump-inducing lyrics of the soaring chorus swell out into the room. It always gives me an overwhelming urge to bawl like a baby. There was a time when I played this song continuously as I threw my heart and soul into making this house a home. If I wasn't doing DIY, I was cooking delicious feasts in this kitchen like a proper wife, then eating it laid out in front of this film, with him jokingly chastising me for turning into such a softie.

I roll my eyes heavenward and swipe my hand across my face. This film always does this to me, even though I know every scene off by heart. I grab a tissue from the box that's next to me and blow noisily into it. I glance back to the TV screen as the handsome young heart throb gazes longingly at the object of his affection. I pick up the remote control and press pause just as their lips clumsily meet for the first time. Then I reach for another biscuit and pop it like a pill, hoping it will soothe my urge to sob.

Stop being silly, Molly, I tell myself sternly. *It's only a film. You're just emotional at the moment; moving is one of the most stressful things you can do. It's right up there with divorce and having a baby.*

The biscuit is suddenly sandpaper in my mouth and I have to force it past the lump in my throat, coughing with the exertion. I instantly imagine myself being found by a neighbour, slumped on the settee, eyeballs rolling towards the ceiling, one hand clasped around my throat with the other clutching the remaining half of the biscuit. Raspberry jam would be smothered tellingly around my gaping mouth, the bloody evidence of my demise.

'Such a tragedy,' my neighbours would say. 'The poor girl died of a broken heart . . . -shaped biscuit.'

I reach back into the packet and stuff another biscuit into my mouth, reassured by the knowledge that it doesn't matter if I get fat anyway. It's not like I'm a teenager, or can have my heart shattered any more than it has been. When you've been through what I have, gambled everything on love – and lost – you're never the same again. Not really.

I press play again and settle back to try and watch the rest of the film but all I can see in my mind's eye is Ryan Cooper.

My first love – and the one I hoped would also be my last.

The Kiss To End All Kisses

There's supposed to be 'a moment' that every girl dreams about her whole life. You know the one; some guy on bended knee offering you his heart. Well, I was never that kind of girl. But even if I had been, the moment turned out to be better than I could have ever imagined ...

'I can't believe we're actually here!' I clap my hands together in excitement and press my face against the window as I take in the city I have been desperate to see for so long lit up like a circuit board in the darkness. I gasp as we leave the Brooklyn–Queens Expressway and crawl across the Brooklyn Bridge. Manhattan rises up before us in our yellow cab; the buildings are inconceivably tall and shiny, I feel like we're looking at them in a hall of mirrors at the funfair. The breathtaking skyscrapers are silhouetted against the navy night sky, like bejewelled teeth in a yawning mouth. Ryan leans over and kisses me on the shoulder then slips his arm around me and I sigh contentedly.

'It's so *cool,* just like in the movies!' Ryan says wondrously, to himself more than to me. I was worried that this holiday we've been planning since we got back together wouldn't be his thing. He's more of a sun, sea and sand kind of guy.

'I'm so glad I'm seeing this city with you,' I say quietly.

Ryan grins as he looks at me, his tanned, handsome face a picture of shock. 'What's this? Has my cynical girlfriend finally become a romantic? Has Harry *finally* become Sally?'

'So what if I have, Cooper?' I say, folding my arms defiantly, jumping as the cars around us begin to honk their horns and our taxi driver yells out the window. I snuggle back into his shoulder. 'What are you going to do about it?'

He laughs. 'You'll see, Molly Carter!' he whispers, threading his arm around me. 'You'll see . . .'

I purse my lips and narrow my eyes at him. What he doesn't know is that I'm also using the chance to study him. I'm drinking in his Balearic blue eyes and palm-frond lashes, the sand-dune slopes of his top lip surrounded by grainy golden stubble smattered over his jaw to match his blond, beachy hair. I've been doing a lot of this over the last six months. I'm still amazed that we got back together after all that happened. But Ryan and I made a promise to start afresh, to treat this as the beginning of a new relationship.

I pull him towards me for a kiss before turning back to look out the window. The bridge has carried us over the Hudson River and lowered us gently into the jaws of the city. For a moment I gaze around at the blur of shimmering buildings, the lights, the line of bright yellow cabs just like ours, and feel like I'm in a futuristic pop video stuck on fast forward. I hold my camera up to my eyes to see this incredible city the best way I know how – through my viewfinder – and that's how I stay, with Ryan's arm thrown over my shoulder as the taxi speeds us further into the glistening, twinkling metropolis.

'Smile!' I shout the following morning. Ryan is standing in front of the Staten Island Ferry sign in the glorious early morning sunlight, a cheesy grin on his face and his index fingers pointing down at his crotch where, over his jeans, he's modelling a G-string that has the Statue of Liberty emblazoned on the front. We have made it our mission to 'do' as many famous sights as we can and have set each other the challenge to pick up the tackiest souvenir along the way. Knowing how competitive Ryan is, he's bound to win. But I have determination and imagination on my side. The best photo wins a prize. Ryan has said if he wins I have to take him to see the New York Giants, and if I win he has to come on the *Sex and the City* tour with me. I reckon he's got the best deal as, to be honest, he'll probably enjoy that, too.

I burst out laughing as Ryan adds a foam Statue of Liberty hat to his ensemble, his arm raised in the air just like New York's First Lady as a bunch of Japanese tourists walk by, recording everything they see. Without a flicker of embarrassment he poses for them as if he's modelling designer clothes. If only his secondary school students could see him now. Cool Mr Cooper the PE teacher, not looking so cool now!

I pull the camera away from my face and sidle up to him as we amble onto the moored ferry. We quickly make our way out to the deck.

'You know,' I whisper, kissing him on the neck and glancing up at his ridiculous outfit, 'I've never wanted you more, Ryan Cooper!'

He pulls me into his arms, pops a matching Statue of Liberty hat on my head and tilts me back, kissing me showily on the lips so that a big group of Japanese tourists gather to take more photos. I blush and hide my face (I've never been comfortable with PDAs) but Ryan lifts me back up again and waves at the tourists who bow to him and politely clap their hands.

Ryan pings his thong and grins down at me. 'Do you admit defeat then?' he asks. Then he pulls a matching foam torch out of his combat trousers and holds it aloft like Lady Liberty herself.

I fold my arms. 'Ohhh, so *that's* what was pressing up against me,' I say. 'For a moment I thought I was in luck ...'

'Admit I've already won the challenge!' he grins triumphantly, brandishing the phallic-looking torch.

'Never!' I reply. 'Not if Carrie Bradshaw's entire Manolo collection depended on it!'

He laughs. 'So says the girl who a few years ago wouldn't be seen dead in anything other than Converse!'

'Hey, I still love my Converse,' I say, looking down at the red ones currently adorning my feet. 'And besides, a girl can change, can't she?'

'She certainly can ... *Harry*,' Ryan laughs.

'I mean who'd have thought it of the spiky 15-year-old girl with the chip on her shoulder, who wanted to rebel against everything and everyone and who thought love was for "Losers, baby",' he says, his fingers making inverted commas. 'Who would have thought she'd become this loving, romantic woman.' He pauses and grins. '*My* woman.' Then he pulls me into his arms. 'I'm just glad my high-risk gamble *finally* paid off!'

I narrow my eyes dangerously. 'Are you implying that I'm *old*?'

He whistles through his teeth and shakes his head. 'Oh no, I'd never do that, I mean you're only twenty-six in a couple of days, although, you *are* now officially closer to thirty than twenty!' He pauses and smiles so that his blue eyes shine. 'And it also means I've been in love with you for over ten years.'

'You weren't in love with me when I was fifteen!' I exclaim, nestling into his arms as the wind whistles through my hair and blows it across his face. I gaze out at the glistening Hudson as I think back to my awkward, mixed-up teen self who could count her friends on one finger and her social skills on . . . none. I was morose, awkward, and so desperate to be different – but only so that I'd be accepted; a contradiction that despite my keen photographic eye, I hadn't been astute enough to recognize.

He strokes my hair off my face. 'I thought you were the most beautiful girl in the world . . .'

'You'd just been listening to too much Prince,' I say with a dismissive smile.

'So', he adds, touching me on my nose, 'why did I tell my mum after our first date that I'd met the future Mrs Cooper . . .'

'You didn't!' I laugh, expecting him to join me, but his expression is serious. 'What did Jackie say?'

'She said if I had, then I should make sure nothing messes it up.'

We lock eyes, the intensity of our gazes an acknowledgement of our recent split and then we smile. We've come a long way since then. I snuggle further into his arms, feeling like there could literally be no better place in the world than here.

What happened to not being bound by the constraints of a relationship? my teenage self shouts in my head, the one that caused my break-up with Ryan in the first place. I think of the list I had pinned to my wall at uni that used to remind me why I'd vowed to steer clear of serious relationships.

Reasons I don't want a serious boyfriend
1. They hold you back
2. Grind you down
3. Then mess with your head

It was a short but succinct list. And yes, I was immature, angry and adamant that no one would ever hurt me again like Ryan Cooper had.

But things change, people change – as do perceptions of people, and now I answer in a language that I hope my teenage self will understand (even if I know it'll make her roll her eyes and stick her fingers down her throat).

Molly Carter + Ryan Cooper = 4ever.

Two hours later we're standing at the front of a queue that snakes around the most famous, filmed and photographed building in the world – the A-list of architecture, The Empire State Building. I squeeze Ryan's hand and he grins down at me as he offers me his hot dog. I take a big bite and he kisses the mustard off the corner of my lips. I laugh. It's like I'm Elizabeth Perkins in *Big* being shown by Tom Hanks just how much fun life can be if only you take it less seriously.

The last few days have been the best, not just of our relationship, but of my entire life. We've floated round the city feeling like we're in our very own romantic movie. '*An Affair to Remember*?' I suggested to Ryan yesterday. But he hadn't seen it. I should know by now that Ryan refuses to watch or listen to anything that was made before he was born – especially not black-and-white movies. I tried describing the story to him, but when I got to the bit where Deborah Kerr gets

knocked down by a taxi on the way to meet Cary Grant at the top
of The Empire State Building, he just said, 'It doesn't sound very
romantic to me, babe!' and added, 'If we were a film I reckon we'd
be more *13 Going on 30*.' He'd grinned and taken my hand as we'd
walked through Times Square. 'After all, *you* were an awkward,
totally uncool teenager when I first set eyes on you and now you're
basically Jennifer Garner! Viva magazine's beautiful editor!'

'Picture editor,' I'd laughingly corrected.

Incredibly, in just four days here we've ticked nearly everything
off my Things To Do In New York List:

- Take the Staten Island Ferry to the Statue of Liberty
- Horse and carriage ride around Central Park
- Go up the Empire State
- Eat cupcakes from Magnolia Bakery
- Spend an afternoon at MoMA
- Go to the Guggenheim
- Go to the Met
- Ice-skate at the Wolfman rink in Central Park
- Carnegie Hall
- Shop (a lot)
- See a show on Broadway
- Have ice-cream floats at Serendipity 3
- Go to Strawberry Fields

More importantly we've fallen in love even more; not just with this
city, but with each other. I feel like we're at the start of a brand-
new relationship. Which is all I could ever have hoped for, after
what happened.

'Come on!' I say, dragging Ryan into the lift and excitedly clapping my hands as it soars ever upwards. 'I can't wait to get to the top!'

'How's this, Cooper?' I yell minutes later, the wind lifting my voice and carrying it over the city's skyscrapers as I pose on the observation deck.

Ryan is standing opposite me, camera aloft, wearing a New York Yankees cap. He looks out from behind the viewfinder and smiles slowly. 'Beautiful. The best thing I've seen in New York.'

'I told you The Empire State would be amazing!' I exclaim.

'I mean *you*, Moll,' he calls back. I pout suggestively to cover my smile as Ryan takes photo after photo before someone approaches him and asks him if we'd like one together. He hands them the camera, strides over to me, turns, hitches me up onto his back and I wrap my knees around his waist, resting my cheek on his neck and laughing. I close my eyes for a second. They say you feel on top of the world up here, that you couldn't feel any higher. And it's true.

'I can't believe it's our last day,' I say sadly as we stroll out of our hotel onto the tree-lined, shop-filled 5th Avenue. The pavement is packed with pedestrians, the road a constant stream of cars and honking yellow taxis. The seemingly endless stretch of limestone-fronted buildings are splashed with exuberant splodges of colour from the billboards, theatre posters and the fluttering flags that accessorize this, the most famous shopping street in the world. And most of the shops are so famous they deserve not just flags, but exclamation marks and their own fanfares too – Tiffany & Co! Bloomingdales! Harry Winston! Louis Vuitton! Pucci! Prada!

And then behind it all, the towering Empire State Building lies like a beautiful discarded stiletto, heel stretched skyward as if to remind its relentless stream of visitors that *it* is the star of the city.

We walk slowly hand in hand towards Central Park and I glance at Ryan strolling along in just an Abercrombie T-shirt, denim jacket and a body warmer. I slip my gloved hand into his and rearrange my scarf. It's unseasonably mild for November but I'm still wrapped up like a mummy compared to Ryan. He's too active to ever really feel the cold.

'And your birthday – you haven't had your present yet ...' Ryan points out.

'I've already had the best birthday ever here with you,' I say, and it's true. Historically I've never liked birthdays; even as a kid I hated the pressure that came with throwing a party: what to wear, who to invite, who would come (if anyone). As a result I've always been low-key about them – especially milestone ones. My 21st passed with a night at the Student Union with Mia and Casey, my 25th was spent at The Crooked Billet in Leigh-on-Sea with Ryan and both our families. But this ... this has been awesome.

'It's been brilliant!' Ryan agrees as we stroll along. 'I want us to do much more of this you know, Moll, see the world, go to new places ... I want us to do it all. Together.'

I squeeze Ryan's hand tightly now and sigh with contentment as I see we're nearly at Central Park. His excitement has been infectious. Ryan makes everything fun. He always has. He never takes life too seriously and finds pleasure in the simple things. In the past I found this frustrating but now it's the thing I admire the most about him. Ever since I started working in magazines, I started needing 'validated fun'. You know, the hot new bar, the best new bag, the most stylish city, hotel, restaurant ... But sometimes this relentless pursuit of the 'new' and 'cool' just leaves me feeling deeply unsatisfied. That's partly what caused our relationship problems before; my constant desire for something more. But I've learned my lesson, I hope. On this trip I've loved discovering the city together, his way. A tucked-away little café we happened across here, a laid-back stroll and a meal at a low-key, romantic Italian in Greenwich Village there.

I chuckle as I recall our sightseeing yesterday. I took Ryan for lunch at Katz's, the deli that featured in *When Harry Met Sally*.

'No way,' he'd said when I'd dared him to re-enact Sally's fake orgasm. '*You* do it, you're the rebel girl.' His voice had taken on a mocking tone, instantly taking me back to our teen roles over a decade ago; him as the town heart-throb, me as the awkward, clichéd social leper. God, I'd hated that time of my life. I wish my teen self could see me now.

I'd folded my arms. 'But I'm *Harry*,' I smirk. 'You've always said so. Which means I couldn't *possibly* swap roles now. Come on, Ry, I'm waiting, you're not *embarrassed*, are you? Worried you'll fail the challenge?' I smile, knowing Ryan won't be able to ignore any sort of dare.

And, just as I knew he would, he'd obliged, his ever-present tan turning a curious salmon colour. How I howled with laughter as Ryan reached his 'climax' and then took a massive bite of his pastrami sandwich, the blush still flushing his cheeks.

'Ry, I will remember that forever!' I laughed as I leaned over and kissed him, then made a face. 'Eurgh, gherkin breath!'

Ryan slows down to a brisk stride as we approach Central Park from the East Side and stroll down the 79th Transverse past the Conservatory Pond and to the Bethesda Fountain.

'It's pretty beautiful isn't it, Moll?' Ryan says quietly, squeezing my gloved hand as we gaze around at the majestic fountain with its centrepiece sculpture, *The Angel of the Waters*. It feels like discovering the prize at the centre of a pass the parcel game after unwrapping layer upon layer of endless little gifts to get to it; the shimmering boat-filled blue lake with row boats and the occasional gondola drifting by, all wrapped generously in a layer of evergreen trees surrounded by the shiny, glittering decorative finish that is the skyscrapers.

Walkers, joggers, snap-happy tourists, cyclists, mums pushing prams, dog walkers, office workers and college students surround us, yet the park doesn't feel crowded at all. It feels as if we're all plugged into the park's very own iPod, our laughter and chatter combine and blends with the breeze, the constant hum of traffic and whir of passing bicycles, to make the perfect soundtrack for the city.

I nod at Ryan because I am too happy to speak. This is the ultimate New York romantic experience. I've seen this park so many times with Ryan, in the romcoms which he has no embarrassment about loving and the *Sex and the City* episodes I adore. We've witnessed some of the greatest fictional romantic moments in history take place. Billy Crystal and Meg Ryan realizing they were more than just good friends in *When Harry Met Sally*, Clooney and Pfeiffer splashing through puddles with their kids in *One Fine Day*, and Cusack and Beckinsale's skating tryst on the Wolfman's rink in *Serendipity*. And now *we're* here. In real life. At last.

I sigh with delight and lift my camera up as I fire off some shots of the wintry sun filtering through the curtain of trees, then I flick the angle and manage to catch a shot of Ryan backlit by it. The way the light falls on his blond hair makes him look positively angelic. I pull him towards me and hold the camera out in front of us for another shot, our cheeks pressed together. By lowering the camera to my waist and tilting the lens up I think I can just get us as well as the glistening backdrop of the skyscrapers peering over the trees. I'm reminded suddenly of what my dad has always said about the John Constable painting of Hadleigh Castle hanging on the wall back home in Leigh-on-Sea. 'It's a man-made structure deferring to the power of nature.' Then I think of Ryan and me and how I took something strong that had been built carefully over time and I nearly destroyed it too. And then I remember how Ryan tried to bring me to New York before...

A rogue tear falls and I swipe it away. Ryan and I have sworn to not bring all that up again.

'I'm so sorry, Ryan ...' I sob, pulling him into a hug.

'What?' Ryan sounds confused, then concerned. 'Hey, why are you crying?'

'I'm sorry, it's just that I was thinking about how perfect this is and that I'll be sorry forever for what I did . . .' I'm properly crying now and Ryan takes me in his arms and holds me.

'Hey, hey, hey,' he murmurs. 'Please don't cry, Molly. I thought we agreed all of that stuff is in the past?'

'I–I know,' I sniff into his shoulder, 'but I can't help . . .'

He pulls away and gazes at me, a smile hovering over his lips. 'Our relationship is better and stronger than ever, Molly, you know that. We needed to break up to appreciate how much we want to be together. I'm *glad* it happened. I am, honest! Please stop looking back. I want this trip, this moment, to be about our future. And it won't be if you keep beating yourself up like this. We were both at fault and we didn't know what we had till it was gone. I'm just glad we realized in time.'

We begin to walk again and Ryan slips his arm around my shoulders, reassuring me how much he loves me, making me smile and then laugh. We've been walking for a few minutes when he pulls me towards him and kisses me.

'There!' he exclaims. 'That's better. Now, I don't know about you, but I can't possibly walk another step without a coffee. I saw a stand over there . . . will you be OK for a minute while I go and get us some? Latte, yeah?'

I nod and sniff and lift up my camera to indicate that I can keep myself busy.

He hands me his rucksack and blows me a kiss as he walks backwards then breaks into a run, streaking across the park like some kind of action hero.

I turn around, snapping furiously as I try to capture the colour and beauty of this pretty pocket of the park. The sun is disappearing behind the silhouetted treetops, creating jewel tones of coral, amber and ruby in the sky. I focus my lens on a sign to

my left and suddenly realize that I'm standing at the entrance
of Strawberry Fields. I shiver, as much with the sense of musical
history as the wintry chill. I glance down and notice the 'Imagine'
mural on the ground ahead, laid in honour of John Lennon after
he was shot in 1980. I walk up to it and gaze at it. My dad would
love to see this. He loves The Beatles.

I hate that I've tainted a single moment of this perfect trip with
bad memories from the past. I want to put it right, focus on today –
that should be my motto. Just focus on how good life is right now.
Suddenly I have an idea. I put down the rucksack and, giggling to
myself, I quickly pull out all the ridiculous novelty souvenir items
we've collected over the past couple of days and put them on one
by one.

I feel pretty silly standing here alone like this, but it'll be worth it
for the look on his face when he appears with those coffees. I adjust
the foam Statue of Liberty crown and wave at some passers-by who
are looking at me out of curiosity. I can't believe I'm the strangest
thing they've seen in this city. I look around. Ryan's been gone for
ages. Where the hell is he?

I busy myself taking photographs of the scenery surrounding
me, finally pointing my camera down and photograph the mural
for dad. My red Converse are just poking into the picture and I'm
still looking down when I hear Ryan's voice.

'Close your eyes, Molly.' His breath warms my forehead as his
hand suddenly covers my eyes. I can hear the amusement in his
voice. 'Nice to see you've dressed up for the occasion.'

'What occ—' he puts his finger across my lips to silence me.
'Ryan?' I whisper through his finger. 'Have you got my latte?'

'No, Molly.'

'Hey!' I protest, opening my eyes momentarily. 'I've been waiting ages!'

'I said, close your eyes,' Ryan repeats firmly.

'I don't know why you're being so bossy, Cooper ...'

'While you're at it, can you please close your mouth too?' The restrained laughter is evident in his voice.

'Charming!' My eyes ping open.

'Are you ever going to do anything I say?' he asks, clearly exasperated now.

'Probably not,' I laugh and he looks pleadingly at me. Reluctantly I squint my eyes shut.

I sigh as I'm cloaked in darkness. 'Now what?'

'Well,' he says, the warmth on my neck disappearing and his voice sounding more distant. 'I want you to open your eyes and look down at your feet.'

I do what he says and see the mosaic again. *Imagine.* It strikes me what a beautiful word it is, full of hope, possibility and belief.

'Now,' he says, his voice sounding strange. 'Imagine for a moment that we're here alone. Imagine that it is just you and me, like this. There's no one else here. Just you, me, the earth, the sky and the sun, stretching out before us endlessly . . .'

'Sounds lovely,' I sigh, opening my eyes briefly. He's not there. I go to turn around. 'Now what?' I close my eyes again and I hear music start playing, the opening chords of a song. I start humming along.

'Now imagine that I am right beside you . . .'

I stop humming. 'But you're not, you're behind me . . .'

'. . . all the time,' he continues determinedly. 'Beside you all the time. From now on. Always.'

I open my mouth and close it again. 'That sounds nice,' I say quietly, trying to block out the voice in my head that's saying, *Is he about to do what you think he's going to do? Oh my God! He is! He is!*

It's then that I realize the song I've been humming along to is John Lennon's 'Imagine'. It is playing somewhere nearby. And not on an iPod, it sounds like a . . . like a . . . string quartet. I open my eyes but I don't turn around. A small crowd of people have gathered and are all looking at me, smiling. Some of them have cameras. I blink and swallow. I want to turn around, I desperately want to, but something tells me to wait for Ryan's next instruction.

'Now,' Ryan says softly, 'imagine that I am behind you, telling you, Molly Carter, that I love you, that I always have and always will, and that right here, right in the heart of Central Park, I want to ask you if you'll accept *my* heart, look after it forever and let me take care of yours. You can turn around now . . .'

I put my hand over my mouth as the tears stream down my face, for once my camera is forgotten as I spin around to see the smiling faces of the string quartet, but still no Ryan.

'I'm down here,' he laughs, and he's there, on bended knee, his arm stretched out and one hand cupping a velvet box, the other hand hovering over the closed lid.

'No!' I gasp.

He laughs. 'I'll be honest, that's not quite the reaction I was after—'

'No! I mean! No, look at me – I look ridiculous! How could you do this!' I kneel down and pummel him in the chest, openly sobbing now.

'I think you look gorgeous,' Ryan laughs, pinging the Statue of Liberty G-string.

'This is not how I planned to look at such a big moment!' I wail.

'You can't control everything, Molly,' Ryan smiles, 'sometimes you have to just roll with it . . .'

I look at him and there is a look of quiet determination that I recognize from when he is battling a wave, shooting a goal or when he's gripping on to the sail of a boat and guiding it back to shore.

'Molly Carter,' he says, slowly, 'will you marry me?' He opens the box and there is a beautiful ring, a cluster of small diamonds on a gold band glittering like a constellation of stars.

'Yes! Yes!' interrupting him as I laugh through my tears. I swipe away my tears quickly and sink to my knees and I grasp Ryan's face and he cups mine and we kiss and there is laughter and tears and it feels familiar but different. So, so different.

Because this is the kiss to end all kisses. It's the kiss that I didn't even know I was waiting for. I close my eyes again and press record in my head, to internally capture the moment that Ryan Cooper puts an engagement ring on my finger. And it is the best present in the world.

The letterbox clatters and, dragging myself away from the DVD, I wander out into the hallway with the lovely original Victorian tiles and corniced ceilings, still keeping one eye on the TV. The removal men should be here soon to finish packing up the rest of the stuff. I seem to have acquired two lives' worth of it: before and after, and they didn't manage to get it all done yesterday. I smile as I think about my purposefully minimal bedroom at uni, bare of any personalization apart from my Annie Leibovitz print of John Lennon and Yoko Ono that was pinned over my bed and the film poster of *Before Sunrise* above my desk. God, I was so serious back then. My duvet was white, my wardrobe full of black clothes. Funny how people change, I think as I look around my messy abode. The thought of keeping anything tidy now brings me out in a sweat. Mind you, most things bring me out in a sweat, these days.

I bend down slowly to the Union Jack 'Welcome' doormat and make a mental note to remember to pack it. I pick up the pile of envelopes, flicking through them quickly, muttering as I do so: 'Bill, bill, notice of bill paid, bill ... doctor's appointment and ...' I pull out the card that has my name and my address written on the envelope in a small, neat print:

Molly Cooper
7 Avenue Road
Leigh-on-Sea
SS19 4BL

I furrow my brow as I study it. It's my old married name. None of my family or friends use it any more, so who ...?

I rip open the envelope and pull out a New Home card. I open it up and begin to read;

Dear Molly,
How are you? I hope you don't mind me writing like this but
I was in contact recently with a mutual acquaintance and
they mentioned you were moving away. I didn't want you to
leave without having a chance to send you my best wishes for
a happy future. I hope you remembered my advice; to choose
happiness and never live with regret. I think of you often and
hope you are all well.

Fondest wishes,
Charlie

I feel my heart contract. The name conjures up feelings and memories I'm trying to ignore today. I glance at the card again. I know it's a nice gesture but find I this contact strange after so long – and after everything that happened. It brings back memories, both good and bad.

The Kiss And Tell

It's funny how someone can come into your life unexpectedly
and instantly make you feel like you can say anything to them,
anything at all. Things you wouldn't dream of telling your
nearest and dearest. And suddenly they become an intrinsic part
of your life without you really knowing anything about them.
That's what happened with Charlie. I bared my soul in a way I'd
never done with anyone.

It feels strange pouring out my heart to another man in a bar like this. I feel like I must have 'Traitorous Wench' emblazoned on my forehead and everyone must know this handsome, attentive man isn't my boyfriend. And we've come to our local pub, for Christ sakes. What was I thinking? I'll never be able to look the barman in the eye again.

'So come on, what's going on?' Charlie says, leaning in towards me and resting his elbows on his knees. His gaze is so tender that it's all the encouragement I need to launch into a melancholy monologue.

'Sorry,' I say, apologizing for the billionth time. 'It's just sometimes I feel like I can't take it any more. I look at him and I don't know who he is, I don't know what he's thinking, or feeling. We're not communicating properly, you know? We're existing alongside each other, pretending everything's OK when it isn't. It really isn't. I know what the right thing to do is, but I don't want to be the one who says it first.' I shake my head, feeling awful for laying all this on him. 'I'm really sorry. I didn't mean to do this ...' I glance up nervously at the busy bar, full of young, Hackney hipsters. I feel old, withered, past it and I'm not even thirty. I glance back at Charlie, not only is he gorgeous, he is so interested and interesting. So caring and kind. Kind of too good to be true, really. If only there were more like him in the world. I blink at him.

'Hey, you know you can tell me anything,' Charlie says, putting his drink down and touching my hand gently. I love how his eyes never leave mine when I'm talking. I feel like no one has looked at me like this for a long time.

'I'm just waiting for him to make the first move,' I say. He studies me closely and then looks down before he speaks. I don't like it when he looks away. Nothing good is ever said when people look away from you.

'Listen, Molly, I know how hard this is for you, I do. But I have to ask this, how much more do you think you can take?'

He looks at me searchingly as he waits for my answer, and now *I* find I can't look him in the eye. I look up at the ceiling, blinking furiously to stop the tears. Then I look back at him, pleadingly. I don't want to answer, I just want him to hug me, hold me.

He must hear my thoughts. He reaches out and takes my hand. I can't help noticing how soft his hands are, not a callous on them. I look down. And he has nice nails. I love nice nails on a man. It shows he takes care of himself.

'Molly,' he says gently, 'I know you don't want to make any decision yet. If you're not ready to go, this can wait. This isn't about me, or what I think. It's about you. If you can't face doing what we've talked about, have you thought about taking a smaller step, you know, moving to your parents or something?' I nod and he squeezes my hand and I catch my breath. 'I know it feels disloyal, but we knew it would come to this ... eventually.' He stands up and lets go of my hand and I suddenly feel bereft. Then he smiles gently and I have this urge to touch him. I want to feel his strength seep into my body.

'I'm always here for you, OK?'

'I know, Charlie.' I look at him thankfully and wonder how I'd ever cope without him. I know it's wrong but I can't help myself and I lean forward and kiss him.

The wine bottles fall into the bin with a clunk and I wince; why is it that the act of pouring wine into a glass is so deliciously satisfying and melodic but the act of getting rid of it smacks of shame and discordancy? Even though I was wise enough to resist its charms at the farewell drinks last night, watching everyone else succumb definitely made me want it more. Like a man you know is bad for you – and I've sure been there before. An image of him appears in my mind suddenly, exactly as he looked the night of our work Christmas party at Soho House. That wolfish, self-satisfied smirk that said 'I will have you', his intense hooded eyes, the sexy shadow of stubble. I thought I'd disposed of him years ago – why now? I clutch the top of the black bag and the wine bottles clatter noisily into a new position. This moving business is messing with my head. I'll be glad when it's all over. I hastily tie up the bag and take it out to the back door.

Just then Sally stalks past, tail in the air – the stuck-up so-and-so. She's welcomed excitedly by Harry, who winds around my legs and purrs at her. She's looking rather bedraggled. Neither of them is happy about the move but they're dealing with it in very different ways. Sally is the errant teen, showing her displeasure by staying out all night whereas Harry's clingy, homely nature has been amplified by the upheaval. But they are united in their bewilderment of the change. I've tried telling them to trust me when I say that we're going somewhere that will be better for all of us, but I'm not sure they believe me. I understand that it's hard for them, but I keep telling them that the end of one thing can mean the beginning of something new. I just hope I'm right.

The Remorseful Kiss

Is there such a thing as a life without any regrets? I've never believed so. We spend our lives aiming for happiness and fulfilment in work, in love and with our friends and family, and yet often our energy is spent lamenting bad boyfriends, wrong career turns, fallouts with friends and opportunities missed. Or is that just me? I admit I'm naturally a glass-half-empty kind of girl, but I know regrets are a burden to happiness and I'm trying to let go of them because I've learned that it's all about choice. You can choose to turn regrets into lessons that change your future. Believe me when I say I'm really trying to do this. But the truth is, I'm failing. Because all I can think right now is: maybe I deserve it. Maybe this is my penance.

'Casey?' I wail after listening to Casey's voicemail message. I'm staggering through the streets of Soho, one of many late-night revellers who have partaken of too much 'Christmas spirit'.

'Please answer,' I moan, hiccupping with tears. 'I know you're probably at work but I need to talk to you. I really, really need to talk to you. I've done something terrible. Something ... unforgivable.' I start sobbing again and press the call-end button.

I gaze up at the Christmas lights. A saucy Santa in a Soho shop window taunts me and in the distance the chorus of 'Santa Claus Is Coming To Town' is being sung loudly by some drunken carousers.

If Santa's making a list right now, he's going to *know* that I've been naughty.

I stumble down the cobbled streets; I can't see straight, let alone walk, and all I can think about is the last four Christmases I've spent with Ryan. He's like a child when it comes to this season, an overexcited puppy who laps up every tradition: the mince pies he starts eating on November 1st, the Christmas cake, mulled wine and other seasonal bounties he dutifully makes weeks in advance, the rich, spicy smells coming from our kitchen as I do nothing more than watch *EastEnders*. Then there are the decorations that, in true Cooper style, are garish rather than glamorous.

Each year, without fail, I come home to find that he's secretly decorated our flat. Just the other day I came home to find tinsel draped over our picture frames, a blow-up Father Christmas in the corner of our lounge and fake snow sprayed all over the windows. Even the flamingo lamp, which I have been unable to dispose of since his mum gave it to us when we moved in

together, had joined in the act and was wearing a Santa hat at a
jaunty angle.

'Ahh, c'mon, Molly,' Ryan had cajoled, wrapping his arms
around me. 'Christmas isn't meant to be fashionable, it's meant
to be fun!' And I relented, as I always do because whilst I'd never
believed it possible, he and his family have finally made Christmas
enjoyable.

Things I love about Cooper Christmases

- Being at Jackie and Dave's and being thoroughly spoiled

- Watching soppy Christmas movies with Ry

- The open-door (and open-bottle) policy for the entire
  holiday

- Lying snuggled in his teenage bed when Ry gets up early
  to go for his morning run along the beach

- Christmas Eve shopping and sale shopping on Boxing
  Day with the Cooper clan (Nanny Door is a sight to
  behold in Next, her elbows are sharper than Joan Rivers'
  tongue)

- My parents coming for Christmas dinner at Jackie and
  Dave's house and being forced to join in the karaoke
  and party games. (Nanny Door is the only person who
  could follow Jackie and Dave's versions of 'Islands in
  the Stream' and their encore 'Save your Love' by Renée
  and Renato with her astonishingly brilliant rendition of
  Jay-Z's 'I got 99 problems but a bitch ain't one' – Nanny
  Door's version is 'I got 99 problems and me hips ain't
  one'

- Missing the Queen's speech

But now, this year, it's all going to be ruined. I swipe away the hot tears that are burning a path down my face. I feel like I'll never be able to look in a mirror again without seeing what I've just done to Ryan reflected in my eyes.

How the hell am I meant to face him now?

The Hollow Kiss

Can you ever truly promise to be there for someone forever? I did and I couldn't keep my word and now, years later, the same has happened to me. Is this reneged-on promise down to karma? I think it's more about learning that in life it begins and ends with you. I mean, yes we all need love and seek support from others, but we need to find it from within first. We're all stronger than we give ourselves credit for. We can cope with more than we think. Survive the worst and, somehow, still find a way to smile.

I can't handle being in the flat any more. I tiptoe around the bedroom, trying not to disturb Ryan. He is still sleeping blissfully, just as he was when I crept in last night. He has rolled onto his side, one strong, muscular arm is stretched over to my side of the bed as if reaching for me in his sleep. His hair is spread over the pillow, overnight his stubble has turned from grainy sand to strands of straw. I want to stand here all day watching him but I can't. I need to get out before he wakes. I can't face him, not yet. I need to work out what I'm going to say, what I'm going to do. I know if he wakes now, I'll want to pretend that everything's OK, I'll want to slip back under the covers, kiss away my disloyalty, make love to him, get lost in the comfort of him, of us, of the only good thing I've ever known.

I quickly scribble a note for Ryan so he knows that I've been home and – more importantly – that he knows that I'm coming back.

> Ry, I couldn't sleep so I've left for work early. I'll be home later.
> I love you.

I raise the biro from the envelope I've been scribbling on. Then I lower it again to add:

> I'm sorry.
> Molly x

I pick up my bag and I look back at our homely flat. It's like looking at a scrapbook of my life. There's the Hadleigh Castle print that my dad bought and framed for me to remind me of home when I first went to uni. I've placed it on the desk in the corner of our lounge and the print of John Lennon and Yoko hangs above it. The Philippe Starck Louis Ghost chair we got as a present to each other when we bought this place sits under the desk. Over the fireplace is the canvas print of the pebbles that I photographed when Ry and I first moved in together at Jackie and Dave's three years ago. The sofa is the white Ikea one Jackie and Dave put in the annexe for us. It's not so white any more so it has a dark-blue throw over it. I turn back to the door and smile sadly. On the back of it is an empty gold picture frame we solemnly put up the night the last episode of *Friends* aired. It was just a short few months ago but it feels like years ago now. None of it feels like it belongs to me any more. I open the door and on my exit, I trip over the Union Jack doormat (another of Jackie's touches) and stumble into the communal hallway, the door slamming shut, without any encouragement from me. It's as if it's spitting me out onto the street with disgust.

My phone rings in my bag and I glance into it, dreading that Ryan's woken up, seen my note and wants me to come back. I look at the screen before answering, the relief desperately evident in my voice.

'Molly?' says a friendly but concerned voice.

'Oh, Casey ...' I reply as a fresh flood of tears pour down my face.

'Hey, shhh, babe, Moll, it's OK! Whatever it is, it's going to be OK,' she says soothingly.

'It won't, Casey, it won't.' I sob, looking back at our front door as I descend the staircase.

'What is it? What's happened?' she asks.

'Can I come over?' I beg, suddenly needing to get away from London, from the scene of the crime. I can't go to work. Not today. I don't care how it looks. I need to be with her, see the beach, breathe in the sea air, get some space to think and work out what I'm going to do and she's the only person who can help me, the only person who knows Ryan and I well enough.

We're walking along the mile-long stretch of Southend Pier, a journey we've taken a million times. Casey is clutching my arm, just like she used to when we were teenagers. Back then it made me feel strong, needed, but now I'm feeling comforted by her presence, like she can take me back to a time when Ryan and I were still happy.

I burst into tears when she picked me up from the train station a little after 8 a.m. She was still in her pyjamas but even these were typically Casey, cute little flannel shorts which she'd teamed with leg warmers, a big pink Gap hoodie that contrasted perfectly with her olive Greek–Italian skin and granite-black hair. We drove back to her place, she made me a cup of tea and I sat on her bright-pink sofa and cried as I told her everything. Then she threw on some warmer clothes and told me we were going for a walk to blow the cobwebs away.

'You know, I've been thinking about this, babes, and I really don't think it's as bad as you think,' Casey says after a rare moment of silence that was only induced by the wind literally taking our breath away.

'You think?' I look at her doubtfully. 'Really? Do you think Ryan will forgive me?' It is a moment of fleeting hopefulness that is swept away by Casey's solemn expression and our bleak seaside-in-winter surroundings.

It's a miserable grey day. The black clouds are rolling in ominously over the estuary, menacing spectres that appear to be coming for me, for my relationship. I have always thought of Ryan like the sun; summer is the season when he's happiest as he can do everything he loves: sport, swimming, sailing, surfing. Summer is the beach; it's eating cockles and sipping wine in the garden, it's sailing out on the estuary or lying on a sun-soaked beach, just like where we had our first real kiss. In winter he seems to recede, diminish. Everything about him becomes paler, more withdrawn.

I ask Casey again. 'Do you think he'll forgive me?'

She takes my hand and looks at me with her sweeping lashes and enormous dark-brown eyes.

'No, Molly,' she says gently. 'If you tell him what happened it will be over. But what I *do* think, and I know you don't want to hear this, is maybe that isn't such a bad thing, you know?'

My stomach wrings with anguish until I feel like I can barely stand up. The pain travels up my body to my chest, squeezing until I can't breathe.

'I know this isn't what you want to hear, babe,' Casey says, 'I know you love each other but you haven't been happy for a long time. You went into that relationship so young – too young, and I know this is hard to hear because Ryan is the best guy there is. The BEST,' she finishes emphatically.

I sob into her shoulder. My body is bent awkwardly to create space between us. I want her comfort but I don't want the physical closeness it requires; it makes me feel like I haven't got this under control. I've never needed her help like this before and I want to pretend I still don't. Because the moment I let myself succumb to her sympathies, I'm accepting that I've majorly screwed up. Casey has seen Ryan and I from the start and hearing this from her has crushed any lingering hope I had that I could work this out. All I've thought about since it happened last night is Ryan. Him. Us. How happy we'd been and how much I've taken it all for granted.

Casey is still talking, but I'm not finding it as comforting as I'd hoped. If I'm honest, it feels weird being given relationship advice by her. It's usually me who is helping *her*; picking up the pieces after someone's dumped her, dealing with the infinite fallout of her infidelities (she's been the cheater, the cheated, but most often the Other Woman).

'You know, it's funny,' she says thoughtfully – which is always dangerous. Thinking *before* speaking or acting is a rarity for Casey. 'When we were teenagers you and Ryan were so different, I never thought you'd *actually* end up together ...'

I gaze back at the 'Pleasure Pier' amusements. Casey and I spent many a happy weekend here as teenagers, playing the slots, eating candyfloss and riding the attractions, but it feels depressingly bleak now.

Then she speaks again. 'I know being with a guy like Ryan helped your confidence when we were younger but you're not a kid any more, babe, maybe you two have just grown up. And apart,' she adds with a sideways glance at me.

'There was nothing wrong with my self-esteem!' I exclaim shrilly. 'I was an incredibly confident teenager!'

Casey tilts her head, somewhat patronizingly and folds her arms under her chest. She looks like a model, stood here on the windswept pier, her sleek black ponytail whipping around her face, fronds of hair sticking to her still-glossed lips. She is the best advert for Ugly Duckling to Swan I've ever seen. 'C'mon, I know you acted all tough to protect me and to stop people thinking you cared, but you were totally *desperate* to be anyone other than yourself. Not that you had it as bad as me though.' She giggles and nudges me. 'Remember those glasses and braces? And my Greek facial-hair problem? Not to mention Mum's obsession with feeding me moussaka every day! Thank GOD for Step Aerobics. And waxing! But you, Molly, you were trying so hard to be different but all you wanted was to have everything that came so easily to other girls: your own sense of style, friends, a boyfriend. You pretended that you hated everything those horrible Heathers from school stood for but I saw the way you looked at them. Even though they were such bitches to us, you wanted to be just like them really. We all did. And Ryan was the ultimate goal. I hate to say this but you changed to fit into his life, and that's when things started going wrong. You and Ryan should have just been a fling, a summer romance – then you should've gone to London, lived on your own, become a photographer, travelled, done all the things you said you were going to do . . .'

I turn away, not wanting to hear any more, but Casey turns me back to face her.

'I'm only saying all this because I care about you, Molly!' Her eyes are glittering, her grip on me pincer-tight. 'You kissed that guy from work and took it further because you're not happy. You want a way out of your relationship and, drunk or not, you went for it. I know you didn't actually *sleep* with him, but be honest – you wanted to, didn't you? And isn't that almost the same? Don't look at me like that, I'm just trying to stop you from kidding yourself any longer. Don't waste any more years with the wrong person just because it feels safe. There's someone out there who is perfect for you in the way that Ryan will never be . . . and someone for Ryan too. Why don't you give yourself – and him – the chance to find out?'

I look away, far out to sea. I want to block out her words, stick my fingers in my ears and sing 'La la la' like I used to do when my mum was trying to tell me something I didn't want to hear. I try to pull away from Casey, but I can't because she's clinging so tightly onto my arms that she's pinching me. But it's her words that are hurting me the most because I know they're true. I look up into the sky just as the rain that has been threatening to fall is released in a torrent by the angry black clouds.

'I need to go home,' I say, staggering back from her. 'I have to talk to Ryan.'

'Molly!' she calls and looks at me with such desperate concern that I step back towards her and kiss her, a quick brush on her wind-whipped cheek, an acknowledgement that even though she hasn't made me feel better, she has helped. But it's a hollow kiss, because it is how I feel: empty inside. I know that I've got to tell Ryan what I've done and I also know that telling him will spell the end of our relationship.

Can't Kiss It Better

'A kiss is a lovely trick designed by nature to stop speech when words become superfluous.' That's what Ingrid Bergman once said and it's true. We kiss to say hello, to stave off silences, to show how much we've missed someone, to show we're glad to be with them. We kiss to stop arguments or to interrupt a conversation we no longer want to have. We also use kisses when we want to pretend that everything is all right. I've been doing a lot of that lately. But it turns out that some things just can't be kissed better.

I open our front door and am immediately engulfed by the warmth and smell of sweet chestnut and Ryan's cinnamon-infused mulled wine spreading through the flat. The familiar sounds of pots and pans being crashed around accompanied by Ryan crooning along with East 17 to 'Stay Another Day'. I freeze by the door and have to stop myself from walking out again.

I walk into our lounge and then I see the lavishly decorated room with the gaudy Christmas tree and the ornaments that seem to have blame etched on their cheaply painted faces. Even the glittering baubles on our tree are doing their best to reflect my shame back at me.

'Molly?' Ryan calls from the kitchen. 'Just a minute! I'll be right out!'

I hold my breath and stand with my head bowed waiting for him to enter the room. I know he'll instantly know what I've done. He'll see it written all over my face.

But instead he walks in grinning cheerfully, wearing a hoodie I bought him last Christmas. He looks as happy as I've ever known him and when he envelops me in an enormous hug, I clasp on to him, never wanting him to let me go. But then I stiffen and shrink away, knowing that what I'm doing is selfish, that I'm deceiving him all over again, making him think that everything is all right when it's not.

Ryan leans back and looks at me, his eyes crinkling with concern. He strokes my cheek. 'Molly, about last night, the way I was on the phone . . . I'm so sorr—'

'Don't, Ryan,' I interrupt, not wanting him to use the words on me that only he deserves. 'Please, don't.' I begin to cry and slump down on the floor. 'I don't want to do this, Ry,' I look up at him pleadingly. 'You have to believe me. But . . .'

Ryan slumps down too, staring at me in confusion. 'What's going on, Molly? It was just a silly argument, but I know I went too far, you had every right to go out with your colleagues after your Christmas lunch. I should have called you today, but I wanted to surprise you, make it up to you. I've cooked you a meal! We're having butternut squash soup followed by roast chestnut and pancetta risotto with a salad of rocket, parmesan shavings and pine nuts, and to finish ... Shit, please stop crying, Moll, you're freaking me out. I know I've made promises that I haven't kept and that's why—'

'Ry ...'

'No, let me finish!' he says slowly and deliberately.

I look up at him desperately, silently begging him to stop talking. He rubs his head wearily. 'I know what a routine our life has turned into. I know I've been stressed and tired and I've taken it out on you. I know I've been selfish. I know that I've expected you to live the life that I wanted, not the one you dreamed of, and I'm determined to change that, so ...' Ryan runs his fingers through his hair and gazes at me, like a child, bursting with a secret and desperate to share it. 'I was going to wait until Christmas, but ...' He runs out of the room and I open my mouth, I try to speak, to stop him. He's back before I can form a word and he slides onto the floor next to me, like a Labrador, panting with eagerness, his face shining with love and hope and loyalty. He thrusts an envelope into my hands.

'In here, Molly, is the answer to all our problems!' he says. 'It isn't a winning lottery ticket, or a trip around the world, not even close, but it's a promise that things are going to change. That our life is going to be different from now on. Well, go on, open it!'

I stare at the envelope blankly, the paper quivering in my grasp. Chicago's 'If You Leave Me Now' is playing on the radio. I'd think it was a sign but Ryan's got Heart FM on. Every song is a bloody love song. I look up, desperate for Ryan to see that he's making this harder. If I open this envelope everything is going to be so much worse.

'Ryan, I can't—' I begin handing the envelope back to him.

'Please, Molly.' He looks at me pleadingly, his eyes full of the knowledge that his life as he knows it is slipping from his grasp and if I just reach out to him, open the envelope, that he'll be able to cling on to it for that bit longer. Make everything safe again.

He refuses to take it and the envelope drops to the floor.

'Ryan, there's something I have to say, something I have to tell you.'

Ryan rubs his hand through his hair in that way he does when he's frustrated and anxious, and shakes his head. 'No, look, you don't understand! I'm going to open it for you!' He bends down and then exhales impatiently as his fingers fumble at the envelope, trying to open it, tearing the paper and thrusting its contents at me as he stands up.

'It's two tickets for New York, flying out on New Year's Eve! I want us to start the year in a place that I promised you we'd go.' His hand is still stretched out. 'I should have done this ages ago but I was so busy thinking about the future that I forgot to look at our life *now*. I got stuck, babe.' He exhales in frustration. 'These,' he thrusts the tickets at me again, 'these are my promise. You can hold me to that. You can hold me to anything, Molly. Molly?'

'Hold *me* . . .' I repeat, sobbing as the tickets drop to the floor.

'Molly?' He grasps me and I fall into him.

I want more than anything for Ryan to hold me and for me to tell him, yes, I'll go to New York with him, yes our life will be different, our relationship will be better, that nothing has changed.

I want to tell him that now I'm faced with losing him, I can see how much I had all along. That it's all I could ever want and I should've realized that a long time ago. I want to tell him what a selfish, materialistic, shallow person I've turned into, how he's a better man than I deserve, how in three years he's taught me to be so much better than I ever thought I could be. But still, it isn't good enough. I'm not good enough. I want to tell him that I don't need New York, or anything else. That doing what I did made me realize that I just want him forever. I want our cosy flat with the crazy Christmas decorations. I want his stuff strewn all over the place. I want to pick up his socks – even his horrible white ones – every day for the rest of my life. I want to be the perfect girlfriend, the girlfriend I've never been and that he deserves. I want to do all of that. Starting right now. I want to give him my list of reasons why our relationship isn't perfect and then my list of why it's worth fighting for. But instead, my conversation with Casey comes into my head and I tell him this:

'I cheated on you Ryan, I cheated on you and I'm sorry.' And then I cry and I kiss his face all over as I whisper the words that I hope will heal the hurt I've just inflicted. It was only a kiss, I didn't do any more, I'm sorry . . .' At this he pushes me away and staggers blindly back into the Christmas tree and brings the whole thing crashing down so that the baubles, the tinsel, Rudolph, everything lies cracked and broken between us. I look around in shock and realize that only the flamingo is still standing. That fucking flamingo.

'I'm going for a run,' Ryan says. And then he's gone, the door slams shut behind him before I've had time to blink.

I phone the person I want to speak to more than anyone – and when Casey doesn't answer I call my mum. I know that she'll make me feel worse than I already do, which, in a sick kind of way, is exactly what I want.

'Hello, Carter reside— Is that you, Molly dear? Are you all right?' she says as I immediately start sobbing.

'No, no I'm not. Ryan and I are over.' And I burst into a fresh set of tears.

'What happened?' she asks briskly. 'Was it something he did?'

'It's not him. It was never him. Just another fuck-up of mine. To add to the many others . . .'

'Oh, Molly, what . . .'

'. . . will people think?' I bristle as I finish her much-used saying. 'Funnily enough, Mum, right now I don't really care.'

'Molly, that's not what I was going to . . .'

But I hang up before she finishes.

What felt like hours later, Ryan came back and locked himself in our bedroom and I did what any British person would do in this situation: I made two cups of tea and I sat staring at the wall, waiting for him to emerge. It took two hours. And when he did he looked different, not like the Ryan I know, but the one I used to see from afar when I was a mixed-up teenager and he was the guy that everyone wanted to hang out with. Cool, relaxed, laid-back, totally unapproachable for a girl like me. He'd retreated. He'd changed out of the hoodie I bought him and I knew then that it was over. He sat down at the opposite end of the room – as far away from me as he could physically get – and threw questions at me like darts.

'Who?'

'When?'

'Why?'

'How?'

'Did you enjoy it?'

'Did you have sex with him?'

'Did you want to have sex with him?'

And crying, I answered him.

'Just a guy from work.'

'Last night.'

'I don't know, because I was drunk . . . no . . . because I was curious. I don't know, Ry, I wish I did . . . maybe I just wanted to try something different . . . I was wrong. I don't want anything different, I just want you.'

'How? What do you mean? On the lips . . . oh, it just happened, I don't know how. One minute we were talking, the next . . .'

'Yes. No! No, I didn't enjoy it! As much as I thought I wanted it to happen, it felt wrong. How many times? Just once. Just. Once.'

'No! No, I didn't have sex with him – what do you take me for?'

I couldn't answer the final question. Not truthfully anyway.

Then he'd flopped back, exhausted from the interrogation he'd just administered. His face was blank. It occurred to me that I once knew every pixel of this gorgeous face and now his expression was reduced to a faded polaroid. He didn't look at me. Not once.

'Ryan? Say something . . . please?'

I say it again now, to try and move this situation on. We've sat here for nearly two hours and we haven't talked, not properly. I tried to go over to him, but he wouldn't let me near him. For the first time it was him who couldn't cope with the physical contact. I never realized how isolating it can make you feel. I come from a family that doesn't 'do' hugging or general acts of demonstrativeness. I thought I was used to it. Apart from Casey, who for some reason was the exception to the rule, I've always bristled when girlfriends or colleagues try to link arms with me. And don't get me started on the 'media air kiss'. I find it hard to kiss the people I love, let alone people I barely know. When I met Ryan, it was difficult to get used to his family's unrestrained affection. I've got better over the years, but it's made me realize again the kind of girlfriend I am with my intimacy issues, my inability to naturally lavish affection like he does. But now I can see Ryan is ready to talk.

'Look,' he says, his eyes unfamiliarly steely. 'I still don't understand why you did what you did, Molly, but, well, you know, . . . maybe you've done us a favour. I suppose we haven't been happy for a while.' He drops his head, takes a deep breath and then looks up at me with a sad smile. 'I guess we were just too young for all this.' He sweeps his arm around our little flat, now our broken home.

'Maybe you and I are just too different,' I say slowly. 'We're not like your brother and Lydia. I mean, everyone saw them as a couple straight away. They got together at the same time and now they're engaged and we're . . .' I look up at him questioningly.

'Carl said he knew they fitted instantly,' he says, looking out the window. I glance out and notice it is snowing. The flakes are softly collecting on the windowpane, settling for just long enough on the glass before being swept away on the wind. Their frailty feels like an ominous sign. 'I thought we did too.' He looks up at me sadly. 'But you need to explore the world, find whatever it is that makes you happy and I . . .' He stumbles, his breath catches in his throat. I get up and take his hand, feeling the need to say one last thing, to explain.

'I wish we'd met five years later, Ry, I wish I . . . I wish I was different. I wish I'd been ready for this, for you. I'm scared that I'll never have anything like this again, that I've thrown away the one big love of my life.'

And Ryan takes my head in his hands and he gently strokes my face, wiping away my tears as his are still falling.

'I'll always be here for you, Molly, always. I'll love you forever, even if we're not together.'

And then he pulls my face to his and our heads meet, like magnets pulled by a force stronger than we can resist. His forehead feels furnace-hot and I feel his breath warm my face, igniting my skin and forcing my lips to lift towards his, like a sunflower, and then he kisses me softly, but it's different to the hundreds, the thousands that have gone before. Because it's the kiss goodbye.

The Squandered Kiss

> The sunlight claps the earth
> And the moonbeams kiss the sea:
> What are all these kissings worth
> If thou kiss not me?

> Percy Bysse Shelley

How many kisses do we waste, brush away, throw away, and then, when they are no longer there, how many times do we wish that we could relive them all a hundredfold? That haunts me sometimes, when I am at my lowest, wondering what Ryan is thinking, what he's doing. I remember when the thought of Ryan kissing someone else was the worst thing that could happen. Now I know that it's not.

'Come ON!' Casey says, heaving me to my feet.

'Noooo,' I grasp at Casey's Hello Kitty duvet desperately, like a baby for its blanky. Outside of work, it's been my constant companion for the past two weeks. I'm sure my body is now imprinted on it like the Turin Shroud. They could reprint it as a design and market it 'Hello Pity'.

'I don't care what you say, Moll, we're going out tonight whether you like it or not! It's New Year's Eve! It's been two weeks since you moved in here and when you're not at work all you've done is mope around the place. You're cramping my style. Look!' She points up at the ceiling. 'That glitter ball is reflecting your miserable face around the room and I can't bear it a minute longer! It's time we wave away the old year – and old men – and welcome in the new! Get your glad rags on, we're going *now*!'

I feebly allow her to drag me into her bedroom, feeling like it's the least I can do for what I've put her through these past couple of weeks. When Casey offered me her sofa to sleep on I jumped at the chance. I wanted to get away from London, from the girl that the city had turned me into. We'd agreed that Ryan would stay in our flat until we sold it because he has to get in to work earlier than me, and often has to stay late to run various after-school sports clubs, but I also knew he'd be spending every weekend at his parents. And I needed to feel near him, even if I couldn't be *with* him.

So I packed my bags and moved in here with Casey, at her new girlie pad. Which was weird in itself. She's always been the one languishing on *my* sofa. I didn't know how we'd handle the new dynamic in our relationship.

And Casey was so excited, she seemed to conveniently forget that I probably wouldn't be sparkling company. Or necessarily deal well with meeting her one-night stands at 7 a.m. in the queue for the bathroom. And worse, on New Year's Eve too (a.k.a the single most depressing night for singles after Valentine's Day). At least on Valentine's Day you're not forced to stay until the bitter end. But Casey is the happiest I've seen her in ages, so I suppose at least something good is coming out of it.

She seems to have used this as a chance to turn back time and is revelling in the delights of having her best friend back. But equally I think she's been disappointed by my reaction to the break-up.

She's expected me to be a sobbing stereotype, lying on her couch in my pyjamas inhaling confectionery, wailing about how I'll never be loved again. But I haven't done that. I won't. I know I've got to get on with it, and I have. Well, except when I'm alone, under the Hello Kitty duvet on her pull-out sofa bed. That's when the tears really come. But other than that, I've thrown myself into work. I even offered to go in between Christmas and New Year – mainly because I couldn't bear spending any more time at home with my parents. Luckily I knew *he* wouldn't be there. He who shall not be named. He's not at Viva anymore, he's been promoted to a new role at Brooks Publishers so he's no longer in our office.

The truth is, I know I'm strong enough to work through this on my own but Casey craves the tears and the drama. I know it's not easy to understand if you're not like me, so I try and give her a bit of what she wants just to get some peace and quiet.

We leave Casey's flat and people are walking past with party hats and blowers and stupid, wacky 2005 glasses. How dare they have fun when I'm feeling like this? I'm standing, shivering at the entrance of Players, the club Casey works at, as she chats to the doormen and waves at the people in the queue, all of whom seem to know her – some of the men pretty well, judging by the way she drapes herself over them in greeting. She confirms this by whispering their 'scores' to me when she comes back over. Casey has been a hit with men for way more years now than she was a misfit teen.

I remember the exact moment when it all changed. When, aged seventeen, her boobs grew out, her body grew up and her hair grew down, all at the same time.

She can get a guy these days, she just hasn't got the knack of keeping them. She pretends that this is fine but I know she'd give anything for someone to love her like Ryan loves – I mean loved – me.

I gulp as an image of him pops into my brain and I valiantly try to swallow the tears back. I can't cry here. Not on New Year's Eve. I'm here to have 'fun', to let my hair down, like Casey says, to do all the things that single girls are meant to do: dance, drink and flirt. All the things I thought I was missing out on when I was with Ryan and that I can't bear to do now that I'm not. My mum was right. Molly Molly Quite Contrary, that's me.

As tears sting the back of my eyes I wonder where he is now, probably down the pub with all his mates. I can see them as clearly as I can see Casey's nipples through her slinky silk top. I did try and tell her to put a strapless bra on, but she wasn't having any of it. And to be honest, she looks amazing. I realize I have no idea how to dress for clubbing anyway. Casey insisted on lending me some of her clothes. So now I look like something out of *Footballers Wives* in an orange, slashed-to-the-navel-dress with sparkly heels that are completely ridiculous, and totally not myself. But that's probably the point.

I feel Casey prodding me. I ignore her, wanting to keep Ryan in my head. I'm pretty sure she's just pointing out another guy she 'knows'. Suddenly, I feel myself being pulled into the club, straight through the VIP entrance and into an area cordoned off with red rope. There are big, lush jewel-coloured sofas and crushed-velvet chaises longues. A smattering of beautiful people are already draped over them, their fake tans and white teeth glowing under the UV lights.

Casey looks wired. She is waving manically and sends me over to a seat right in the corner. 'Sit there, babe!' she says brightly, in a high-pitched voice. 'I'll um, I'll just get us some drinks!' And she disappears, leaving me to sit on my own. A guy immediately swaggers over, in a try-hard outfit of a fitted white designer T-shirt, with Gucci sunglasses hung over the V-neck. The T-shirt is pulled taut and tucked into his tight faded jeans to enhance his gym-honed body and to reveal his ostentatiously displayed Hermes belt, presumably. None of this hides the vacant expression he's wearing as his main accessory.

'Hey girrrrl, you're too pretty to be alone,' Hermes Guy drawls, looking back at his mates and giving a thumbs-up sign.

I raise an eyebrow: 'And you're too stupid to realize that I want to be.' He looks startled, but undeterred.

'What's your name?'

'Effoff.' I smile, through gritted teeth.

'That's pretty! Effoff! I ain't heard that before. Is it Swedish?'

I snort in derision and wave my hands to dismiss him. He slopes off back to his mates, looking more than a little bit confused.

Just then Casey arrives with a bottle of champagne. 'Here we go! I thought we'd start with something bubbly to get the party going!' Her eyes hover around and then return to me. 'Here's to being young, free and single . . . and to, er, meeting *new* men!' She pours me a glass and I down the lot. I'm going to need it tonight.

An hour later, I've consumed pretty much an entire bottle and I'm on the dance floor working some moves out to 'Crazy in Love'. And I'm doing a pretty darned good job of it too! In my head and with a bottle of champagne inside me and in this dress, I reckon I can basically pass as Beyonce herself. I'm now re-enacting the video, with Hermes Guy who's happily taken the role of Jay-Z. I was a bit harsh on him earlier. He's actually really, really nice and I am looking well hot, so *why* does Casey keep trying to pull me off the dance floor? Now I can see why she gets pissed off when I try and stop her from having fun. I thought I was being protective; I realize now it's just *annoying*.

'Hey!' I say, as she tries to steer me back to the VIP room. 'What are you doing? I'm having a lovely time, dancing with whatshisface over there. Did you see me?'

I do a version of the booty dance but add the leg and arm waggle Mia and I created at uni for good measure. 'Uh oh!' I sing tunelessly as I edge back onto the dance floor. 'This is fuuuuun, Case! Look at me, I'm having fuun!!!!' And for some reason, known only to me, I start doing the Robot.

Casey shakes her head and beckons me back over. 'Come on, Moll,' she pleads. 'Let's go and sit back down. I've bought us another bottle!'

'YAY!' I squeal. 'But I'm going to finish dancing first, OK? Because I'm *good* at it! Look!' And then I start flailing my arms around feeling as free and uninhibited as I've felt for ages. It's 11 p.m., it's New Year's Eve and I'm young, free and single!

'Please,' Casey begs, trying to drag me away. 'Molly, please come with me before you see . . .'

'Before I see wha— Uh . . . oh.' I've hooked my hand around my ankle and my hand is behind my head, when I turn around and see him. Ryan. Across the dance floor. Kissing someone. A girl. A tall, blonde, beautiful girl.

A girl that's not me.

'I'm sorry,' Casey says sorrowfully, slipping her arm through mine and trying to lead me away but I am stuck to the floor. 'I tried to warn you.'

Everything seems to stop then, the music, the people, and I swear it is just him and me in the room.

Oh, and her.

I stare for a moment, I see him look up and over at me. He stops kissing her and pulls away. She says something but he shakes his head. She walks off. Then he raises his hand to his forehead, rubs it and sweeps it over his head like he does when he's anxious. Then he looks at me, sorrowfully. I can't move, I want to move but I can't.

I just stand there, on one leg, like a . . . flamingo, staring at him as the song changes and Casey tries to pull me away again.

'Don't do this to yourself,' she says, taking my head in hers and forcing me to look her in the eye. 'You were doing so well. Come on, let's go now, Molly.'

I lower my leg, still staring at him. I wish I hadn't seen it, but he's single, he can do what he likes. So I just nod at him and I turn, and as I look back he raises his hand to his lips, as if to blow me a kiss. But instead, he just drops his hand so the kiss falls to the floor and he disappears. I want to run over there and scrabble around on the floor, like I do when I'm looking for a lost contact lens. I want that kiss. I want him. Why did I throw it all away?

I wail into Casey's armpit in the taxi as she strokes my hair. Part of me thinks at least Casey's finally got what she wants, a bawling best friend she can look after.

'I know you don't want to hear this,' she says, still stroking my hair, 'but maybe what just happened is for the best. I mean, now you can finally move on and accept that it really is over between you, can't you, eh?'

I nod but what I'm actually thinking is I would have preferred to live in ignorant bliss, hoping he was in the same state I am, desperately missing me as much as I miss him.

I press pause on the DVD and push a visibly miffed Harry off my lap, suddenly overcome by the guilt of how much I have to do. What the hell am I doing being distracted by a film? It's just like when I was a kid and Mum used to militantly make me clear up my room every Saturday morning, and I'd wind up secretly watching *Going Live*.

I brush the cat hair off my leggings and walk into the kitchen, put my mug in the sink and grab the marker pen I left on the island unit last night. I need to label some of the newly packed boxes from last night with my clear and simple system: Charity Shop, Ship or Storage.

It's the smell that does it. I close my eyes and inhale the pungent petrol-like smell as I take the lid off the pen. Ryan would often spend evenings sprawled across our lounge floor, drawing up various player formations on big sheets of white paper for upcoming school football matches while I read my photography books.

This scent is, in a way, stronger and more memory-inducing than his Hugo Boss aftershave and for a long time after he left, when I smelt that particular scent I'd find myself turning and following the wearer in case it was Ryan before realizing what I was doing and hastily retreating.

But unlike that, this smell brings pleasure as well as pain because it doesn't just make me think of Ryan. It takes me back to my school days; Casey and I giggling during lessons and then scribbling notes to each other in our exercise books about boys we fancied. And of course, it reminds me of home. My parents. The smell of Sharpies infiltrated our house as they laboured tirelessly over homework books with their red pens.

I look in an unmarked box on the kitchen counter, full of random kitchen gadgets and scrawl 'Charity Shop' on the side. It may seem like I'm wiping a lifetime of memories out, just like on a whiteboard, but it's in order to make way for new ones.

The Worst First Kiss

There are certain givens when it comes to falling in love. Take the first kiss. No one ever wrote about the path of true love starting with a terrible kiss, did they? Would Juliet have been quite so infatuated with Romeo if he'd just stuck his tongue down her throat instead of doing all that balcony stuff? Or if Jack had drunkenly snogged Rose at that below-decks party instead of tenderly kissing her whilst making her fly on the bow of the ship? Would it still have been the biggest grossing film of all time? Maybe Shakespeare and all his romantic writing contemporaries (and James Cameron) thought a bad first kiss was just too obvious a sign that the relationship was doomed from the start. At times, I've wondered the same thing.

'Oh GOD, not him,' I mutter darkly, spotting the familiar figure of Ryan Cooper approaching as I try desperately to hide behind my mum. It's a cold, bleak Saturday morning and Mum's dragged me out on a Christmas shopping trip to Southend in a bid to 'bond' with me. I'm hating it because generally I do everything to avoid being seen in public with my parents because they're so embarrassing and so miserable.

They haven't *always* been this unhappy but things have recently hit an all-time low and it's really *pissing me off* that neither one of them has the guts to just put me out of my misery and leave. But Dad's the head teacher at Westcliff, where I go, and Mum's head of English at Thorpe Hall, the local private school where Ryan Cooper goes. They're both well known in the community.

They're only together because of some misplaced sense of social standing (and because no one else would have them). They can barely be in the same room as each other any more. Mum's always in the kitchen, cooking, marking, moaning at me. Dad's always in his office, looking at his paintings and his books, but mostly looking out the window, as if he'd like to be anywhere but here with us. So they continue with this ridiculous web of pretence. The older I get the more I see it and the more I hate being around either of them.

But Mum won't give up. She insists on trying to find out what 'makes me tick'. (I am so tempted to say one day, 'Sex, drugs and rock and roll . . .' just to watch her *freak out*.) And I know she only wants to go shopping so she can try to get me to buy some clothes that she approves of (loafers, A-line skirts, roll-necks). I don't know how many times I have to tell her that I *like* my old, holey jeans, my battered Converse and array of flannel shirts, army-surplus jumpers and short skirts.

'Shall we go to Topshop dear? Or Mrs Selfridges?' She smiles desperately at me now and tries to link my arm. I swiftly pull it away.

'*Miss* Selfridge,' I hiss. 'And I wouldn't be seen dead in there.' I lift my Nikon F50 to my face from where it permanently hangs around my neck. It's an early Christmas gift – and their attempt to buy my approval. At least now I can escape my miserable present by focusing my attention (and my lens) on my future career as a photographer. It's all I've wanted to do for as long as I can remember. Mum and Dad tell me that the reason there are hardly any photos of me as a toddler was that I'd always run around to whoever was taking the photograph and stand behind it too, desperate to see what they were seeing. I picked up a camera for the first time aged four. It was Christmas and I can still remember looking through the little square window and secretly loving the fact I knew exactly what to do without anyone forcing me to learn. I didn't need lessons, unlike the ballet I'd been sent to once a week since I was three. With this, I could just look and click. And I seemed to understand instinctively how to do it well. There were no chopped-off heads in my pictures, even at that age. That camera became my third eye. I walked around looking through it all the time. I remember thinking, when I was about seven, that it was like Dad's glasses, it made me see better. Now I realize that it was because my photos captured real emotions instead of the fake ones people always seemed to portray for everyone else. It made me feel powerful, like they couldn't keep any secrets from me whilst I was looking through it. I didn't always take actual photographs though – Mum and Dad rationed my films to two a month, but I'd pretend, seeing, visualizing, adjusting, framing. As I got older I'd write notes in a book about light, shadow, composition and focus, and I became obsessed with famous photographers like Henri Cartier-Bresson, a master of candid photography who developed the street-style reportage photography that I'm inspired by.

And now, seeing the wet, rainy High Street of Southend

shimmer through my viewfinder makes the day – not to mention this shithole seaside town – seem brighter somehow, turning it from something depressing into something beautiful. Sometimes I wish I could have the camera permanently attached to my eyes. Life looks so much better through it. Plus there's the added bonus that it would hide my face enough for Ryan Cooper not to spot me.

'Mrs Carter!' he calls, hitching his sports bag up on his shoulder and increasing his pace as he swigs sexily from a Lucozade bottle.

Shit. He's seen us. I busy myself changing the film in my camera, so I don't have to acknowledge his presence.

'Shouting at me in the street?' Mum mutters. 'What will people thi— Ryan *Coopah*!' Mum trills as he appears in front of us. Mum uses her best Standard Received Pronunciation voice whenever she's around fellow teachers, her students or their parents.

'Alright, Mrs C?' Ryan grins, lighting up the street with his smile, and then peers over at me. It's not the style I like – way too clean-cut – but I have to admit he's looking kind of hot in a hooded top, baggy jeans and trainers. And smelling nice, too. All freshly showered. I glance at his Puma bag. He must've had a match this morning.

'Hi, Molly. I haven't seen you around for a while. How are you?'

I don't answer. I just turn away, lift my camera up and pretend to be busy snapping photos.

'Shouldn't you be at home doing your coursework, Ryan?' Mum says tightly.

'It's Saturday,' Ryan responds politely, glancing at me through his curtains. 'I've just had a game of footie and thought I'd come into town.'

'Time and tide wait for no man,' Mum replies archly. 'We all know you have a very bright future ahead of you in the sporting world, Ryan. The school is proud of your achievements, but you need a good education to fall back on if the – what do you call it – the 'Beautiful Game', doesn't work out, hmm?'

My skin burns with mortification. Can't she switch off her teacher act just for a second? Can't she see I'm literally *dying* of embarrassment here in front of the hottest guy in town?

'You've got your A levels coming up,' she continues primly, 'and your recent essays suggest ...'

Clearly not.

'Mum, leave it,' I hiss furiously. 'You're not at school now.' She glances at me, her lips pinch and her cheeks flush – a striking contrast to her normally pale, unmade-up complexion.

'It's OK,' Ryan smiles. 'Your mum's right, I *am* always training. It's my dream to play pro for Southend by the time I'm eighteen, y'see – so that only gives me a year!' He nods politely at Mum. 'But Mrs C is spot on. I need to get my head down this term. I wanna do well in my A levels and with a great teacher like your mum, I'm hoping to get a good grade in English at least!' He grins at us and I turn to look at her, shaking my head as surprise flickers over Mum's face and her pursed expression softens into a smile.

'Oh Ryan, you're too kind,' she blushes. Jesus, he's even worked his charm on my mum. Is there no limit to this guy's powers? She touches his arm gently. 'It is every teacher's dream to inspire their pupils ...'

Oh God, I feel a *Dead Poets Society* moment coming on.

'As the great Joseph Conrad once said, "A man is a worker. If he is not that he is nothing."'

'Never was a truer word spoken, Mrs C,' Ryan replies sagely and I shake my head at him from behind my mum's shoulder. He is taking the piss, surely? I try and catch his eye but he appears to be busy listening to my mum's impassioned speech so doesn't notice.

'You know, Mrs C, you must be exhausted walking round town after such a busy week at school,' Ryan says, once she's finished her monologue. 'Why don't you treat yourself to a cup of tea somewhere? Molly and I could mooch around Topshop then come and meet you in about an hour, yeah? Would that be cool?'

Mum looks predictably startled and negative. But then she looks at me, and then back at Ryan. 'Well, yes, that would be coo— I mean fine. I am rather tired, I must confess. I'll maybe go and browse in the bookshop. Yes, that's what I'll do . . .' And she pulls her embarrassing grandma-style plastic scarf over her head, zips her anorak up and goes to kiss me on the cheek. I dodge out of the way and she turns and walks off down the rain-soaked street.

I stand still, slightly flummoxed by the situation I now find myself in.

'Alone at last,' Ryan winks when she's gone.

'That was a sly move,' I say as I stride off down the High Street, hoping he'll get the hint and give up. He doesn't.

'Well, I have a way with women,' he laughs, easily catching me up. 'Especially teachers. They love me.'

I see him look at his reflection in a shop window and inwardly gag. *God* he loves himself, not without reason, but still. '*I* thought the great *Ryan Cooper* would be way above the whole teacher's pet routine . . .'

'Not if it gets me time alone with a girl I like,' he grins.

'Your mates aren't around now, Ryan,' I say. 'You don't have to *pretend.*'

He frowns and shrugs, like he doesn't know what I'm talking about. I turn and take a picture of a couple kissing outside a café.

'What are you taking photos of?' he asks.

'Just stuff. I take photos of everything.'

'What about me?' He jumps in front of the camera and performs a series of cheesy catalogue poses, laughing unselfconsciously at himself as he does so.

I lower my lens and stare at him unflinchingly. 'Sorry, I should have clarified. I take photos of everything . . . that *interests me.*' I lift my chin and stalk past him.

'Oooh, that hurt,' he says, clutching his stomach and staggering around as if I'd stabbed him. I try not to smile as he bounds back over to me. 'So do you fancy hitting Topman with me? I want something new to wear tonight to The Grand.' He pauses and flicks his blond hair out of his face with his hand. 'Are you going?'

'Not allowed,' I say. Then I mentally kick myself.

A smile hovers over his lips. 'From what I've heard, that has never stopped you before.'

He's right. I've been going to pubs and clubs since I was fourteen. Not that my parents know. The drainpipe outside my bedroom window comes in pretty handy and they're always too busy doing their marking or reading or listening to their embarrassing old 60s' music to notice I've gone. I turn and walk towards Topshop, biting my lip to hide my delight as Ryan follows me.

'Guurghh.' I stick my fingers down my throat as Ryan steps out of the changing room wearing a pair of denim dungarees.

'What?' he says defensively.

'Why is one of the straps flapping over your shoulder like that? I can see your nipple!'

Ryan looks offended. 'But it's really fashionable,' he pouts prettily. 'Robbie Williams looked well cool in them in the 'Pray' video. And all the girls love *him* . . .'

'Not *all* the girls,' I reply with a grimace. 'Seriously, take my advice and take them off. NO, not here!' I flap my hands and cover my eyes as he starts to undo the other strap.

Ryan grins. 'I knew you couldn't resist me . . .'

I fight back a smile. 'Get back in your changing room! Go!' I order.

'Make up your mind, Molly Carter, you either want me or you don't.' He grins.

I manage to stay poker-faced despite the unexpected fireworks in my pants, and Ryan shrugs and then retreats back inside.

'You know,' I call, as I examine my chipped plum-coloured nail polish, trying desperately to reduce my heart rate at the thought of him undressing. 'I was under the illusion that it's *girls* who are obsessed with shopping, not wannabe local football stars.'

He pops his head round the changing-room door and I see a flash of bare chest as he pulls on a sandy-coloured suede shirt. I can feel the blush spreading over my cheeks, and I immediately lean down and closely inspect my trusty scuffed Converse, which I've customized and which I'm wearing with a long black skirt and a crushed-velvet black bodysuit. I like black. And not just because it's the only colour that doesn't clash with my self-cut and hennaed hair.

'I didn't think Topshop was your style,' he replies with a grin.

I fold my arms. 'You think you've got me all sussed, don't you, Cooper?'

He shakes his head. 'Nope. I haven't got a clue about you, Molly. That's why I like you, babe.'

'I'm not your babe,' I reply snitchily.

He raises an eyebrow and his crystal-blue eyes sparkle mischievously as he folds his arms and gazes at me. 'No, you're not.' He pauses and grins. 'Well, not yet,' he says, and he closes the door behind him again.

I turn and grab a couple of dark, checked flannel shirts hanging on the rail and thrust my hand through the door, turning my face away but not before I get a glimpse of his smooth, tanned chest once more. 'Here, try these. Wear them open over a T-shirt for a more grungy look and hopefully it'll stop you looking like such an Essex boy. No offence.'

'None taken.'

I feel his hand brush mine as he takes them and a volt of longing shoots through my body. 'I know you love me just the way I am.'

I tut and turn away, hoping he didn't notice that I didn't correct him.

Half an hour later we're sitting in a café just off the High Street. I feel like pinching myself to check this is really happening. So I do.

'Ow!'

Holy *shit*. It is.

'Are you OK?' Ryan asks.

'Oh, um, yep, just, you know, banged my ankle on the table.' I suck in my breath and rub my leg. He looks under the table at it and winks.

'Can I help with that?'

I blush. *Pull yourself together, Molly Carter! Emily Davison did not throw herself in front of the winner of the Epsom Derby so you can sit here simpering at a boy.*

'No. I'm fine,' I answer primly. 'Now what were we talking about?'

'You were telling me about your parents,' he says, leaning forward and resting his elbows on the table.

Somehow he's managed to make me tell him things that I never imagined revealing to anyone other than my diary. He seems to have this knack of asking the right questions, like he already knows the answers. Maybe it's because at seventeen he's nearly two whole years older than me. He's much more mature than boys my age. I love how he listens so intently, with his head slightly tilted to one side so his sandy curtains flop into his eyes, his cheek resting against his knuckle so his eyelashes brush against it and his lips parted slightly as if to offer soothing words of encouragement at any moment.

'Can I ask you something?' I say, swirling my straw around in my Coca-Cola. I don't do hot drinks.

'Shoot.' Ryan blows on his hot chocolate before taking a sip and a cloud of froth lands on his upper lip. I resist the overwhelming urge to lick it off. *Control yourself, Molly!*

'Why do you act like such a macho prick when you're actually really sensitive?' I look up and see him grinning at me.

'I'll answer if you explain why you dress like you're ugly when you're actually really beautiful.' He leans forward and gently removes my glasses.

I snatch them back in case he realizes that they're fake lenses. 'You are a giant cheeseball, Ryan Cooper!'

'I just want to look at you without anything between us.'

I crack up laughing and bang my hand on the table, my silver moonstone rings clatter on it satisfyingly loudly. 'That's the worst line *ever*. Where did you steal it from? Some terrible eighties romcom?'

'What if I did?' He leans back and puts his arm across the leather banquette. 'Can I tell you a secret, Molly Carter?' He leans forward across the table so his lips are inches from mine. 'But you have to promise not to tell anyone.' I raise a pencilled eyebrow expectantly.

He takes a deep breath and looks around furtively. 'I am a romcom addict,' he whispers dramatically, his eyes glimmering mischievously.

I can't help it. I burst out laughing.

He looks at me with mock offence. 'Hey, this is serious. No one can know though, OK?' he whispers, looking around again.

'Why?'

'I'd have thought that was obvious!'

'No,' I laugh, '*why* do you love them?'

'You really wanna know why I like them? I like that you know how it's all going to end, that there aren't any big surprises. People follow their hearts and everything works out.'

I prod him across the table. 'So what's your favourite romcom then?'

He answers instantly. '*Top Gun*, obviously. Tom Cruise is the nuts ...'

I roll my eyes and he hurriedly adds: 'but you name them, I've watched 'em all. *When Harry Met Sally, Pretty Woman, Sleepless in Seattle.* What about you? What's your favourite?'

I gaze at him unflinchingly. 'None of them, I don't believe in all that love stuff.'

'Really?' He smiles. 'I don't reckon you can knock it till you've tried it,' he murmurs.

I look down and sip my Coke loudly. 'I want a career instead of being stuck at home being someone's wife. Cleaning up after someone doesn't seem like much of a happy ending to me.'

'Whooo,' Ryan whistles. 'That's the most cynical thing I've ever heard! You remind me of someone from a film ...' He snaps his fingers. 'Harry. That's it! You're just like Harry Burns!'

'I am so not.'

'Are too.'

'Am not.'

'You only think you're not, Molly.'

'I do not.'

'Do too ... Ha!' He snaps his fingers and points at me and I look at him quizzically.

'You're smirking. Why are you smirking?'

'Because I *knew* you liked romcoms too.'

'I do no—'

He is still smirking and I realize he's got something on me. 'Then why are we re-enacting a scene from *When Harry Met Sally* right now?' he says triumphantly, banging his hand on the table and pointing at me. I go to protest my innocence. 'Harry,' he says warningly, the grin still evident on his face, 'I've got you sussed. I reckon your dislike of romcoms is as fake as those glasses you wear.' He winks at me and I shut my mouth.

*

We're walking through the town and I keep pausing to take snaps of the glistening reflections of shops in the puddles – and the people that are passing them. I love how it makes the town look like it is floating on water, like a less romantic version of Venice. I imagine the credit in an art gallery 'Southend *In* the Sea' by Molly Carter. Ryan is waiting patiently beside me.

'So I guess I don't need to ask what career you want then,' he laughs, folding his arms and tipping his head to one side.

I nod, lift my camera up, focus it and quickly take several shots of his face, doing my best to capture the softness of his expression, the way his blond hair perfectly frames his face, the intensity of his blue eyes and those soft, plump lips . . .

'You could sell photos of me when I'm a famous footballer.'

I raise an eyebrow, just like Casey taught me to do. ''Course I could,' I say dryly. 'I forgot I'm in the presence of the next Gary *Lineker.*'

He grins and jogs on the spot. 'First step, The Shrimpers, then England!' He leans closer to me and adds, 'And I'm much better looking than Gary Lineker, right?'

I roll my eyes. 'Vanity will get you nowhere, my friend.'

He turns.

'So what *will* get me somewhere then, Molly?'

I lift my camera to cover my face and start snapping his, capturing a montage of shots of him sweeping his hair out of his eyes. He leans forward so his features fill my frame and I snap that too. It is the closest thing to kissing him I can imagine.

'I thought you said you didn't take photos of things you weren't interested in?' He laughs.

I peer out from behind the viewfinder and find myself smiling. 'I don't.'

Casey and I are standing outside Leigh-on-Sea's premier drinking establishment, The Grand, shivering with nerves and cold. She's wearing a white embroidered bra-top that's barely containing her curves, a black ribbon choker and tight blue hot pants that she's sewn some patches on to. And she's wearing lace-up, knee-length boots. She's pulled her dark hair off her face in a little quiff and her make-up is all bronze eyes and cheeks and deep-red lips. Aside from the mouthful of metal and the glasses, I think she looks properly beautiful.

In contrast, I'm about as dressed-up as I get in an ankle-length black satin slip that I bought from a charity shop, which I'm wearing over a faded black The Smiths T-shirt and my trusty Converse. I've pulled my red hair off my face into a bun and unleashed a can of Elnett on it, and I'm still wearing my new dark-rimmed glasses – just to prove that I'm not trying to look pretty for Ryan. The effect I'm going for is 'grungy Kate Moss' but obviously way less supermodel-ly than her. I'm not *completely* deluded.

'Do you think they're already here?' Casey says, trying to peer through the window.

'I don't know, but we have to remember to play it cool, OK?' I'm bluffing – I'm horribly nervous about seeing Ryan. And a bit worried about how he'll be in front of Casey and his friends. And how Casey will be. No boy has ever shown an interest in either of us, which is one of the things that we bonded over when she started at Westcliff two years ago.

''Course! I don't know how to play it any other way!' she says, crossing her eyes and panting like a puppy on heat. I smile and squeeze her hand. 'Now,' she says, pulling a serious face. 'Remember the BFF song?' She holds out her little finger and I link it with mine. I wrote 'our song' to the tune of 'Electric Dreams'. I was trying to write our BFF list of rules the first time I went to her house and her mum was playing it and the melody just seemed to fit. I sing it now unselfconsciously because a) no one is around and b) I've had two shots of Southern Comfort from Casey's mum's extensive drinks cabinet. She gets through

it so quickly she never notices when we have some too. Even
if she did, she wouldn't care. I grin at Casey as I begin to sing
tunelessly:

> 'We've only got each other right now
> But we'll always be around
> forever and forever no matter
> What they say (they say, they say)
> We'll never let love get in the way
> Or spend another day
> Without saying "I love ya"
> And we always will (we will, we wi-ill)
> Dum dum de DUUUUUH . . .'

Casey joins in for the unchanged 'Electric Dreams' chorus and we
both crack up laughing. Then we clasp hands and squeeze through
the doors. The pub is packed and we find ourselves immediately
swallowed up by the heaving crowd and smoky air. The Grand is
the most popular pub for Leigh's teen residents. It's an impressive,
Victorian building on the Broadway. Dad told me those dead
comedians Laurel and Hardy played here or something. Full of
interesting facts like that, my dad is.

The place is full of 16-year-olds so we fit right in. I look across
the bar and immediately spot Nikki Pritchard and her gang, 'the
Heathers' Casey and I call them, snarling over at us. They're swinging their hips suggestively to some crappy Kylie song and doing
their best to get the attention of every guy in there. It's pathetic. I
can't believe I was ever friends with them. It was only for a fleeting
period, before Casey joined Westcliff High and saved me, but it
was long enough.

'Perhaps we should go,' Casey says, grasping my hand, and I
know she's seen them too. Ever since they ganged up on her in her
first week at Westcliff I've felt the need to protect her. 'We'll never

find them in here anyway,' Casey shouts into my ear, pulling me back. Just then we hear a voice soaring over the music and I look over and spot Ryan waving us over. Then I look at the Heathers who have witnessed this and are giving us dirty looks across the room.

'Oh my GOD!' Casey hisses gleefully. 'Is this really happening?'

'Over here, Molly!' Ryan calls for good measure. I turn and drag Casey towards the bar.

'Where are we going?' Casey asks in confusion, craning her neck back at Ryan Cooper and Co. 'Aren't we going over? Oh my GOD, I can't believe Ryan Cooper wants *us*! This is the best night of my life it's . . . Hi! HI RYAN!' She shouts and waves at him as I try to pull her arm down. 'Hey, what did you do that for?'

'We're acting cool, Casey!' I chastise. 'Two Southern Comforts and lemonade,' I say to the barman who barely glances at me before serving me.

Casey smiles as I pass her the drinks. 'Gotcha,' she smiles and readjusts her bra-top to expose more of her abundant cleavage. I look at her doubtfully as she leads us towards the five-strong gang that makes up Ryan's posse.

'Hello boys,' Casey drawls and sticks her chest out in a brazen attempt to imitate the Wonderbra billboard campaign that every-one's talking about. Is this her version of playing it cool? I go to pull her away then I look at her bright, friendly smile that is unencumbered by awkwardness or attitude, and realize I could probably learn a lot from her. She's just herself and I love her for it. I kind of envy her, too.

I watch Casey chatting amiably to Alex Slater, a tall, dark-haired, dimple-smiled lad who girls seem madly keen on. Including Casey it would seem, judging by her body language. I glance across and see he is standing next to a shorter, broader, dark-blond guy with spiky hair, who looks a bit like Ryan but much beefier. Casey whispered when we first spotted them all that he's Carl, Ryan's brother, before she abandoned me to chat up Alex. There's also a little guy in a hat, dribbling over every girl on the dance floor – he's called Gaz I think, and some other cute, floppy-haired Mark Owen lookalike, called Jake, dancing along to Baby D's 'Let Me Be Your Fantasy'. Casey glances over and nods her head in the direction of Ryan. Clutching my drink desperately, I shuffle over to him; he stood back a little from the group. *Think Casey. Be like Casey,* I mutter under my breath.

I stick out my chest and lift my slip up to show a bit of ankle and then drop it again. Oh *God,* I give up. I am basically my mother. The genetics are too strong. I'm going to be a virgin for*ever.*

'Hi Ryan,' I drawl huskily. 'Fancy seeing you here,' I then shout enthusiastically over the music, just as the song finishes. Ryan's wearing the flannel shirt I picked out for him in Topman. I pluck at his sleeve awkwardly and look up at him. 'It looks go-oo-od on yo-o-ou,' I say. My voice has suddenly, inexplicably, taken on an unnaturally high-pitched staccato.

'Erm, thanks,' he replies, smiling passively and swaying a little on his feet. His mates all grin like loons at each other. I take a sip of my drink and look around awkwardly.

'I didn't think I'd shee you here,' Ryan slurs, his eyes losing focus a little as he lurches in close to me. I take another gulp for Dutch courage. Clearly I have some catching up to do.

'No?' I reply in my best flirtatious fashion. 'I thought you'd think I was a sure thing.'

Another silence. Someone snorts and slaps him on the shoulder and Ryan turns and laughs openly. I see one of them – Carl, I think – whisper something to Ryan. If I lean forward I can just work out what he's saying: '. . . dare you to kiss her . . .'

A dare? I stagger back. Humiliation and anger surge through my body as I mentally chastise myself. *Stupid, stupid me.* I glare at him, turn and walk off as fast as I can.

'Molly, stop!' I feel a hand grasp at my arm and he pulls me around. His friends are still laughing in the background and he looks embarrassed. 'I'm sorry, it's just dead hard with my mates here an' that, but I just want to say ...' For a split second I see his face lunge towards mine and I remember how sweet he was earlier in the day and how much I wanted to kiss him. Then his mouth is yawning towards me, his nose hits mine and his lips crash-land awkwardly. He grasps me close to him and kisses me, urgently, firmly, then moistly as he rotates his tongue like a hamster in a wheel. I squeeze my eyes shut and try to enjoy my first ever kiss but all I feel is waves of dismay at his drunken, public lunge, so different from the sensitive, romantic, tender experience that I've seen in the movies ...

I push him away as his jeering, cheering, leering mates circle around us. Ryan looks at me in confusion and panic as he tries to focus on me.

'Whass wrong, Molly?' he slurs.

I look at the crowd that has gathered around us, the sneering faces of the Heathers loom out at me and I see they've surrounded Casey and are goading her about her weight and clothes. I shouldn't have left her.

Tears prick at the back of my eyes and my throat swells so much I can't speak. They're all laughing at the fat Greek girl and the stupid goth who thought they stood a chance with the local pin-up. I lurch over towards Casey, grasp her hand tightly and I break free, pushing my way through the crowd trying to get us as far away as possible from Ryan sodding Cooper, his mates and those bitches. We lunge through the doors and the cool, salty breeze of the sea air claws at my exposed skin. And as Casey and I stumble towards the bus stop, I can hear him calling 'Molleee, Molleee,' and with the laughter still ringing in my ears I make a vow to myself that I'll never trust anyone other than Casey again.

9.45 a.m.

The phone has been ringing for at least a minute, and panting with the sudden exertion of hurrying down the stairs I put my hand on my chest. I look down and realize I'm still holding one of my old diaries after finding a box of them. I've been reliving my teen years for the past half an hour, rather than getting ready. Bad Molly. It's been hilarious and heartbreaking reading my angsty entries. I glance down at the open page and re-read it.

3rd March 1995
Saw RC outside school. He was with his usual gang of mates posing in front of all the stupid Year 11 Westcliff girls who were swooning over them like they were the frickin' Brat Pack. C got all excited and said RC had looked over at us. She reckons he fancies one of us. I didn't tell her that he'd actually looked over because the Heathers had walked past at that precise moment and did the mocking two-fingered bunny ears sign over our heads. C is so deluded, I let her live in her bubble as it's a much nicer place than in mine. She's my best friend but sometimes I wonder how she can be so naive. I envy her sometimes. I mean, I know she has it pretty hard what with her mum and everything. But no one has it as hard as me. My life sucks.

15th May 1995
Mum and Dad had another row again. I wish they'd just put us all out of our misery and divorce. I mean, what's the point of being married if you detest each other? Life would be so much easier for me if they lived apart. I'd be popular, gets loads of presents at Christmas and Mum would HAVE to let

me get my ears pierced. I'd threaten to live with Dad full-time if not. (Although, knowing her, she'd probably take me up on it.)

I swear, right here, right now, that I'm NEVER going to get married. I'm just going to be a successful career woman and have loads of boyfriends that I use for sex and then dump. I just need to get started with one. It's so depressing that I'm nearly 16 and still haven't had one. I'm dying to get rid of this pesky virginity. Even Casey's done it now. I blame RC. He's made me even more of a leper than I was before. I HATE HIM!!

The phone is still ringing and I answer it gasping, 'Hello?' breathily, as I close the diary, my head still full of my poor, angry teenage self.

'Awight, Molly love,' says a gruff but friendly Essex voice at the other end of the line. For one panic-inducing moment I think it's Ryan's dad – maybe he thinks I've got more of Ryan's stuff? – but then I realize it's just the removal man.

'How's it all going?' he asks. I look guiltily around the house hoping that my mum has secretly visited in the last half an hour I've been aimlessly pottering. Nope, still in a state of absolute chaos.

'Um, all's good here, really good!' I reply in a jolly tone that belies the sheer panic I'm feeling. I tuck the phone under my ear as I sweep a load of paperwork into a box, seal it with some masking tape and mark it 'Ship'. 'Er so when do you reckon you'll be here?' I add flippantly, as if it doesn't matter a jot to me when they arrive because I'm *so* organized.

'Thass wot I'm calling to tell ya, love,' he says cheerfully, 'we'll be wiv you in fifteen, awight?'

'GREAT! See you then,' I squeak enthusiastically. I put down the phone and take a deep, yogic breath calming myself with the thought that it's probably an occupational hazard for removal men to see people in this state. I can't be the worst they've witnessed. And if I am . . . sod it, I've got bigger things to worry about. Like leaving my friends, my family, my entire *life* behind on a crazy whim. Have I lost my mind? What the hell am I doing?

The Never Let Me Go Kiss

You know how some people think of their life in 'movie moments'? They walk down the street with an internal soundtrack playing, or imagine themselves as a romcom character whenever they go on a date? Well, not me. Up until I met Ryan I never thought my life could be anything like a movie, and then when we got together it felt too comfortable to be anything epically romantic. At points I was desperate to, dare I say it, be swept off my feet. Maybe it was working in women's magazines but I, Molly Carter, found myself hypnotized by Woman's biggest enemy: 'The Fairytale Ending'.

There's nothing like being on a plane for twenty-four hours to get some serious time to reflect on your life. Despite my best efforts to stop thinking about Ryan and the mess I made of our relationship by watching three films in the last ten hours (*Mean Girls, Pride and Prejudice* and now *Brokeback Mountain*), eating two in-flight meals (both of which professed to be chicken but tasted like cardboard) and drinking two small bottles of Australian Chardonnay (does wine go to your head more when you're at 30,000 feet?), I'm thinking way more than is advisable when seated in the middle of a bunch of strangers and facing the prospect of a future alone whilst watching a heartbroken cowboy cark it in a caravan.

I swipe away a tear and think about the three weeks I've just spent with my best friend from university, Mia. I booked it after seeing Ryan kiss that girl on New Year's Eve. I needed time away. Time with sorted, sussed Mia with her great job, incredible lifestyle and cavalier attitude to love. She doesn't even remotely believe in it and even *she* admitted that she thought Ryan and I were meant to be together forever. She told me that if I felt so strongly that the break-up was a mistake that I should just tell him. So I did. Over email, which was probably the wrong thing to do but it doesn't matter because I know it's not going to make any difference.

I didn't hear back from him.

I've just got to face the fact that Ryan and I are over and move on. I put the eye mask on and try desperately to go to sleep so I can forget what a mess I've made of everything.

I come out of Arrivals with the rest of my fellow long-haul travellers, too exhausted and too busy tripping over my stupid boho skirt (bought in a moment of break-up madness) to even think about looking up. But then, just as I'm rubbing my sore ankle, I look around and notice all the people who are being greeted by loved ones. I can just imagine the montage of photos of the greeting couples, but I resist lifting up my camera, concluding that I'm not in the mood to photograph other people's happy reunions.

I sigh, muss up my fringe and pull my hair back into a loose ponytail at the nape of my neck and wearily pick up the handle of my huge suitcase again, thinking about the next leg of my journey and wondering how I'm going to summon up the energy to get on the tube and then back to Casey's flat. And then go back to work tomorrow.

Work. I'd almost forgotten what that was like. My suitcase crashes into my ankle again and I swear under my breath, then quickly lift my camera to my eyes, unable to resist it this time. I start snapping photos of the people greeting each other, the hugs, the cries of joy . . .

And then, through the viewfinder, I see him.

He's standing next to a tall, well-built man who is holding a huge placard that says 'I love you!' and that Ryan is pointing at.

I look in amazement at Ryan who is smiling at me. He stares at me for a moment and then points again before slowly opening his arms. He grins and then I am running, laughing, crying, stumbling, swearing, but mostly crying. I run, dragging my massive bloody suitcase behind me, camera banging into my chest and my heart pounding out of it. My bra strap slips down my shoulder, my skirt tangles around my knees and if I'm not careful I'm going to fall flat on my face in front of everyone, but none of that matters because now . . . now I am back in my Ryan's arms.

I throw my body against his, entwine my legs and arms around him like he is a tree, a magnificent, grounded oak tree and I am a bird who has found her way back to her nest. I'm clinging on to him and I can't speak.

'I've been waiting for you,' Ryan whispers at last.

'For how long?'

'All day, six months, a lifetime . . .'

'Me too,' I answer. I look up at him, at his face that I know better than my own, at his eyes which are bluer than the Sydney sky and his lips which I've kissed so many times and yet not nearly enough times at all.

'I don't want to be another day without you, Ryan,' I say at last. 'You're all I want, you're all I ever wanted but other stuff just . . . got in the way. I–I'm so sorry for what I did—'

'Shh,' he says, and he smiles and I know I'm forgiven. 'This is a fresh start, OK?'

I nod and wriggle my camera out from between us as Ryan kisses me.

'I'm never going to forget this kiss,' I mutter into Ryan's lips as I hold it out and take a photo of the moment I didn't dare dream would ever happen.

'And I'm never going to let you go again,' Ryan says, and I forget all about capturing the moment on film and instead savour his lips in a way I have never done before, and that I swear to myself I will do forever more.

Sealed With A Kiss

You know how you have a year where it feels like everyone you know is getting married and you end up pinging drunkenly from one wedding to another, dancing wildly, behaving badly and secretly wondering when it's going to happen to you? Well, I never had that. I'd only ever been to one wedding before my own. And even though I was overjoyed to be back together with Ryan, I still retained a bit of my in-built Carter cynicism about it. But this was a Cooper wedding, done the Cooper way. I was back with my first love and little by little over the period of that beautiful, emotionally charged day, I found myself understanding what the fuss was all about and feeling that perhaps, just perhaps, I could do the whole 'I do' thing, too. One day ...

We're in Ryan's teenage bedroom at Jackie and Dave's house, getting ready for Lydia and Carl's wedding. Lydia is using the annexe that Ryan and I lived in (was it really only four years ago?) as her bridal suite – before we make our way to the venue. I'm quickly hopping into my outfit while she has her make-up done, before going back in to help her get into hers.

'You'd better be careful or you're gonna upstage the bride!' Ryan kisses my neck, pinches my bum and winks at me in the mirror. I laugh as he spins me round to face him so I nearly fall out of my hot-pink dress.

I put my hands on his chest as he brushes his lips over mine and groans, before nuzzling his nose in my neck.

'God, I wish we were staying in a hotel,' he murmurs, rubbing his hands up and down my body. 'I would rip off this dress right now and . . .'

'Now, now, spaghetti arms!' I chastise, channelling Baby from *Dirty Dancing* but feeling more like Julia Roberts, pre-*Pretty Woman* makeover, in my too-tight pink frock. We're interrupted by Ryan's mum's 'dulcet' tones.

'RY! MOLLEEEEEE! Come down and have a glass of pink champoo with us, darlin's! It'll soon be time to go!'

'You go,' I say to Ryan, kissing him on the lips and tying his pink cravat that sets off his deep tan acquired through holidays, sailing, football and, much to my disapproval, sunbeds. 'I need to go and do my bridesmaid duties! There!' I pat his neck and look at him approvingly. 'See you at the altar, best man!' And I wave my fingers at him and disappear out of his bedroom door, leaving him to begin the lengthy task of styling his hair.

I run down the stairs, passing the extensive black and white gallery of photos of the Coopers, now featuring Lydia and I. I still can't believe I'm up there. I asked Ryan if I'd been removed during our brief hiatus, but he'd assured me that Jackie had left me up. And after the way she'd greeted me with a big hug and an emphatic, 'It's *so* good to have you back, my darlin',' the first time I came over, I actually believed him. And despite my initial misgivings I feel honoured to be Lydia's bridesmaid too.

'Are you sure?' I'd said when she asked me four months ago. 'I mean Ryan and I have only just got back together ...'

'You're not planning on splitting up again, are you?' she'd replied matter-of-factly, flicking her blonde extensions off her bare shoulders as we'd worked our way through our pizzas in Ugo's, our favourite local restaurant, one Saturday afternoon.

'No *way*,' I'd said emphatically, and necked a large mouthful of wine.

'Well then, of course I'm sure. Besides, it's not like you're he only one ... I've got eight!' I'd burst out laughing as she'd leaned in and whispered, 'Jordan's got nothin' on *this* wedding!'

I'm nervous as we wait in front of Leez Priory, watching the flock of hired peacocks strut past us ('Wicked idea of Jackie's!' Lydia said when we got out of the pink Cadillac). We're waiting for the nod from the registrar to walk down the aisle (and by aisle I mean 'pink carpet'). I'm nervous for Lydia – I know how long she has waited for this moment, she and Carl have been engaged for two years *and* had a baby – but I'm also nervous because I know that this is the moment that everyone will know that Ryan and I are serious, that we're back for good.

As the strains of James Blunt's 'You're Beautiful' begin to play from the string quartet inside, I can't help but laugh at her audacity to choose this as her wedding march. It's typical of Lydia to be so wonderfully carefree and confident. Lydia turns around and winks at us all and I cradle little baby Beau, an absolute pudding of a boy (who, confusingly, is wearing a pink babygro to fit in with the colour theme), and we begin to walk.

I can't deny it, I love seeing all those girls' faces as they watch us come in. Especially when I realize that Nikki Pritchard is there. Single, mum-of-three Nikki Pritchard, who Lydia used to work with at the beauty salon. The same Nikki Pritchard from Westcliff High who was head of the Heathers. I love the gasps of astonishment for Lydia's white dress 'with a twist, babes'. The twist being that it's tight and short, has a hot-pink sash and shows off her brilliant legs and bright-pink Jimmy Choo shoes. 'I did not pay five hundred quid for these babies to hide 'em under some big blancmange,' she'd said when she had her fitting.

Then I see my mum and dad and they smile at me fondly, which makes me want to cry. And then there's Ryan, standing next to Carl and to my surprise, my breath catches in my throat, my chest heaving out of my low-cut dress with all the love I feel for him. I blink back tears as I see how hard Carl is working to hold it together. I see Ryan put his hand on his big brother's shoulder and Carl clings on to his fingers for a moment, and Ryan then nudges him towards Lydia, who grabs Carl's hand and practically drags him into a pre-wedding snog. Ryan looks back at me, his eyes dancing with happiness.

'Time for the wedding breakfast!' calls Jackie, a vision in fuschia pink, strutting alongside the peacocks on the lawn in front of the marquee in her high heels and even higher fascinator, her blonde layered bob styled to perfection.

It's all brilliantly bling but completely lovely because Lydia and Carl are so happy and in love and they couldn't give a toss what anyone else thinks. Even my mum and dad seem to be enjoying it, in their own way. Jackie insisted I pass on an invite to them, too. 'You're practically part of the Cooper family, my darlin', which means so are they!' I spotted them briefly squeezing hands during the ceremony and they even smiled at the rude jokes in the speeches in between the tentative sips of the single glass of champagne they'd each allowed themselves. Pity they've failed to spot Dave topping up their glasses every time they look away.

I smile as Mum comes over now, uncharacteristically wobbly on her feet.

'So, Molly dear,' she says, briskly tapping her hat, which is perched primly on her short hair. 'Do you think it's about time I bought another of these?' She winks and I laugh and wag my finger at her as if I am the school teacher. I have never seen my mother wink. I should ply her with champagne more often. I think of how disapproving she used to be of Ryan and how far she and I have come in our relationship since my awkward teenage years, and I know it's Ryan and his family we have to thank for our easier, warmer relationship.

I watch as Mum sways back to Dad's side. I'm not alone for long.

'You alright, Molly?' Ryan's lovely Nanny Door says, handing me another glass of champagne. I smile as I take it from her, genuinely pleased to have the chance to chat with her. She's always been my closest ally. She slips her hand through my arm and we wander over to a table to sit down. She looks adorable in a pale-blue trouser suit and I compliment her on it.

'Oooh, the colour matches my eyes, doll – and my rinse!' She's being self-deprecating. I remark how well she's matched it with some silver shoes and a big silk scarf, and she smiles serenely, clearly pleased by the genuine compliment. 'Well, I model my style on Jane Fonda, dear. Her exercise vids still keep me young, y'know! Between that, me pelvic floors and a monthly trip to Champneys, I'm in pretty good shape! Anyway, enough about me, what about you, Molly? You were looking a little lost there if I weren't much mistaken.'

'No Nan, I was just taking it all in . . .'

She leans in closer and winks. One of her false lashes has slipped. 'Thinking what you and Ry will do differently on your big day, eh love?'

'No!' I exclaim and then laugh, because I kind of was.

'No shame in that, doll,' Nanny says, taking a sip of her champagne and smacking her pink lips together. 'Sometimes it takes losing someone you love to realize just what you've got. Of course, the ideal is to never lose them at all but, well, that's not always so easy, is it, dear?' Her voice drifts off and I know she's thinking of her Arthur. I take her arm and she smiles brightly. 'Now, d'you fancy a dance? I love this song!'

'Hey, gorge,' Ryan says drunkenly as he leads me back onto the dance floor later (I needed a rest after Nanny Door; she was unstoppable once she got up there).

I nod my head as Mum twirls past with Dave to Kanye West's 'Gold Digger' and Dad and Jackie jive by.

'Check John out!' Ryan chuckles.

Just then Dave spins my mum around and delivers her into Dad's arms just in time for a slow dance to 'Hey Jude'.

Ryan squeezes my waist as we watch them, clearly so much happier doing their little waltz together than the fancy moves the Coopers were making them throw. My throat aches as I realize that this is exactly what their marriage is, a slow waltz and they have, in their own way, been enjoying it all along. It's me who's always wished they'd dance faster and fancier.

'Ehhh, Ry, Molly!' Carl says in his The Fonz voice as he lurches over to us and throws his arms around our shoulders, closely followed by Alex who clearly thinks he's Patrick Swayze, and Gaz who appears to be marching across the dance floor like Doody from *Grease.* 'Isn't this just the best day ever! When are you gonna do the deed, eh?'

'I'd *love* to do the deed wiv *her*,' Gaz says with a chortle, tilting his pork-pie hat in Lydia's best mate's direction. 'Watch this!' And he marches over to the bridesmaid who is gyrating in the middle of the dance floor. We watch as Gaz taps the girl on the shoulder and she immediately turns around and snogs him.

'No *way*!' Alex yells.

Everyone bursts out laughing. 'Don't think that means you can avoid the question, bro,' Carl says, ruffling Ryan's hair just as Lydia dances up and throws her arms around us.

'Come on,' she says, jumping up and down just as the DJ puts on 'We Are Family'. 'All the Coopers together!'

Ryan kisses me on my head as the three of them begin to bounce.

'But I'm not a Cooper!' I protest, feeling my feet being lifted up off the floor as Jackie and Dave join us.

'Not yet,' Lydia whispers, and I blush.

'Bou-KAAAAAY TIIIIIIIME!' Jackie screeches across the dance floor at the end of the song and I watch as the female guests streak past me, an orange lightening flash of fake tan, all yapping excitedly like a pack of Chihuahuas. Lydia gets up on the stage in front of the band clutching her pink floral bouquet complete with pompoms, and Ryan nudges me with his elbow.

'Aren't you going over?' he whispers.

'Nope, I reckon I'm safer back here,' I say, folding my arms for good luck.

'Are you READY?!' Lydia screeches and holds up her bouquet of fuschia roses as if it's the Olympic torch. 'ONE, TWO, THREEEEEE!'

I watch as the bouquet soars in slow motion, over all the girls' heads, their faces shine with hope, then turn to frustration, and then disappointment as it flies over and beyond their reach. And then I feel Ryan push past me and I watch in astonishment as he leaps athletically into the air to catch it. Then Ryan lands and turns around, brandishing the bouquet and grinning broadly at me. He runs over and slam dunks it into my arms before doing a lap of the room, like he's just won the FA Cup. Then he appears in front of me again, throws his arms around me and kisses me as the room erupts into cheers.

I cover my face in embarrassment and he pulls my hands away from my face so he can kiss me. Lydia waves at me from the stage delightedly and Carl gives a thumbs up. I spot Jackie and Dave in another corner jumping up and down and clapping. I feel my skin prickle and my face turn the same colour as my dress.

Ryan laughs. 'Sorry, babe, I just couldn't resist . . .'

'Couldn't resist showing off!' I chastise, but I smile and I slip my hand into his.

He winks. 'I just know how bad you are at sport. You'd never have caught that! Most girls would be thanking me.'

'Ah,' I interrupt, 'but you forget, Cooper. I'm not like *most* girls . . .'

He grins and cups my chin, pulling me in for a kiss. 'I know, Molly Carter. That's what I love about you.'

I wander into my empty bedroom, wrapped in a towel. I take a moment to look around. It may not look like much now with the mattress on the floor and everything in boxes, but of all the rooms in the house this is the one I'll miss the most. It's been my haven over the past few years. Ryan and I used to joke when we first got together that if it weren't for work, we'd just stay in bed forever. I'm not sure he expected me to ever carry through my threat. After he went, I lay here for days on end, weeks even. When I'd pulled myself together and could leave the house, I'd still spend my evenings here, going through old photo albums. Because I'd painted the bedroom the same duck-egg blue as our old kitchen, I could almost pretend we were still living in our flat – before everything went wrong.

I redecorated a couple of years ago. I wanted to start afresh, find Molly *Carter* again, so I painted the room a rich mulberry colour. It felt cosy, womblike. It said 'single' not 'sad'. The now-bare balcony windows were framed by thick, lustrous gold curtains; over the bed was the same print of John and Yoko I've had since uni. Stacked around the edge of the room were piles of photography and art books, and my dressing table next to the balcony doors. That's still there complete with a couple of framed photos I haven't wrapped up yet. One is of my mum and dad on their wedding day. I go and pick it up. I gaze critically at the picture. I used to hate how serious they look but now I appreciate how hard marriage is, how much a couple has to face together in a lifetime. And how solid you have to be to stay together through all those ups and downs. I am in awe of them. Not just for staying together but because of how strong they've been for me.

I rip off some bubble wrap from the roll that's lying on the floor and look at the picture one more time before wrapping it, noticing how my dad gazes into the camera lens with his wistful smile that I know is his version of heart-burstingly happy. I pop the picture in a box marked 'Ship' and glance outside.

The January morning has lifted its blanket of darkness and the vast sky is now stonewash blue with a filter of bright, white sunlight peeking through. It is going to be a beautiful day. I smile and open the doors, stepping out to where my wrought-iron table was placed until it was packed up along with the two chairs. I have sat there for uncountable hours in all weather, the changing seasons reflecting my changing state of mind. The winter rain mixed with my tears, the spring breeze blew away my misery, the summer sun healing my broken heart.

I hop back in and head over to the fitted wardrobes. I open a door and gaze at the contents on one side as I rifle through.

My jeans are thrown haphazardly in a way that would make a Gap sales assistant faint. My favourite grey skinnies are packed away so I root around for my other fail-safe denim option: dungarees. I know, I know, the item of clothing style forgot, but they're so *comfy*. And as my mum would say, 'You're moving house, my dear, not going on a fashion parade'. Funny how eventually you really do start turning into your mum. And most surprisingly, how you don't actually mind.

I pull them on and look in the mirror that is leaning against the wall. I barely recognize myself. OK, so I *thought* the dungarees were comfy but cute in an ironic 1980s Demi-Moore-in-*Ghost* kind of a way, but I now realize I look more like Meryl Streep in *Mamma Mia*. I giggle at the thought and I unselfconsciously replicate a few Abba moves in front of the mirror, singing the chorus of the title song under my breath. I'm interrupted by the doorbell just as I get to the broken-hearted bit.

The Welcome Kiss

I'd never really understood that phrase 'bosom of the family' until I met Ryan's. Probably because my family's 'bosom' always felt meagre in comparison to most; the love was small, contained, more of a Kate Moss double-A cup than the Baywatch bust I longed for. Their love didn't seem to cushion or protect me, or spill out showily. When I was young I wondered if I'd ever know the kind of ostentatious shows of affection that 'normal' families seem to have. And having rested my head in the Coopers' ample cleavage, I felt like I'd got it at last. I was home. Since then I've realized that my family's love was always there. It still lay a heartbeat away. I just didn't get close enough to hear it.

I'm standing nervously on Ryan's parents' doorstep in the salubrious street in Marine Parade, a.k.a the rich part of Leigh-on-Sea. The house is an impressive double-fronted, Edwardian detached property with a huge stone driveway and two big stone lions guarding the front door. There's even a fountain in front of the house. No wonder he still lives at home. He's probably got his own *wing*. This is not at all what I expected. Suddenly I am petrified. My finger is hovering over the bell as I summon up the courage to press it, silently cursing my boyfriend of a week. I mean, what was he thinking asking me here already? And what was *I* thinking saying yes?

I press the doorbell and take a deep breath. I feel completely inappropriately dressed. I refused to ditch my Converse when Freya the fashion editor tried to get me to wear some heels. However, I did concede to ditching my parka for this grey funnel-neck coat. I muss up my fringe so it covers my eyes a little, throw my shoulders back, adjust my bra and wipe my hands on my jeans. On the advice of Lisa, the beauty editor and my desk buddy from work, who is determined to get me out of my make-up rut, I've slightly femmed up my overall look by ditching the heavy kohl and I'm all pink-glossed lips and blushed cheeks. When I left my flat I thought I almost looked pretty but now I realize I just look stupid. I wish I'd just been me, but more than that I wish I'd said no to Ryan when he asked me to come.

I hear someone walking towards the door. This is *madness*. I'm about to turn and walk back down the front path when the door swings open and a vision of glamour with bleached blonde hair wearing a Juicy Couture tracksuit opens the door. She looks more LA than Leigh-on-Sea.

'Molly? Hiya! I'm Jackie, Ryan's mum. I'm so glad to *finally* meet you, darlin'!' She throws her arms out and envelops me in a hug.

Finally? I've only been seeing your son for a week!

Molly?' she repeats, pulling back with a dazzling white but warm smile. 'Come in, darlin'! Don't be standing there on the doorstep, you make the place look messy!'

She laughs as she ushers me in, the gold of her watch face and Tiffany heart-locket necklace glowing like the sun.

I look around the hallway, desperately hoping Ryan will appear when Jackie spontaneously envelops me in another highly perfumed hug. Isn't this how boa constrictors kill their prey? Just when I think I might pass out, she pulls away but holds on to me tightly at arm's-length and studies me appraisingly. I slide my eyes to the left and right to see if I can see any sign of Ryan in my peripheral vision. Just then she lets me go and I resist the urge to rub my arms.

'Now, darlin',' she smiles as she heads towards the giant staircase, 'you have to excuse me still being in me slopsies!' She gestures at her pink tracksuit. 'I've just been throwing some lunch together and now I'm going to put some make-up on . . .'

She looks like this without make-up?

'. . . get dressed and come back downstairs.' And she disappears up the stairs, calling, 'Make yourself at home, darlin'!'

I gaze around me. Where the hell is Ryan – well, apart from emblazoned all over the walls? Everywhere I look there are huge portraits of the family. There are several of Ryan's mum and dad with their arms wrapped round each other, in one they look like they're actually French kissing. Then there's Carl and Ryan photographed through the years. In the hallway are gigantic blown-up studio prints of each of them as babies, naked and sitting on a shagpile like something from an Athena poster. There's a cute one of Ryan as a toddler on the beach in his wetsuit standing next to Carl. They're there on the beach again as teenagers, both running up the sand, wind whipping their hair after a sailing session. There's a montage of Ryan grinning mischievously in his football kit, clutching various trophies. In one of the pictures Carl's arm is thrown proudly and protectively over his little brother's shoulder. There's photographs of the whole family all tanned and smiling on holiday, and another studio portrait but this time of all four of them wearing white shirts and blue jeans where they clearly couldn't sit still long enough for the photographer to take a classic picture of them, so instead they are mid-hysterical laugh, like someone has told a joke. *Or they've taken a look at their matching outfits*, my (rude) teenage self points out.

I stand awkwardly staring at them all and practically faint with relief when Ryan finally appears.

'Molly! I didn't realize you were already here. 'MUM!' he bellows. 'You should have told me Molly was here!'

Jackie peers round the bannisters at the top of the grand spiral stairs, now wrapped in a towel and brandishing various make-up brushes. I quickly avert my eyes.

'Sorry Ry-Ry, I thought you knew. Besides, Molly's a big girl, I told her to make herself at home. She's one of the family now, right, darlin'? Ooh, introduce her to Nanny Door, will you?' and she disappears again.

I looked sideways at Ryan. *'Ry-Ry?'* I mouth.

'Ignore her,' he grins good-naturedly. 'She's just trying to embarrass me.'

An hour later and Ryan has shown me around. He told me on the tour that Dave and Jackie bought it twenty years ago and put a big extension and conservatory on so it now boasts five bedrooms, a beautiful kitchen-diner with an enormous island unit and shiny granite surfaces, as well as a cavernous lounge, dining room, cinema/games room and a gym. If my mum saw it she would literally vomit with a mixture of jealousy that she doesn't live in such luxury and immense snobbery about their interior-design style. It's

all glass coffee tables with fresh flower displays, huge modern appli-
ances, an enormous state-of-the-art cinema and sound systems, a
gigantic hot tub in the garden, vast black leather sofas and bold,
oversized statement chairs. It's garish and not at all to my taste, but
strangely, it works.

We walk back into the lounge and Ryan introduces me to
Nanny Door, a spritely septuagenarian who's been widowed for
ten years with ocean-blue eyes and a smile just like Ryan's. She
lives down the road from Ryan's parents, is fiercely independent
but comes over for lunch every weekend.

'Hello lovey, my name's Doreen,' she says, putting down the
newspaper and heaving herself out of a pink throne. 'But you can
call me Nanny Door. Everyone does. Bleedin' ridiculous thing,'
she grumbles at the chair as she stands up. 'Who does Jackie think
she is, Posh bleedin' Spice?'

'Nanny Door!' Ryan admonishes with a laugh and I can't help
but join him.

'I heard that, Mum!' shouts Jackie from another room and
Nanny Door cackles mischievously.

'Anyway, pleased to meet you, Molly.' I have to say, you ain't
what I expected. I thought you'd look like that Helen from *Big
Brother*. Oooh, she did make me laugh. Did you watch it, doll?' She
affects a Welsh accent and widens her eyes. "I love blinkin' I do!"
Ah ha ha!' she cackles. 'Ohh, it were *classic*, weren't it?' She chuckles
again and then shuffles closer and studies me with her piercing gaze.
'You're prettier than her though, dear. All Ryan's other girls have
been blonde before, ain't they, Ryan dear? And a bit lacking in the
old woo-hoo . . .' she taps her head '. . . brain department. But you
look like you've got your fair share of marbles!' And she smiles up
adoringly at her grandson who towers over her. Ryan throws his
arm around her shoulders, kisses her on the head and leads her into
the dining room where lunch is being served.

Jackie is wearing what looks like a black lurex minidress, with a gold snake-style belt around her impressively trim-for-her-age waist. Dave's come home from a job and changed into a pale-pink Ralph Lauren jumper and jeans, and Carl crashes in with his new hairdresser girlfriend, Lydia. He's absolutely besotted by her, and rightly so. She's got this incredible presence, not just due to her incredible figure. My teenage self definitely wouldn't approve – if I'd met her in school I'd have probably labelled her as just another 'Heather' but I'm surprised to find myself instantly drawn to her. We sit down in the light-flooded dining room and Jackie brings in a real ready-made spread. And when I say ready-made, I mean it's literally silver-foiled Waitrose ready meals all the way. It's kind of a relief.

'The first thing you have to know about Jackie,' Dave announces proudly as he digs into a silver-foil tray that has been put on a grand silver platter, 'is that she don't cook. In fact, we actively encourage her not to cook. Firstly, because she's too busy keeping us all on track, making herself look beautiful, doing her charity work, running my accounts and keeping the house looking nice. But also because she's *bloody awful* at it!'

'Well that's good,' I laugh, touching Ryan on the knee. 'At least he won't ever expect too much from me, I can't cook either!'

Jackie smiles good-humouredly at me. 'Good on you, Molly babes!' She turns to Dave.

'You'll fit right in here, gal,' Nanny Door says to me, digging into her overflowing plate like she hasn't eaten in weeks. 'Every weekend I come here praying that my Jackie ain't tried to make anything herself. I don't know who she gets it from.' Her wicked smile suggests that she knows only too well.

'Well, culinary skills or not, it didn't stop me falling in love with her, did it, Jacks?' says Dave with a loving wink at his wife.

'Oh Dave, you big softie . . .' Jackie flaps her hand, her diamond-encrusted eternity ring catching the light as she does so.

'I knew it as soon as I saw her walking down Southend Pier with her mates. It was 1969 and she was wearing this tiny minidress and white wet-look boots.'

'And he had this luscious long hair and a tight roll-neck on with flares,' Jackie adds dreamily. 'He told me I looked hip, offered me a cigarette and then kissed me.'

'I was only seventeen, but I knew I'd met the girl I wanted to marry,' Dave continues. I note how they tell the story as seamlessly as relay runners. 'When you know, you know, right Jacks?' he says, offering her the story baton.

'You do, Dave,' she says with a smile. 'And we did.'

'Hey Dad, I bet if you'd known Mum couldn't cook you'd have changed your mind about marrying her!' Carl pipes up with a deep laugh but Dave just looks lovingly across the table at his wife. It is like the rest of us are no longer in the room.

'Nothing would have changed my mind about this girl,' he says solemnly. 'As soon as I saw her, I was a goner.' And he takes his napkin off his lap, stands up and blows his wife a kiss across the table. I watch in disbelief and a little bit of horror as Jackie stands up and pretends to catch it and put it down her cleavage. I want to laugh, but I sense that this would absolutely be the wrong thing to do. Then Dave shakes his head as if he's just come out of a trance and smiles widely around the table at us all as he lowers himself back down into his suede-backed dining chair.

'They say the way to a man's heart is through his stomach, but I'm living proof that ain't true!' And he picks up his knife and fork as if with these words he has just gained philosopher status.

'The only living proof I can see is that fast food ain't good for your waistline!' chips in Nanny Door with a cackle and everyone laughs, including Dave.

'Ryan learned to cook out of necessity more than anything, didn't you, bud?' Carl says, rolling his eyes at his dad. 'Has he cooked for you yet, Molly?'

I smiled. 'No, there's been a lot of talk, but no action so far . . .'

'Ooooh!' chorus Jackie and Dave.

'No, what I meant was . . .' my voice trails off and I stare desperately at Ryan, but he's too busy laughing to save me. Instead, Nanny Door stretches out her hand to me and squeezes it. 'We laugh a lot in this family, darlin',' she said. 'You'll soon get used to it.'

And that's when I start laughing too.

It doesn't take me long to realize that despite the lack of cooking skills, Jackie is not to be underestimated. After lunch I watch in amazement as she efficiently marches around her house, the sergeant major to Ryan, Carl and Dave's soldiers. She organizes Ryan's teaching calendar and after-school coaching. She files Dave's invoices whilst advising Carl on negotiating a fixed-rate mortgage on the three-bed property he's hoping to buy. Half an hour later she's looked at the plans of his house, proposed an extension, found a spare slot in Dave's diary for his company to do the build, called her solicitor and asked him to work on behalf of Carl, organized a charity event at the school, called a gardener to mow Nanny Door's lawn and contacted a local furnishings store and asked for them to send carpet and fabric samples for Carl's future house. That he hasn't even bought yet. She's a one-woman marching band, and she doesn't play a duff note.

'Your mum's a force to be reckoned with,' I say to Ryan later that afternoon as we're lazing on the leather sofa in the lounge.

'I know,' he smiles, 'she's pretty amazing.'

I lift my head off his chest and look at him. 'Do you think they like me?' I ask, suddenly desperate to be accepted into the bosom of this warm, loving family that's so far removed from my own.

'I *know* they do,' he replies, and strokes his finger across my cheek as he draws me in for a kiss.

When it comes to saying my goodbyes that evening, Jackie pulls me into her arms once again whilst Ryan is busy bear-hugging his dad and swapping football banter with Carl. But this time I'm ready for it. I'm surprised to find I even enjoy it.

'It was lovely to meet you at last, darlin',' she smiles and brushes a little clump of my fringe off my face in such a maternal way that it makes me want to cry. I'm not sure I've let my own mother ever do that. The last time I let her touch it she was trying to tug it into two tight, neat plaits. That was just before I cut it all off and dyed it Molly Ringwald red.

'It was lovely to meet you too,' I reply with a shy smile. 'Now I can see why Ryan has always been so reluctant to move out . . .'

I glance around the hallway again and instead of being disparaging of the giant photo displays, it becomes clear that this is a genuinely happy family. It makes my throat ache when I think of the single, stilted wedding photo of Mum and Dad that sits on our mantelpiece next to a particularly horrifying school picture of me looking like Wednesday Addams.

Jackie laughs and hugs me again. 'My boys are my life,' she says. Then she holds me out at arm's length and studies my face carefully like she did earlier, her carefully painted pink lips now drawn into a serious line. 'I just hope you're ready for Ryan to be yours. He's fallen hard for you, Molly darlin', and I don't want him hurt. My little boy isn't used to heartbreak. He came out of the womb smiling and I want him to stay that way.'

I shake my head dutifully, wanting to please her so badly.

Jackie smiles and kisses me on the cheek, leaving a pink imprint, and turns back to her son. 'You got a good one here, Ry,' she smiles.

Ryan doesn't answer he just strides over and kisses me full on the lips as his family whoops and cheers around us.

'That's one for the wall!' Jackie says, clapping her hands in delight. 'Get the camera, Dave!' she says. Maybe we have more in common than I thought. 'Now do it again!' she cries. And Ryan and I stand in the doorway and kiss. I never thought I'd say this but maybe I could get used to these PDAs after all.

As Ryan shows me out of the house, his mum standing behind him, I realize that we've just become an official couple. But I'm not sure who made the final decision: Ryan or his mum.

Just Can't Be Away From You Kiss

It's impossible for anyone to understand the complete lure of love until you've been in it. Before Ryan I was the Queen of the Commitment-phobes. I swore I'd never give myself wholly to a guy, that I would keep my independence, retain the biggest part of me for myself, my career and my best friend, Casey. My main concern in life was to have freedom, excitement, adventure and travel – not love.

Funny how things can change in a heartbeat, isn't it? Because suddenly Ryan was there and all I wanted was to be with him all the time. He was intoxicating, addictive. In those early weeks, being with him was more alluring than anything else I could have imagined; you could have offered me a flight to the moon and I wouldn't have gone if it had meant being apart from him.

I know some people are dubious of someone experiencing a volte-face like this. But I bet they just haven't been there yet themselves. They haven't felt that overriding thrill of meeting the person that they want to spend every minute of every hour of every day with. Someone who understands you more in a few short weeks than the people who have known you your whole life.

But I was always burdened by the feeling that this kind of sudden, intense relationship wasn't meant to happen to a girl like me. I just didn't believe I deserved it.

Now? Now I would give anything to feel that way again. That's why the best advice I can give anyone is to not be afraid to give love your all. Even if you end up hurt or bruised, it is, as Tennyson acutely observed, and I duly realized albeit too late, 'Better to have loved and lost than never to have loved at all.'

I'm in the place that has become the most natural and comfortable place in the world for my body in the past four weeks, spooned in Ryan's arms on his black leather couch and sipping on a fresh berry smoothie that Ryan has made. Well, not *his* couch, it's his parents'. It's a Saturday afternoon and we're at his house. It's where we've been for the past three Saturdays, spending every delicious moment of the day together. After wasting so many years actually getting together, now we're like children with sweets, gorging on the pleasure of each other's company.

'Molly ...' Ryan says softly into my ear. 'Can I ask you something?'

'Sure I say', turning my face up towards him. He strokes my hair and nuzzles his lips into my neck and I close my eyes in rapturous delight.

'You know how much I love being with you like this, don't you?' he whispers.

'Mmmm,' I reply, as he kisses my neck again. I love it too. I open my eyes and glance at the film that I've been so easily distracted from. Saturdays have become our movie days. Today we've watched *10 Things I Hate About You*. We're now watching *The Champ*, which apparently is one of Ryan's all-time favourites.

I twist my body around so I'm facing Ryan and realize he's been crying.

Ry sniffs. 'It just always gets me this film. And then I was thinking how happy I am with you and it made me think, Molly, I was just wondering how you'd feel about ...'

I sit up as Dave walks in. 'Alright Champ, you're not crying at this mush again, are you?' he chuckles and rubs his youngest son's head affectionately.

'Argh, geddoff, Dad,' Ryan pushes him away good-naturedly,

and Dave jogs around the sofa and fake-pummells Ryan's stomach. 'C'mon, son, gimme your best pop!'

' You know I'd never take a swipe at an old, out-of-shape man! 'Now Dad, can you give us a minute . . .'

'Old!' Dave exclaims, ignoring Ryan's hint. Ryan rolls his eyes and smiles apologetically at me. I'm desperate to know what he was trying to ask. 'I'm only forty-seven, mate! And I'm in peak condition!'

'Pops, you're embarrassing Molly, stop now!' Ryan laughs. 'If you stopped eating all those big breakfasts, you'd look alright for your age. But you need to start exercising. You built a gym in the house – why don't you use it?'

'Ahhh, these fitness lunatics, Molly, they're always trying to convert those of us who are perfectly happy as we are, am I right?'

'I hear you, Dave, I hear you,' I smirk at Ryan cheekily. 'Just because he spends his life running around a football field telling people what to do, he thinks he can do it to us too!' I smile, thinking about how easy it always is being here and how at home I feel. Dave is raising his eyebrows in confusion at his son and as I glance back at Ryan I spot him pulling a desperate 'privacy please' face.

'Well, ahem, so,' Dave says, edging out of the room. 'I should go and leave you kids to . . . you know, it. I've got things to do. Busy, busy, busy that's me, eh, Ryan? Busy working hard to pay for this big house that could easily fit more people . . . ha ha. Anyway, must go!'

I laugh as I settle back into Ryan's arm on the sofa. The film has been paused and for a moment we sit in silence. Ryan coughs and I look at him.

'Sorry about that,' he smiles.

'Don't be. Your dad's great.'

'Yeah, he is.' He takes my hand. 'So, Molly . . . there's this thing I really need to talk to you about . . .'

'Hello my darlin's!' Jackie appears in the doorway and Ryan

groans and buries his face in his hands. 'Can I get you kids a little tipple?'

'No thanks, Mum,' Ryan replies uncharacteristically edgily.

'Are you sure?' She comes and perches between us on the couch. 'A little cheeky Saturday afternoon glass of vino? Or a beer? Tea, coffee? Coke? Milk?'

'No thank you, Mum,' Ryan says, 'we're just happy *talking*, you know?'

Whatever hint Ryan is trying to give his mum, she isn't getting it.

'Maybe we can get a Chinese and watch *Who Wants To Be A Millionaire* together tonight then?' she says brightly. 'We haven't had a proper family night for ages.'

Ryan leans across and smiles at his mum. 'That'd be nice, thanks. *Later* sounds good.' He looks at her straight in the eyes and then she throws her hand over her mouth and giggles.

'Of course! Silly me! Yes! I must go and . . .' she looks at Ryan desperately. 'Cook dinner?' And she skips out of the room.

I settle back on the sofa again and go to press play on the remote but Ryan stops me. 'Do you mind staying in tonight?' he asks, stroking my fingers.

'Course not! You know I only come here so much because I'm in love with your family!'

I go to press play again but Ryan stops me, again, and leans over me, kissing me gently on the lips.

'Good. Because, well I was wondering . . .' Ryan looks at the door as if checking for any more interruptions.

I stroke his hair. 'What's this all about, Cooper?'

'I just had this crazy urge to ask you something, Molly,' he says. 'I wanted to say it earlier, it's something I've been thinking about and I know it's not been long but . . .'

I pull myself up so my head is resting on the arm and look at him quizzically. 'What?'

'Move in with me, Molly!'

'WHAT?' I am struck sideways with shock. This is not what I expected. We've been dating a month. The best month of my life. But only a month. And I'm not meant to have a serious boyfriend. Especially a serious boyfriend who I've known since I was fifteen. It's not part of my Life List.

Ryan turns my face to his and looks into my eyes, all joking now gone.

'Give notice on your flat and move in with me, babe. I wanna be with you all the time.'

'You're crazy!' I exclaim.

'I'm not crazy!' he laughs. 'I'm in love. I love you.'

My jaw drops open, I'm sure I am dribbling. I am dumbstruck for the first time in my life. He Loves Me! Me! The social leper with a bad haircut and attitude! Me! The girl whose camera was her best friend until Casey came along. The girl who was convinced her first kiss was a humiliating dare. The girl who thought she'd never get the guy. *The girl who dreamed of more than what a man could give her*, my teen self reminds me.

Not any more, I tell her. That was then. Now all I want is Ryan.

'So what do you say?' he presses.

And I don't know why, or where it came from, or why I'm not listening to my gut instinct that is saying I'm too young, I've got too much to do, too much I want to achieve. But somehow, without me even thinking it and for once, propelled by my heart, not my head, nor my mouth, my answer comes out of my mouth.

'YES!' Final answer. We kiss and I feel like a millionaire.

The Kiss Over The Threshold

It's a strange thing to have your future all wrapped up in a parcel and tied with a bow when you're twenty-two. 'Here's your perfect man, life, home!' But I grabbed it because I knew a good thing when I saw it. There was no doubt in my mind, not back then anyway.

We're standing in the sweeping driveway of the Cooper's house and in front of the enormous double garage that Dave has spent the last two months converting into a one-bedroom flat for Ryan and me.

Jackie smiles at us all. 'I announce this garage – I mean Ry and Molly's annexe – officially OPEN!' She cuts the red ribbon that she's put across the brand-new door, and Ryan, Dave, Nanny Door, Carl, Lydia and I clap and cheer. Despite the cold January weather, a flood of warmth bursts through my body. Jackie waits for the clapping and Carl's shouts of 'Shag pad!' to die down to speak again.

'Ry and Molly,' she begins, clasping her hands together as if she is the Queen giving her annual speech. Dave stands beside her silently with his arms folded over his ample stomach, blue eyes twinkling with a mixture of amusement and pride. 'I just wanna take this opportunity to welcome you both to our house,' Dave glances sideways at her and she gets the hint, 'I mean, your house. And your new life together as a co-habiting couple! And my Dave and I wanna wish you all the love and luck and happiness in the world, my darlin's. And to say, you know where we are if you need us . . .'

'Yeah, too bloody close!' calls Carl. I giggle as Dave unfolds his arms and jokingly clips the back of his eldest son's head.

Ryan takes the key which Jackie has put on the end of the red ribbon, unlocks the front door and we step inside.

'So, what do you think?' Dave is grinning at us as we stand in what used to be their garage, turning around in amazement to look at the beautiful modern living space he's transformed it into.

'Dad, it's wicked!' Ryan exclaims and throws his arms around him. They slap each other on the back and turn to face me, one arm still hanging over each other's shoulders.

'It's incredible, Dave!' I kiss him on the cheek and he squeezes me tightly. And it is lovely, it really is. It's such a sweet thing they've done for us. I still can't believe it was only two months ago that I left my rented flat and moved into Ryan's room at his parents' house.

I always said I'd rather die than move back to Leigh, turns out I just needed to get sick. Lovesick, that is. Not everyone was as happy as I thought they'd be about our decision though.

The Saturday after Ry asked me to move in with him, I went round to Casey's mum's café. I thought she'd be as excited as me when I told her my big news. The lunchtime rush was over and Toni, Casey's mum, had said she could take a quick break. It upsets me that Casey's still working there. It's always busy (due more to Toni and Casey's flirting skills rather than their serving ones) and I know she didn't get the grades for college, but she's quick-witted, funny, and I know she's got far more going for her than being her mum's greasy-spoon slave.

'Is that such a good idea?' she'd said quietly, gazing into her tea when I told her my news.

I tilted my head and looked at her. 'What do you mean?'

'Well, don't take this the wrong way, but . . . it's just a bit soon, isn't it? You've only been going out a few weeks!'

I'd bristled at this. Raw nerve. 'But Case, I've known him for *years*. He's not just some random that I've met in a nightclub and gone home with, you know.'

I hadn't meant for this to be a dig, but I knew as soon as it came out of my mouth that's how it sounded. Casey had coloured at my words, her olive skin taking on a dark berry tinge that matched the café's walls. I'd flapped my hands apologetically. 'Sorry, that's not how I meant it to come out.'

She'd smiled graciously. 'It's alright, Moll, I *know* I jump almost instantly into bed with men – mostly because I'm worried they'll change their minds – but that's my point! I jump into bed, not their *houses*. And especially not their *parents'* house.'

'I know it's fast, Case, but it already feels like we should have got together a long time ago. Now we are, neither of us wants to waste any more time.'

'OK,' she'd smiled at me, but it held none of its usual sparkle. 'I'm just looking out for you, babe. BFFs remember?' She links fingers through mine and I smile, thinking of our childhood, child*ish* devotion to each other. 'I just wanna make sure you know what you're doing. You've never shown any signs of wanting to live with a guy before, and it's a *really* big deal. You know how much you love your own space, you sure you're going to cope with being with someone 24/7?'

'We'll both be working. It won't be that different at all,' I'd said brightly.

Casey had just raised her dark eyebrows and stared at me, her uncharacteristic silence speaking volumes. 'And what about your mum and dad?' she'd said after the long pause. 'Do they know yet?'

I'd shaken my head at this. 'No! I haven't spoken to them for ages! You know me and my folks, ha ha!' I am trying to lift the mood because I hate that Casey is the one bringing me down. I expect it of my parents, but not Casey.

'Ryan wants us to go round there together soon as he doesn't want Mum finding out from someone else, it would be super-awkward at school for Ryan otherwise, what with them working together and all.' I still find it weird that Ryan's a teacher. Ryan Cooper a teacher! A PE teacher. It's like Danny Zuko ending up as Coach Calhoun.

'So when are you going to?' she'd pressed. 'Tell them, I mean.'

'Soon, today, now. Argh! Can I have something stronger than a Coke before I go?' I groan. 'I'm going to need it.'

'They'll be cool about it. Ryan's a diamond guy – and he's a teacher. Not much to complain about there.'

'Yeah, but we're not *married* . . .' I make the sign of the cross and roll my eyes. Casey knows how much I struggle with my parents' religious beliefs.

Casey had laughed and hugged me as I'd stood up. 'I'm glad you're happy, I am, babes. I just thought it'd be me first, I mean, you're meant to be having the career, I'm meant to have the husband, remember?' She pulls away and gazes at me intently. 'Just remember, you're only twenty-two, you don't have to rush into anything . . .' And she tapped her left finger and then patted her stomach.

'What? NO!' I'd exclaimed. 'Don't be crazy, Case! I'm only moving in with him, there's loads we want to do before we even think about that stuff!'

'You've talked about it then,' Casey had said quietly.

I'd blushed. I didn't want to admit that Ryan and I had planned our entire life out one night when we were in bed, said all the places we wanted to go, all the things we wanted to do, named our babies, our cats, even numbered our grandkids. We'd written it all down as a list in my diary. Molly and Ryan's Life List. Ryan figured it was time for a new one, now the one I wrote at uni is a bit out of date. And not much had changed from the original. Not really. We'd laughed a lot as we swapped the pen between us, adjusting each other's comments.

Molly's Life List and Ryan's!

Go to Australia

Live in New York - go to New York

See the shops, sights and museums and see a New York Giants game!

Be a photographer!!!

Go to a cup final (er, you can do that on your own!)

See Take That! Live (impossible unless we go back in time,

Ry. They've broken up and Robbie will NEVER get back with them. So get over it!)

Go to a film premiere!!

Meet Tom Cruise (Ry, you are not and never will be the Goose to Tom's Maverick.)

Buy a flat in London (or Leigh?!!)

Then buy a house in London (or Leigh ☺)

Have babies some day soon, at least two. A boy and a girl!

And then the banter had begun.

'OK Ry, boy name – go!'

'Champ.'

'No WAY! He'd get bullied.'

'Yeah babe, Champ Cooper, you gotta admit it's a winner's name! OK, what would you call a girl, then?'

'Xanthe.'

'Bless you – but what's your girl's name?'

'Ha ha, very funny. That's her name, Ry. Xanthe. Xanthe Carter . . . it's cool and different. Not like boring Molly.'

'OK, if you say so, babe, but it'd be Cooper. Champ Cooper and Xanthe Cooper, OK?'

'Done. What about dogs?'

'I prefer cats. What about Harry and Sally?'

'Ooh, I like it!'

I looked at Casey. No, I'd thought, best I don't tell her about that.

'Just think, Case!' I'd said instead, enveloping her in a warm hug, 'we'll see loads more of each other now!' She'd nodded in acknowledgment of this then smiled dully and extricated herself from my embrace, turning her back on me as she'd started loading the dishwasher.

Telling Mum and Dad hadn't been much better. Even though Ryan had come with me and had used his abundant charms to warm them up, praising their 'lovely house', asking Mum about school and Dad about art exhibitions, the atmosphere had still been decidedly frosty. I'd looked at my perfectly ironed, primly presented, old-before-their-time parents sitting opposite us. We'd held hands smiling at them as they stared seriously back, clutching onto their teacups, digestive biscuits perched on the saucers (oh, how I wished that once, just once, Mum would buy an interesting, fun biscuit like, say, a Jammie Dodger). Suddenly, my mouth had twitched and I'd snorted, trying to fight back an awful uncontrollable urge. It's a knee-jerk reaction of mine when I feel uncomfortable. Luckily Ryan is used to it.

When Ryan explained that we were moving in together Mum had just pursed her lips and stared pointedly at my (bare) left finger and Dad smoothed down his hair and looked out the window, as if he wasn't even there. No changes there.

'I presume you know that we don't approve of living together before marriage,' she'd said, directing her primitive, prurient view at Ryan.

Ryan had smiled and nodded. 'I appreciate that, Mrs Carter, and I respect your beliefs, I do, and I hope you know that I sincerely believe marriage will be the next step we take. I love your daughter and see us being together for a very, *very* long time.'

I'd glanced at him, then, slightly freaked out by the way the conversation was going. We were too young to be talking about marriage! But Ryan squeezed my hand gently and I felt immediately calmer. He wasn't about to propose or anything – thank God – he just knew how to handle my parents. I decided to leave him to it. If I opened my mouth it would only end in an argument. Like always.

'Well, Patricia dear, it does seem to be the modern way,' my dad said slowly, smoothing his combed-over hair again and opening his book. The conversation over in his eyes. My dad is a man of few words. When he does speak it always feels as if he has spent hours ruminating on his words before putting them in a sentence. Sometimes it can make him seem almost prophet-like, at others, like a mute.

My mum had tutted and fiddled with her cross. 'I suppose I can't stop you, I know my daughter well enough to realize that would only make her all the more determined to disobey me ... I never have been able to control her. But I can't say I'm not disappointed.' She'd paused and glanced around the room, before her pale-grey eyes settled on mine. 'I had just hoped for so much more for you, Molly dear.'

How dare she? I'd thought. What could be better than Ryan? I'd opened my mouth to say something sharp but Ryan just laughed and put his arm around me.

'It's one of the things I love about her, Mrs Carter. Your daughter has big dreams and trust me, I don't intend on holding her back.'

'WAHEY!' Dave pops a cork on a bottle of Moët and pours it into our glasses.

'To Ryan and Molly!' The Coopers all cheer and we clink glasses as I look around at our lovely little home. I feel like there should be a cartoon-style sparkle coming off every surface as I look at it. It's so *new*. New paint, new parquet floors, new furniture. It feels as new as our relationship.

'Oooh, I nearly forgot!' Jackie says, putting down her glass on the coffee table and handing us a present. 'It's a little house-warming gift from me and Dave!'

'Nothing to do with me!' Dave interjects holding his hands up. 'I built the place, that's my gift!' He winks at us and throws himself down on the brand-new, white Ikea sofa.

'Aaahh, thanks Mum!' Ryan says as she hands it to him, 'you shouldn't have.'

'No, Jackie, you really *shouldn't* have,' I add, trying to hide my horror as Ryan pulls out the gift from the wrapping paper.

It is a big, bright-pink, plastic, flamingo table light.

She squeals and claps her hands. 'It's a bit of fun, innit? I thought it'd look just lovely here.' Jackie plonks it next to the TV, a.k.a the place where no one can miss it. 'I bought it because it's pink and I thought the place needed a bit of brightening up. Dave wouldn't let me loose on the interiors, said we should keep it 'minimal' so you two could make it your own.' I look at Dave gratefully and he winks again and silently sips his fizz, letting his wife do the talking as usual. 'I also thought it was appropriate,' continues Jackie with a wistful smile on her face, 'because flamingos mate for life.' And she takes both of our hands and squeezes them, a single tear dropping from her eye. She is nothing if not dramatic.

'I thought that was swans?' says Carl, looking confused.

Jackie sniffs and flaps her hand dismissively. 'Swans, flamingos, they're all the same!'

My mouth twitches a little and I look at Ryan, but he is gazing gratefully at his mum. In the last three months I have learned to accept as Gospel anything that Jackie says or does. Which means – *oh dear God* – the flamingo has to stay.

'It's a lovely thought, Mum,' Ryan says. 'We love it, don't we, Moll?'

'Umpff,' I say, taking a swig of champagne to drown my response. I've never been a good liar.

I open the door with a beaming smile. 'Come in, come in!' I say brightly to the two familiar men, making a point not to mention their hour delay in any way whatsoever – I dread to think the state they'd have found me in otherwise. I can smell a vague but distinct whiff of greasy spoon on them, which makes me want to hurl, but I manage to contain myself.

'Tea, one sugar, am I right, Bob?' Bob gives a thumbs up. 'And two for you, Ian?' I smile at his teenage son, praying he'll turn it down. After all, they don't need a tea break just as they've got here do they?

Amateur error, Molly, amateur.

'That'll do nicely, Miss,' says Bob. 'It's been one of them mornings.'

I tootle off to the kitchen. When I return to the hallway they've already started lifting the boxes there.

'Right boys,' I say, clapping my hands which instantly makes them put down the box, as I hoped it might. 'So my plan is for us to finish off upstairs today if that's OK? There are some final bits to pack up in the bathroom and two bedrooms, the mattress needs to go and there are quite a few boxes up there. Some of them are marked for storage; you'll be taking those first. My dad will meet you at the storage facility to pack it all in. The others are to be shipped. Make sure you check with me if you have any doubts on anything whatsoever. There is a system!' I chirp. 'Even if it doesn't look like it right now!'

They glance around at the mess the house is in as if to say, *Call this a system, love?* I can see what they mean. There are all sorts of random bits still lying around, not to mention the DVD playing again in the background. It doesn't exactly look like I'm taking this move seriously. But I am.

I am moving – and moving on.

The Domestic Bliss Kiss

At university I used to lie in bed in the house I shared with Mia and three distinctly grubby boys, thinking about the years I had ahead of me to live alone in blissful solitude. I dreamed of living in a little North London pied-a-terre or an East End loft. I'd wallow in my own minimalistic style, drink white wine on the sofa and have candlelit bubble baths just like single women always do in films and books. All this was so much more exciting than the thought of living with a guy, which, as far as I could tell, started with a metaphorical adventure in the Ikea bedroom department and ended in old age (or divorce) by the hotdogs and Swedish biscuits. This did not sound like a particularly palatable prospect to me. And then came Ryan ...

'Ryan, I'm home!'

'I'm in the shower,' he calls.

I walk through the front door of our converted garage, throw the keys in the beautiful shell Ryan gave me in Ibiza and which I've proudly put on display on the Ikea sideboard in the hall. I notice it has a new, garish floral display on it, too. Jackie keeps popping in once a week and 'doing an Elton' as I call it. She says every home needs fresh flowers. I say every home needs a Do Not Disturb sign. Obviously I don't actually *say* that, I just think it.

I walk into the lounge and flop on the white couch, exhausted after my week-long commute but blissfully happy to be home. We've only been here for a month, but there is honestly no better feeling than walking through this front door every night. I've spent the last few weeks turning it into our home, painting the walls the exact shade of duck-egg blue Ryan and I wanted and carefully putting together photo collages and hanging them up the stairs: photos of me and Ryan, him and his friends, me and Casey, our amazing holiday, and it occurs to me how different I am since meeting Ryan. I'm such a people person these days! Ryan says it is his ongoing project to immerse me socially, not just with *his* friends and family, but my own. So Casey and I are seeing lots of each other again. I even make more effort with my parents.

I still like my own space though. And I've spent most weekends pottering around home shops whilst Ry is at the football or at the pub, finding little vases and cushions and putting finishing touches to all the rooms, so it looks like it could come straight from the pages of a magazine. I love it, but it still doesn't feel like home. I don't want to sound ungrateful but I feel like we're playing grown-ups in a Wendy House in Jackie and Dave's back yard.

I pop Ryan's shoes by the door, and pick up his socks that are strewn in the lounge. Then I shake out the fake fur rug and lay it back down on the floor, adjust the candlesticks on the mantelpiece and straighten the big blown-up picture of the pebbles on Leigh beach that I took the day we moved in and gave to Ryan as a present. Much as I'd love a cool *ELLE Deco*-esque flat with quirky, vintage furniture, I've accepted that this brand-new annexe is not the place to do it. Not least because, really, it's Jackie and Dave's brand-new annexe. I know that from the way Jackie checks it meticulously whenever she comes round, occasionally adding a framed photo of her and Dave, or one of the boys. So the décor is more them than me. But that's OK. I know we won't be here forever. I stare at the pebbles print for a moment, proud of the thought that went into it. I wanted something that represented where Ryan and I grew up, where we live and where we fell in love. I'd etched our initial into each stone and photographed them when he wasn't looking. Then I'd popped the stones in my pocket before we walked home. It was my way of combining our ways of collecting memories: physical (his) and photographed (mine). These stones are the starting point of our joint memories – we can keep adding to the collection as we make more and more.

Ryan was speechless. He isn't particularly creative, apart from in the kitchen, so he's kind of in awe of what I do (his words, not mine). He has the stones on his bedside table now.

'I don't have an original idea in my body,' he said once when I praised him for making me another amazing culinary feast. 'I can copy a recipe down to the last letter, buy a cool outfit that I've seen in a magazine, or quote a line from a movie, but I can't come up with anything myself. 'You have this incredible way of seeing the world, Molly. It's one of the things I love the most about you.'

I accepted the compliment but wasn't sure I agreed. Ryan's view of the world is like a sunny holiday snap. He's bright, uncomplicated and completely exposed. Whereas I am black-and-white, heavily laden with emotion and complex in composition. But I guess when those photographs are placed next to each other, they become a perfectly balanced album.

I feel him before I see him, his arms winding their way around my waist, his nose finding the crook in my neck where it fits perfectly.

I turn round and smile. *Home*, I think as our lips meet. I pull away and look at him, still marvelling that he's mine. He's freshly showered from school and ready for a night out. His hair is closely shorn, and he's wearing a tight, V-neck T-shirt and baggy green combats with box-fresh white Adidas trainers. He looks gorgeous. But I'd love him if he were fat, bald and ugly. As much as I'm sure people think Ryan Cooper is all about looks, I know better. I know because he chose to go out with me, Molly Carter, ex-teen outcast. So trust me, if he were all about looks he would not be with me. Part of me can't help but still wonder why. My life's like a teen film come true. Molly Ringwald, eat your heart out. I didn't need *Sixteen Candles*, Jon Cryer or a pink dress. I just needed Ryan Cooper.

I glance over at the dining-room table that is covered with muddy football boots and kit, his school paperwork spread everywhere, bottle of Becks perched precariously on top, and resist the urge to have a tidy up. I've had to become less anal since moving in with him, not just because he's so bloody messy but because put simply: Ryan loves stuff. He keeps *everything*: ticket stubs, receipts, magazines, he's even got his old eraser collection from when he was a kid. There are piles of things all over the place which I've suggested putting away or 'editing' but Ryan insists they stay. It's like he's lined our nest with all his old memories. It's sweet, really.

'Aren't you meant to be going to the pub with the boys?' I say as he pulls me into his arms for another kiss.

Ryan nods. 'Yeah, but I couldn't go without seeing you first. How was your day?' He throws himself down on the couch and takes a swig of beer before handing it to me. I snuggle up next to him.

'Brilliant! Jo, the Aussie picture editor, says I can go on the cover shoot next week with her,' I say excitedly. 'I've done loads of work for it, finding the location and suggesting a photographer, but I never thought I'd get to go myself. Picture assistants don't usually, and I've only been in the job four months!'

'That's brilliant, babe,' Ryan smiles. 'Is it anyone famous?'

I shake my head and take a sip of his beer. 'No, it's a model shoot, but it'll be fantastic experience. The photographer is someone I've admired for ages. He's shot for all the big magazines and done some amazing fashion campaigns. It'll be great to see someone like him at work.' I turn and look at him. 'Anyway, how about you? Did you manage to get Year Eleven to do their GCSE coursework on time?'

Ryan nods over at the pile of papers on the table. 'Only just. I'm worried some of them aren't taking it seriously enough. I reckon I'm going to have to get tougher on them.'

'I'll believe that when I see it!' I laugh. Ryan has a brilliant relationship with his students. He says he doesn't want to be a boring, uninspiring teacher that they can't talk to. He's most comfortable running around a field, revving them up to perform and encouraging them to love sport. Telling them off for not listening and learning about the biology of the human body isn't his strong point.

Just then the phone rings. Ryan pulls on his jacket and downs the rest of his beer, leaving it on the mantelpiece before striding over and kissing me goodbye. I hold his hand and walk over with him to the front door, gasping as the shock of cold February air envelops us. He kisses me again, mouths 'I love you' and I pick up the phone just as he disappears from my vision and into the fog.

'Case!' I squeal, tucking the phone under my chin and heading over to the freezer to get out some pizzas. 'When are you coming over? Now? Cool! No, Ryan's gone out with the boys so I'm a pub widow tonight!' I laugh and grab a bottle of Chardonnay from the fridge. 'What? No, of course I want you to come. What part of "pub widow" didn't you understand? I've got pizza, wine and I'm ready for a girlie evening with my best mate. It's been a long week! Alright, see you in half an hour!'

I put the phone down, throw some posh crisps in a bowl with some dips alongside, put out some olives and pour myself a large glass of wine. When Ryan isn't around to cook for me, my eating habits revert to university-style nutritional debauchery.

'Case!' I exclaim opening the door and giving her a big hug before ushering her in.

'Hiya, Moll,' she smiles. 'Wow – this place looks amazing!' She turns around, gazing at the walls covered with photographs and pictures as if searching for something in particular. 'Where am I then? Oh, you put that one up, Moll? It's gorge of you but I look totally hammered!'

'You *were* hammered,' I laugh.

'OK, fair point, but at least put up one where I look *cute* and hammered. I know there are plenty of those!' She giggles. She carries on nosing around the flat.

'Um, has the local church got any candles left for Sunday worship?' she jokes, gazing at the fake fireplace which has a stack of candles burning brightly in it.

'Ha ha, I'll have you know that church candles are *very* stylish,' I say.

'I'd prefer a glitter ball myself,' Casey replies, 'or, like, proper flashing disco lights! Yeah, that's what I'd have if I ever get to move out of my mum's shithole!'

'Glass of wine?' I offer, picking up the bottle.

'Ooh, aren't you the little homemaker!' Casey chuckles, throwing down her fake Burberry bag and wandering around the place. 'Have you got any vodka? It's Friday night and I wanna go dancing later. Wine just sends me to sleep. It's the drink of the middle-aged.'

'Um, I'm not sure, maybe in the cupboard?' I say, pointing at the corner kitchen unit. But I thought we were hanging out here this evening?'

'We are for now, but the night is young. Just because you've settled down and are boring doesn't mean the rest of us have to be! Surely you weren't planning on us staying in all night, were you?' She gazes at me incredulously with her heavily mascaraed eyes. She still hasn't realized that she's beautiful enough without it. That's what happens when an ugly duckling turns into a swan. It has taken some time for her style to catch up. I wish I could let Freya, our fashion editor, loose on her and dress her in something less . . . tacky. Then I'd scrub off the fake tan that she doesn't need on her gorgeous Greek–Italian skin and get rid of the cheap highlights in her hair.

'Um, well I just thought we could have pizza, watch an old eighties movie, like we used to, you know, *The Breakfast Club* or *St Elmo's Fire* or something, drink some wine and have a proper catch-up, like the old days!'

'Bo*r-ing*,' Casey yawns, sounding exactly like she did when we were fifteen. 'No offence, babe, you may be wallowing in marital bliss but some of us have had a hard week at work and need to let off some steam. Mum's given me a rare night off and I don't want to waste it!' She grabs a bottle of Smirnoff and pours a large measure into a highball glass before adding a token splash of orange juice. 'Up yours,' she says, raising it before necking half of it. 'So how's married life treating you?'

I blush. 'Stop it, Case, we're not married!'

'As good as,' she winks. She looks around. 'I feel like I'm sitting in a replica Ikea display!'

I nod shyly, taking this as a compliment. 'I never thought I'd say this, but I love it, Case! It couldn't be more perfect. I love coming home to him, waking up with him; I love our little weekend routines. Last week I even attempted a Sunday roast,' I say proudly. 'I completely burnt it. But at least I tried!'

Casey splutters in her drink. 'Fuck me, you're freaking me out now.' She grabs my face and looks into my eyes. 'Where's my best mate, the one who couldn't cook, said she was never going to settle down and live with a man. What happened to you travelling the world, being Miss Independent? Next you'll be telling me you actually *like* living in Leigh!'

She looks at me and I make a guilty expression. 'Shut UP!' she gasps.

'Well, I can't help it, I do!' I pour myself another glass of wine and settle back on the sofa with a piece of pizza.

She shakes her head in disbelief.

'I don't know, maybe it's just a novelty, but I really do like it. I don't want it to be forever. When we can afford it, we'll definitely upgrade to a place in London.'

'Upgrading, eh?' she says wistfully.

'How are things with Toni anyway?' I ask, suddenly aware of how different our home lives are. Poor Casey, I know how desperate she is to get her own place, get out from under her mum's shadow.

Casey shrugs. 'The same, she's busy with all her men and leaving me to manage the caff – and the boys. Without me the little shits would never go to school.' She looks up through her dark eyelashes and smiles. 'I've got some news though. I've got a new job.'

'You have? 'Where? Doing what?' I yelp excitedly.

'It's at Players, the brand-new club in Southend!' she squeals back. Casey pours herself another large measure of vodka. 'It's going to be wicked! It's opening next month and they want to make it this really cool, really exclusive place, you know like a West End club. They want a couple of girls to work on the door, doing the guest list and stuff. And one of them is gonna be me! They like the fact that I've lived here all my life, I've got service industry experience, I know the scene and lots of people. I can't wait to start! Just think, Moll, my job is *actually* going to be clubbing! How cool is that?'

I raise my wine glass to toast her new job and take a sip. She's so happy. I don't want to spoil it by saying that I'm not sure working in a club environment is going to be the best place for her.

'Now, how about you get changed and we go out and check out the competition? I can call it research!'

'What's wrong with what I'm wearing?' I say, gesturing at my ankle-length black dress and boots that I wore to work today.

'Let's be honest, what's right with it? You're twenty-two and you're dressed like a nun!'

'Freya, the fashion editor, says this is very fashionable right now, actually Case! Long is the new short, you know.'

Casey adopts a posh voice. 'But "Fraiya the Fashion Edit*ah*" doesn't live in Essex, does she? Come on,' she pleads. 'Get out those fantastic legs of yours, put on some heels and let's go clubbing! Come on, it'll be a laugh, just like the old days, you know, when you used to be *fun* . . .'

The Bittersweet Kiss

Just like creative people always say you only remember criticism not praise, I've discovered that in times of distress it's the bad things that stay with you longer than the good. Just like I could (will) never shake that bad first kiss between Ryan and I, now I can't shake the bad memories. It's so bloody frustrating. All I can think about are the arguments I started, the times I nagged him unnecessarily, or administered one of my stony silences when he'd done something to annoy me. They're all there, etched on my brain. I'm like a self-harming teenager: I know I should stop, but I don't want to. Each pain-inducing memory feels good, like I deserve all of this because really, I didn't ever deserve him.

I squeal as The Verve's 'Bitter Sweet Symphony' comes on in the student union bar and accidentally spill my Snakebite over my Converses.

'I blurrey LOVE this song, girls!' I slur, throwing my arms around Casey and Mia.

'Thanks for coming down, Case and makin' my nineteenth birthday so brilliant! It jus' wouldn't have been the shame without you!' I lift up my camera and take a snap of the three of us above our heads as I know it's always a more flattering shot. Especially when you've drunk as much as we have. Then I close my eyes, throw my hands in the air and begin to jump up and down. Although this proves to be hard as my trainers keep sticking to the beer-soaked floor and my drink keeps slopping over me. I open my eyes again. All around me students with long hair, wearing dark baggy clothes and with extra bags under their eyes, are dotted around. I fit in here. For the first time I belong. Only my friends seem to stick out. Casey in her black PVC miniskirt and baby-pink T-shirt and Mia, my new best mate who I met here on the very first night. She is wearing a white tailored shirt with black crease-fronted, boot-cut trousers and pointed red Karen Millen boots. We literally couldn't look more different if we tried.

I wave at Mia and she lifts her white wine and shakes her blonde Posh Spice-inspired bob.

'Chin chin!' she laughs.

'Hey, Mi,' I shout, staggering forward a little.

'I'm *hot*!' she yells. In her posh voice it comes out 'haught'.

'WHAT?' Casey shouts but we ignore her.

'Yes, it is a soupçon too hot in here, isn't it what!' I shout back, hamming up her posh accent. She puts down her wine and comes over and we look at each other before shouting, 'No, *I'M* hot!' and then crack up laughing. Mia is holding her sides, practically on the floor with laughter.

Mia was the first person I met in the student union six weeks ago and I was instantly drawn to her. She stood reading *Vogue* at the bar, clutching a gin and tonic. I walked up to her, ordered myself a vodka and Coke and then turned to her. Before I could say a word she waved her hand across her face and said, 'I'm hot.'

'Yes, it is a bit hot in here, isn't it?' I'd politely replied, not knowing quite where to take the conversation, my social skills still being somewhat underdeveloped.

Then she beamed at me, a full-throttle, gleaming Mia mega-watt smile and said, 'No, *I'm* hot,' and then we both burst out laughing, the ice well and truly broken.

Six weeks on and it's our signature saying – and is now accompanied by a waggly-armed chicken dance.

Casey looks at us both blankly and then shrugs before striding off. When we've finished embarrassing ourselves Mia goes to pick up her drink.

'Hey, it's gone!' she says. And then she looks across the room and sees Casey has got her face attached to the guy Mia was flirting with earlier – and she's holding Mia's wine glass out like a trophy over his shoulder.

'That girl is trouble, you know,' Mia says darkly, and goes to the bar.

Mia's not as ice-maidenlike as she can appear. She's fun to be around but she is a force to be reckoned with, too. She's an only child like me, and her parents are both successful lawyers, so she was brought up by a series of nannies. She only hears from her parents about once a month but it doesn't seem to bother her. She's got a long-term boyfriend at home but she lost interest in him soon after we got here.

'I'm too *young* to be tied to one man – unless it's in *bed*,' she said to me on the Sunday morning at the end of Freshers' week, when we were lying on mine watching Ruth snog Kurt Benson in *Hollyoaks*. 'From now on I'm going to have my men how I have my alcohol . . .'

'Um, short and straight up?' Mia likes hardcore liquor, no mixers for her. She's always the one downing tequila shots at the bar – and still standing at the end of the night.

'Nope. Try again.' She smiles.

'Er, on the rocks . . . and with a twist?' I say again.

'No, Molly,' she'd added with a sassy smile, 'super-strong and disposed of in seconds. In fact,' she says, sitting up, 'I think I'm going to phone him right now and tell him it's over between us.'

'Are you sure?' I'd said, pulling my ancient The Smiths T-shirt over my crossed knees. 'I mean you've been together three *years*, you lost your *virginity* to him.'

She'd looked at me with a wide-eyed, innocent gaze. 'Oh yes,' she'd said emphatically. 'I always knew it wasn't going to be forever.' And she'd picked up her Nokia 6160 and curled her feet underneath her as she quickly struck her fatal blow to her first ever relationship.

I was shocked, but I related to her emotional detachment too. Not with any actual relationship experience – I hadn't had a boyfriend yet – but I felt the same about the guy I'd lost my virginity to, aged sixteen. It was utterly premeditated on my part and utterly crap too.

The problem is, *I* haven't quite got around to going there again either. I mean obviously I had *plenty* of opportunities during Freshers' week, but after being so reckless that first time, I thought maybe this time, you know, I'd try saving it for someone who I actually like.

I spot him across the room staring at me as I'm trying to restrain Mia from pulling Casey by her hair off the guy she's snogging. A tall, reed-thin, dark-haired Richard Ashcroft lookalike leaning against the wall, cigarette dangling out of his mouth, his skinny arms hanging down almost to his knees. His eyes are blue, bright blue, and his lips, whilst thinner than I'd like, are really nicely defined. He waves at me, well, either that or he is clearing a viewing hole through his sheet of middle-parted greasy hair and then looks down, another big clump of his hair falling over his eyes again. Fuelled by alcohol and my newly found confidence of being a proper grown-up *19-year-old* university student, I nudge Mia and mouth, 'Watch this,' and then I stumble over towards him, swinging my hips whilst pulling up my charity-shop-bought, satin mini dress so that it reveals the holes in my tights, and pulling down my sleeves on my sloppy mohair jumper so that it falls off my shoulder.

We don't talk for long. Only enough to exchange names ('Marcus' – but he pronounces it Mar*coos*), where we're from (him: Buckinghamshire, me: London – I just couldn't *bear* to say Essex), A-level results (me: three As – I know, so much for rebelling, huh?, him: three Bs), and our degree courses (me: Photography, him: Fine Art). Then he bends his neck down to get to my face level, which is hard, given our height difference, kind of like a pelican trying to get a fish, and he kisses me.

It's a curious sensation. Curious because for those five minutes when I saw him, approached him and then talked to him, I really, *really* fancied him. He's just my type, according to the list I'd drawn up before I came here:

Things I Want From a Boyfriend
• Clever
• Cool
• Not from Essex (V. IMPORTANT)
• Must have nice lips
• Blue eyes
• Not be emotionally retarded
• Or culturally challenged

But his kiss is disappointing, not because it's bad, but more because this image of Ryan Cooper pops into my head, and I feel like I'm being haunted by this memory of him kissing me in The Grand. And even though it was terrible and humiliating, I can't help but wish that Marcus was him. Which is unbelievably annoying. Seriously, I haven't thought about the guy for weeks. Well, days anyway. Apart from earlier when we were at the bar getting drinks and Casey mentioned that she's seen him around town with his little boy band of merry men. Well, she mentioned it because I casually asked . . .

'Aha,' she'd said, her green eyes glittering as she sipped from her bottle of Hooch whilst simultaneously staking out the room for prey. 'Still thinking about Ryan Cooper, even though you're surrounded by all this fresh meat?'

'Uh, like yeah right, *no*!' I'd said defensively.

'So you're not interested to know that he asked after you when I saw him down at Tots the other night.'

'Did he?' I'd replied, nearly dropping my cider.

'Only to try and get closer to me though, *obviously*,' Casey had laughed wickedly and winked. 'I mean, what guy can resist the charms of Casey Georgiou!'

And these days, it's true. Casey, in true 80s chick-flick makeover style *has* gone all gorgeous. Last summer, the weight fell off and her Greek genes finally kicked in. Here at uni, where (apart from Mia) we're all washed-out white, weary and wearing black, she is like a ray of sunshine. If Mia and I are 'hot', she's sizzling.

And according to her, I can't get enough of Ryan Cooper – even though I'm kissing someone else. Clearly I need to up the action to *really* get him out of my head once and for all.

I grab Marcus by the hand. 'C'mon,' I murmur. 'Let's get out of here.' He doesn't complain.

I wish I could say the earth had just moved for me in my halls bedroom but as I lie here, flat on my back being spooned by Mar*coos*,

I think I've discovered the hard way that a posh arty type doesn't necessarily make the best lover. It's all been longing, heartfelt gazes and not enough action. Not nearly enough action, actually. I lift my wrist up and glance at my watch. God, did it last eight minutes? It didn't feel as long as that. Oh no, hang on, the bit when he cried probably made it feel longer.

I look up at the upside-down image of John Lennon coiled around Yoko Ono pinned above my headboard, and then sideways at Marcus. His pale, skinny, shuddering body is wrapped around me and I watch as his breathing evens and slows and he falls asleep with his mouth open like a singing choirboy's. I lie there, stiff as a board, wondering if I might have met the John to my Yoko and just not realized it. Maybe I should give him another chance? The passion might not be there yet but he ticks all the other things on my list. And he *has* had a hard time lately. His parents broke up while he was doing his A levels (which is why he only got Bs, he said) *and* they had to sell their French ski lodge to help pay for the divorce.

Oh *Puh*lease. Who am I kidding?

I look up again, not at Yoko and John but this time at my *Before Sunrise* poster. But instead of Ethan Hawke, all I can see is Ryan sodding Cooper. I think of our first – and last – kiss.

The Lost Kiss

'A discarded kiss is a moment of love lost forever.' (Molly Carter, today)

Imagine if you counted the kisses you've thrown away. You know, when you've presented your cheek instead of your lips, rolled over in bed after an argument, ran out the door without time for a goodbye. Annoyingly, when you're not together any more those are the kisses you always remember. So many missed kisses – where do they go? I imagine them as a collection of crosses in the sand; a kiss graveyard full of buried treasure. Some stolen, some lost or overlooked, some carelessly thrown away, all waiting to be found.

I fling my bag down on my desk, take off my leather biker jacket and loosen the tasselled scarf I've wrapped around my neck before starting up my computer. The big, usually bustling office is eerily empty. Stripped of the fashionable people, music and gossip streaming through it, it suddenly occurs to me how grey, dingy and *office-y* it is.

I settle down at my desk and luxuriate in the silence. I don't get much of it these days and I realize how much I miss it. Apart from my commute, I'm literally never on my own and standing in a packed train doesn't really count as 'me time'. So this is actually a treat for me. No one gets in to work before 9.30 a.m. at *Viva* so I know I've got the place to myself for at least an hour before my car comes. I've got an important celebrity cover shoot today – my biggest creative challenge since becoming picture editor nine months ago – at a studio in Kentish Town, and I wanted to come in to the office first to make sure I'm properly prepared. Suddenly I'm slammed by my younger self, berating me.

So bor-ing, Molly Carter! What happened to the girl who wasn't going to conform? It's like we've turned into MUM.

I haven't! I haven't turned into Mum. I look at my reflection in the mirror.

A scarf, Molly! I mean, seriously?

It's a silk designer scarf! I reply in my head defensively. From a sample sale!

Designer schminer. Next you'll be wearing it around your head.

I pull it off, feeling hot all of a sudden and I grab my Pret A Manger latte, taking a long sip while I'm waiting for my computer to start up, hoping the caffeine will work its rejuvenating powers on me quickly.

Coffee, Molly? We HATE coffee! It tastes rank, we've always said so!

I put it down and rub my eyes. It was so hard getting up at the crack of dawn this morning, leaving Ryan snoring contentedly in bed, but it's an all too regular occurrence these days. I went to kiss him on the lips but he rolled over, grunted what I think was a goodbye, and sunk back under the duvet and into a deep slumber. He has this incredible ability to barely stir when I leave the house these days. Six months ago we'd manage breakfast, or at least a cup of tea in bed before I left and definitely a kiss (we swore we'd never say goodbye or goodnight without one). But his increased workload and my recent early starts have meant that this has fallen by the wayside. I miss them, I feel a bit lost without them. Without it I find that my morning cloud takes longer to lift and I don't function as well. It's weird to think that one person can be the sole arbitrator of your happiness. But he's totally the umpire in our love match; the only person who can calm me down no matter how close to the baseline my mood has swung. He can make me feel like a champion when my confidence has taken a knock. He lifts me over the net whenever I'm feeling low. He—

Sport metaphors, Molly? We hate sport! We can't hit a ball or catch one! We've never picked up a tennis racket in our life!

As I wait for my computer to start up, I resist the urge to phone him. He'll be cycling to work now anyway. Sometimes I don't think he appreciates how hard commuting is. He has it so easy in comparison. Mind you, I do get a nice home-cooked meal every night when I get home, so – as Casey keeps telling me – I don't have much to complain about. He really is the perfect guy. Well, except for the snoring. And the relentless channel hopping. Last night I swear we watched four programmes simultaneously. Oh, and his socks, which he leaves everywhere.

I put thoughts of Ryan out of my mind and glance down at the call sheet resting on my desk, and take a deep breath to steady my nerves. This is going to be the most stressful day I've ever had at *Viva*. It's my first big project since Christie promoted me to picture editor. We're photographing eight new stars for a gatefold 'Next Big Thing' cover for our bumper August issue. The entertainment team have managed to secure the biggest new young names in music, film and TV and I've spent the last month liaising with their PRs to get them all in the same studio, on the same day and at the same time. Which, as anyone who has ever dealt with a celebrity will know, is no mean feat. To be honest, much as it all sounds glamorous, it's the least favourite part of my job. I much prefer shooting real women who have achieved something or overcome some kind of odds. They're the people who should be inspiring a generation of women, not a load of vacuous celebs. I can't tell you how many times I've felt genuinely overawed by women we've photographed who have set up businesses, overcome health scares, helped others or started campaigns. The women who have done something worthwhile. And I like to think I'm good at making them feel comfortable in front of the camera. I love watching them relax, dropping their guards and their insecurities for me and the photographer. I can't deny I wish it were me taking the pictures but, for now, I'm learning. On shoots I'm always soaking up what the photographer is doing as much as I am doing my own job. Sometimes it's hard to be standing so close to my dream, but I know I'm lucky to be getting such practical experience.

Anyway, because of this shoot I've come into work at the crack of dawn most days and have been staying late for weeks now, dealing with location changes, celebs dropping out, trying to get them back in, securing the best photographer, having meetings with Seb, the art director, and Christie about the concept. Fingers crossed the hard work will be worth it. That's what I keep telling myself anyway, when my stress levels keep rising. I know Seb was particularly dubious about me being at the helm. He's this really cool, experienced guy, but he's also the silent, brooding type. I think he saw me as a glorified work experience and I've had to work really hard to gain his approval. But I think I've proved that what I lack in experience I make up for in creativity and dedication. And we've bonded over our joint hatred of the office music (we both love Jeff Buckley and Radiohead) and he's been telling me about some recent exhibitions he's been to see. I realize I might have misjudged Seb a bit. He's not up his own arse and aloof, he's just less ... people-person-y than I'm used to.

I click on Outlook, just to check that there aren't any last-minute emails from our cover stars pulling out. It's quite hard to use a keyboard with your fingers crossed. I exhale as I realize that there is only one email. And it's a welcome one.

Molly!!!!

How are you?!!!??? How's Viva, how's Ryan? And Casey? I miss you – but not enough to come back! Can you believe I've been here two years in September? Life is fab here in sunny Sydney, like one long holiday. I know how you love a list so I thought this might help you realize why you HAVE to come out here asap:

Reasons why Oz is better than boring old Blighty

The weather is hot (and so are the men)

The surf is big (and so are the men)

The beaches are beautiful (and so are the men)

The clubs are wild (and so are the men)

The culture is ... Oh, sod the culture, Molly, the men are fucking AMAZING!

You can get a natural tan instead of the fake ones you Essex-types are so used to!

I laugh at this; Mia knows I have never touched fake tan in my life. I think of her list and then look at the lists currently resting on the desk in front of me and feel enormously depressed. One is my work list, the other a general to-do list. I read the second list and with pen in hand, I scrawl another one:

To-do list
Pick up dry cleaning
Call parents
Buy birthday present for Jackie (something pink?)
Call student loans company
Go to Tesco (milk, teabags, OJ, fish)
Red gas bill (tell off Ryan, he was meant to pay it)
Council tax
Renew tax on car
Renew monthly train ticket
Wash Ryan's football kit
BOOK HOLIDAY – AUSTRALIA?

I stare at the last words I've written, hating the question mark that I've added at the end. I don't know why our plans for going on a big trip together have been sidelined yet again. The other night Ryan mentioned going on holiday to his parents' place in Portugal this year. Part of me is starting to think he doesn't even want to go on a big trip any more.

I sigh and look at the list of things I've got to organize for the shoot today. To be honest, looking at it is equally depressing. Especially when I look back at Mia's list. It doesn't help that the teen me keeps rearing her head.

How did our life become so dull, Molly? We had such big plans!

It's called growing up, I shoot back. Everyone's life is like this. I sit back down and read the rest of Mia's email, hoping it'll make me feel better while I'm waiting for my cab, but deep down knowing that it won't.

*

The magazine is doing brilliantly, Moll. I still love my job, even though I've been here two years, and the editor is amazing, too – and she's pregnant! Which means I'm in line to be acting editor! Can you believe it! Me? An editor? And I'm only 24!!!

Why, why, WHY haven't you booked your ticket yet? I want to take you RAGING (that means having fun in Oz. But you should already know this if you watch Home and Away.) COME TO AUSTRALIA (sorry, that's the last time I'll mention it! Promise!). Remember our Life Lists? Anyway, must go, I've got a feature to edit before 5 p.m. – then it's time to hit the beach and the bars!

Love you, miss you (book your ticket NOW!!!)

Mia xxxx

I stare at the last paragraph for a while, picturing the Life Lists Mia and I wrote one drunken evening in our first year at uni:

Molly's Life List
Travel around Australia – with Mia!!!!!
Live in New York
Be a photographer
Have a successful exhibition
Own my own place
Stay single until I've achieved all my ambitions

Mia's Life List
Travel the world (Australia? With Molly!!!!)
Be a magazine editor by age of 30
Own my own place
Stay single . . . forever!

See Molly? She's ticking things off her Life List. She's making the most of her twenties, what about you? Stuck in Leigh, in the place we swore we'd never go back to once we left for college. What happened?

Life happened, OK? Love happened. It's not my fault that Ryan and I fell in love before the mid-twenties watershed. You'd think we're actually offending people with our cohabiting happiness. So what if I've only slept with three men in my life? How many more notches on my bedpost do I need?

God, why am I thinking about this now? I shake my head and close down my email without replying and glance at my watch. Five minutes until my car is due. I quickly open up Google and type in 'Flights to Australia'. I just want to look, to check the price, to see what the possibilities are.

My heart pounding with excitement, I start jotting down flight dates, times and prices. I'm going to talk about it to Ryan when I get in tonight. Or maybe I'll just be spontaneous and book them now! I glance down as my work phone rings and I sigh.

'The car's here? OK thanks, I'll be right down.'

I grab my bag and dash away from my desk, leaving my computer beaming like a beacon.

'This is going to be one full-on day,' grins Seb as I fight my way through the studio doors, laden down as I am with suitcases and bags. 'I hope you're ready for this, Rookie.'

'Ready as you are, *Veteran*,' I retort. 'Are you going to help me with all this or what?'

'Or what, I'm afraid Molly. I am *far* too important to be handling baggage.' And he sinks back on the leather sofa, puts his Adidas-clad feet up on the glass coffee table and continues reading *Esquire*.

'The amount of girls you've got on the go, Seb, I'd have thought you're used to dealing with baggage,' I say cheekily. I've learned that the best way to deal with Seb is with banter. It's the only language he understands.

'The only "baggage" I deal with is on the Louis Vuitton scale of luxury,' he drawls, referring, I assume, to his taste in women rather than his taste in handbags.

'Oh, I see,' I say, heaving the suitcase into the changing room. 'Overpriced and overexposed, you mean?'

He smiles slyly, his white teeth bared and grey eyes glinting like a fox who's just spotted its prey. 'I mean, over here . . .' And he stares at me.

I turn away, heart racing, cheeks traffic-light red. 'Let's get to work, shall we, Seb?' I say. 'There's a lot to do today.'

He lounges back, arms stretched over the back of the sofa and a confident smile creeps over his face. 'Too right, there is.'

'How does it look, Moll?' Seb calls over. I'm peering at the computer screen at James the photographer's last set of shots as Seb and James adjust the lights before the next celeb arrives.

'Great, but I think in the next shot we need to make it all look more urban.' I think for a second. 'What about shooting against that exposed brick wall instead of the white backdrop. Or even . . .' I start gabbling as the idea strikes me . . . 'or even, you know, the balcony outside?' I rush over to the fire escape and open it. 'It's got that great East London panorama, almost Meatpacking-esque. Kind of reminiscent of that Jean Shrimpton shoot David Bailey did for *Vogue*? What do you reckon?'

Seb turns slowly and looks at me, his eyes working his way up my body disconcertingly and settling on mine, 'Moll, that's a fucking STUPENDOUS idea! Beautiful *and* bright, huh?' and I'm annoyed to feel a flicker of satisfaction, despite his sexist remark. He points lazily at me and grins. 'I reckon you just graduated, Rookie.'

I pretend to throw a mortarboard in the air, thrilled at his praise. When I look back he is still staring at me. I watch as he and James start moving the camera equipment and the big lights. I love how he got my vision instantly. It's nice being on the same creative wavelength as someone else, especially someone as experienced and talented as him. It validates me, makes me feel more confident and in control.

I reckon my 15-year-old self would be proud. This is glamorous and exciting! Shooting famous celebrities for the number one women's magazine!

Celebrities? she hisses back at me. *Glamorous? Not exactly changing the world, are we?*

But we could almost be in New York right now!

But we're not, we're in East London.

It looks like New York though!

And we're not taking the photos.

But I'm practically directing the shoot – which is *even better*, right?

Wrong.

Ah, I give up. I never did like my 15-year-old self anyway. No wonder my mum and dad thought I was such a pain in the ass.

It's 7 p.m. and Seb, James the photographer, Lauren the make-up artist, Freya and I are all flopped on the sofa, drinking Prosecco and celebrating the end of a brilliantly successful day.

'We did it!' Freya exclaims, leaning her head on Lauren's shoulder in exhaustion. 'We only went and did it. Eight celebrities in one day. Surely that's a record?'

'I'm not sure *Vanity Fair* would agree,' I laugh, taking a long, satisfying slurp of Prosecco and closing my eyes so I can properly enjoy the sensation of the alcohol hitting my bloodstream. God, I need this drink. I realize I've been utterly strung out for weeks. I feel a sudden urge to call Ryan. I want him to share in my success. I slip away from the group and call Ryan from the corridor.

Our home phone rings a few times before going to answerphone and I know immediately where he is. So I call his parents.

'Awight?' says a gruff voice that sounds just like Ryan.

'Hey, Carl!' I say brightly. 'It's Molly. Is your brother there?'

'Ryly!' Carl says cheerfully. He gave us this new nickname when he decided one night at the pub that Ryan and I are Leigh-on-Sea's very own version of Bennifer.

'Please, you *know* I only answer to "Molly from the Block",' I say with a smirk. I love the banter I have with Carl. He feels like the brother I never had.

Carl guffaws. 'Ha, ha, classic! Ryan's here, I'm thrashing him at Subbuteo.'

'That's the only place you'll ever beat him at football,' I laugh. Carl had to accept a long time ago that Ryan's sporting prowess way outdoes his. Luckily his ego can take it.

'That hurt, Molly, that hurt real bad. Here's your worse half now. See ya!'

The studio door opens and I slide out of the way, as Seb appears holding my glass of Prosecco.

'Hiya, babe, how are you doing?' Ryan says as he comes on the line.

I mouth my thanks to Seb as he hands the glass to me and he hovers there for a moment next to me. I try to deafen the sound of my heart beating in my chest. Probably just the post-shoot adrenalin.

Yeah right, Molly, or maybe you just fancy the pants off him.

I take a swig out of my glass and rest the stem against my knees, steadfastly looking at it, and not Seb. I mustn't look at Seb.

Seb and Molly sitting in a tree, k-i-s-s-i-n—

I mentally tell my teen self to shut up.

'I'm good ... the shoot went well!' I blurt out rather loudly and overenthusiastically. Seb grazes my ankle with his foot and I look up and he grins and gives me a thumbs up as he leans against the door, doing nothing to hide the fact he's listening to my private conversation. God, his arrogance is sexy.

'Oh, was that to-*DAY*!' I can tell by his voice that Ryan has taken a shot at goal mid-sentence. Clearly his stupid table football game is more important than my career.

'Yes, Ry, it was today,' I say, rolling my eyes at Seb.

'Boyfriend?' he mouths and I nod. He mimes having a ball and chain around him and I laugh and lean over and smack him. As I pull my hand back I notice it is shaking slightly.

'Molly?' Ryan says. I realize he's asked me a question. 'I said how did it go then? Was it worth all the hard work?'

'I think it's going to be our best cover ever!' I reply, stifling a giggle as Seb mimes shooting a hoop and then clasps his hands together above his head in a winner's pose.

'That's great!' Ryan says. He's still playing Subbuteo. 'So are you on the train now then?'

'No, we've just finished. We're all having a drink here then I'm going to come home.'

'Aww, babe, I really wanted to hang out with you tonight. I've barely seen you these past few weeks.'

'I know, Ryan, I'm sorry,' thinking that we see each other way more than most couples I know. I cross my legs in front of me, absent-mindedly tapping the toes of my soft, buttery-brown suede boots against each other to scuff them a little. I look up at Seb and roll my eyes and he raises his eyebrow, pulls a face and slips back into the studio, pulling his fake ball and chain behind him. I rest my head back against the wall but turned towards the studio, where I can see everyone having a laugh. Seb has his arms crossed and is nodding his head to The White Stripes. I love that band. I glance at my watch.

'Listen, Ry, I er, I've got to go, there's still some packing up to do.' There isn't but I want to go enjoy myself. 'And er, it'll probably take a while so don't worry about dinner for me . . .' Suddenly I feel like staying out and getting pissed. In a way I haven't done for months.

Because you're so fucking boring ... Oh sorry, I mean 'responsible' these days.

It's called being in love.

It's called being under the thumb.

Who asked you anyway?

'OK,' he sighs. 'God, I miss you, babe. It sucks that we've both been working so hard lately.'

'I know, Ry,' I say, suddenly seeing an opportunity. 'Maybe we should book a holiday?'

'What?' Ryan says, and I hear him cheer as he scores a goal and Carl shouts brotherly abuse at him in the background.

'I said maybe we need a holiday!'

'We're going to Mum and Dad's place in Portugal with them and Carl and Lyd, remember? We could ask Casey, too, if you like. It'll be such a laugh!'

'Well, I was thinking about somewhere else actually ...' I say tentatively. 'On our own.'

'Ibiza again then?' he offers cheerfully. 'Or the Canaries?' His voice jerks with the exertion of each shot he's playing. 'The islands, not the football team obviously, haha!'

'But we talked about going to Australia this year, remember? On New Year's Eve? We said we'd definitely do it!'

'No, Moll*eeey*,' he says, his voice wavering as he presumably takes another shot at the goal. 'We said we *could* do it but you've just been promoted. How do you think your editor will feel if you ask for six weeks off?'

'So what are you suggesting?' I reply tetchily. 'No holiday at all?'

He laughs flippantly, which suddenly fills me with annoyance. 'Calm down, babe! Like I said, we'll just go with my parents this year.'

I can barely contain the anger I feel at Ryan.

Seb's face appears at the window and he gestures at another freshly opened bottle of bubbly. 'Let's not talk about this now,'

I retreat to stop myself saying something I'll regret. 'I'll see you later, OK?'

I stare at my phone for a moment after I ring off, and then drain my glass and walk back into the studio. Seb pours me another and smiles at me as I down half of it.

'Fancy staying out for a bit then?' he raises a thick, dark eyebrow and stares at me challengingly.

I think of Ryan at his parents' house, playing Subbuteo like an overgrown teenager. 'Yeah, I do actually, Seb,' I say, as I take another greedy gulp. 'I really do.'

Several hours later, I open our front door woozily and creep in, putting my keys down on the sideboard next to a particularly garish bunch of gerberas. The lights are all off downstairs – all except one. The flamingo. I unplug it and put it in the kitchen bin. Suddenly I feel like a rebellious teenager again and it's kind of fun. But just as I turn around and head for the stairs I freeze, imagining Jackie's tragi-comic face when she notices it's gone. I walk back slowly, pull the flamingo out and put it back next to the TV. I stare at it accusingly before walking quietly upstairs to bed.

The Let's Compromise Kiss

When I was younger I didn't like the word 'compromise'. It was a word my parents used a lot and as far as I could tell it just meant accepting second best, not being brave enough to go for what you really want.

Now, I've learned that compromise is what binds people together. Compromise is sharing and conciliatory, it is loving and kind and unselfish. It opens its arms to another person and takes a step halfway between what it wants and someone else's wishes and dreams.

'Here we are then, our new home!' I gesture wildly around our new one-bedroom flat that we actually OWN and then look out the window. 'Hello Hackney!'

I turn around and grin broadly at Ryan, who, along with his dad and brother, is heaving the last of our boxes through our (OUR!) front door. Jackie has disappeared. No doubt she's nosing around the place. I try not to get wound up, but fail. This is our place and I want Ryan and me to have the chance to do it our way this time. Mum and Dad are here, too, as ever, visibly uncomfortable. Mum is clutching her handbag in front of her and fiddling with her silk neckscarf as she looks around and tries her best not to look disapproving. I am so thankful for that, it kind of makes me want to hug her, but I don't. Dad is smiling blankly and I know although he's here in body, in his head he's somewhere else entirely. Probably at whatever exhibition is on at Tate Britain. I watch Ryan's family look around, wide smiles scrawled clumsily over their faces like a child's attempt to emulate happiness with a crayon, whereas I'm the kid at Disneyland for the first time, bursting with excitement and happiness. *This* is what I wanted.

'It's really . . . um . . .' Carl begins and then trails off.

Dave picks up the lead. 'It's very . . . well, it's really . . .' He is clearly trying – and failing – to find something positive to say.

I hear Jackie poking around the kitchen, then she enters the lounge in her pink tracksuit, her nose leading her round the room like a poodle looking at a particularly undesirable kennel.

'It's not fit to live in, darlin's!' she exclaims, not mincing her words. 'There's damp on the walls and dirt on the floor, the rooms are tiny and have you seen the bathroom? There's no *shower*! I mean, my boy can't live in these conditions! You have to come home now! I won't be able to sleep knowing we're leaving you here, don't you agree, Patricia?'

Mum stiffens and looks at me as she pulls her scarf through her fingers.

'I'm sure Molly and Ryan will make it very homely, Jackie,' she replies tautly. Jackie shakes her head mournfully and plays with her heart locket, drawing attention to her oaky, tanned cleavage. 'I still don't understand why you wouldn't let us help you so you could afford something better?' She looks at Dave despairingly for support.

'Jacks ...' Dave says warningly as he catches my infuriated expression. As does Ryan, so I quickly rearrange my face into a smile. I don't want to upset him. But sometimes Jackie crosses the line from interested to interfering. Luckily Ryan steps in. It's unusual but welcome support.

'Because we want to do this on our own, Mum,' Ryan says patiently, putting down his box and walking over to hold my hand. 'You've helped us out so much – too much – over the past couple of years, letting us live in the annexe rent-free. This is the best we could afford and it's not forever, we're not planning on having kids here. Although ... it may do for the conception!'

Ryan laughs and then clocks my bewildered expression. 'Look, Mum, the problems are only cosmetic and we've got the money to get them fixed. Honestly, it isn't as bad as you think ...'

'It'll look much better when all their stuff is in it, Jacks,' Dave agrees, squeezing his wife's shoulder affectionately.

'*If* it fits,' she sniffs, looking around the place disdainfully and fiddling again with her necklace. I'm not sure why I didn't see it before but Jackie can be just as snobby as my own mother. And at least my mum doesn't try to hide the fact. But Jackie presents herself as a woman of the people – as long as the people are new-money middle-class.

'Well, we may have to downsize on our stuff a little, Jackie,' I say, thinking of the hideous plastic flamingo light and resisting the urge to do an air punch. 'But honestly, don't you think it's wonderful that we've managed to buy a really great one-bedroom, ground-floor flat with a garden on a good road in an up-and-coming area of London? Kirstie and Phil would be proud!' I pause and look at her pleadingly. 'We were kind of hoping Jackie and Dave would be, too?' I can't believe I've resorted to this. She loves being talked about in third person.

Dave laughs and flings his arms around us. 'We *are* proud of you, we *are*. We're just sad that you're leaving us.' He turns to Ryan and looks down at him with the same disarming smile that he's passed on to his youngest son. 'I think your mum was hoping you'd be living at home forever, Ry. Me too, if I'm honest, mate.' I search Ryan's face for signs of crumbling; as much as he's tried to hide it I know he's been dreading the moment when we finally leave the Cooper nest. But, to give him credit, he agreed to my demand to move to London. I flush when I recall the argument I started after I confronted him about not wanting to go to Australia. I told him I was bored, that Leigh and his parents were stifling me and that if we didn't do something drastic soon I felt like I'd explode. It sounds so harsh now I think about it, I just felt so let down by him. I thought he wanted what I wanted. Left to his own devices he'd have lived at home forever, spent Friday night at the same pub with the same mates until his dying days, going to the footy every Saturday . . . I was saving him from himself. This life, the one I could see was right for us, suited us so much better.

'I'm twenty-six, Dad.' He puts his arms around me. 'Me and Molly, well, we need to make our own way. He looks at me and smiles weakly. He looks tired but that's just because we haven't had a summer holiday this year what with all the looking for a new job for him, and a flat for us, buying it and then packing up all our stuff. Once I'd pointed out that he was right, going to Australia wasn't the answer to our problems, but that moving to London was, he'd agreed. We'd decided that although he could commute easily enough from Hackney to Leigh, the best thing for us as a couple would be working and living in the same city. And with his experience at a school like Thorpe Hall, he could get a new teaching job easily enough. 'I'll really miss the kids,' he'd said sadly, 'and seeing the guys at the weekends, and Sunday lunch with you ...' But then he'd grinned. 'But in the long run I'll get more time with you so it'll all be worth it.'

'We *could* come back at weekends!' I'd said tentatively, wanting to offer him a compromise, something to make up for taking him away from the Mother Ship. He'd visibly brightened then, his face beaming in that irresistible way that had made a million hearts melt before mine. I'd hugged him tightly, thanking my lucky stars for such a wonderful, supportive boyfriend and trying to contain my excitement that we'd finally be moving to the big city.

'We'll get the best of both worlds! And buying a flat in London would be an investment in our future! It's time we stopped relying on your parents for everything.'

He'd nodded his agreement and kissed me. 'You're right. I want you to be happy and if moving to London is what it takes, then that's what we'll do. It's the perfect compromise!'

'I love you, Ryan,' I'd said, offering up my lips to him. And he'd lowered his and given me an earnest kiss.

He does the same now as my parents, Jackie, Dave and Carl exit our building, the Coopers' conversation blaring like a flock of honking geese as they head for their white Mercedes that sticks out so conspicuously on the run-down, grey Hackney street.

'Well, here we are, babe,' Ryan says as he pulls back from me and looks mournfully out of the window as they drive off with a screech of tyres, a toot of the horn and the sound of the radio blasting out of the window.

I smile, close my eyes and greedily inhale the silence. I feel like I have been starved of it for years. I look around at the desolate lounge, a room that I can already see forming in my head with a dark feature wall, some big photographic prints, more daring colours than our annexe, more of me, more of us. I coil my body around Ryan and I lock my arms around his neck as he draws me up around my waist, a half-formed smile hovering as I kiss him longingly on the lips.

'We're going to be so happy here, Ry, I just know it,' I say, pulling back and gazing into his eyes. I can see the doubt forming. I know Ryan. I know every blemish, freckle and mole. I can feel his emotions change with every word, blink, breath, kiss. I know he's unsure. Not about me, but about living here. I know he's worried about his new job in an academy school in East London. This is the biggest challenge that Ryan's ever faced. But I know this move is going to be the making of him. And the making of us.

The Grown-Up Kiss

I heard this song on the radio recently by this American band called The Ataris. The song talks about how growing up is better than being a grown-up and it struck me that although my teenage self would probably vehemently debate that point, right at this present moment I concur completely. Being a grown-up sucks.

'Hey, honey, I'm home,' I say, as I slam the door behind me and peel off my biker jacket and scarf. I walk into the small galley kitchen where Ryan is busy cooking up a storm. I sniff. Mmm, Thai curry.

I'm trying not to think of the final *Lord of the Rings* film premiere and after-party I was invited to tonight. I said no because Thursday nights are our 'date nights'. Monday to Wednesday evenings Ryan has various sports clubs and football training sessions to run, or he has to oversee after-school detention. But Thursdays are sacred because on Fridays he goes back to Leigh to see his mates before playing football on a Saturday. It was one of the terms of agreement of our move. I was meant to go every week and occasionally I do go back with him (mainly to hang out with Casey), but frankly, the two of us have more fun here, so if she's not working at Players she stays over here and comes out with me and my work mates. They think she's hilarious. Everyone loves Casey.

'Since when did you get so sociable?' Ryan ribbed me last week when I told him I couldn't go back to Leigh with him as I was going out with them.

'Since I started following your rules,' I replied. 'Number one: family always comes first.'

'Correct,' Ryan had said with an approving smile.

'Number two: fun should *always* take precedence over finances. You won't care about your bank balance . . .'

'. . . on your deathbed,' Ryan had recited.

'Number three: the pleasure that can be gained from the company of friends is priceless. Never turn down an opportunity to see them even if you don't feel like it.'

He'd added a side note with a jokey chuckle: 'As long as you remember that the person you have to hang out with the most is me!'

I'd smiled because I know he's not actually joking. It's funny because sometimes it feels like he wanted me to be more sociable and now I *am* he isn't always sure how to deal with it. I felt I needed to remind him why it's important, not just for me but for my career.

'Number four: networking is the best way to get ahead in life.'

Ryan had nodded. 'But not always the best way to get happy,' he'd added with a serious tone to his voice. 'See point one: family comes first.'

I'd wrinkled my brow in annoyance. I *know* he'd prefer me to go back with Leigh with him. But all *my* friends are here and Friday nights are a chance for me to prove I'm more than a boring old Charlotte – as in the prim-and-proper one from *Sex and the City*. My colleagues gave me this nickname after I turned down one after-work drink session too many. No matter how much I tell them I'm actually the *anti*-Charlotte, I just happened to meet someone who changed my mind, I couldn't change theirs. Not without proving I can have fun *and* hold down a relationship. So that's what I'm doing.

It's hard though because I'm the only person in the office in a proper relationship. Seb's a serial dater, Freya changes boyfriends more often than she changes outfits, even our editor Christie is single. And *she's* in her mid-thirties. To them I am an exotic creature with an alien lifestyle.

And to be honest, at times it still feels pretty alien to me. Or at least, it is to the 15-year-old me who still can't believe that this is actually *my life*. She pops up at work, usually when I'm in the middle of sorting out some budget or staff problem. And I feel the need to explain to her that the dreams you have as a teenager aren't necessarily the ones you have as an adult.

Here she is again now, glaring at me contemptuously as I sit down at the breakfast bar and wait to be served my dinner.

What a cosy, safe and comfortable little life we've got. Why the hell didn't you let us go to that premiere? It would have been brilliant! What kind of bourgeois freak would choose this over that?

Sometimes she pops up when I'm out with Ryan, pointing a camera at us and then holding it to one side as she eyes us up disbelievingly, like we're the oddest couple she's ever seen. She mouths '*Him? Really?*' and then rolls her eyes, and then points out the women who are turning to stare at him as we walk by and I'm hit by a wave of paranoia again. I know that's just her, the cynical teenage me who didn't believe I was good enough for someone like Ryan Cooper. I don't think like that now. I know that I'm what he wants. And he's what I want.

Steam is whirling around the brightly painted room like clouds over a clear blue sky and I wave my arm around, trying to waft it – and her – away at the same time. She disappears, but not without a final curl of her lip at the domestic scene.

'Mmm, that smells delish!' I say brightly, wrapping my arms around Ryan and nuzzling my nose into his navy Duffer St George hoodie, drinking in the scent of him and trying to dispel the disloyalty that I feel when teenage Molly is in the room.

I peer over his shoulder and into the saucepan that's sending out such deliciously spicy, fragrant scents.

'I was feeling a bit under the weather, so I thought I'd knock up a batch of my special Thai broth,' he says, taking a swig from a bottle of beer.

'Yours or Jamie Oliver's?' I say with a sly grin. 'And is it flu or *man* flu?' I know from experience how crap Ryan is when he's ill.

Ryan turns and prods me in the stomach, before kissing me on the forehead. 'Oy, where's the sympathy and the gratitude for me slaving over this pucker tucker, eh?!'

'It IS Jamie's recipe then!' I laugh jubilantly.

'Yeah, alright,' he admits. 'But I've added a little "Ryan Cooper" twist! Scallops, tofu and my own secret, creamy ingredient . . .'

I raise my eyebrow and he rolls his eyes. 'Just taste it, Moll!' He scoops some up on the ladle and offers it to me with an expectant smile. I notice that the skin around his eyes crinkles like raffia paper. We're getting older.

I open my mouth and sip, in what I hope is a sexy way. 'Mmm,' I moan, feeling the fragrant broth slip down my throat and through my body, warming me from inside out. Suddenly I feel this overwhelming wave of lust overtake me. It never ceases to amaze me that this can happen when you've been with someone for two years. I put the ladle back in the pot and reach up and grasp him around the neck.

'Fancy satiating my appetite *before* dinner?' I murmur, and I put my hand on his crotch suggestively and kiss him on the mouth.

He responds to my kiss, but as I press my body up against him, he pulls away.

'Come on, Moll, let's eat,' he says. 'I don't want my extra-special Thai noodle broth that I've slaved over to be ruined!'

'Er, o-kay, *Mum*,' I say facetiously, trying not to let it bother me that he's choosing soup over sex. He turns and reaches for an open bottle of wine from our stainless-steel fridge for me. I grab a wine goblet from the oak shelves and a couple of our nice bowls and chopsticks from the drawer and I start setting them up at the breakfast bar.

'Shall we eat in the lounge instead?' he says. 'We can sit on the floor on cushions around our coffee table and pretend we're in a Japanese restaurant . . .'

'. . . whilst eating Thai food?!' I laugh. 'Are you sure you should be a teacher, Ry?!'

'You know what I mean,' he snaps. He hates it when I criticize him. He may be super-fit, but he definitely needs thicker skin sometimes.

'Hey, I was just kidding,' I say with a laugh.

'Well. Don't.'

I hold my hands up, taken aback by his defensive tone. 'OK,

OK, I'm sorry, really. I won't ever do it again.' He looks over and smiles apologetically.

'Sorry, Molly, I'm just tired … this new job is really taking it out of me. The kids … well, let's just say they're not exactly an easy bunch. No, that's not fair, most of them are … they're just not what I'm used to. I shouldn't take it out on you though.' He comes over and kisses me on the lips gently and then starts serving our dinner.

I lean against the kitchen units and watch him move around the kitchen with the ease that he passes a ball around the football pitch. He is such a natural chef, confident and sure of every moment, and watching him now, I can't help but remind myself again of how lucky I am to have him. To have *this*. We've only been here three months but this place feels more like home than the annexe ever did. Above the working Victorian fireplace in our lounge is my pebble print that I gave Ryan when we moved into the annexe, to remind him of his hometown. On the wall opposite, above our big sofa, I've blown up a photo I took of us on a windswept Southend beach – my hair has blown over my face and we are laughing hysterically. And there, next to the TV, is the flamingo light. I've tried to sneakily remove it on many occasions but it always seems to find its way back, like a boomerang.

Despite that pink eyesore, this flat is 100 per cent us, and that's why I love it. And Ryan seems to have adapted his own style over the past few months too. About time too – he's twenty-six and he'd been dressing – and living – the same since he was seventeen. Living here has made him more individual, more interesting, more *grown-up*, which makes him sexier than ever, although I have to admit he is also more stressed. His new job is very different to Thorpe Hall and I know he's feeling it.

I sit on the floor cushion he's put down for me, face hovering over my steaming bowl of soup like a Bisto kid. 'I've had a hell of a day …' I sigh.

'Me too,' he interrupts, gazing into his bowl and stirring the broth slowly and methodically. 'I'm really worried about this student of mine . . .'

I glance at the sofa where piles of books and papers are spread all over it – clearly he was mid marking before he took a break to cook dinner. Even though I no longer have to commute, he still gets home long before I do.

'Do you want to talk about it?' I ask tentatively, dreading the answer as I know I'm about to get an evening of passionate teacher talk – rather than passionate sex.

And as Ryan begins to tell me all about his day, and I take a long slurp of wine and listen to him, I realize this must be what parents feel like, as I hear him talking about his students as if they were his own kids.

At 10 p.m., tired, cranky and with our date night clearly a damp squib, we get into bed. I'm lying in my brand-new (unbuttoned), blue-and-white striped pyjamas, waiting for Ryan to return from the bathroom, hoping we can rectify the evening. I lift my head a little as Ryan enters the room wearing just his white Calvin Kleins, and I feel a shiver of lust. I smile at him and he turns around, pulls on a pair of tracksuit bottoms and pulls out his papers, which I now notice he'd put on his bedside table. He throws a quick glance at me, and grins before he starts to sing 'Walking in the Air' in an Aled Jones falsetto as he begins his marking.

I look down at my pajamas – the object of his ridicule – and reach for my magazine, hitting him with it before I do up my buttons and, with a heavy sigh, start flicking through the pages without absorbing a thing. My body may be in bed, but my brain is half having sex and half out on the town at the big premiere after-party with my colleagues. Having fun. Like 24-year-olds tend to do. 'Night, Ry,' I lean over and we have a quick peck on the lips, like I've occasionally seen my parents do. Then he goes back to his marking.

I give us a C. For Could do better. More effort required.

'We're starting on the spare room now!'

'Thanks, Bob!' I call up to him as I cling on to the magazine I'm holding. I sniff and wipe away a tear. Who knew a box of old magazines would make me weep? It's an issue of *Viva* from December 2004. I reckon I'm mostly crying because of the gorgeous laughing cover model who is wearing a short, tight, sequinned dress and a party hat, and who is so far removed from me and my life that she may as well be my *daughter*. When did I get old? And why the hell didn't I wear dresses like these when I had the body to? What's even more galling is that I actually remember Freya forcing me to try on that exact sequinned dress in the fashion cupboard. I kept my Converse on and told her I felt ridiculous in it, although I remember being surprised at how good it actually looked. God, I wish I had photographic evidence of that. I wouldn't get it over my knees these days.

I pop a Jammie Dodger into my mouth (I am determined to finish the packet as well as the packing), and keep flicking through. Has it really been eight years since I worked on this issue? I flick through the pages, marvelling at how I know exactly what news pages, feature or fashion spread comes next. It's remarkable how much of your past stays with you, without you realizing. I can understand remembering big life events in detail, like weddings, or engagements, or birthday parties, or holidays, but this was a month of my working life, almost a decade ago. But all the memories of it are still there, as clear as day. The shoots, the work and the sheer effort that went into it all, the conversations we had when choosing the cover model, the music we listened to on the office stereo. How closely we worked as a team . . .

I throw the magazine down like it's on fire, when I suddenly realize what Christmas this issue was from. I hurriedly pick up another issue. This is much better. October 2000. The very first issue I worked on after starting at *Viva* as an intern. I was straight out of uni, young, hungry and ready to take on the world.

The Never Ever Kiss

You know how magazines seem to think that when you're in your twenties you should be constantly ticking things off a 'Things to do before you're 30' list? Well, what if we had a 'Things not to do before you're 30' list too?

Mine's easy, it would read like this:

Do not stop kissing Ryan Cooper

Which is weird, because when I was twenty it would have read like this:

Do not kiss Ryan Cooper ever again

And, of course,

Do not ever put a boy before your best friend

'Eeeeeee! Oh my God, oh my God, you're back! I can't believe you're actually here! How was the train? What time did you get in? What have you been doing? Am I the first person you've seen? Where—'

'Woah! Can I come in before I get the third degree?' I laugh, stepping through Casey's front door, as familiar as my own.

'Well, at least you're *getting* a degree, that's more than me! What's the gossip? Any boys I should know about or that I need to *get to know*? Are you still seeing Mar*coooos* or is there anyone else? I need to know all the sordid deets, *especially* the sordid deets! Don't leave anything out! Apart from the boring lectures. I get enough of them working at the caff!'

I laugh, already feeling overwhelmed. Casey throws her arms around me and gives me a big squeeze. She grabs my suitcase and drags me indoors. 'Oh, and you need to tell me when exactly you're going to become a world-famous photographer like I've always known you would be. I need to check my diary so I can plan my trips around the world with you! God, Moll, we have sooo much to catch up on! I've missed you loads since I came to visit last. It was wicked fun, wasn't it? Even though that Mia clearly doesn't like me much, she's just jealous though, 'coz we're BFFs!' I balk a little at the baby-ish phrase. 'Do you ever see that boy I snogged, the one she liked?' she giggles. 'You know, worked behind the bar, cute, Irish. What was his name? Michael? Mickey? Mark? Whatever. He was studying something weird. Fine something . . . art. That's right. Massive cock. That's the one, ha ha. But never mind that, I want to hear all about you!' She throws herself down on the stained couch, not without throwing off days-old dinner plates and boys' clothes – and some men's too. Toni's clearly got some guy on the scene. Again.

I look around at Casey's home that she still shares with her mum, her two brothers, who must be eleven and thirteen by now, the various rodents that they keep (pet rats, gerbils, hamsters – the place stinks of them). Not to mention the various rodents that their mum dates on a cyclical basis (the place stinks of them, too). They live in a small three-bedroom bungalow on the Belfairs estate, which they seem to explode out of. There's stuff everywhere: games consoles, DVDs, CDs, books, clothes, games. My mum would freak out at the chaos and I have to admit I constantly restrain myself from organizing, tidying or doing the washing up. But that's a constant battle of mine anyway. My mum spent the first twelve years of my life ingraining her orderly nature in me and I've spent the last eight years trying to undo it. I'm pretty sure by the time I hit twenty-five I'll have managed it. It all started when I finally refused to wear my hair in those bloody plaits for one more day. I remember so vividly the moment I vowed to be my own person because it was the morning after I overheard my parents arguing. I was up late, swotting for some test I desperately wanted to do well at, when I overheard them talking in the lounge. They said that being together was a mistake 'except for Molly'. They talked about splitting up and I vividly remember sitting on the stairs listening to my mum's shrill, raised voice reverberate through from the room below, with my fingers crossed, actively willing the moment one of them would just put us all out of our misery and say, 'Let's get a divorce'. Not a normal reaction for a child of twelve, you think? But I saw divorce as an opportunity to be more like the other girls at school – and as an excuse to ramp up the teen angst. Divorce got you sympathy, attention and friends. Their divorce could define me, by making me less of an outcast. Yes, I'd be the product of a broken home but the way I saw it, it was pretty shoddily glued together. But then their voices went quiet and Mum said something like, 'I think we should stay together, for Molly's sake,' adding, 'after all, what

would the vicar – and the board of school governors think?' The
next day it was like nothing had happened.

At that point I had a moment of searing clarity. I looked at my
plaits, my terrible clothes, thought about my lack of friends, the
relentless taunts by the Heathers, and my lack of freedom, and it
suddenly occurred to me that if my parents' life choices for themselves were so wrong, then the ones they were making for me were
pretty shitty, too. They'd chosen to stay together because of their
misguided desperation to be seen as the 'perfect family'. So I'd have
to live under the penance of their pious beliefs. I didn't respect
them any more and I wanted them to know it. I was going to be
me from now on. After a change of image involving me shouting
at my parents a lot, wearing a shorter skirt to school, as well as lots
of make-up and some serious attitude, I spent a shaky few weeks
trying to fit in with 'the Heathers' after they showed a fleeting
interest in my makeover moment, but I soon realized that I was
just their toy. Someone to prod and poke and tease and get to do
their dirty tricks, like shoplifting stuff for them. I felt so stupid,
so weak-willed. I hated that they'd sucked me into their idiotic
clique. I just wanted a friend who I could just be 'me' with. Once
I'd worked out who 'me' really was.

Enter Casey Georgiou.

She swept into school like a big breath of fresh air. Casey Not-
so-Gorgeous, the Heathers immediately called her. But in my eyes
she *was* because she was unselfconscious about her curves, and
seemingly impervious to their cruel, stupid taunts. She seemed
so happy, with her crazy plastic hair clips and bright-pink patent
rucksack. The nasty jibes just seemed to bounce off her; she seemed
so carefree and fun-loving and completely different to the vacuous
dummies I'd had to put up with for so long and, more importantly,
she was so different to my introverted, serious self. She fascinated
me. I was desperate to get to know her but she was only in two
of my classes – art and textiles – I was in top sets for the rest. She

smiled at me often – but then, she smiled at everyone. For the first week I hovered around her, choosing a desk near but not next to her, not really willing to believe I was worthy of having a friend of my own, but feeling like she was the best option I'd ever had. I loved that she was always giggling and chatting in class and always came in with a big beam on her face. I was sure she'd be batting friends off like flies, unlike me. And then it happened. One afternoon I was walking past the playground, camera held up to my eyes as usual, trying to look busy rather than alone, when I heard a big ruckus from the playground. I glanced down to see the Heathers surrounding someone. Their arms were flying up and down, fists clenched. I could see their ugly scowls as they raised their hands for the next blow. I couldn't see their victim, but suddenly I saw the discarded bag and recognized it immediately. I flew down the steps, camera banging against my chest as hard as my heart was. And then, with strength I didn't know I possessed, I launched myself into the group. I'll never forget how she looked when I got to her. Her long black hair was swirled out on the tarmac like an oil spillage, I couldn't see her eyes as her hands were covering them but her lip was cut and bleeding, her shirt was ripped so her flesh and her bra were exposed to the entire school, she'd pulled her plump legs up to her tummy and she lay there, looking like a poor, discarded shrimp. I yelled, 'MURDER!' at the top of my voice (it was the first thing that came to mind), in order to clear a space around her. It worked, they all ran away and then I sank to my knees, pulled a clump of folded tissues out of my bag and a bottle of water. I dabbed her lip and whispered that everything was going to be all right, and slowly she'd pulled down her hands and heaved herself up into a sitting position, and blinked at me before her poor lips broke out into a painful smile.

'You saved my life!' she'd gasped, and enveloped me in a hug.

But as I helped her up, holding up my fists to anyone who dared come close, I felt she'd saved mine.

From that moment on we were inseparable. We waited for each other after class, spent every breaktime together, I even purposely dropped grades in a couple of subjects so we could be in the same set. I'd been planning on doing it anyway, just to piss Mum off – now I had an even better reason. I helped her with schoolwork, she helped me to relax and be myself. For the first time, someone liked me for *me*. It was a revelation.

'Molly!' Casey squeals now as she gestures to the small space next to her on the couch. 'You look wicked!'

I glance down at my fitted black T-shirt and long denim skirt that I'm wearing with – yep, you've guessed it – Converse. My style is still basically the same, mostly black, mostly long, but these days I like to show off a little bit of my shape, too.

'Ooh, I love your hair! It's grown! You're almost back to your natural brunette! If you had it feathered, and highlighted, you could totally have a Rachel cut!' I pull a face. This was not a look I'd be aiming for. 'Although you'd need my Greek nose.' She sticks her face up against mine and turns us to face the mirror in the hallway and I can't help laughing. 'See! Told you!' she exclaims. 'Oooh, we can watch loads of *Friends* over the holidays. It's my favourite programme EVER.' She pauses, but only to draw breath. 'I'm desperate to see *There's Something About Mary*! I love Cameron Diaz, I wish I were just like her, don't you? She actually makes me wanna get my hair cut short! And maybe dye it blonde?' She shakes her long, dark mane.

'You look gorgeous as you are, Case!' I smile.

'Ahhh, you just always expect to see me with old braces, bad hair and Greek–Italian puppy fat! Hey!' she snaps her fingers. 'I'm the Monica to your Rachel!'

'You were never fat, Case,' I point out. 'Just ... curvaceous.'

'Well, thank God for step aerobics! And straight teeth! I passed one of the Heathers in the street the other day – Nikki, do you remember? She's up the duff! Again! Who's Not-so-Gorgeous now, huh? Ha ha!'

'I haven't heard that name for a long time,' I say, mentally rewinding the months since I left Leigh to go to uni in London.

'God, I've missed you so MUCH!' Casey leans over and squeezes me tightly. Her hair is pulled back with lots of little brightly coloured bulldog hair clips and they're digging into my cheek. I pull away.

'We only saw each other a few weeks ago!'

Casey pouts. 'Yeah well, that's way too long. We used to see each other every day!'

I squeeze her to let her know I've missed her, too. She knows I'm not one for ostentatious emotion.

'Molly!' exclaims Casey's mum as she walks in from the kitchen and stands with her hip jutting out, chewing gum.

'Hi, Toni,' I smile politely. I know Casey finds her embarrassing because she's not like other mums.

'Make Moll a cup of tea please, Mum!' Casey demands as I throw myself down on her sofa.

'Make it yerself sweetheart, I'm going aht. I gotta hot date.'

'Another one?' Casey mutters sullenly.

'Don't be sore just 'coz your mum gets more action than you! I can't help it if men find me irresistible. I'm off to an Ann Summers party at that posh house on the Marine Estate. Whatsername. Jackie Cooper.' My chest constricts at that name. 'Ooh, her husband is well fit, I'd give him one!'

'UGH,' Casey says as her mum slams the door behind her. 'Seriously Moll, be thankful that your parents are the way they are. Can you imagine having a mum like mine who talks about shagging all the time? It's so embarrassing!'

'So how long are you back for?' she then asks excitedly, throwing her legs over mine and stretching out languidly.

She smiles at me hopefully and I dread giving her my reply. 'Just a few days to be honest, Case . . .'

'Oh, you're not off to stay with Mar*coos* are you?' Casey says, curling her lip. She never did take to him.

I shake my head. 'Nope. I broke it off. Eight months was as long as I could stand with him! I reckon that's the first and last long-term relationship for me.'

'So you're single?' Casey squeals. I nod. 'And ready to mingle?'

'I guess so.'

'YAY! We are going to have so much fun! So, hang on, why aren't you staying here longer if you're not with him any more?'

'I've got a work placement at a magazine in London for six weeks starting next week, so I'm going to stay at my uni digs for the summer.'

'A magazine?'

'It makes sense for me to get some experience on a picture desk. It'll give me loads of photography contacts, too.'

'Ooh, I know!' she says, sitting up on her knees and clapping her hands together excitedly. 'I could come and work at the magazine, too! I could be, you know, one of those people who shop for a living! Or even better, their party correspondent.' She adopts an American accent and holds the TV remote up to her mouth as if it is a microphone. 'This is Casey Georgiou reporting from the Oscars where I'm currently snogging Brad Pitt.' She clutches a cushion to her lips and kisses it passionately and I laugh. 'Speaking of Brad Pitt,' she says, putting the cushion back in its place, 'I know another guy who all the girls fancy who's looking forward to snogging – I mean seeing – you . . .'

'Who?' I rack my brains trying to think of anyone in Leigh who could possibly want to see me. Being away from home has made me realize the size of the chip I had on my shoulder. It was more of a potato wedge.

'A certain local football star who drives a nice car and is a *total* hottie . . .'

'Oh. HIM. Is he still living round here?' I sniff.

'Wow, Molly, you can still hold a grudge better than anyone else I know!' Casey raises her perfectly pencilled eyebrow. When did she get so good at applying make-up, I wonder?

'I haven't thought about him in *ages* actually,' I say defensively. 'I had a boyfriend, remember? I look at my fingernails so she can't see I'm lying. 'Besides, I've got a right to hold a grudge – he totally humiliated me.'

'He only kissed you, Molly.'

'Badly.'

'That's not a crime is it? If it was, every teenage boy should be locked up!'

'OK, I'll rephrase that. He kissed me badly as a dare, in front of everyone!'

'Yeah well,' she continues flapping her hand dismissively, 'clearly you haven't thought about him AT ALL since.'

I make a face at her. 'I haven't. Apart from to recall the deep-rooted humiliation that's printed to my core like a stick of Southend rock. Other than that, I can barely remember his name.'

'Whoooee,' Casey whistles. 'He got you *baaaad*. Well, I happen to know he's up for grabs, and a bit down on his luck . . .'

'Oh?' I say, suddenly intrigued.

She nods and rubs lip balm on her lips. 'He can't play football any more, hurt himself at his trial for Southend. He's still living at home and has had to have loads of physio and stuff. Lucky physio!' she laughs. 'Hey maybe that would be a good job for me?' She wiggles her hands. 'Put these magic fingers to good use! Anyway, it's sad for him but good for you, eh Moll? I mean, bruised egos make them vulnerable. That's what I find anyway when I hoover up other girls' sloppy seconds. It makes them dead grateful.' Her face clouds over and she puts on a bright smile. 'When it comes to cheering up men, I'm like Leigh-on-Sea's very own Saint . . . Mother Lady . . . you know whatshername. She's old, or dead, and she always wore that hat. Blue and white it was . . .'

'Mother Teresa?' I offer, struggling to keep up with Casey's train of thought. I'm out of practice.

'That's her! Yep, I'm her, but younger and hotter and with better make-up and less clothes! So yep, if you don't want him, let me know, 'cause I, Saint Casey Georgiou, will go and lay *my* healing hands on him ...'

'Cas*ey*!' I laugh, trying to hide my annoyance at her persistence. 'What's your obsession with Ryan Cooper anyway?' I ask as I settle back on her sofa and close my eyes. 'Change the record.'

'OK. Consider it changed. And he probably wouldn't be interested in you any more with your new hair and your future magazine career, and your swish London ways. Leigh lads like to keep it local, remember? They always stay close to home.' I roll my eyes in acknowledgement of this truth. 'So babes,' she continues, 'what shall we do tonight?'

'What about The Sun Rooms or Club Arts in Southend?'

Casey groans. 'Oh God no, not that divey old alternative music place you always insisted we go to.'

'It was better than Tots.'

'If by "better" you mean "not as much fun" ...'

'What do you suggest then?'

'I was thinking about a little walk down memory lane ...'

'I can't believe you brought me here!'

Casey and I are standing on The Green in Leigh-on-Sea, gazing across at the boats that are moored there. Clusters of teenagers are scattered over the grass, and I can see hazy silhouettes of people down on the beach and on the boats, too. The June evening sun is bathing everything in a soft, lemony light that makes me feel like I've stepped into a photo album, one that I wasn't fussed about opening because it has lots of terrible haircuts, clothes and bad memories. I grab hold of my Canon EOS and hold it close, for support and comfort more than anything else. This green was the scene of so many embarrassments, my parents insisting on picnicking here with me – complete with deck chairs, gingham picnic blanket and windbreaker – when everyone else was smoking Silk Cuts with their mates. Not to mention the rejections, the boys who laughed at me and Casey, the girls who called us names. It feels too soon to return here, those years, those memories are too close. I've spent the last two years trying to erase them with my shiny new London life.

'Well, it's summer, where else would we go apart from the top deck of the *Bembridge*? We used to have so much fun here, didn't we?' Casey grins. I raise an eyebrow at her and smile – a trick she taught me – always lifted by her ability to see sunshine through the rain.

'I guess you could call it that, Case,' I reply drily. She glances at my camera which I'm still clutching to put it in front of my face, not to take photos, but to hide behind. This place makes me feel like the vulnerable, awkward teenage me instead of the confident, outgoing and worldly woman being a university student has made me. Casey tugs at my arm. 'Oh, take one of me, Moll, you can put it on your photo wall in your room, next to the one of you and Mia! Or you could put it on the cover of that fancy magazine you're doing work experience at! What's it called? *Viva Forever*.' She starts singing the Spice Girls' hit and swings off an old Victorian lamp post and, with both of us laughing, she pouts at the camera as I take a series of shots of her with the sea shimmering in the background. Then, bored already, she leaps over to her bag. 'I've got all the supplies we need, too.' She flips it open to reveal a large bottle of cider and forty Marlboro Lights. 'C'mon, Molly, for old times' sake?' She holds out her hand and, to my embarrassment, begins to sing something from a different lifetime. I glance around hoping no one is close enough to hear it.

*'We've only got each other right now
But we'll always be around*

forever and forever no matter
What they say . . .

Come on, Molly, join in!'

'They say, they sa-ay,' I mutter obediently, not wanting to hurt her feelings but hoping she'll follow suit and lower her volume. She beams and continues singing loudly.

Then she grabs my hand and whilst I pull back at first and shake my head, after a moment, I give in, swing my camera over my back and we run down the hill, laughing as she sings the chorus loudly and people dive out of our way.

We're lying on the top deck of the boat feeling the familiar, fuzzy-edged happiness from the cider inhabit our bodies as we gaze at the stars.

'Can you believe we're twenty?' Casey says wondrously. 'Nearly twenty-one! It's so old! Properly grown-up. It feels like only yesterday that we were lying here, wondering if we'd ever get a boyfriend . . .'

'. . . and now here we are, thinking the same thing!' I laugh, lifting my cigarette to my lips. Despite my earlier misgivings, I am actually starting to enjoy this evening.

'Speak for yourself!' Casey blushes and falls silent for a second in a most uncharacteristic manner.

I gape at her. 'What?'

'Oh, nothing, I mean, you know, we don't need men! We've got each other! And that's all we need! Right? BFFs forever!'

I sit up and shake her on the arm. 'Are you seeing someone?' Her face is guilt-ridden. 'Why didn't you tell me? Is he from the café?' Despite my nagging her to do something else, Casey's still working at her mum's place. I know it's because there is a continual stream of young male kitchen staff that Toni employs to work alongside her and her daughter. I'm pretty sure that's what is keeping Casey there anyway.

'No, he's not.'

'So where did you meet him? In a club, bar, what?'

'He's someone I've known for a while, actually,' Casey says, studying her stick-on French-manicured fake nails. I look at my own chipped, dark nail polish and sit on my hands to hide them.

I laugh, stubbing out the cigarette next to me. I nudge her gently. 'Come on, spill it, sister, you're making me think you don't want me to know who he is.'

Casey looks uncomfortable. 'Well, he's thirty-nine . . .'

'An older man,' I tease, unable to hide the disapproval in my voice, 'there's a surprise.' Casey is nothing if not predictable. Her absent father has given her a lifelong fascination with father figures. 'And what does he do?'

'He's a plumber,' Casey says. She is being reticent, which is unlike her.

'So where's he from?' I push.

'Um, well, around here actually.'

I frown. 'But we practically know everyone here.' I look at her. 'Do I know him?'

Casey doesn't say anything. She just gazes away in the opposite direction.

'What's his name? Casey?' I try and turn her face to look at me but she looks up at the sky instead.

'Oh, look Molly! At the stars! Up there! Wow, aren't they pretty and sparkly, you know, like diamonds.'

'Casey . . .' I interrupt.

'Oh OK,' she sighs and looks at me uncertainly. 'It's Paul Evans.'

It takes a second for his name to register.

'What?' I gasp. 'As in the *married* plumber with *two kids* Paul Evans?'

'Yes,' she replies before adding defensively. 'And OK, so he's married, but they've not been happy for ages. Years actually. And he says he's going to leave her.'

I roll my eyes and pull out another cigarette.

'Don't pull that disapproving face on me, Moll,' Casey grumbles, 'you look just like your mum. And don't judge until you've seen us together either. You should see how he looks at me.'

'I can imagine,' I reply drily.

I throw my arm around her. My sweet, beautiful, naive, desperate-to-be-loved friend.

'Just be careful, Case, I don't want you getting hurt again. You know you have a habit of going for the wrong type.'

'I can't help it that I go for older guys, I prefer them to be mature, you know? I would've told you sooner,' she garbles as her long-held secret tumbles out, 'but I just knew you wouldn't approve. You slag off anything to do with Leigh these days – even more than you used to!'

'I've just moved on.'

'Moved on from me,' Casey mumbles.

My face drops in horror and I throw my arm around her and squeeze her tightly. 'Don't be silly, Case!' I say, wishing I were better at all this reassuring stuff.

'I miss you, you know, Molly,' Casey says quietly.

I clutch her hand, feeling guilty that so many weeks have passed without my calling her, let alone coming to see her. 'Me too. And I'm happy for you, Case, I am. But remember, I'm your best friend, so as far as I'm concerned no man is *ever* going to be good enough for you.'

'I didn't say he was Mr Right, but he's Mr Better Than Nothing, OK? Besides,' she continues, 'I need something to fill in all the spare time I have now you're at *uni* being a boring *student* and *studying* all the time, with your clever new *friends*...'

Casey looks over her shoulder at me and smiles and I know she's just joking. She can never stay mad or hold grudges for long. It's one of the things I love about her and one of the many reasons we're so different. 'And he's not how you remember anyway, Moll!'

she says pleadingly. 'Yes, he's a grown-up, but so am I now. So are we. I mean, you're not the girl who ran out of The Grand after Ryan Cooper snogged you.'

'Thank God for that!' I laugh.

A figure looms out of the boat's shadows. 'Thank God for what?'

Casey scrambles to her feet. 'Ryan! I–I, er, didn't know you'd be coming tonight!'

I glance at him and away dismissively. I'm shaken but not surprised by his appearance, it's just another reminder of why I moved away from this place. Nothing's changed, same people, different year.

'What a surprise!' Casey exclaims in the worst case of overacting I've ever seen. 'Is Alex here too? And the others? Gaz and Carl and Jake? Ooh, there they are! She waves at them and then stands staring pointedly at Ryan. I'm not sure what she's waiting for. Ryan smiles down at me and then looks back at his mates.

'Hey, Case.'

'Yeah, Ryan?' she simpers. I roll my eyes.

'Alex really wanted to talk to you I think.' And before I can blink, let alone tell her to stay right here, she's off.

'Casey!' I call, but she doesn't look back. I look up at Ryan. I'd forgotten how tall he is. And broad. In the couple of years since I last saw him, he's bulked up. He has proper yachting arms, ripped and strong, which he's showing off by wearing a vest top. His skin is nut-brown and his mid-nineties curtains have been replaced with a gelled David Beckham style. I can't deny it. He's still pretty hot. But, I tell myself firmly, I much prefer boys with brains bigger than their biceps, who know more about art and culture than who's on top of the football league.

He grins down at me sheepishly. 'Well, well, well, Molly Carter.'

I look away, hoping to show my disinterest. 'It's good to see you.' He bends down and nudges my knee. 'It's been a long time.'

I move my legs away and busy myself by adjusting the settings

on my camera. 'Yeah well, I don't get back to Leigh much. I live
in *London* now,' I add pompously, suddenly feeling the urge to
prove myself.

He smiles. 'That's cool.'

'Yep,' I reply curtly. 'It is.' I look around desperately, trying to
find an excuse to leave. Ryan clearly has other ideas. He sits down
next to me and then leans back on his elbows in a way that suggests
he doesn't plan on moving any time soon.

'So what do you do in London then?' he asks, taking a swig of
beer.

'I'm doing a photography degree. At the London College of
Printing.'

I'm showing off, but I don't care.

'There's a whole college dedicated to *printing*?' He laughs and
I stare at him solemnly. 'I'm just kidding. That's wicked. It's a
properly good college, isn't it? And it means you're one step closer
to that dream of being a photographer. Good for you!'

'Thanks,' I say, shocked that he remembered our conversation
from all those years ago. I look around desperately for Casey and
realize that we're surrounded by snogging couples. The *Bembridge*
has always been Leigh's local haunt for young, amorous teens.
Which makes seeing him here even worse. Brings back bad memories. 'So what are you up to?' I say politely, but disinterestedly,
thinking, *Not much if you're still hanging around here.*

'I'm about to start training to be a teacher at college,' he grins.

'There's a whole college dedicated to teaching?' I retort sarcastically, and he laughs and holds his hands up. I look at him
quizzically. Guys like Ryan Cooper don't become teachers. 'So
why would you want to go and do that?' I laugh, then clock his
hurt expression and remember what Casey told me about his
injury. 'I mean a teacher – wow! That's very . . . er . . . *noble* of you.'

'Well,' he begins slowly, gazing at me intensely. 'I believe that
children are, y'know, our future.' He pauses and then stands up

slowly, his eyes sparkling mischievously at me and breaks loudly
into Whitney Houston's song, causing some of the surrounding
snoggers to stop mid-tongue.

I pull him down and shush him, punching him on the arm as
he laughs gleefully.

'Now you *are* taking the piss,' I pout, twirling my cider around
with the hand furthest away from him, the other clenched on the
deck tantalizingly close to his.

'So what happened to your dream of being a footballer?' I ask,
thinking back to our long-ago conversation when I bumped into
him with my mum and he took me for coffee. Unsurprising really,
back then it felt like the biggest thing that had ever happened to
me. How pathetic.

'I got badly injured during my trial a while back,' he says matter-
of-factly. 'Tore my cartilage in my knee and had to have surgery.
Bang went the idea of going pro.'

'Oh, that's awful!' I exclaim, wondering why he doesn't look
more bothered about it. The way Casey told it, it was a local
tragedy.

He shrugs and smiles. 'It happens. It wasn't the end of the
world.' A shadow flickers over his face momentarily. 'Besides,' he
leans towards me to whisper, 'I'm not sure I was as good as everyone thought I was. Reckon it was definitely a case of confidence
over talent.'

'If your kissing was anything to go by, that's probably true.'

Shit. Did I just say that?

Ryan laughs. 'Ahh, well that addresses the elephant in the . . .
boat. About that night at The Grand, I'm sorry.' He pauses and
looks at me sincerely. 'But it wasn't what you thought, y'know.'

'What, shockingly abysmal you mean?' I say sarcastically.

He stares at me and smiles a little sadly. 'I meant a dare. It
wasn't a dare.'

'What was it then, double dare, or maybe a physical challenge?'

I retort. 'If it was, you failed.' I love goading this guy. It's too easy.

'Ouch,' Ryan clasps his chest and scuffs his trainers on the ground. 'Right in the heart, and ego. I'm not sure which hurts the most.' He looks up and grins cheekily. 'Are you gonna kiss it better then?' he presses.

'And why on *earth* would I want to do that?'

He winks. 'Because if first is the worst, that must mean second will be the best ...'

I look around for Casey. Where is she? 'So, er, what are you doing for the summer?' I ask awkwardly.

'I'm going to Australia for a couple of months,' he says excitedly. 'I'm going to be a deck-hand on a boat that sails around the Whitsundays. I leave in a couple of weeks. It's going to be wicked!'

'Wow!' I exclaim, genuinely impressed. 'I've always wanted to go to Australia. Me and my mate Mia have said we're going to go and live in Sydney one day. It's meant to be an amazing city, loads to do!'

'Yeah,' he grins. 'I thought I should have my fun on the other side of the world, so I don't have to hold back! I need to behave once Mr Cooper is officially unveiled to the world. Well to the kids of Essex anyway!' he laughs and looks at me.

'I'm starting my PGCE back at uni in September, straight after I get back from Oz. I'm looking forward to it too. Teaching isn't a million miles away from what I wanted to do, not really ...' I look at him doubtfully. 'You never know, I may end up *teaching* the next Gary Lineker, rather than being him!'

His generous mouth lifts into a cute smile. We stare at each other, remembering a past moment shared. An awkward silence descends like the night breeze, cooling the atmosphere.

'Come on, let's walk,' Ryan says, getting up and extending his hand to me.

'We're on a boat,' I laugh, 'there's only so far we can go.'

'Let's just go and look at the view across the water.'

I stand up and blink, suddenly realizing just how much the cider has gone to my head.

'Wooo,' I say, swaying a little.

'Hey,' Ryan puts his arm out to steady me. 'You OK?'

'Yep, just felt a little woozy there for a little bit.' I giggle. 'I'm OK now.'

We carry on walking and I realize he hasn't moved his arm. I stiffen a little. I'm drunk but not *that* drunk. If he thinks he's going to take advantage of me again, embarrass me in front of all these people, he's got another thing coming.

'You know,' Ryan murmurs, his breath warm against my ear. 'I've always regretted what happened that night in The Grand.'

'Me *too*,' I say emphatically. 'I expected it to be bad but it was the worst first kiss EVER!' I giggle again. I *never* giggle. What's wrong with me?

Ryan gapes at me. 'It was your *first* first kiss?'

'Mmmhmm.' I nod and then stop when I realize any vigorous movement makes my head spin. I must be drunk. 'Didn't you guess?' He shakes his head and I prod my finger against his chest. 'Well Cooper, unlike the *rest* of the boys in this town it must have escaped your notice that as a teenager I was NOT the hot piece of ass that I am now.' Ryan bursts out laughing. 'Hey, it's not funny! Iss true. I know you kissed me for a dare. And I also happen to know that I have bloomed in the intervening years ... Oh, yes ...' I shake my new, longer, darker locks off my shoulders and prod him in the chest again. 'I bet you're kicking yourself now, aren't you, huh?' I bat my heavily liquid-lined eyelashes for comic effect.

Ryan catches my finger and pulls my hand to his chest.

'I didn't kiss you for a dare, Molly Carter,' he murmurs. 'Is that really what you thought? That it was some sort of stupid bet?'

I nod – and then burst out into a fit of uncontrollable giggles again.

Ryan doesn't join in. 'I kissed you because I really liked you,' he says solemnly. 'I just happened to do it badly. The boys will never let me forget it either. "Shit Snog" Cooper, that's what they call me. Imaginative, huh?'

'Sounds about right to me,' I smile and then immediately narrow my eyes. 'But don't try and lay on the charm now, Cooper. I'm not going to feel sorry for you.'

Ryan holds his hands up. 'I swear, Molly, I like – I mean,' he coughs, 'I liked you.'

I fold my arms and stare pointedly at him. 'So why do you regret that kiss then?' I prod him again jubilantly. 'Ha! Smooth talk your way out of that one!'

Ryan turns and gently brushes my cheek then leans back and whacks me on the bottom. 'Because, you hot piece of *ass*, what I was *gonna* say if you just let me finish, is that if I could wipe out that moment six years ago when I kissed you so embarrassingly badly, I would do it all over again. And,' he leans in slowly, 'I can guarantee it would be much, *much* better.'

I burst out laughing again at the corniness of his line and am horrified when I notice that a little bit of my spit has landed on his face, but Ryan doesn't seem to notice.

'The soft ripple of the waves would be like background music . . .'

I contain my laughter to a derisory snigger. 'It's an estuary, there aren't any waves.'

He stares at me for a moment then his eyes flicker out to the distance. 'We'd gaze out across at the glimmering lights of Leigh-on-Sea . . .'

'Hardly Paris, is it?' I say, folding my arms, my mouth twitching a little with the effort of disguising my smile.

Ryan takes a step closer to me and untangles my arms, gripping lightly on to my wrists then lifting them up. I feel a snort of nervous laughter building. 'I'd hold your arms out like this, so you could feel the wind in your face, just like Leonardo di Caprio did with Kate Winslet in *Titanic* . . .'

'HAAAAARRRRRRR!' I explode with giggles, but they simmer to a stop as Ryan, still holding my arms, slides his body behind me. I shiver as he presses himself gently against my back, the urge to giggle now completely gone. He smells so good. Hugo Boss, I think.

'The *Bembridge* is permanently moored.' I mutter, trying not to show how affected I am by his touch, his scent and the feel of his breath on my neck. I turn and look up into his eyes. I feel like I've been cast with an enchantment. 'There wouldn't be any wind . . .'

He ignores me. 'And then,' he says turning me round to face him and putting his finger over my lips, 'I'd lean forward . . . like this . . . I'd cup your face with my hands . . . like this . . . and I'd slowly lean in and . . .'

'Ryan!' A shrill voice interrupts our moment. 'I've been looking for you *everywhere*!' I feel the cool air hit my body as Ryan quickly moves away from me. A tall, blonde girl sidles up to him and lays her hand territorially on his arm.

'We've been waiting for those drinks you promised us.' She flirtatiously drags a finger down his arm, across his waist and threads it through his trouser belt-loop. She tugs. But he doesn't move.

'I'll be right there, Stacey, I'm er, I'm just catching up with an old friend.' She tugs again and looks at him beseechingly and I seize the opportunity when he turns to talk to her to slip away.

That was close, I think as I run down Gypsy Bridge and on to The Green, not stopping to let Casey know I'm leaving. He nearly did it again, luring me in like a fisherman dragging his nets in with his well-practised pick-up lines. And I was there, in the palm of his hand, flailing around all breathless and bug-eyed. And I nearly bought his whole 'wounded footballer turned sensitive high-school teacher' act. For a moment there I thought there might be more to him than his fake tan and white trainers. I should've known better.

Once a player, always a player.

I'm furious with myself. I mean, trying to recreate *Titanic*? How pathetic is that? I hate that movie anyway, I mean, look where it got Kate Winslet; clinging on to a floating bit of debris in the middle of the Atlantic Ocean. And if *that* isn't a fitting metaphor for love, then I don't know what is.

I'm washing up the kitchen paraphernalia I've left out until today. The single saucepan, the cutlery, mugs and all the wine glasses from last night. I dry them and then carefully put each of them on pre-cut pieces of bubble wrap. It is so *weird* packing everything up like this – especially in this room, which has always been so crammed full of stuff. Weird, but liberating. I finish drying up the pasta maker that I made ravioli with last night and pick up the floating food debris from the plug with one hand. Glancing back I notice some stubbornly stuck bits of pasta on the machine that I haven't quite managed to wash off. I scrape at the cutters with the Brillo pad and when I'm satisfied that it's gleaming I pack it in its original box. As I look at it I'm suddenly struck by a memory so vivid it transports me to another time, another place.

The Girls Just Wanna Have Fun Kiss

Do me a favour will you? Break a rule today, go crazy, live in the moment. Open your heart. Now open it a little more. Love big, love even bigger. Don't be afraid to stand up, to shout it out, to be heard. Say I LOVE YOU. Give it what for. Give love what for. For me. Because I didn't. And now I can't.

That is all.

(But that is nowhere nearly enough.)

The doorbell rings persistently and I put down the pasta maker I've just been furiously scrubbing with a Brillo pad. I love Ryan's homemade ravioli but I hate washing up the bloody machine. I wipe my hands on my skinny grey jeans and open the front door. The overcast October day streams in – along with the ray of light that is Casey. No matter what the weather, you can always rely on her to be sunny. She has that in common with Ryan. Maybe that's why I was drawn to them both? In many ways they're really quite similar.

She beams at me and then throws her arms out to reveal her bright-pink overnight bag and a bottle of champagne. She's wearing a short, plunging, emerald-green dress with bare legs and over-the-knee boots. A bit much for a wintry lunchtime girlie day, but she gets away with it.

'Let's get this party started!' she squeals, stamping her feet and lifting the bottle in the air over her head.

'Case, it's not even lunchtime!' I laugh as we kiss each other jokingly on the lips and I take her bag off her. A passing car honks and she immediately turns around and poses in the doorframe, arms in each corner, one knee bent and pulled to her chest. The car, with two young guys in the front seat screeches to a halt and I drag her inside, both of us giggling irrepressibly like teenagers.

'I'm so excited you're here!' I squeal, embracing her in a big hug.

'I know, Moll!' she grins. Her hair is really long and poker-straight and has been dyed blonde. She can carry it off but it just doesn't look like her. I prefer her natural dark hair. It made her stand out. 'I can't believe I've got a whole weekend off! It's mad! Hey, isn't Ryan here?' She walks into the lounge and looks around the room, which is perfectly tidy – the biggest giveaway to his absence.

'He's gone back to Leigh for the weekend. There's a Southend FC match on today, they're in League Two of the Coca-Cola Cup, they've been doing really well since Tilson was appointed manager last year. Ryan reckons ...' I glance at Casey and she rolls her eyes and yawns.

'Moll, I did not come here to talk football. I came here to see you, get drunk and find me a man. Now, can you help me with that? Or is Boring, Brainwashed, Football-Widow Molly here to stay?'

'Sorry,' I grin at Casey. 'I don't even realize I'm doing it any more.' Ryan's obsession with his childhood football team has, by osmosis, made *me* knowledgeable. I think I might even understand the offside rule. I don't think Casey would be impressed. 'So what do you fancy doing? I'd really like to see the Edward Hopper exhibition at Tate Modern, the way he painted light is so inspiring, I mean it's almost photographic—' I burst out laughing at Casey's curled lip and petulant expression. 'I'm *kidding* Case, just kidding. I'll go to that on my own!'

These days when Ryan's back in Leigh, I wake up on a Saturday morning, browse through the *Weekend* section of *The Times* whilst the coffee maker is warming up, working out what cultural event takes my fancy. Then I shower and head into town, always going via a market: Broadway if I fancy a young, hip vibe; Spitalfields if I want something a bit fancier; or Borough market, if I want to surprise Ryan with some great ingredients to make one of his incredible dishes.

My camera is my only companion on these trips. I relish the time alone to morph into the bustling weekend city-life, making myself invisible so I can photograph the rich canvas, the cutaway of London's core. I grab a sandwich for lunch and then visit a gallery or an exhibition, or take a walk along the Serpentine, or I head somewhere that I can observe people living and breathing the city's pulse: the skaters down on Southbank, the shoppers on Sloane Street. Then I might sit in a little pavement café, like Bar Italia in Soho and have an espresso whilst I flick through my day's photos before going home. I call Ryan for a chat and then go out for tapas with the girls from work, or, if Casey's down, we head out to a cocktail bar and then a club. I miss Ryan, but I love this time too. It's a day in my week where I feel most like me.

Sometimes I am skewed by guilt that twists me over hot coals of doubt as I think about how I promised Ryan when we moved to London that I'd go back every weekend. But I can't. I find it too stifling. And one of us should be making the most of what London offers at weekends, right? And I only promised to go back because I thought once he was here he'd change. But it's like he's on a bungee umbilical cord and it keeps pinging him back to Leigh-on-Sea. Whenever I complain he reels off his 'Family comes first' speech to me.

And besides, absence makes the heart grow fonder. Everyone says so.

The truth is Ryan and I have realized we like doing different there and slumps back, spilling some over the floor. I quickly get up and go to the kitchen to get a cloth, wiping round her feet whilst she lifts them up like a teenager. I suddenly have an image of my mum doing the same and I throw the cloth down on the floor in disgust.

Two hours later and Casey and I are wandering around Camden.

'No wonder you like it here,' Casey giggles, pointing at a stall that's selling fringed, mirrored sequin bags.

'Hey,' I say, picking a bag up and throwing it over my shoulder. 'I'll have you know these are the height of fashion these days! Kate Moss has got one just like that!'

'Only ten years too late for you then, babe,' Casey giggles. 'Didn't you have one when you were fourteen?'

'I can't help being ahead of my *time* darling,' I say faux pompously, and we burst into laughter. It's lovely spending time with Casey, but ever since Ry and I moved to London, and we see each other less, we're only really comfortable when we're talking about the past, drawing on shared memories of our childhood when the bond between us was so strong that we couldn't imagine anyone or anything ever coming between us. But th

I put the bag back and we continue walking silently around the market, with me picking up the occasional thing either for the flat, or for me. I like the long, gypsy-style tiered skirts but when I point them out to Casey she pretends to vomit into her takeaway noodles. She then picks up a suede miniskirt and holds it up against herself. I look at Casey chatting animatedly to the stallholder, flirting confidently like the pro she is. The girl knows how to talk, that's for sure. I watch her now as she throws her head back and her chest out and laughs with total abandon as the young, attractive bloke looks at her with lustful approval. He touches her bum, and she doesn't flinch, despite it making *me* do so. But she just winks provocatively and takes a step closer. Maybe I'm just a prude but this sort of thing makes me uncomfortable. I've been with Ryan for so long that I can't remember what it's like. Am I just getting old and boring?

What do you mean 'getting'? Hate to break it to you but you've been there a while.

I feel the cold grip of doubt clinging to my heart and I look away, taking a sip of my coffee to make myself look busy while Casey *gets* busy. I think of Ryan and wonder what he's doing right now. Then I realize I don't need to wonder. I know. Because I always know what he's doing, I know his routine – our routine – by heart. Every single day.

So do something different! Something crazy! Be reckless for once, act your age not your European shoe size!

Suddenly I feel the urge to do something crazy and spontaneous. I approach Casey and the over-familiar stallholder. I put down the skirt that Casey is still clutching and throw my arm possessively around her.

'Would you mind not flirting with my girlfriend?' I say vamp-ishly, resting my cheek against to hers. Casey looks at me and grins.

'Oh, babes,' she says breathily, looking sideways at the stallholder who is now salivating at both of us. 'I thought you might like me in this, I know miniskirts get you hot!' And she plants a lingering kiss on my lips for full effect.

Then we stagger off, managing about five steps before breaking into fits of giggles. I hold out my camera and tilt it above our heads and still laughing, we pose touching tongues.

Right then I vow it's time to start having fun again, to start living.

We emerge from the tube and into the sunshine at Waterloo station. The IMAX cinema dominates over a grey, urban concrete city. It's started to rain and Casey looks up and throws her arms out and starts spinning around on the spot until she's dizzy, like kids do. I join her and we start laughing as everyone walks past us with bemused expressions. We stop and grasp on to each other.

'What are we doing *here*?' Casey says, looking around disapprovingly. Admittedly it's one of the less appealing parts of London, but it's one that I hardly ever go to and for that reason it is beautiful to me. It makes me feel like I could be anywhere. Like, say, New York, perhaps? God, I'd love to have lived there. There's still time, I guess. I'm only twenty-five.

Only twenty-five.

I grasp her arm and start weaving through the streets purposefully. I'm not 100 per cent confident that I know where I'm going, but part of the adventure is the journey, not the getting there. Ryan's always felt like a final destination for me, the point at which I rest. He was the first place I came to so I didn't travel far to find him. Since then we've accelerated round the Monopoly board of life, passing Go, missing the chance cards and settling with a house on the very first square we landed on.

And I'm trying to ignore my teen self, but recently, her voice is getting louder and more persistent, asking me if what I've got is enough. I'm not asking for the life equivalent of a hotel on

Park Lane, but I can't help but wonder if I settled too early, that I got the Old Kent Road when I could have had Regent Street. I push this terrible, disloyal thought out of my head. Everything's OK really, I just need to have a little bit of fun.

'We're here!' I exclaim as we arrive at a small door.

Casey looks around, clearly confused. 'Um, where's here?' she asks doubtfully.

'Here is ... the edge of the world!' I say obliquely, but dramatically throw my arms out wide, fuelled by a wave of excitement. 'Come on,' I say, grasping her hand.

'Molly, what the hell are you talking about?' Casey grumbles as she follows me inside. 'I thought we were going shopping, or drinking.'

'We *are* going drinking,' I reply, 'around the world!' I gesture up at the sign and smile brightly at her, suddenly doubting my decision. 'Welcome to ... Vinopolis!' I say the last bit weakly.

Wine tasting? Is this really being wild and crazy and spontaneous?

I continue regardless, desperate to prove my idea is a good one as I'm beginning to have doubts myself. 'You come here, buy a ticket and travel around the world tasting wine!' I explain. Casey doesn't answer. 'I-I just thought it'd be a fun and informative way to spend the afternoon! I've always wanted to come here but Ry doesn't like wine, so ...'

'You brought me knowing that I do?' Casey laughs good-naturedly. 'Not that I care where it's from,' she adds, 'I'll drink whatever booze you put in front of me!'

'Well, prepare to be educated, Case,' I smile. 'You never know, you may leave this place a proper connoisseur.'

She looks at me, a blank expression on her beautiful face. 'babes, have you seen the way I drink wine?' And I laugh as she mimes glugging it down her neck.

*

We're in France, trying a selection of Burgundys, going against the well-known wine-tasting advice to spit out what we taste.

'Mmm,' Casey says, rolling a large gulp of wine around her mouth in a supposedly professional and refined manner. She swallows and looks up, as if searching for the perfect analogy. 'It tastes like ... I'm getting a little hint of ... a definite soupçon of, yes hang on, yep, I've got it ... GRAPE!'

We're practically rolling around Spain when I feel somebody tap me on my shoulder.

'Fancy seeing you here, Rookie!'

I frown at Casey, who raises an eyebrow at me, and I turn around quickly. Seb is standing with two of his mates, grinning widely at Casey and me. They are all wearing almost identikit matching ensembles of indigo jeans, designer trainers and V-neck monogrammed jumpers. With their messy media hair and stubble they look like triplets.

'Hi Seb,' I smile, actually feeling pleased to see someone I know. At least Casey will see that I have got a social life, too. 'What are you guys doing here?'

'Ahh, you know, just taking in some culture. We like to do something a bit different at the weekends, so we have this Saturday lunch club,' Seb explains. 'We each choose something different to do every week, something none of us have ever done before. This was my choice. I love a bit of wine tasting, don't you?'

'I've never done it before, actually,' I reply, in equal parts embarrassed by my admission and impressed by this group of guys' inspiring approach to weekend living. You wouldn't get Ryan and his mates doing the same.

Casey clears her throat next to me and I glance at her, suddenly her tan is too fake, her dress too short, her boots too high for a Saturday afternoon. I feel embarrassed.

'This is my ... b-b- old friend, Casey,' I say. The word 'best' stuck in my throat at the very first consonant. Casey doesn't notice and raises an eyebrow and a hand in Seb's direction and gives him a long, sexy smile.

'Please to meetcha,' she purrs. 'And who are your mates?'

'Oh, sorry,' Seb says, waving his hands. 'Molly, Casey, meet Nick and Matt.'

'Hey,' they chorus coolly, and give us easy smiles.

'So have you been to many countries yet then?' Seb asks, folding his arms.

'Only Ibiza,' Casey replies before I can stop her. 'And I'm half-Italian and half-Greek, although I'm not telling you which bits,' she winks. 'Have you guys been there yet? Italy or Greece, I mean, not my bits . . .' I glance at her in horror but they're all laughing at her joke so I join in.

'*Aaaaghhh!*' I squeal. I am sitting on the back of an Italian Vespa, zipping through the streets of Rome with my hands around Seb's waist. I'm, if not drunk, then very, *very*, merry. We have been in Italy for ages. In fact, we only left it once, to go to South Africa and Portugal and then decided we liked it so much we wanted to come back to drink more Chianti and have another go on the scooter.

'It's just like *Roman Holiday*!' Seb calls over his shoulder.

'Is it?'

'You, know, *Roman Holiday*? Gregory Peck, Audrey Hepburn . . . you must have seen it?'

'Nope,' I call back. 'I've always wanted to though.'

This is true. It was on my list of Films to Watch before I met Ryan, but then we started dating and despite getting him to watch some films I like, he point-blank refuses to watch any that were in black-and-white.

Seb swivels round on the scooter so we are facing each other. I shift back on the seat and gulp, suddenly aware of our close proximity. I look around for Casey, but then remember she said she was going to take the guys to Greece.

'Hey!' I exclaim as I point at the video screen that is still showing us zipping round the cobbled roads of Rome, despite the fact that Seb the driver is facing me. 'Dangerous driving!'

'Sod that,' he grins, folding his arms and staring at me intently. 'I want to know how a mag girl, a *picture* editor of a magazine no less, has never seen *Roman Holiday*? It's a style classic! A beautifully shot piece of cinematic photography!'

I shrug, feeling incredibly self-conscious all of a sudden. 'I don't know,' I reply, looking down. 'I guess that one just passed me by.'

'You've been to Rome, though right?' Seb asks curiously.

I shake my head, feeling more foolish and culturally inept than ever, not wanting to go into the detail of my childhood spent trawling the UK's seaside towns, going from one bleak B&B to another. Or my holidays with Ryan's family in Portugal. Suddenly it all seems so parochial. Seb's stubbly jaw drops open, his greeny-grey eyes barely containing their disbelief. 'You love photography, though, right?' he asks. I nod. 'Then you absob-loodylutely *have* to go to Rome to photograph St Peter's Square, the Sistine Chapel, the sights and sounds of the city, the flamboyant Italians drinking espressos in the marketplace, the lovers kissing in front of the Trevi Fountain . . .'

I stare at Seb who is talking with such passion about this beautiful city and I am overwhelmed by this feeling of longing. Not for Seb, I'm longing to see more of the world, more of *life*.

Seb clearly notices that I have gone quiet. The glass I'm holding that contained a delicious Montepulciano is empty and he takes it, dismounts the scooter and puts it on the table in the middle of the room. Then he grabs my hand, lifts me off the Vespa and carries me into the next room.

'Come on, Rookie,' he says, planting a kiss on my forehead. 'I'm going to show you the rest of the world!'

Seb leads me into California and grabs me a glass of Zinfandel. 'You've no idea what you've been missing,' he says. He raises his glass to mine and downs it, shaking his head and laughing, exuding an air of danger and excitement.

And with a jolt and a pang of regret I realize that Seb's got it wrong, the problem is that I know *exactly* what I've been missing. And now I've seen it, I'm not sure I can go back to the ignorant bliss I've been living in.

'What's going on?' Casey whispers across at me, from where we're sitting in Century, the private bar on Shaftesbury Avenue that Seb is a member of. We're sitting in a corner, with Nick and Matt, having one of the best nights I've had in a long time.

'What do you mean?' I ask innocently, smiling woozily at Seb as he brings over a bottle of champagne and then returns to the bar.

We glance across at Nick and Matt opposite us. Seb is chatting to another friend at the bar.

'We're going up to the roof garden for a min, boys!' Casey chirps. 'Don't miss us too much!' She grabs my hand and marches me into the lift and upstairs where she sits me down and stares at me. 'Seriously, babes, what's going on? You seem really ... different. Is everything OK with you?'

'Mmmhmm.' I nod unconvincingly and look away.

'What I mean by that is everything OK with you and Ryan?' She taps me on the shoulder and as I turn to look at her I know that she can see, just from looking at me, all the frustration and the doubt I'm suddenly feeling about my relationship.

'Blimey,' Casey says, shaking her head. 'I thought you two were unshakable. The perfect couple.'

'Nobody's perfect, Case ...' I say sadly.

'Do you still want to be with him?'

And I find I can't answer her. All I can think is, what happened to that young couple head over heels in love? We got stuck, that's what. Stuck in jobs, stuck with commitments and responsibilities, stuck with a mortgage in our mid-twenties when we should have been having fun. And now I can't help but think that if I'm still on the Monopoly board then perhaps it's time I played my Get Out of Jail Free card.

The Kiss My Dignity Goodbye Kiss

Why is it that we're meant to know what we want to be and the type of person we want to be with, before we've even worked out exactly who we are? I turned my back on so many opportunities, experiences and life routes. I spent most of my life trying to look like I knew what I was doing, act 'mature', be the grown-up. I wish I'd spent more time being free, seeking adventure, doing things wrong instead of trying to control everything so much. I wish I hadn't tried to live my life by ticking things off a to-do list and just focused on to-day instead. Maybe then I would have been more ready for the grown-up stuff when it came along so much sooner than I expected. I know you're not meant to have regrets, but that's mine.

'I can't believe we're *here*! Ibiz*aaaaaa*!' Casey exclaims, saying that particular word exactly as she says 'Tequila*aaa*' and in the same fake Mexican accent. She abandons her suitcase by the door and launches herself on one of the twin beds in the sparsely decorated hotel room. She rolls over and locks her hands behind her head, her dark hair fanning out over the white sheet, belly-button ring glinting against her already tanned skin. In her bikini top and white denim hipster skirt Casey looks like she got dressed to go clubbing, not get on a plane. Mia is channelling her inner Liz Hurley, wearing expensive, white boot-cut jeans, cork wedges and a sheer, floral chiffon top with a white camisole underneath. I'm looking the most laid-back of the lot of us in my cut-off denim shorts and footless tights (I'm not about to get my pasty legs out), a Topshop vest and my favourite bright-green polka-dot sunglasses.

'This is going to be an am-azing holiday girls!' Casey squeals. 'Sunbathing by day, clubbing by night, meeting guys, drinking cocktails, no college work to worry about for you, no waitressing at the restaurant for me, just fun fun fun! Oooh, I can't wait to go to Eden! I've heard so much about it and then there's the foam parties and El Divino.'

'Yeah well, I think Molly and me are more Café del Mar/Pacha kind of girls, rather than Ibiza Uncovered, you know,' Mia says, somewhat coolly.

Casey pulls a face at her and then smiles at me. 'Come on, Moll!' Casey scrambles up and drags my other suitcase over to the bed next to hers. 'Are you going to start unpacking or what? It's time to par-*tay*!!'

I laugh, buoyed by her excitement, and allow her to drag me over to the other bed.

Mia hovers by the door eyeing up the small, uncomfortable-looking sofa by the wall next to the balcony.

'Oh, so sorry Mia,' says Casey, following her gaze but not sounding sorry at all. 'We've hogged the best beds, haven't we? We can always swap halfway through the week.'

Mia smiles stiffly, like she knows this will never actually happen, and then walks in and sets about unpacking her suitcase neatly into the wardrobe. As well as being classy, clever and composed, Mia is also a neat freak. She literally couldn't be more different to Casey. The atmosphere is strained and I can't help but wonder if this has been a terrible idea of mine. I'd hoped that a girlie holiday would bring my two best friends together. Mia and I have just graduated, for God's sake – this is supposed to be *fun*. And it definitely won't be if I have to spend the next week playing piggy in the middle. I know Casey was a bit put out when I suggested that Mia came along, but I thought I'd convinced her that three young, single girls together could have lots more fun than two.

I reckon we can all teach each other a thing or two about being single, as we come at it from different angles. Mia's single *completely* out of choice, I'm single due to my high expectations and Casey doesn't have a problem getting the guys; it's keeping them that's the problem. This holiday isn't just about celebrating mine and Mia's graduation, it's about celebrating our *freedom*. No. Men. Required.

A sudden soft, island breeze lifts the thin gauzy curtains that are pulled across our balcony and parts them a little. I have a sudden urge to see the sea and gaze at the beauty of the island. I bound over to the window and open the curtains. And as I do, we all stare in horror at our view.

It isn't a sparkling turquoise sea, or a flaming Ibizan sunset. It's a . . .

'COCK!' squeals Casey.

'COCK!' gasps Mia.

'COCK!' I shout, pointing at the apartment-building wall

opposite our window, which has an unmistakably large, four-foot-high penis scrawled over it – complete with spiky pubic hairs. We all collapse on the floor, cackling hysterically.

'Come on, girls,' Mia says when we've finally calmed down. 'Let's get drunk.' She links both of our arms and we squeeze out of our hotel door and I feel a glow of warmth, not just from the stifling humidity of the evening, but from the thought that this holiday might just work after all.

The music is thumping in the small, sweaty bar that is one of many small, sweaty bars that line the main drag or the 'West End' of San Antonio. We're standing around a table, a large pitcher of Sex on the Beach is in front of us, which has prompted a pathetic amount of chat-up lines from blokes of varying ages and degrees of attractiveness. Obviously, I told them where to go which was received with loud boos and jeers – from Casey and Mia. It seems the one thing they agree on is that they'd like some of what we saw out of our hotel window. So much for a week of girlie bonding.

'Come on, Molly,' Casey begs as I bat another group of guys away. 'You can't expect us to not talk to any men at all. Think of all those holiday romances we could be having! There are some proper cuties here. Look at him over there!'

She smiles and bites her straw seductively as the sleazy old bar owner winks at Casey and beckons her over. I grab her arm as she makes to go, a natural reflex of mine. I've had too many nights out where Casey has made a beeline for the oldest/sleaziest man in the room. And just because we're older now, doesn't mean I'm about to stop protecting her.

'No, Casey! Seriously, you have no idea where he's been. And he's way too old for you.'

'He can't be more than thirty-five. And think how much of the world, of *life* he's seen …' She sighs and wiggles her fingers at him in a Marilyn Monroe-esque flirty wave.

'I am,' I say, pulling a face – and her hand back down. 'And that's what grosses me out.' I turn to Mia who is looking over at him like there's a bad smell under her nose. 'Back me up here Mia, you agree with me, right?'

She shrugs dispassionately. 'Depends. I mean, if she's just looking for a fuck—'

'Mia!' I exclaim.

'What? They're two consenting adults, after all.' She plays with her straw absent-mindedly. 'She's just drawn to him because her dad walked out. It's called father fixation or abandonment angst or something. Maybe a good seeing to from Signor Sleazebag over there will make her get over her issues. You never know, it could save her a fortune in therapy in her thirties.' She pauses and downs most of her drink and pours herself another from the pitcher. 'But if she's under any sort of ridiculous illusion that he'll fall in *love* with her and they'll end up happily ever after, well, then she's even more stupid than she loo—'

I elbow Mia but it's too late. Casey glares at her and looks sulkily away. There is nothing she hates more than being told she's stupid.

'I think it's time for a toast!' I say brightly. 'To my BFFs!' I start singing mine and Casey's song to placate her. 'We've only got each other now and we'll always be a-round . . .' I was hoping this would lift the mood but Casey just glowers at me, and then at Mia who is looking at me like I'm a freak. I stop singing mid-sentence and just clink their glasses. 'Here's to having a great girlie holiday. And remember . . .'

'We're *hot*?' Mia says, waggling her arms and legs as Casey rolls her eyes.

'*Of course,* that, but I was going to say, no letting any guys come between us, OK?'

Casey nods. But only when I prod her. Mia does too, but then immediately thrusts her glass at me as a young guy starts thrusting against her. I turn and put our drinks on the table and when I look back she's snogging his face off. Great. I turn to Casey but she's disappeared. I look around as a cheer erupts from the middle of the dance floor and I suddenly spot her, doing the limbo in the middle of it, much to the delight of all the guys who have surrounded her. I sigh, pour myself another drink from the pitcher, and down it in one.

'Ughh,' I groan. The three of us are lying on the beach, in the heat of the midday sun, trying to burn the alcohol from our bodies and the memories of our drunken night from our minds. It's not working.

I lift my sunglasses and turn on my side. 'Please tell me I didn't actually snog that really ugly 18-year-old who was hovering around me all night.'

Mia moves from her graceful sun-worshipping position on her towel, arms placed carefully by her side, hands palm-up, legs parted and turned out like they're in second position, bikini straps tucked underneath her.

'No, Molly, you absolutely, definitely, did not in any way snog Gerard, that really ugly 18-year-old with the pizza-face and perspiration issues,' she replies sarcastically, slipping her hand into my bag, which is lying between us, and holding up a piece of paper she's taken from it that has Gerard's name, home address and phone number, and email address.

Casey snorts with laughter and then sits up and holds her head between her hands. 'Ugh. Moved. Too. Quickly.' She pops on a sun hat and rests back on her elbows making her tummy look impossibly taut. 'And you absolutely, definitely, did not then proceed to snog his best mate which then caused a fight and resulted in us all being thrown out of the bar.'

I put my hands over my face. 'Oh *God.*' I groan. 'I blame you both. You're bad influences on me. This was *meant* to be a No Guys Allowed trip, remember?'

'Uh,' Mia says, wincing as she opens one eye and raises a finger.

'Firstly, do you really need to speak so loudly?' She mimes turning a dial down and I reach over and hit her. 'And secondly. Ouch. Hurts. To speak.' She lowers her arm. 'To be honest, Molly, my aim is to get as much horizontal action as I can over the next week. Once I stop wanting to hurl.'

'Yeah, well, I still think you let me down,' I grumble. 'If you hadn't abandoned me with that pitcher of alcohol, I never would have ended up in that mess.'

'Correction,' Mia says, wagging her finger, 'you let your*self* down.'

'And your knickers . . .' Casey adds gleefully. 'Over there on the sun lounger, remember?'

'NO!' I squeal, and sit up, grappling to tie up my bikini straps to protect my modesty. 'I didn't! I *know* I didn't do that. I'd remember, wouldn't I? Wouldn't I?' They both look at me with falsely sympathetic faces.

'Chill out, babes,' Casey says as they start laughing. 'We're just winding you up. It'd take more than your body weight in alcohol to make you lose control THAT much.'

'Well anyway, that's it,' I say decisively, picking up my book and smacking Casey with it. 'No more drunken encounters for me.'

'So what are you going to have instead?' Mia says, lifting her sunglasses and arching her eyebrow imperiously.

'Some beautifully romantic holiday love affair,' Casey giggles, knowing this is as unlikely for me as it sounds.

'Nope. Neither. This,' I point at my now kaftan-covered body, 'is off limits. Particularly here.' I point at my heart.

'Don't you mean there?' Casey winks and points at the black triangle of material covering my nether regions, just visible through the full-body cover-up I'm wearing. Mia laughs and I fling my arms out and hit them both.

'There too,' I say defensively. 'Now, if you don't mind, I'm going to read my book.' And I try to drown out Casey's incessant chatter about the hot Spanish bartender by getting completely lost in *Atonement.*

Later, I'm laying on my lilo, head turned to one side, eyes half closed. The late-afternoon sun is warming my back and I'm mindlessly watching my fingers create intricate patterns of ripples in the water, listening to the *twinkle, ping* that the water makes, accompanied by the gentle *thwack* of the waves against the rubber lilo. I feel like I am in the midst of a grand orchestra of the elements, with the sun as the conductor and the sea as the string section. Over on the distant beach the melodious laughter and chatter has become the background chorus. It's blissful out here on the ocean, uninterrupted by anyone. I'm alone with my thoughts, drifting in the endless calm of the ocean. Just me . . .

'ARGH!' I shout as I am unceremoniously thrown off the side of my lilo by something banging into me. I emerge from under the water and cling on to the inflatable with my eyes still closed, kicking my legs and spluttering as I smooth my hair out of my eyes and wipe my nose. 'What the—'

'FUCK! I'm so sorry!' a male voice gasps. I hear a splash and someone swimming over. Then I feel a pair of hands grab at my body.

'Get OFF!' I yell, blinking wildly and rubbing saltwater from my eyes as I try to scramble back onto the lilo, smacking off my invisible attacker's hands which, to be fair, appear to only be attempting to propel my legs back onto the lilo. I simultaneously try to hit him and grasp my bikini bottoms, which are slipping down in an alarming fashion. 'Stop manhandling me!' I splutter as I get another mouthful of sea. 'I can get back up myself!'

'OK, OK! I was only trying to help.'

I heave myself up on the lilo and sit astride it, trying to regain some of my dignity by pulling my bikini bottoms out of my bum.

'You could at least apologize for crashing your lilo into me,' the voice says from behind me.

'Crashing into *you?*' I splutter. 'Are you kidding?' I look over my shoulder and glare down indignantly as I take my first look at the idiot driver of the other lilo who is treading water next to me.

'Ryan?!' I exclaim.

He looks up and bursts out laughing.

'Fuck*ing* hell! Molly Carter!'

His broad, tanned shoulders are glistening above the surface of the water. His blond hair is cropped short, making him look older and more rugged now that he has lost the last bit of puppy fat off his face. His skin is the deep acorn-brown of someone used to spending lots of time in the sun, with paler skin just visible underneath the sandy prickles of his stubble. His blond eyelashes are all wet and stuck together, his blue eyes as turquoise as the sea we're surrounded by and I notice the very tentative beginnings of laughter lines around his eyes.

'I should've known it was you, Cooper,' I say coolly. 'You were always showing off in your Golf GTI. No wonder you can't steer a bloody lilo either.'

'Hey, as far as I could tell, you had your eyes shut!' he retorts. 'I'm pretty sure that would constitute an immediate fail in the Lilo Driving Test. Didn't you read the Ocean Highway Code before you came out on your vehicle? At least I'm a qualified sailor.'

I'm reminded of our last meeting a year ago when he was about to set sail for Sydney. I'd like to say I haven't thought about him since then, but I'd be lying. It's weird. He got under my skin that night on the *Bembridge*, more than I thought possible. My heart is now racing uncontrollably, I can't believe that we've met here in Ibiza of all places. What does it mean? Are we being drawn together, like the romantic equivalent of tectonic plates? Or is this Casey's doing again?

I look over to the beach and see a distant figure in a bright-yellow bikini standing up with her arm held out like a sailor's, looking out to sea.

Hmmm.

Ryan grins at me and then pulls himself back up onto his own

lilo with ease. I try not to look but can't help noticing how his
well-defined stomach muscles contract and his biceps bulge as he
does so. There is a tiny smattering of moles in the middle of his
chest that I have an urge to touch. I put my hand in the sea and
splash water on my face to try and prevent any blushing. I think
it might be too late.

'What the hell are you doing out here anyway?' I say, paddling
my hands in the water, mainly to give them something to do, but
also to try and encourage us further into shore. I realize that we
have drifted somewhat.

'I'm here with the lads,' he answers, brushing his hands over his
head and leaving diamond droplets of glistening water in his golden
hair. 'We've been coming here for the last four or five years, since
we were eighteen.'

'Of course you have,' I reply sarcastically, glancing down and
self-consciously readjusting my plain black bikini top to ensure it's
covering (what there is of) my boobs properly.

'What is that supposed to mean?' Ryan folds his arms and looks
at me.

I stop paddling, framing my eyes as I squint up at him.
'Nothing, it's just, well ... the boys in Ibiza, it's a bit of a cliché,
isn't it?'

He shakes his head and tuts. 'You haven't changed, Molly. You
still like getting on your high horse even when you're straddling
a lilo, don't you?' he says, flicking his hand into the water and
splashing me in the face.

'Hey!' I laugh as I splash him back. 'You're only defensive
because it's true!'

'We come here for the beautiful beaches actually.'

I snort.

'Oh OK, and the women too,' he adds. 'But what's wrong with
that? We're young, free, single ...'

Tick, tick, TICK, I find myself thinking as I'm reminded of my updated secret Things I Want From a Boyfriend list. So secret, I haven't even shown Mia or Casey. It is squirrelled away in my diary. I've been honing it for years.

Things I Want From a Boyfriend
- Young. Not toy-boy young, but a couple of years older is OK
- No ties, can do whatever they want, go anywhere, travel the world etc.
- Single. No boyfriend-stealing allowed EVER (See BFF List)
- Hot. So I'm shallow, shoot me
- Exciting career. (What goes well with a photographer? Roadie? No they're always old, sweaty and overweight. Music producer? Maybe. Artist? No needs to be a job that's . . .)
- Well paid. So I'm shallow, shoot me (again)
- Well read. I don't want to date no idiot innit
- Cultured
- Cook? Because I can't. And I don't want to starve
- Nice family? (Not all that imp. But would do my head in if they were as dull as mine)
- Hot. Ryan Cooper hot

God, Ryan Cooper's hot.

Stop it, Molly. Stop.

'And what about you,' he says. 'Who are you here with?'

'Just a couple of girlfriends . . .'

'Oh yeah,' he teases. 'The *girls* in Ibiza, eh? Anyone I know?'

'A friend from uni, and Casey . . .' I notice Ryan twitch a little when I mention her name.

'Oh you're here with Alex aren't you, I take it things didn't end that well between them last year.'

He nods. 'Yeah, I think he thought they were just having a casual thing, but she got serious and it freaked him out.'

Sounds about right. 'I wasn't around when they broke up, but I know Casey was pretty upset about it,' I say as I paddle. 'She reckons he dumped her for no reason. Do you think we should try and make sure that they don't know the other is here?'

'Nah,' Ryan says, rubbing his hand over his face and through his hair, the sunlight catching on his watch and making it sparkle. 'We're grown-ups. I don't want us lads running out of bars as you all come in. Casey and Alex have seen each other around Leigh since. I'm sure they'll be cool.'

'I forgot what a small town it is,' I say wryly, leaning forward on my lilo and paddling more to get momentum. 'Everyone always knows everyone else's business. It's part of the reason why I left.'

'And part of the reason why I stayed,' Ryan laughs. 'I like knowing everyone in the town, I like that people care about my family, help out if we're in trouble or remember me from school. I like that my mates all still live round the corner from me.' He pauses. 'And I especially like that I can get my washing done by my mum whenever I want!'

I laugh and splash him. 'Found it hard washing your own pants in Australia, did you, without your mum around to do it for you?'

Ryan lies forward on his lilo and smiles cheekily. 'Not really, I don't wear them.'

I try not to blush. 'I'm amazed you came back,' I say instead. 'It must have been so hard.'

'Not really,' he smiles again. 'I didn't go in the end.'

I look at him for signs that he's kidding, or is at least embarrassed by this admission, but he's just grinning into the sun, soaking up the rays like a superhero who uses it as his source of power. How could he not have gone? What an opportunity wasted. There must have been a big reason.

'Oh, that's such a shame,' I say sympathetically. 'Did something happen?' I pause, waiting for him to tell me about an amazing job opportunity, then realize it could have been something more serious like a family illness, a heart attack or cancer or something, or maybe it was that football injury again. Poor guy.

Ryan glances across at me and shakes his head. 'Nah, I just decided not to go. I knew I'd miss my family and my mates too much so I just hung round Leigh for the summer. It was brilliant. I trained the sailing cadets and became coach for the under-14 local football team. Did you know I got a job as a teacher back home, too?'

I shake my head.

He gave up a summer in Australia to stay in Leigh? What is this guy on?

'Where?'

Ryan grins. 'Thorpe Hall.'

My mouth drops open as he mimes straightening a tie. 'They couldn't resist employing a former star pupil. I start in September. Hey – does your mum still work there?'

I nod silently, still trying to digest each statement as it comes.

Ryan laughs and touches my knee with his hand. 'She'll be my colleague now, how weird is that?'

Really weird.

'Yeah,' he continues, 'I'll have to stop myself going into the sixth-form common room instead of the staffroom at lunchtime. Luckily as I'm a PE teacher I don't reckon I'll get caught up in too much teacher politics – and I'm planning to be as much a mate to the students as a teacher. I can't wait.'

I widen my eyes and nod, still in disbelief that Ryan Cooper is actually going to be a *teacher*.

'God, this is weird,' I say, swiftly changing the subject. 'I mean fancy bumping into each other here of all places!'

Suddenly a thought occurs to me. 'Hey, do you think Casey and Alex set this up. You know, us both being here, in Ibiza?'

'Why would they do that?' he frowns.

'Well, Casey has always been obsessed with getting me and you together for some reason, I've no idea why . . .' I am sure I'm blushing. 'I think she had visions of a cosy foursome when she and Alex were still a couple.'

'That's crazy,' Ryan replies. 'We barely know each other.'

He's right. We've only met a handful of times over the past few years. But despite this, seeing him would always stir up something unexplainable inside me. Not just lust but something more, it was like he could see inside me.

The day we first went for a coffee and I told him how I felt about my parents, told him my innermost secrets, shared our dreams and our fears, I felt he knew me better than almost anyone else. Despite all the years that have passed, when he looks at me as he's doing now, it still feels exactly the same. I feel like I'm fifteen years old again; I feel like a teenager. A teenager in . . . love.

I look away, desperate to get back to the girls. All of a sudden I feel out of my depth, but the golden, sun-kissed beach and bay might as well be the moon, they look so far away.

I start splashing my hands desperately, like a dog.

'We're not getting anywhere like this,' I say, looking at the stretch of sea before us.

'Aren't we?' Ryan replies sliding into the water. He pauses and raises an eyebrow. 'Then maybe we should change direction . . .'

He swims over to me, one powerful arm rising out of the water after the other, and he puts one hand on the pillow of my lilo.

'Lie down, Molly,' he says softly.

'I bet you say that to all the girls,' I joke, wobbling a little.

He rolls his eyes, but a smile creeps out. 'Just do what I say, will you?'

I comply. I am aware as I lean forward, that his gaze lingers longer than entirely necessary on my pale chest as I lie down on my even paler stomach. I don't complain. Instead I find myself saying, 'You won't let go, will you?'

'Never,' he answers. There's a prolonged pause as we look at each other. 'Are you ready?' he says, and I nod. Then he turns and with one strong, lean arm he swims and pulls me along and I'm no longer drifting alone in the middle of a great, vast ocean.

The Judas Kiss

Have you ever wanted a kiss so badly that you felt you couldn't bear the not knowing how it'd feel any longer? Have you spent hours imagining the moment as it will happen; that delicious slowing down of time and the shortening of breath as the space between you lessens, giddy with anticipation and lack of oxygen and desire and expectation? Have you imagined the feel of that person's lips, their tongue, their breath mingling with yours?

Have you then found yourself in that exact situation only to discover that the anticipation was way better than the act itself? That it was the not kissing that was so intoxicating in the first place?

And then have you ever come to the conclusion that turning a silly fantasy into a reality was the single biggest mistake of your life?

'Wooohooooo!'

A loud whoop reverberates around the restaurant as Christie stands up, party hat slightly skew-whiff on her otherwise perfectly coiffed head. She's grinning widely, lip gloss shining like one of the brightly coloured baubles that adorn the restaurant's tree. The entire editorial staff of *Viva* have descended upon The Gaucho Grill, an Argentinian steak restaurant that is tucked away in a basement on a little side street off Piccadilly, for our Christmas lunch. The restaurant is a vegetarian's worst nightmare – and a Christmas traditionalist's (there's not a turkey to be seen – apart from several jokes in the crackers that could definitely be categorized as such). The seats are covered in cowhide and large slabs of steak have been served to each and every one of us, along with creamy mash, thick-cut chips, plump grilled tomatoes and mushrooms on skewers. Endless empty bottles of wine – an excellent Sauvignon from the Norton region that Christie picked, and an even better Malbec, chosen by Seb – are strewn over the long table, along with discarded crackers, and party hats. Dessert has been picked over and Seb and his deputy, Dominic, are even puffing on cigars whilst the rest of us have moved on to Caipirinhas. Seb had made a point of explaining each brand to Dom, and shown him exactly what to do whilst talking passionately about his travels to South America. He'd expertly cut the end off the Cohiba cigars he'd chosen for them both and lit them, then handed one to Dom who managed to cough and splutter his way through a couple of puffs, trying to regain some semblance of cool by proceeding to just hold and not smoke it for the next ten minutes, whilst Seb expertly puffed, chatted, joked, bantered and blew it out like a cigar connoisseur. Not that I was watching him or anything. Oh, who am I kidding. I haven't *stopped* watching him, or thinking about him, or imagining what it would be like to kiss him since that day in Vinopolis two months ago. I have tried to focus on Ryan and our relationship, tried to tie the strands of it back together again to work out if I am just having some sort of mid-twenties crisis (it's an official condition, we did a feature on it in last month's issue). But still I am drawn to him.

Only Casey knows about my doubts. She's listened and advised when I've called her in the middle of the night at the club, or woken her up with my woes. I feel awful that I am even talking about it with her. It's like I've betrayed Ryan just by expressing my doubts. Part of me wonders what I'm waiting for, if I was that certain, surely I'd just go? But he's the only person that I've ever loved and, in person, he's my perfect fit. It's just on paper that things go wrong. I even wrote a list the other night when he was sleeping peacefully next to me, one arm thrown possessively over my body.

Reasons Ryan and I aren't compatible

He likes sport, I like culture

He likes staying in, I like going out

He likes cooking, I like drinking

I like travelling he likes ... going home

I'd ripped up the list feeling like I'd just betrayed Ryan. I got out of bed and called Casey immediately, knowing that she'd still be up, to ask her what she thought.

'I dunno, Moll,' she'd said gently. 'I always thought you and Ryan were meant to be. But maybe you weren't meant to be forever?'

I haven't been able to get that sentence out of my head since.

The waitress brings over three ice buckets now and positions them along the table as Christie grins beatifically at us all while I neck my cocktail.

'Being a typical American wallflower, I know I'm not often prone to making speeches . . .' she begins, and we all laugh. Christie loves the sound of her own voice but at least she understands irony. 'But I thought I'd give it a try. Anyway, I just wanted to say thanks to you all for your incredible hard work over the past year. *Viva*'s success has been unprecedented.'

'Wooohooo!' we all cheer again as the waitress begins pouring the champagne. Christie pauses, waiting for her to finish so she can focus on the rest of the speech.

'But that isn't the only reason I wanted to say a few words today.' She takes a deep breath. 'As I'm sure you've all been aware, there have been quite a few closed-door meetings recently . . .' There is a murmur of nervous laughter from us all, an acknowledgement that we all knew something was afoot. But we know from her wide smile that this is anything but bad news. 'The MD of Brooks Publishing has decided that in order to secure *Viva*'s future, we need to keep transforming ourselves. Websites and blogs are becoming a crucial part of the industry. Consumers want more of an instant hit – so the technical team are in the process of developing a website for *Viva* that will launch at the same time as a weekly magazine format in March. We've been working on the dummy for the past two months and it's been approved. As of January, *Viva* will be a weekly magazine.'

Christie laughs at the sight of approximately thirty jaws hitting the table. I glance across at Seb and he winks at me knowledgeably, clearly he was in on this secret before the rest of us. I smile and look back at Christie, trying to ignore the increased beats per minute of my heart. He looks strangely at home in these surroundings, smoking a cigar like he was born to do it, whilst reclined on a cowhide seat, cigar smoke weaving sexily into the darkness, like a young Matt Dillon.

I try not to but I can't help a nonchalant second glance back, and when I do he just stares at me intently, the shadows dancing over his face making his eyes look even more intense and hooded. He rubs his hand across his chin and smiles lazily. I smile back.

Christie is still talking and I focus again on her, knowing that this is really important to my job, my future.

'Aside from the new magazine format, Brooks are throwing everything at this online launch to make us the go-to website for young women in the UK.' She pauses and looks down the table at us all. 'Obviously this will mean more work for you all – with not much reward at first. Until we employ an online team the content will all be coming from you. Who better than the award-winning *Viva* team to bring your knowledge, your creativity and your inspiration to the website!'

An audible groan ripples down the table as we translate her words: more work, no more money.

'It's going to be an exciting and exhausting few months in the office.' Christie beams perkily at us all. 'But I don't want to talk about the hard work ahead at our Christmas lunch. Today is about celebrating a brilliant team, an incredible magazine and an exciting future.' She raises her glass. '*Viva* 2005!'

As we all cheer and join in her toast, I can't help but feel a wave of excitement. I feel like I'm at the heart of something big, full of potential and possibility. Right now, I love my job, my colleagues, my boss, this champagne, Christmas . . . I look in my bag and pull out my phone. It's 6.30 p.m. and I have three texts from Ryan, all of them asking where I am and when I'll be home as he's cooking dinner.

Shit. I forgot to tell him that it was my work Christmas lunch today. I text him back deftly. 'At work Christmas do. Not hungry so go ahead and eat without me. M xx'

I press send and pick up my champagne glass just as my phone begins to ring.

I squeeze out of the cowhide banquette, then dash up the stairs and out into the bitterly cold early evening. I answer it just in time. I'm panting as I say my greeting.

'H-H-Hel—'

'What took you so long?'

'—lo,' I finish, and am then stunned into silence by Ryan's abrasive tone.

'Well?' Ryan prompts and I shake my head, trying to focus on our conversation.

'I was down in the basement of the restaurant, I've come outside as it's too noisy down th—'

Once again Ryan doesn't let me finish. 'It's nearly seven o'clock, Molly, I've already made dinner – why are you only just letting me know you're not going to be back?'

'I'm sorry,' I say, feeling instantly annoyed at myself for apologizing. I am reminded of living under the ridiculous curfews my mother set. 'I forgot it was the office lunch today and I lost track of time . . .'

A group of Christmas party revellers stagger past me on the street, four girls with their arms linked, wearing tiny dresses and big smiles. They look young, way younger than me – or maybe not? I look closer. No, they're probably mid-twenties, too, they just seem younger. They haven't got a care in the world. Nowhere else they have to be, no one expecting *them* home for dinner.

Shivering, I tuck myself out of the way, in front of the fire-exit. I realize I should have brought my coat outside. Not just to protect me from the cold night air, but the atmosphere of this conversation, too.

'Well,' Ryan grumbles, 'are you coming home now?'

I look at my watch and am suddenly jolted by what I can see, not just the time of night, 7 p.m., but . . .

The *time*: the twenty-first century.

The *time*: my three-year relationship.

The *time*: my mid-twenties.

We're meant to be having the time of our lives, Molly. It's my teenage self again. *Tell him we're not coming home yet.*

Suddenly, I feel overwhelmed by the urge to laugh, to laugh hysterically. Must be the alcohol because this really isn't funny.

I take a deep breath, and fuelled by the fizz of excitement at Christie's news, the sparkle of fun that the possibility of a night out could bring, and – most of all – by that last glass of champagne – I say the word that I should say to Ryan far more often than I do.

'No,' I reply defiantly. 'I'm not coming home yet, Ryan. I'm with my colleagues having fun at my work Christmas party. It's only early, so I'm going to go out with them after this, something I don't do very often—'

'Ha!' Ryan splutters.

'What's that supposed to mean?' I reply dangerously quietly, partly because I have spotted two of my colleagues who have come out for a sneaky cigarette.

Suddenly I have the urge to join them, even though I haven't smoked since Ryan and I got together. I turn away, slink back into the darkness because I don't want them to hear my discussion with Ryan, but also because I don't do shouting. I've always been the quiet, brooding type, while Ryan likes to talk about things endlessly, usually with a smile on his face, which just winds me up even more.

Which is why, even as I ask him to explain exactly what his 'Ha' meant, I know that I am leading him into a dark corner. Ryan clearly doesn't realize this. If he does he chooses to ignore it.

'It *means* that you go out all the time. After-shoot drinks, press launches, "work meetings", you're hardly ever bloody here. And if you are around it's when I'm back home.'

'It's not *my* fault you keep running "home" to Mum and Dad at weekends,' I shoot back. 'Most 27-year-old men have untied their mother's apron strings by now and want to hang out with their girlfriend at the weekends, not their parents.'

Ryan laughs, but it is not a happy sound. 'Fucking hell, Molly, I *do* want to hang out with you. *Je*-sus. I just want to hang out with you back home in Leigh, you know, like you promised ... remember? It was meant to be the compromise.'

I defy my own rules and raise my voice. 'In case you hadn't noticed, Ryan,' I hiss, 'our *home* is in London, it has been for over a year now. And I *have* compromised. A lot.'

'Is that really what you think, babe?' he replies.

'Don't call me babe,' I snap.

'We made an agreement, remember, *Molly*?' he emphasizes my name sarcastically. 'I moved up to London for *your* career, not mine. Don't you think I'd rather live back in my hometown, where all my friends and family are, where my life was? Working at a school where I don't have to worry about there being possible stabbings every day? But I don't because I know living here makes *you* happy. But you were meant to compromise by coming back to Leigh with me at weekends. But you haven't, not for months. And then on an evening when we *can* spend time together, you tell me at the last minute that you're out with your work friends! Jesus!'

He sounds like those cartoon voices on a phone or Woodstock from Peanuts. Wah wah wah wah. I understand that yes, at times I have let my side of the bargain down, but I'm not going to *admit* that, because his nagging tone is just making me more stubborn than ever. Besides, I can't admit that the only reason I agreed to the London/Leigh split-life proposal that Ryan made when we bought our flat was that I didn't really think Ryan would actually *want* to go home all the time. I thought London would spark his sense of adventure. That he'd meet new friends, like I have. I thought he'd meet guys like, you know, like Seb and Dom, or Matt and Nick who Casey and I met the other month. Guys who were interested in more than going to see their local football team play every week and hanging out with their schoolmates. I thought London would reignite Ryan's love for travel, that he would see the rest of the world that was out there and it would inspire him to see more; more cities, more countries, more places. But it hasn't. Ryan hasn't changed, if anything London has made his aspirations smaller than ever. All he wants is his old job, his old home.

It suddenly dawns on me that Ryan was never going to change. Not really. Because I realize now that, forget Australia, *anywhere* would be too far from Leigh – including London. No, the only person who changed in this relationship was me. I changed for Ryan because I wanted to be with him so desperately. I thought that if I moved back to Leigh, I could want less, aspire to less. But I couldn't. Now I *do* want to go out. I want to have *fun*, I want to embrace the city I live in and the opportunities it offers me. I want to move forward. I want that more than anything.

More than Ryan? My teenage self asks softly.

The silence crackles down the phone between us. Now Ryan's rant is over, I hear him crashing pots and pans around the kitchen like some demented apprentice of Marco Pierre White.

'Shit!' he expostulates suddenly.

'What's wrong?' I ask dully, distracted by what I'm feeling, what I'm thinking.

'I just burnt my fucking hand draining the fucking clam linguine . . .' he mutters petulantly.

And I can't help it, but I snort with laughter loudly. I try to disguise it but for once, I can't. I can't help but be struck by the ridiculousness of this argument. The ridiculousness of us both.

'I can't believe you think this is funny, Molly,' Ryan says coolly.

'And I can't believe you don't,' I reply. And with that, I ring off. It is the first time I have ever put the phone down on him. I feel as rebellious as I did when I cut my plaits off and dyed my hair red all those years ago.

Feels good, doesn't it?

Yes, I think. *It does.*

And as I descend the stairs and head back into the dimly lit basement restaurant, I'm swept up in the tidal wave of my party who are coming up the stairs.

'Mollleeeee!' they cry. 'We're going to Soho House! Are you coming?'

I catch Seb's eye and he winks lazily and folds his striped Paul Smith scarf around his neck and pulls the ends through the loop. And as I nod I vow that from now on, I, Molly Carter, am going to do whatever I damn well please.

Three hours later, after more drinking, laughter, piss-taking and determined flirting with Seb, who has been a willing reciprocator of my attentions, I feel that not only do I deserve this fun, but I want, no, I *need* more.

Finally, you listen to me!

My 15-year-old self was right all along. Relationships clip your wings, tie you down, make you old before your time. Just like my parents. Why not live a little? I'm young, relatively attractive and I now realize that I've basically been living like a Stepford wife.

So do something about it! No one would blame you – you deserve this! You deserve some uncomplicated fun!

The alcohol I have consumed has succeeded in casting dark shadows over my relationship and yet it has bathed me in goddess-like light. Right now I feel like the sexiest, most beautiful girl in the world. And trust me, unless I'm with Ryan, that's not a familiar feeling for me.

No saying his name, no thinking it, even! You're a twenty-first-century woman who can do what she wants, when she wants and doesn't have to answer to anyone but yourself! That's feminism! That's what the suffragettes fought for, remember?

Only when I am standing on Old Compton Street after coming out for some fresh air with Seb, do I take this thought process one step further. I'd be lying if I said I hadn't gone to sleep next to Ryan imagining this moment but never did I envisage I'd ever do anything. But now I can't imagine holding back a second longer. Seb and I are talking, then he steps closer, leans in, and for a moment I know I have a choice, a split second of doing the right thing, or the fun thing.

I blink, smile, and then he cradles my head, pulls, and presses his lips that I have been thinking about for weeks against me and slips his tongue inside my mouth. And I respond with all the enthusiasm of a girl who hasn't kissed a man's lips other than her boyfriend's for three years. I shut my eyes and my brain, and for a moment I become someone other than Molly Carter. For once I'm racy, sexy, spontaneous and rebellious, I'm Molly Ringwald in *The Breakfast Club*, I'm Demi Moore in *St Elmo's Fire*. I press my body hungrily against Seb, wanting this kiss, this moment, to transport me to somewhere exciting, adventurous, somewhere different from the safe, stable life I have been trapped in for so long. I realize that kissing Seb like this is making me feel young for the first time in years.

It's only once I have thrown myself drunkenly into a taxi alongside Seb, my limbs locked around his waist as he half carries me through his front door, only when I am half-naked and spread-eagled beneath him on his couch and the fug of alcohol and party-season adrenaline subsides, that I realize that unlike Ryan's, Seb's lips feel thin, ungenerous, not at all sexy. And the kiss now feels not fun and rebellious, but shameful, repulsive even.

I pull away, gagging slightly as I realize that Seb's breath tastes bitter, of alcohol and stale cigar smoke. And then I'm hit with a wave of sorrow so great that I have to push Seb off me. Tell him to stop. That it's a mistake.

'I'm sorry, Seb, I don't want this ... I thought I did. I thought for a stupid, idiotic moment that I wanted something different and I do, but not like *this*. I don't want to do this to my boyfriend. He doesn't deserve it.'

Seb tries to pull me back to him but I push him away and I start crying, big racking, body-convulsing tears, and he is backing away. He's looking at me like I'm mad, and I don't blame him, because I sound mad, like a crazed woman who has no idea what she wants. Who has lost sight of anything that is of any importance to her. Which I have.

And then I stagger to my feet, put on my shoes, pull on my dress and my coat and I stumble through the front door of his flat, out into the street of a part of London I don't know. Any care for my safety went the moment I betrayed my boyfriend.

'Hey, Molly, let me call you a cab at least,' Seb calls from the doorway. But just at that moment, like a divine intervention, a glowing amber light appears in the street. I throw my hand out and hop in, give the driver my address and then, as we pull away, I guiltily glance back for a second to see Seb shake his head and slam his front door shut. I lean my head back on the seat for a moment and close my eyes. But then the ZORB-like spinning begins and I open them again and start scrabbling around in my bag, looking for my phone. But I can't find it. I think for one terrible, vomit-inducing moment that it's lost, or I left it in the bar, that I'll have to go back to Seb's and I start sobbing.

'Lost,' I cry, and I know that I'm not talking about my phone any more.

I'm still crying and scrabbling through my bag and then, dizzy with relief, I find my phone and I fumble through the address book, my fingers stiff with cold, my heart frozen with regret. And I call the only person who can help me. The only person who will understand, who will listen without judging – my best friend in the world, Casey.

12.10 p.m.

I put the pasta maker in the box marked 'Charity shop' and glance around the kitchen. I'm still not a natural cook, probably never will be, but with the help of Ryan and some friends (Jamie, Delia, Nigella, Gordon) I've become passable. I won't ever win *Masterchef* but I can potter around in here, making nice hearty casseroles and fresh pasta dishes to my heart's content. Given that it has never been finished, it's become the real heart of this home. For a while I didn't have any photos up in here. They were all packed away under the stairs, partly because of the ongoing redecorating (a line of paint testers are still splodged on the wall but were never decided on), and partly because I didn't need to look at them every day any more. But then they gradually crept back until a vast array lined the walls in an impressive framed montage. But this new wall of memories had one major difference: it was from the past eighteen months only. It was my way of looking to the future. A couple of the photographs still remain and I lift them down now and slip them out of their frames. I left them till last as I want to carry them in my purse, for safekeeping.

I glance at the one in my hand now: three women at a wedding, having the time of their lives. One is beaming particularly brightly, looking like a Greek goddess in a white gown. I think of Casey and wonder what she's doing now. I wish she was here. But no point thinking like that now, I made a decision to do this on my own.

I pop the picture in my purse, and pick up the other grainy, black-and-white shot. I look at it carefully, trying to make out the image of the person in it, and then put it in my purse, too.

I sit down at the 1950s Formica kitchen table that's full of my paperwork. I've spent so many moments in this room, looking through my photographs on my laptop, carefully selecting my favourites from editorial shoots or just for my own portfolio. I glance at the credit card bills lying on the top of the plastic folder. Meals out, drinks, nights in, hotels around the country, trips to art galleries, trips abroad; it is the credit card bill of a woman determined to make the most of her life while she still can. I think of how much I've packed into such a short space of time.

The landline starts ringing again and I hurriedly put the bill back and put the lid on the box. Why do I still act like I'm tidying my bedroom and my mum's going to pop up at any moment and say, 'How are you getting on?' and find me faffing about. I'm nearly thirty-three, for God's sake!

'Hello?' I answer.

'Molly.' Just the sound of his deep, reassuring drawl makes me instinctively touch my necklace, twirling it around my finger like the act might bring me closer to him. 'I just wanted to call to see how you're getting on? I feel so bad for leaving you, but you know how it is . . .'

I sure do. I know there'll always be someone who needs him more than I do. But I'm OK with it.

'I'm fine! Really! Not much more to do now,' I say brightly.

'Listen, babe, I know how hard this must be for you.'

'It's fine,' I laugh. 'I'm used to it.' I realize how that sounds. 'Honestly,' I add gently, 'don't worry about me. I'm a big girl.' I pause. 'How are things at the hospital?'

'What time will the removal men be there?' I notice how expertly he changes the subject back again.

'They're already here, they're just finishing upstairs,' I reply. 'Like I said, it's all under control.' I want to tell him not to worry, that this is something I need to do on my own anyway. But I can't bring myself to say it.

'Thanks for ringing,' I say instead.

'Molly?' he says softly.

'Yep?' I say hopefully.

'See you later. I love you, OK?'

The Single Kiss

'Molly Molly Quite Contrary', that's what my mum used to call me. I'd decide I wanted something and then as soon as I got it, instantly change my mind. Ballet lessons, aged five, turned to horse-riding lessons aged five years and two months, which turned to swimming and then back to ballet again. Then there were the pets. I wanted a rabbit, then a cat, then a dog (I got none of them as by then my parents were used to my flighty ways). My only constants were my camera and Casey. The only things I have ever stuck to.

And then there was Ryan. My perfect man, the love of my life. I wanted him, got him, then got a bit bored and threw it all away. I had to go all the way to the other side of the world to work out all I'd ever really wanted was waiting for me back home.

Our screams reverberate around Sydney airport, apparently even drowning out the Arrivals tannoy. People tut at us and strain their ears as Mia and I jump into each other's arms and whirl each other around in a circle. I'm crying, Mia is not. She's always been emotionally tough – even more so than me. It's the posh girl in her. She once told me she's only cried once since she was a child. And that's when she went to boarding school at eleven. Since then, not a single tear. It was one of the many things I related to immediately; she didn't need people, more importantly, she didn't need me. But she wanted me as her friend anyway.

I've experienced an emotional switch since Ryan and I broke up and I saw him kissing that girl in the club. I can't seem to *stop* crying these days. The slightest thing can set me off, an advert on the TV, a mushy romcom because it reminds me of Ryan, who'd merrily mop his eyes during our movie-marathon Saturdays. Now *I* sob every time I see people in love, whether it's in the street, on TV, in a film, in a music video, and I cried when Brad and Jen announced their separation. I cry when I walk past a happy family sitting in a restaurant, I cry at happy-ever-afters and tragic endings. I cry at cute dogs and I cry at crying babies. Sometimes I wonder if he has experienced this emotional transplant too. Perhaps he has become a hard, cynical man who doesn't believe in happily ever after and in finding the one, because they'll only go and cheat on you, like I did with him. This thought tears me into two; one side of me can't bear the idea that I might have done that to him, but the other secretly hopes this is the case. At least that means he won't have fallen in love again easily. As much as I've been trying to get on with life for the past few months, my biggest fear has been hearing that Ryan is seeing someone else. After seeing *that kiss*, I know it's only a matter of time.

'Molly Carter, are you CRYING?' Mia says in astonishment. I can't believe how different she looks – still beautifully polished, but so much more laid-back and happy.

'No, yes, no, shit, it's just been a long flight. I'm overtired,' I say, swiping my hand across my eyes in embarrassment and pulling down my sunglasses over them. I do a little involuntary hiccup and stifle a sob as I look around the airport and see all the *Love, Actually* moments as all the happy travellers embrace their friends and loved ones, and I snort unattractively as the tears flow again. This does not go down well with Mia.

'You've been hanging around Casey too long. Looks like you got here just in time.' She picks up my suitcase and frogmarches me over to the exit. She's never seen this Molly before, who cries at the drop of a hat and who had to move in with Casey in Southend of all places because she couldn't be on her own. I was meant to stay in our flat, but in the end Ryan agreed to because I just couldn't bear the thought of being there without him. But being in Southend, so close to our hometown, a place that IS Ryan, is unbearably hard, too. I know he's there every weekend. And being a small town there have been various rumours, you know, girls he's dated, girls who want to date him, but nothing serious, so far. But I hear everything. It is torturous but I don't want it to stop. At least while I am hearing about him, he is part of my life. To hear nothing would also be unbearable. I can't win. I even wrote a list on my laptop to work out what I should do and everything pointed to here.

My Pull-Myself-Together Plan
1. Do something drastic (Cut hair? Lose weight? Gain weight? Change jobs? Change countries? Think Life List e.g. New York/Oz)
2. Surround self with good friends who won't let me feel sorry for myself (Casey? Girls from work? Mia)

3. Get as far away from Ryan as possible (Oz?)
   Preferably get some sun (Oz)

I'd paused before writing the final entry and then I'd typed it in caps and underlined it.

4. BUY TICKET TO OZ

'Hey,' Mia says, shaking me brusquely. 'Come on now, Molly! Pull yourself together!' She sounds like my mum. It is weirdly comforting. 'You're in Australia now, *no one* cries here. There's no need to because the sun is always shining. For the next three weeks you're going to have fun! No moping! No worrying about work, you're going to meet men in Manly, drink beer on Bondi Beach, and if I have anything to do with it – have sex in Sydney ...'

I must be wearing a horrified expression more plainly on my face than I realize because Mia puts her hand over her mouth. 'Oh no, that sounds really weird, doesn't it? Obviously I don't mean I'll be *involved*, just that I'll be encouraging you ... not while you're doing it or anything, like a sex cheerleader, oh no ... ugh.' I can't help but laugh and Mia smiles. 'That's better, that's what I want to see! Laughter! Happiness! You're on holiday in Australia! At last! You can tick it off your Life list! Woohooo!'

I mirror her whoop, albeit less enthusiastically. We step outside the terminal into the blazing sunshine, despite this being, according to Mia, 'average' weather for winter.

'Look,' she gestures, the passion for her adopted home country apparent in her eyes – as is her pride and excitement in showing it to me. 'You're in Australia now, land of the free! And you *are* free, Molly, free and single! You *wait* till you see the men over here. They are seriously ripped ...'

'Yeah, well,' I say a little primly. 'I'm not sure I'm here for that. I just want to hang out with you and—'

Mia interrupts me with a disapproving squeal. 'Arggh, stop being so bloody *British*, Molly! You're single, to be honest, I think a good fu-u-uc—' she clocks my expression and changes the direction of her sentence to something less graphic, 'fu-u-un is just what you need!'

She takes a sideways appraising glance at my appearance and makes it obvious that I fall short of her standards. I know I look a mess, especially after twenty-four hours on a plane.

And then there's Mia. Her years living here have transformed her from an uptight, perfectly turned-out Brit to the epitome of glossy, laid-back Aussie glamour in her trademark white jeans and bright, surf-brand halterneck top – but this time she's in Havaianas flip-flops instead of heels. Her hair is still long, perfectly blow-dried and caramel-blonde. Her nails are manicured to perfection, both on her hands and feet, but her face is relaxed and shining and she exudes absolute confidence, radiance, relaxation and happiness. Clearly life Down Under suits her.

In the same way that life as an unfaithful, single, emotional mess doesn't suit me.

Mia grasps my arms and stares into my eyes, one expressive eyebrow raised in a combination of compassion and frustration.

'You, Molly Carter, have to let yourself go.'

I nod. Harsh, but fair.

'I know you've had a tough few months, but it's time for you to pick yourself up and start again. I want this trip to bring back the old Molly, the Molly who embraces life and opportunities.'

She squeezes my hands tightly, and gets that determined expression in her eyes that I saw at uni, as she gives me a pep talk.

'I'm going to make it my mission to send you back to the UK stronger, happier and more sure of yourself than you've ever been,' she says determinedly. Then her face softens for a moment as she takes my hand. 'I can't bear to see you like this, Molly . . . it's just not *you*.'

My bottom lip wobbles and I smile and brush my hand over my long, bedraggled hair which I've pulled back off my face with little plaits. I should take a picture for Mum, she'd love it.

'That's the problem, Mia,' I say sadly, 'I just don't know who I am without him.'

Mia purses her lips and grips me tightly.

'You are a strong, talented, passionate, beautiful, independent woman Molly.

You have so much going for you, so much to offer. You have the world at your feet, a whole host of possibilities. You have no ties – do you know how amazing that is? To be twenty-five and to be able to do anything you want! Stop wallowing in the past and focus on the future. Because there *is* a future without Ryan, I promise there is.' Mia squeezes my hand, lifts the handle of my suitcase and leads me out into the burning sunshine that warms my skin, if not my spirit.

Two weeks later and I feel like I've been fully inaugurated into the Australia fan club. Mia's loved showing me her life and I've loved seeing it. From her gorgeous flat in Manly, a cosmopolitan little suburb across the water from the bustling city, to the incredible sea view from her bedroom window, her friendly local bar that serves the best cocktails, to the lovely local deli she gets her breakfast smoothie from every morning. Then there's the incredible, idyllic beach that is minutes from her front door and the scenic, sun-kissed boat trip she takes to work every morning.

'It beats the tube, doesn't it?' she'd grinned as I sat, with my hair billowing around me, gazing across at the breathtaking Sydney Harbour Bridge, and over the water, the Opera House with its distinctive white sails making it appear to be bobbing over the Disney-blue water. And then the panoramic view of the city's shimmering buildings stretched up in front of us like a mirage. It's a sight I've dreamed of seeing for so long. And the relaxed, contented smiles on the commuters' faces show that it's something they're grateful to see every single day.

'It sure does,' I'd replied. And I meant it. This city is everything I dreamed it would be. Breathtakingly beautiful, cosmopolitan and friendly, it has embraced me like an old friend, made me feel like I'm a part of it, even though I am a mere acquaintance – and turned me into a happier person than I was when I arrived. I've gone jogging on the beach every morning, I've taken scuba diving lessons whilst Mia was at work, I've bought fresh local produce from the farmers' market and cooked in a way that I never thought I could, maybe because Ryan was always too busy doing it. I've spent hours in the city on my own, taking hundreds of photographs which I've sent to Christie and the girls at work. I've been to art and photography exhibitions on my own and Mia's taken me to her favourite restaurants for lunch and to the cornucopia of cool bars she frequents. She even took a few days off so we could go on a boat trip round the Whitsundays. I've felt lighter than I have for months.

I love how free I feel over here. I don't have a family to feel guilty about, Casey isn't nagging me to go out, there are no work friends I have to make the effort with (or avoid, in Seb's case). It's the first time I've felt happy for years. And I remember why I liked it so much. It's also the first place I've felt under no pressure to make other people happy.

Here, you are unencumbered by pressure. If someone asks you what you've been up to and your answer is 'hanging out at the beach' or 'having a couple of schooners', it's OK. It's alright to while away the afternoon in a bar, or at a market. It doesn't matter if you haven't seen the latest exhibition or visited your parents for three months. Here, there is no doctrine that says you should work for ten hours a day, every day. I haven't written a to-do list since I got here. The no. 1 Aussie Life Rule seems to be if the weather is good then of *course* you should go surfing and hang everything else.

It's a blissfully relaxing way to live and I can see why Mia loves it so much.

And having the time to take photos has made me realize how much I missed it. I know it's the next thing I have to focus on in my Life List. After getting over Ryan.

And having distance from my family has made me miss them, too, I even phone my mum and dad as soon as I wake up to tell them so – which must be a first.

Mum's making Dad's favourite dinner of shepherd's pie. 'I only do it to get him out of that office of his,' she says brusquely. 'He'd spend all day there if he could, in his little world, surrounded by his comforts, his books and his art. But that's OK,' she adds benevolently, 'if it makes him happy.' It suddenly hits me that Leigh-on-Sea is Ryan's Constable picture, the place he feels happiest and most inspired. I blink back a tear. At least my mum had let my dad keep his Constable painting. I took Ryan away from his and made him feel guilty whenever he tried to go back.

'Mum, I just want to ask you something.' I take a deep breath. 'Are you happy with your lot? You know, with Dad, with me?' I blurt out quickly.

'Of course, I am.' She laughs.

It's not the answer I expect. I know I need to get more, to chip away at Mum's façade, the one she puts on for everyone.

'I mean, has your life been enough for you?' I ask quietly, already knowing the answer. 'Because it's never felt like it has to me.'

I hear her draw breath, actually winded by my words. 'Really? Well, I-I didn't, I don't mean to ...'

'I'm asking you to be honest with me, Mum. Stop putting on an act. I can see through it. I always have.'

She immediately puts on her teacher voice. 'Molly Carter, stop being ridiculous!'

'Mum, I overheard you and Dad saying you'd stay together for my sake. I *heard* you,' I say quietly. 'I was about eleven or twelve ...

I was sitting on the stairs and you and Dad were arguing. Well, you were shouting at him, telling him you should split up, he was just taking it, like he always does ...'

'Oh, that!' Mum says. 'That was just over some nonsense or another. We had a cuddle in bed that night and I apologized. Your dad knew I didn't mean it and it was forgotten by the next morning.'

I stare at the receiver in my hand and shake my head. 'But ... but I thought ... I thought ...'

'Molly, your dad and I were never going to split up, not even in our worst moments and yes, there've been a few. Our struggle to conceive another child for one.'

I'm genuinely shocked and then saddened by this admission. I'd always presumed they didn't want any more after me. How could I have been so self-absorbed?

'Your dad and I fit. In our own awkward way, we fit. We're not massively demonstrative like Jackie and Dave, or probably the most exciting parents in the world. I know I was rather strict and your father was too laid-back and yes, that caused tension. I was stressed with work and I took it out on your father when he didn't appreciate that my job, my position, was equal to his. And that I was *also* having to do all the things that mums do: cook tea, make you eat it, take you to ballet and music classes, or horse-riding lessons, or whatever hobby had taken your fancy that particular month. I had to buy your clothes, sew name tags, wash your school uniform, makes costumes for school plays. He just had to work ... and dream. And sometimes the dreaming bit was really frustrating for me. It's why we agreed he'd go and do it in his office, where I couldn't see him just sitting there, doing nothing, whilst I was so busy doing so much. But, as he pointed out to me, it was my choice to be that busy. I could have taken on less, been easier on myself ... and on you. I know how much I've expected of everyone. And I know that made life hard. I just wanted the best for you.'

'And do you think you got the best for yourself?' I ask quietly. 'You didn't end up in your dream job, or with a rich man, or with your dream house. Or even your dream family.' I add, thinking of the child they failed to conceive.

'No,' Mum admits. 'But I ended up with the one thing that everyone wants above everything else ...' She coughs. I know talking like this is hard for her.

'What's that, Mum?'

'Love, Molly dear.'

I cover my mouth to subdue my sobs as she continues to speak.

'Loving someone means having the confidence to know that you won't be happy all the time, that they *can't* make you happy all the time. It's a totally unrealistic expectation. And sometimes, in a marriage or a long-term relationship ...' she pauses, and I know she's directing this part of the conversation at me, 'well, you need to learn that. When your father's fed up, off he goes to his office, or he drives up to London and goes to some exhibition. And when he comes back, he gives me a kiss and everything is OK. He knows I have a temper. It's one of my downfalls. But he knows I don't mean what I say half the time.'

I don't say anything because suddenly so much makes sense.

'No matter how frustrated I sometimes feel, I've always been very sure that I didn't want anything else. And your father has always known that. I'm sorry I didn't convey that to you.'

'But how did you know that you didn't want anything else?' I ask, suddenly desperate to know that secret.

Mum is quiet for a moment. 'Because Molly, your father has always made me far more happy than unhappy. I'm not a maths teacher dear, but I think that's the best possible equation you can hope to get. Not very romantic, I know, but it's the truth.' She sniffs and I wonder if she's crying too. 'And anyone would be lucky to have had a percentage of the happiness I've had.'

I'm crying. I'm 10,000 miles away and suddenly all I want is a hug from her.

'You miss him a lot, don't you? Ryan, I mean,' Mum says tentatively, each of her words like little baby steps towards me. We are not used to talking in this way with each other.

I snort, and wipe my nose. 'What do I do?' I sob.

'You tell him, Molly, my dear. You just tell him.'

And so that morning, I put down the phone and I open up Mia's laptop, and for the first time since I wore plaits and that stupid sailor dress, I do what my mum tells me to. I agonize over every word, every comma and phrase. I delete two paragraphs and start again. I try explaining why I did what I did. I try apologizing first, and then last. And then I ditch the entire document. Because I can't put into words what I feel. And then it comes to me. I frantically search Mia's desktop for the old photos we were looking over the other night and which, being the crazily organized freak she is, she has scanned and put into yearly and monthly files on her computer. Pictures from uni and from nights out, and her leaving party when she came to Australia. And then I open the folder marked July 2001 and I look through the pictures of that life-changing holiday to Ibiza, and I find the series of photos that she took of Ryan and I, on the beach, playing volleyball, his arms wrapped around me, both of us gazing at each other like we were castaway on some private island. Young, carefree and completely, unashamedly happy. I open an email, type in Ryan's address then just write 'Love' in the subject heading and attach the pictures. I don't write anything else. I just sign my name and put one, single kiss underneath. And then with one click, I send it.

I open the cupboard under the stairs and curse as the mop and bucket fall on me.

'Ouch!' I yelp, rubbing my nose. I prop the mop against the door and peer inside at all the stuff I'd put in there five years ago and forgotten all about. Packing up this place has sometimes felt a bit like a Russian roulette version of a treasure hunt, with cherished and painful memories hidden all over the place. It's actually going to be a relief when they're finally gone.

I scrape my hair back into a stubby ponytail. I pull out a box and sit back on my haunches as I peer in at all the hundreds of ticket stubs, receipts, programmes, flyers and cards. I pick up one. It's from Rossi's and I smile: the date is 6th August 2001. Our very first date. Next I find the tickets to the Take That comeback gig at Wembley Arena in 2006. That was such a brilliant night. I'd never seen Ryan so happy. There are also handfuls of cinema ticket stubs. I pull out a ticket and feel my eyes prickle as I realize it's for the last film we went to see together: *Knocked Up*. It was hilarious and sad and poignant and ironic all at once. I remember clutching Ryan's hand, crying, but not knowing if it was with laughter or sadness. I put the stub back and shut the box. I don't go through any more. I don't need to. Instead I pull it out and write 'Storage' on it. Then I drag it into the hallway. It is pretty heavy and I have never been the strongest or fittest of people even in my youth, never mind now. So I heave and tug, gasping with exertion and feeling my precious necklace banging against me with every pull I make, like a prodding finger reminding me of its presence in my life. I clutch it and smile.

The 'Til Death Do Us Part Kiss

For a girl who never thought she believed in marriage, once I came around to the idea I wondered what the hell had held me back for so long. All this time I'd been afraid of the permanence of the institution, the finality, the absolution.

One person for the rest of your life.

Now I know that this isn't always possible.

I'm woken by the dawn urgently prodding my eyelids and forcing them open, jolting me into immediate action as my body instinctively responds to what my mind hasn't been able to forget all night. I'm getting married today. I sit up and clasp my hands to my chest and try to contain my squeal of excitement. I'm getting married today!

I glance down at my sleeping partner and am tempted to wake her, but Casey is lying so serenely beside me and looks so peaceful with one arm gracefully flung over her head, that I know I can't. Not yet. Instead, I lean over to my bedside table and grab the pad which I left there last night.

My Wedding Day (MY WEDDING DAY!) List
Take photos of the sunrise
Have mani-pedi
Get married!
Have breakfast with Mum, Dad, etc.
Get married!
Put thank-you presents in Mum and Dad's hotel room,
Lydia's, Jackie's etc.
Get married!
Give Ryan's present to Carl
Get married!
Get make-up done
Get married!
Pick wild flowers for bouquet and for bridesmaids'
corsages and headbands
Get married!
Remember to take bridesmaids' presents down to reception

Text Carl to check he has rings
PUT ON DRESS
Get married!!!
Get married!!!
Get married!!!

I glance at my watch. It's not yet 6 a.m. but I slip out of bed and go over to the window. The silvery tip of the sun is bashfully peeking up behind the sea, casting everything else in silhouette, as if the rest of nature is bowing to its power. I desperately want to capture its big entrance properly in a photograph so that this day will always be mine, to have and to hold, forever.

I quickly whip off my pyjama shorts, leaving on my lace vest top I slept in, and I pull on the cropped, white Audrey Hepburn-style jeans I was wearing last night for the meal I had with my brides-maids and my parents. I tie the scarf that I've pulled through the waistband and put my hair up, slip on my Converse (some things never change) grab my camera and creep out of the room. Casey stirs and turns over in bed; I hold my breath but she doesn't open her eyes and I silently shut the door behind me and run down the corridor, long ponytail flying behind me, desperate to catch the moment before it goes.

As I step out of the hotel and onto the beach and lift my camera to my eyes, I find that with every flash my head is a Rolodex of memories flicking furiously through the years that have led Ryan and I back to this place where we had our first *real* kiss. Some I can find immediately, others are filed miscellaneously and require a more methodical search through my memory. Others I've pur-posely mislaid or put in dusty old boxes at the back of my mind because I don't want any bad ones spoiling this perfect day. I've always been good at putting things into lists and boxes, never more so than now.

As the sun rises it lights up the Ibizan sky in glorious

technicolour, ringing the few feathery plumes of clouds with gold so that they appear to be wearing celestial wedding bands. I sit down on a sandbank and fold my arms across my knees, smiling as I think of everything that lies ahead, the life I am going to embark on as Ryan's wife.

I look across the beach and catch a glimpse of two windsurfers out just beyond the bay and I know without question that it is Carl and Ryan. It would be exactly Ryan's wish to begin the day like this and I'd recognize the slant of his body as he leans away from the sail, the curve of his legs, his hold, anywhere. I've watched him so many times over the years, so many holidays already, and so many more yet to come. I smile and watch the brothers for a moment, feeling an illicit thrill at seeing my husband-to-be on our wedding day and am then struck by a prick of superstition. Is it bad luck? But surely it doesn't count if they don't see you?

I turn my head, just in case. I don't want to jinx anything. I stand up and brush the sand off my jeans and pick up my trainers, but I can't resist one last glimpse at them. It looks like they are sailing into the sun's tail, trying to catch it as it ascends out of the ocean and into the sky – and it wouldn't surprise me if Ryan managed it. I laugh, feeling my stomach twirl like a majorette's baton and I scramble up the bank and back across to the hotel, suddenly desperate to get this wedding in motion.

'Morning,' Casey yawns and stretches as I come back into the room, clutching a tray of fruit and coffee.

'Hey, sleepyhead, time to get up. I'm getting married today!' I put the tray down and jump on the bed as Casey groans and tries to pull the sheet over her face.

'God,' she says bleakly, 'if you're this excited at' – she glances at her watch – '6.22 a.m., you are going to be completely bloody unbearable by this afternoon!'

'I'm *allowed* to be unbearable,' I laugh. 'I'm the *bride* remember!'

I hand her a mug of coffee and she pulls herself up and sips it slowly.

There is a knock at the door and Mia and Lydia burst in screaming. They're both wearing pink Gap hoodies. I wish I had my camera, I never thought I'd see Mia looking so Essex.

'You're getting married! You're getting married!' they chant.

Jackie, my mum and Nanny Door follow them. Jackie's wearing a pink satin dressing gown and has an eye mask on top of her head. Her make-up is already applied, or perhaps she hasn't taken it off since last night. I know she, Dave, Ryan and Carl all went out for dinner with the boys somewhere in the Old Town. Nanny Door is already dressed although I do hope it's not her wedding outfit as she appears to be wearing a pink velour tracksuit. My mum is wearing a flannel nightie, a pink cardi and an embarrassed smile. I get the impression that Jackie dragged her here, mainly because my mum would never willingly be seen in public in her nightie. I want to give her a hug but Jackie has dived on the bed and is trying to have a playful pillow fight with me. Every time I try to speak to Mum I get a mouthful of feather-filled cotton in my face.

'Jack-Jackie, stop it, you'll spill my coff—' I give up. Lydia, Mia and Casey have now joined in but in the midst of the carnage I manage to slip off the bed and over to my mum. I pour her a coffee from the pot – black, just how she likes it, and I take her arm and we wander out onto the terrace.

She looks out at the spectacular view of the Mediterranean and it occurs to me I have never been on a holiday like this with her. So I know that my wedding, on a frivolous, sun-soaked party island is completely out of her comfort zone. But I'm really touched that even after her initial and obvious disappointment that we weren't getting married in a church, she hasn't criticized our choices, or tried to encroach on our day.

'How are you feeling?' she asks now, her pale, unmade-up lips curving into a gentle crescent.

'Nervous, excited, I can't wait to be married to him,' I reply truthfully.

Mum nods and taps her short, carefully cut fingernails on the balcony rail. 'Well, that's all a mother could ask for,' she says. I nod and smile. She pulls her cardigan around her, even though it isn't cold and gazes out at the horizon. I know she's feeling uncomfortable and exposed in her nightie. 'Look, Molly, you should know by now that my view on love has always been very practical. My list of things that I wanted was the following . . .' She clears her throat and starts to reel them off like a shopping list. 'Someone good and kind, loyal and trustworthy, financially secure and had the same beliefs as me.' She looks up, her sharp grey eyes are watering slightly. This is what your father is and what love is for me. And it's more than enough.' She sniffs and dabs her eyes. 'It's this sea air.' She looks at me again. 'But some people want the passion, the one big romantic love.' She gently raises her hand and touches my face. 'And some people really deserve it. You have so much to give and you and Ryan are so good for one another. You really love him don't you, Molly?'

'I do,' I say, as much a practice for my vows as a reassurance of my own beliefs. I repeat them because I like how they sound. 'I do. It-it scares me sometimes how much I love him, Mum. I don't want to ever lose him again.' I'm startled to find I am crying.

'Well, that's just silliness,' she admonishes, swiping her hand across my face to dismiss the tears, as if they were a class of unruly pupils. But there is a gentleness in her expression and her action. 'I know he is a good man, but Molly, believe me when I say this, he isn't perfect, no one is.' She pauses, then. 'The secret to a strong marriage, Molly, is to not lose yourself in it. We come into this life alone, and we leave it alone. The only true constant, is yourself . . .' Her sentence trails off and I know in her head she's adding, 'and God' but she knows saying it out loud would wind me up.

'That is the saddest thing I've ever heard, Mum,' I say, shaking my head.

'No, it isn't, Molly,' Mum says with a smile that I used to think was pious but I now think is simply conviction. 'It just means that the only person your happily-ever-after is hinged on is you. Don't put that pressure on Ryan, or your marriage. It's the mistake so many people make.'

She leans in and kisses me on my cheek. It is quick and dry, as if she has forgotten how to do it. 'Now,' she claps her hands like she is calling a class for register. 'We'd better get going, hadn't we? We want you to look ...' She stops, as if struggling to find a suitable word to describe her only daughter.

'I think the word you're looking for is *beautiful*,' I say, linking my arm through hers and turning towards the balcony doors. Compliments have never come easily to Mum. I'd have hated being her pupil; if it was anything like being her daughter, you had to kill yourself to get a 'V. Good'.

She brushes her hand gently over my hand and shakes her head as she looks at me. 'You're already beautiful, Molly. You always have been. And clever and creative and remarkably sensitive and wise. But today, you will be *radiantly* beautiful.'

Swiping away a tear I let her lead me back into the room.

Jackie, Nanny Door and the girls are all giggling conspiratorially in a corner. Casey has now got a pink hoodie on too and I raise my eyes, suddenly suspicious that something is going on. Jackie's eyes light up as she spots us and she steps forward and hands me a little package. 'An early wedding-day gift for you, darlin'! Open it, open it!'

Mum goes and stands over with them as I rip open the paper and pull out a beautiful white satin kimono. My initials, MC, are embroidered beautifully on the front. I love that they will stay the same even after I'm married. There isn't much difference between Carter and Cooper, so I plan to change my name to Ryan's. I've always said it's something I'd never do and I don't know what changed my mind. Maybe it's because I know how important it is to Ryan. And because I like being part of the Cooper clan.

'It's beautiful!' I gasp. And it is. It is clearly the highest-quality silk, it is cut beautifully and the initials are sewn on with what looks like Swarovski crystals.

'Turn it over! Turn it over!' squeals Jackie. I see my mother purse her lips, but something tells me it is because she is trying to disguise a smile, not disapproval. I twist my hands so I can see the back and 'Mrs Cooper' is sewn on in crystals too. I burst out laughing as I look back up and see that they have all turned round and are standing in a line with their backs facing me. Each of the things they're wearing – even Mum's pale-pink cardi – has been customized with different words. Jackie is standing at the far left of the line. Her silk dressing gown is just like mine, except it is cerise pink and says MILF on the back.

I put my hand over my mouth as I splutter out a laugh.

'What does that acronym stand for?' asks my mum innocently, leaning round so she can see from her far end of the line.

'What's an acronym?' asks Lydia, wrinkling her nose.

'It means the short version,' I explain to Lydia as my mum mutters something about 'the youth of today' and 'education going to pot'.

'Um, well Trish, what it stands for is … "Mother-In-Law … Forever"?' Jackie says, trying to keep a straight face as I continue to laugh.

Nanny Door is next. She winks at me over her shoulder as I read out the inscription on the back of her velour tracksuit top.

'Nanny Door-in-Law!' I laugh. 'Brilliant!'

'I thought of it meself,' she says proudly. 'It rhymes an' everything!'

'Mine says "BFF",' Casey says. And I smile at her.

'Mine says "Brides*Laid*",' Mia says, and my mum tuts audibly. 'Because I want everyone to know that I am single and available.'

Lydia uses both her index fingers to point at the back of her hoodie. Hers says 'Super SIL'.

Finally, my mum's cardi says MOB on the back. 'This *acronym*,' she says pointedly, 'stands for "Mother of the Bride".'

I laugh and pull mine over my shoulders and go and join them, pushing into the middle of the line and throwing my arms around them. Jackie and my mum throw their free arms around each other and we huddle together to create a circle, and I feel myself beginning to well up as we have a big group hug.

'Thank you, everyone. I love it.'

'I'm glad you do, darlin',' Jackie pipes up. 'It was either that or that diamanté-studded vibrator, wasn't it, Nanny Door?' And we all fall about laughing.

Even my mum.

I'm sitting in front of my mirror as Lydia applies the last of my make-up.

Me, Mum, Dad and the bridesmaids had a lovely breakfast out on the hotel terrace and everyone has dispersed to their rooms to get ready. I've sent Mum off to deliver my present to Ryan – a watch engraved with our initials and a kiss – and Lydia is just putting the finishing touches to my make-up. Casey is getting ready in the bathroom. I'm going to slip my dress on any minute. The wedding is in just under an hour and the butterflies are flooding my stomach. I've had a text from Ryan this morning that was simply a screenful of kisses.

'There!' Lyd says as she puts the finishing touches to my face, a little shimmer on my cheeks and under my eyebrows and on the bow of my lips. 'The perfect beach bride!' I glance in the mirror and gasp. My tired, stressed face has been transformed with her magic touch so that my skin is golden and dewy, my once-heavy eyes are wide as saucers and the sea-green of my irises is complimented by the sandy sweep of shimmering eye shadow she's applied to my lids. My eyelashes look inexplicably long and dark, separated a little with minimal mascara so that they look like they're wet from the sea. My hair flows in loose, flowing waves from a centre parting, down to just past my chest, and the front section is pulled off my face by two little plaits (a detail I added especially for my mum) tied at the back of my head and then decorated with the flowers from my bouquet. It has been a long journey from my awkward, red-haired, black-clothed teen self to this. I twist my head and throw my hair over my shoulders so I can see it cascade down my back. Then I stand up and look at Lydia.

'Are you ready to put it on, babes?' she says with a smile. I nod and look over at my dress that is hanging from the wardrobe door. I walk over slowly, reverentially, and carefully take it down and lay it on the bed. Then I slip off my dressing gown and call out to Casey. She's been in the bathroom for ages.

'I'm putting it on now, Case!' I call excitedly.

'Be right there!' she yells back. Then I hear the toilet flush but she doesn't emerge.

'Will you help me?' I ask Lyd, desperate to have this beautiful gown on, unable to wait a moment longer.

'Of course. Shouldn't we have photos of this though? Shall I get the photographer in here?'

I shake my head at Lyd. I decided before the big day that I don't want 'before' pictures. I want the day to begin when I step out in my dress, ready to marry Ryan.

Lydia holds out the white gown carefully, ready for me to step into. I glance at the bathroom again, but still no Casey. I hope she's alright. I slip off my dressing gown. I don't want today to be too much for her. Not after everything she's been through recently.

'Now, step right here,' Lyd says.

I shiver as the light gossamer material of the ivory Grecian-style dress slides up over my body, and I close my eyes as Lyd secures it at the back.

'Oh, Molly,' she sighs and steps back. My hands are shaking

uncontrollably and I take three big deep breaths before I open my eyes and look in the mirror. The dress is everything I dreamed it would be. Romantic, relaxed but beautifully bridal too. The Grecian style makes me feel like a goddess, I love how the gathered, rolled shoulder straps and floaty, feminine skirt allows me to get away with the plunging V-neck line. There are also two swathes of silk floating out from both of my shoulders instead of a train, and on my back, there's a little bit of extra special detail, a little nod to my roots.

I hear the bathroom door open and I turn around.

'Molly,' Casey says, cupping her hands over her mouth. 'You look beautiful!'

I smile and hold out my hand to her, wanting her to know that so does she. Tears spring into my eyes as I think about just how far both of us have come to get here, and how long it has taken for us to learn to be comfortable in our skins.

I glance back at the mirror and she comes and slips her hand into mine as we both stand in front of it. I turn to Casey and grasp both her hands and lift them out wide; she looks at her feet in embarrassment. It's the first time I have seen her in the dress I chose for her and I feel a secret jolt of joy that I've done so well. I found it shortly after I came back from New York as a newly engaged woman. Before I knew if she would even be at the wedding, let alone be my maid of honour.

'You look incredible, Case,' I say through my tears. The bright burst of orange is perfect against her dark skin and tawny eyes. Her dark hair – natural once again – is swept up into a messy chignon, with tendrils coming down, and the coral cascade of chiffon that falls in a waterfall from spaghetti straps around the neck, to her thighs, makes her look demure yet beautiful in a way she always said she never could. Especially after what happened that night. I can picture her now, as I could when I bought it, walking barefoot across the sand, blazing a fiery trail like a

Monarch butterfly. She still looks like my Casey. But a grown-up version of Casey.

I realize that I couldn't have got married without her. It just wouldn't have felt right. All my dreams, all my aspirations for the future are as linked to her as they are to Ryan. She's been there through it all. And been through more than I'll ever know. We're both still gazing in the mirror at ourselves when Lyd steps forward. I know she's sensed that we need a moment alone.

'I'm off to put on my dress. Although I'm never going to pull off orange like you've done, Case!' And she kisses us both and then slips out of the room.

We stand in hushed silence for a moment, just inspecting ourselves in the mirror. I feel like we're seeing two reflections. In one we are our teenage selves, complete with Casey's little hair clips and her pink plastic rucksack, me gazing through my badly cut and dyed fringe, stabbing my DM-clad toe into the ground sullenly. And then there's the one of us now: all grown-up, happy, beautiful, holding hands – BFFs forever, just like we promised.

'You're getting *married*,' Casey whispers, and I squeeze her hand.

'I know, weird, huh?'

'Not weird,' she says, wiping away a tear. 'It's right. It was always meant to be you. I mean, come on, we both knew it was never gonna be me first.'

'I reckon you're just seeing how I *do* so you can better it!' I nudge her and she nods.

'There'll be way more bling for a start, *way* more,' she laughs.

'Hey, I got bling!' I say with a smile, turning around so Casey can see the back of my dress where there's a wishbone-shaped strap of dazzling Swarovski from my shoulders down to the V of the dress on my lower back. Something I knew that Ryan – and his mum – would like. 'You can take the girl outta Essex . . .' I giggle.

'It's perfect, Moll,' Case says, tears streaming down her face. 'You're the most beautiful bride that has ever been.'

I lean across and pick up something from the dressing table. I smile and mime pulling my shoulders back and lifting my chin, and Casey mirrors my movements. Her eyes are glassy with tears as I gently pull a fallen piece of hair back from her face and pin it up with a beautiful orange butterfly clip so that it looks like it's hovering in her hair.

'Repeat after me,' I say softly. 'I am beautiful . . .'

'I am . . .' she trails off.

'Beautiful,' I prompt firmly.

'Beautiful,' she whispers.

'And like this butterfly,' I continue, 'I am free.' The words suddenly stick in my throat as a tear falls from her eyes as she repeats the first part of the sentence. 'Free to love and *be* loved,' I finish, stroking her hair as I let my hand drop to hers. She doesn't say anything, she just looks down and I squeeze both her hands. 'And you *will* be loved, Casey, I promise you will be. And not just by me and Ryan, either.'

She nods and then looks at me, as if for the first time.

'Oh, Moll,' she says, 'you're getting married!' And we both burst into tears.

'*No!!!!*' cries Lydia, rushing into the room in her short, orange satin number. 'You'll ruin the make-up! Quick!' And she starts dabbing at my eyes furiously as Casey and I wave our hands at our faces to try and stop the tears coming and, giggling, we run to the bathroom to make sure there are no streaks down our faces.

As we stand in front of the mirror, still laughing, the years fall away again and it is just me and Casey, two awkward teenagers who needed each other more than anyone else in the world.

'Are you ready?' Mia says, squeezing my hands as we prepare to step onto the beach and make the long walk towards the bay where

Ryan is waiting with Carl. I look at the three girls, standing there in their beautiful dresses and I smile excitedly.

'How about you, Mr Carter?' Casey asks, and he splutters a little, unused to being asked or having the chance to answer without my mum there.

'Ah, well, yes, I am, certainly, although, I wonder, is there a lavatory around here somewhere?'

'Dad!' I groan, slipping my hand through his arm. 'You should've gone before.'

'Ah well, yes, that is true, certainly. It must be the nerves. Or, ahh, the age . . .'

'Just take a deep breath, you'll be fine,' I say.

'Shouldn't I be the one giving you advice?' he says. 'In fact I did prepare something . . .' He fumbles around in his pocket, takes off his half-moon glasses, mops his brow and puts them back on. 'I know you're not, ahhh, a *traditional* girl but, ahh, this is an incumbent part of my father-of-the-bride role and so I do feel that I, um, ought to say a few words . . .' He is still fumbling in his pocket.

'You don't have to, Dad,' I say gently.

'Yes, but I *want* to. I want to give you some marriage advice. Although, I have, um, purloined this from someone who could put it far more eloquently than I.'

I look at my dad and feel a jolt of love, for my serious, introspective, socially averse father who has frustrated me for years, but who is more like me than I ever have been prepared to admit. And I'm willing him on now, hoping that he will find the right words, the words that will make sense of our relationship, his marriage, this moment. It is a lot to expect.

'Darn it,' Dad says, pulling various bits and bobs out of his pocket. 'I've lost it. Oh, well, I think I can recall . . . yes . . . I can.' He turns to me and his speckled eyes glisten. 'I-I have taken the liberty of changing the personal pronoun from me to you.' He clears his throat and begins to recite.

'Let you but live your life from year to year,
With forward face and unreluctant soul;
Not hurrying to, nor turning from the goal;
Not mourning for the things that disappear
In the dim past, nor holding back in fear
From what the future veils; but with a whole
And happy heart, that pays its toll
To Youth and Age, and travels on with cheer.
So let the way wind up the hill or down,
O'er rough or smooth, the journey will be joy:
Still seeking what you sought when but a bo . . .'

(He stumbles slightly.)

'Ahh, I mean, when but a girl,
New friendship, high adventure, and a crown,
Your heart will keep the courage of the quest,
And hope the road's last turn will be the best.'

I kiss my father on the cheek, grip his hand, and clutching it tightly we begin to walk towards my husband, my future, murmuring my wise old dad's refrain for marriage, for life, for happiness under our breath. 'O'er rough or smooth, the journey will be joy . . .'

We walk past my mum, who smiles at me. Then I pass a sobbing Jackie and a beaming Dave. There's Freya and Lisa, Jo who has flown from Oz to be here, and even Christie, who has come with her husband. There are a handful of uni friends, and of course, Jake, Gaz, Alex and some of Ryan's colleagues from Thorpe Hall and his Hackney school. But I barely register any of them because all I can see is Ryan. He looks as gorgeous as ever in his sea-blue suit and white shirt, bright orange flower in his lapel.

I get to Ry's side and he looks down at me with a grin on his face. 'You made it then,' he murmurs.

'Did you really think I wouldn't?' I ask, my heart soaring up to the sky.

He raises an eyebrow. 'I'd be lying if I said no, but that's only because I've been here since our very first kiss.'

'Second,' I remind him, curving my lips into a wry smile and glancing around at the shore where we kissed for the second – and the best time.

'First,' he grins. 'I knew from the start. It just took you a bit longer to catch up, *Harry*...'

I shake my head and slip my hand into his as we turn and face the minister.

'I'm not Harry,' I say. 'There's no more Harry. Just Molly. Molly Cooper. Now, shall we do this?'

Snap!

We kiss again, for another camera, another photo, another piece of video shot by a guest. So many photographs, so many moments captured: the sand, warm between my toes, dress billowing behind me, Ryan's arms around mine, the sun beating down on our backs as it starts to sink behind us, a glass of champagne thrust into our hands. People come up to us to chat, congratulate, kiss, hug. Casey, Mia, Jackie, Carl, Lydia, my dad, our wonderful friends and family. Even my mum comes and takes us both by the hands. Then she turns to Ryan and smiles benevolently at him.

'How funny it is to think that I'm your very own MILF now, Ryan dear!' Mum says proudly and pats his hand.

He stares at her, and then me, unable to hide his horror. I can't stop the impending snort of laughter I feel coming on. I drag him away from a bemused Mum, telling her I'll explain later, and telling him that I'm saving him from my mum's amorous advances. And then we run, hand in hand, me trying not to spill champagne over my dress, on our way to the hotel, where fairylights hang from the trees, a canopy of stars above us in the glow of the Ibizan sunset.

An intimate dinner for forty, a relaxed tapas meal, our friends, our family, each other. It is everything I've ever wanted.

'Do you feel different?' I ask as we sit, later that night, on the beach, a bottle of champagne between us. It is 4 a.m. We have danced and kissed and laughed and kissed and danced and kissed some more. Some of our guests have gone to bed, others have gone on to a club. We went to bed – and then got up again – not wanting our day to end. We have decided to come here to watch the sunrise on the first day of our marriage. I am drunk and deliriously happy. Drunk on love.

I prod him. 'Not listening already, huh? It didn't take you long to settle into married life!' I laugh. 'I *said*, do you feel different?'

'Yeah, it's weird,' Ryan says, tilting his head thoughtfully. I watch his lips moving slowly as he speaks, then he rubs his ankle. 'It feels like I've got this massive weight, right here,' and he clutches it and groans, miming as if it is an unbelievably heavy ball and chain.

'Hey!' I smack him on the arm and then clamber up on him, enjoying the feeling of the cool sand between my toes and the heat of him. 'I'll show you what a heavy weight feels like,' I giggle, as I straddle his chest and pin down his arms.

'Oh, please do, Mrs Cooper,' he moans, 'please, please do ...' And then he pulls me over in the sand until he is on top of me.

He gazes down. 'Molly Cooper,' he says softly, smiling as he releases the unfamiliar coupling from his lips. 'This feels different because it feels like ... forever ...' He pauses, waiting for my affirmation. 'You know?'

'I know,' I smile as I stroke his forehead. 'I know.'

1.10 p.m.

'Hey, Miss? Miss? Where d'ya want this then?'

I glance up at the blotchy, overworked face of Bob, who is blithely coming down the stairs with what appears to be my dressing table on his back, whilst his younger apprentice is carrying a single box as if it is the heaviest thing in the world. I hear my mobile ringing in the kitchen and am tempted to go and answer it, but whoever it is will have to wait.

'Are you OK, Bob?' I say, rushing over to his aid, but he waves me away.

'I'm fine, gal, used to lifting bigger than this. Just tell me where to put it, eh?'

'Oh, yes, sorry, in the van. It's going to storage.'

'Don't need a fancy dressing table any more, eh luv?' he winks.

'I'm a woman, I'll always need a dressing table like that,' I laugh. 'I just can't take it where I'm going!'

He staggers out of the front door and minutes later he's back. 'Well, luv, that's the last of it from upstairs – what next?'

I glance at my watch and then at his red face and my stomach, which is growling with hunger. 'Lunch!' I answer, and his face brightens even more – but this time with relief.

'That's music to my ears, luv,' he grins. 'I'm gonna have a sit-down in the van and read the paper.'

'You're welcome to stay in here if you like, I'll rustle up a sandwich . . .'

'Nah, don't you worry, my lunch box is in the van. The wife packed it for me, gawd bless her. But if I don't come back in, you know she's put arsenic in me BLT! Ha ha— Oof!'

I open the door to let him out, just as someone is about to knock on it. I squeal as I kiss my sister-in-law, and then usher Bob out into the driveway. I squeeze her, then bend down and grab my nephew. 'Beau-Beau!' I wrestle him into a reluctant hug. At seven and a half and with all the nonchalance and coolness of a kid twice his age, he considers himself *way* too big for a special Auntie Molly hug. Luckily my 5-year-old niece, Gemma, isn't as discerning. She's thrown herself at my legs squealing with delight. I close my eyes and kiss her blonde hair, trying to soak up the moment so I can remember it in the future.

Beau appraises me with his sharp blue eyes, so like his Nanny Jackie's and his uncle's, and then makes his summary of me, like Simon Cowell after a particularly dire *X Factor* audition.

'You look sad,' he says honestly.

'Beau!' Lydia scolds. 'You can't say that!'

'It's OK, Lyd,' I say with a laugh as I crouch down to his level. 'Well, Beau,' I reply with equal sincerity and just a hint of a smile, 'you're absolutely right. It's because I'm going to miss you all very much. But I'm excited too because I know that I'll be very happy in my new home.'

'Just like Uncle Ryan is?' Beau says, without blinking.

I glance up at Lydia and she looks away. I nod and usher him in. 'Now Beau, do you fancy an apple juice and a Jammie Dodger? If I've got any left,' I add guiltily as I glance into the lounge and spot the empty packet of biscuits I've already worked my way through this morning.

'We're not staying long,' Lydia says, throwing off her leather jacket and hanging it over one of the two chrome-and-red 1950s diner stools that stand in front of my little island kitchen unit. They're being given to the local charity shop. 'I was just walking down The Broadway and thought I'd swing by here as I just couldn't face last night being the last time we saw you. *And* Beau begged to see you again. Believe it or not,' she adds.

We giggle as we glance into the lounge. He couldn't look less bothered to see me. In the five minutes we have been speaking he has unplugged the DVD, located the Playstation that I bought especially for his visits and has found the already sealed-up box that contains all the games. And ... oh yep, he's opened it.

'Make yourself at home, won't you, Beau-Beau!' Lyd calls sarcastically, and then shakes her head apologetically at me.

'Don't worry, Lyd, I already knew that he only loves me for my gadgets,' I say, just as Beau comes running into the kitchen shouting, 'Auntie Molly! Can you make me a smoothie in your special whizzy blendy thing? Oooh, and what about making ice cream just like we did last time? That would be so cool. Ha! Cool, get it?'

'I rest my case,' I laugh, lifting the just-boiled kettle and pouring hot water into the only two spare mugs that aren't yet packed. I realize that one says 'Keep Calm & Carry On' and the other says 'The Only Way Is Essex'; I was given them as a leaving gift from Lydia.

'Beau!' Lydia scolds. 'I told you Auntie Molly is very busy today packing up her house. We've just popped by to see if there's anything we can do, not unpack her stuff again!' She turns to me as I hand her a cup of tea. 'Gem, go in there and play with your brother, OK?' Gemma totters off obediently, her blonde ponytail bouncing perkily. '*Is* there anything I can do, babes?' Lydia asks.

'No,' I shake my head, and then glance at my watch.

'You don't *look* stressed,' Lydia points out as I sit on a kitchen chair and put my legs up on another. 'How are you feeling though, really?'

'Oh you know ... sad, weird, numb.'

I've become pretty adept at describing my emotions. Now I see every feeling I have as a snapshot that I can flick through instantly, each one replaced quickly by the next one in the pack. I've learned the hard way that emotions can be as disposable as the old plastic Kodak cameras we used to take our holiday pictures with. Happiness is as transient as sadness.

'Well that's perfectly understandable!' chirps Lydia in her characteristically bright way. 'But I know it'll all be alright!'

'So do I,' I say with a slight defensiveness that I didn't know I felt. It passes as quickly as it arrives. 'Don't get me wrong, Lyd, I'm ready for this but still . . .'

'I know, Moll,' Lydia says unusually quietly, leaning over the table and stroking my hand.

'I'm just worried I'm going to feel really alone, you know?'

'Are you *mad*?' Lydia gasps, laughing with the authority of someone who knows better. 'Lonely is the last thing you're going to be. Trust me. I know it's scary going somewhere new, but you know people there already and you're going to make new friends so quickly. It's what always happens. *We're* the ones that are going to be lonely without you.' She looks down at her hands and a tear drops from her eye onto them. She runs a finger under her eyes and rolls them heavenward. 'I'm so sorry, I swore I wouldn't do this. I just feel like I'm losing you, too . . .'

'Don't, Lyd. You're not.' I stand up and walk over to the dresser in the corner and open the drawer. 'Besides, I've got just the thing to help us stay in touch.' I pull out my old Canon digital SLR. 'I want you to have this.'

'Oh Moll, I can't—'

'Yes, you can, I've got a new one. I want you to take photos of you, Carl and the kids, silly photos, things you're doing every day and I want you to upload them here once a week. I go over and grab my laptop. I tap in a few words and in an instant, a Tumblr document appears with the words 'Lydia's Blog' at the top. I quickly take a picture of her, plug the USB cord from the camera into the laptop and upload the picture. She's pulling a face and her mascara has run.

'That's hideous!' she snorts.

'I don't care. I'm the only one who is going to see it and read it. You can just post pictures if you want, or if you need to talk, about anything, you write and I promise I'll write back as soon as I can, OK? It'll be like I'm still just down the road.' I squeeze her hand and Lyd gives a watery smile, before pulling out her make-up compact and reapplying.

'Ooh, I nearly forgot. Here's mine!' I open up a matching blog page, turn the camera around, pull a face and quickly upload the picture. 'I'll post pictures of all the things I'm doing. It'll be brilliant!'

'Well, I guess you're the expert.' Lydia's lip wobbles and then the tears come again. 'It won't be the same, Molly, but well, it's better than nothing. It's a lovely idea, thank you, Moll.' And she kisses me on the cheek and we sit holding hands for a moment.

'There's something else I want to give you, Lyd, something I want you to cherish. I've wanted you to have it for a long time. I take my hand away and then put it back on the table and open it up, so my palm is facing up. In it lies a glittering antique diamond ring.

'Oh Molly, your engagement ring, no!' Lydia cries and shakes her head. 'I couldn't, I just couldn't!'

'Listen to me, Lyd,' I say firmly, pressing it into her hand. 'It's what I want. This ring is a Cooper heirloom so it's not mine to keep.'

'But Ryan, he gave it to you ...'

'Which makes it mine to give away. Just because things didn't work out as I'd hoped ... well, I don't want to take it from here, from Nanny Door, and from Jackie. Can you imagine if I lost it in transit? They'd kill me! The ring is a part of this town as Ryan is.' I pause. 'Perhaps Beau will want to have it one day, when he falls in love. He's going to be a little heartbreaker too, I reckon ...'

Lydia nods, and that's when our tears really come.

'I can't believe this is it,' Lydia says as she stands on the doorstep.

I grasp her closely to me, mostly so Beau doesn't see us crying but he's too busy playing Angry Birds on Lydia's iPhone anyway.

'It isn't goodbye. Remember our blogs and you all have to come and see me!'

She sniffs, her eyes shining brightly. 'Too right.' She kisses me quickly on the cheek, stares at me for a moment and then smiles as she puts her arm round her son's shoulders.

'Come on Beau, Gemma, it's time to go! Say goodbye to Auntie Molly now please.'

Beau looks up and smiles with that irrepressibly cheeky Cooper smile, and throws himself into my arms. I close my eyes, remembering all the hugs that have gone before, as a baby, a toddler and a little boy. When his delighted shouts of 'CUDDLES!' instead of 'bundle!' would be the only warning that would precede him launching himself on my bed when I stayed over at Lydia and Carl's.

They turn away and I hear Lydia ask for her phone.

'Awww, Mum, I thought I could keep it to play on until we get home!' he whines.

'I never said that, you cheeky sod!' she exclaims as she totters down the path in her stacked patent heels, taking the noise, chatter, life, but not my cherished memories, away with them.

The Snatched Kiss

Do kisses fade like polaroids if you don't pay attention to them? I have kissed and been kissed so many times and yet unsatisfyingly few are imprinted on my memory. Only two or three from my childhood remain but I know there must have been many more. But I cherish the handful I remember like they are precious jewels. There's the proud kiss my mum and dad simultaneously gave me on each cheek after I'd taken my first Holy Communion. I remember standing in my white dress and veil, toes scrunched nervously in my little satin ballet pumps as their lips pressed to each of my beaming cheeks. It felt like their kisses had dried and would be forever imprinted there, like the flowers I used to press between the pages of books.

And if I close my eyes I can conjure up the smattering of gentle, soothing kisses on my fevered cheek and brow my mum gave me when I had chickenpox. They felt like angels' wings healing my poor, spotted skin. And I can vividly recall the giant smacker I gave her on her lips (they tasted faintly of Bakewell tart) when I came running out to her after my very first day of infant school. It took her by surprise so much that it sent her toppling backwards. I'd never seen my mum spread-eagled in an ungainly fashion anywhere – and I was horrified. But to my surprise she laughed it off, got up and then kissed me on my head. My mum's surprised me a lot these days. Every time I think of her, I experience a Ready Brek warmth to my body.

Then there are the passionate, romantic kisses of my life – most of which have been with Ryan. One particularly hard evening I lay in bed counting how many kisses I had shared with Ryan over our years together (yeah yeah, I know I'm sad – so shoot me – as

I used to say when I was a teenager!) and the number came into the thousands. But if I add up how many of those I can instantly recall? Of course I remember the important ones: when we first met, moved in together, got engaged, got married ... but the day-to-day kisses? The ones where we told each other without any words or fancy surroundings or ostentatious ceremony just how much we loved each other? Just as with the endless facts and figures I learned in school and that have since flooded out of my brain, only a few remain. The only conclusion I can come to is that I just wasn't concentrating hard enough.

'Can you just look at this before you go?' I call as Ryan whirls through the flat, swooping up his books, football boots and his bike helmet as he goes. He stuffs half a slice of toast in his mouth and dives towards me, delivering a kiss to my cheek as he pulls at his diary that I realize I am sitting on. I tilt so he can get it and then wave my list in front of his nose, desperate for him to look at it. This is not just any old to-do list I'm trying to show him. It's The Master Wedding List, or, as Ryan calls it, The List of All Lists. I made it when I started to feel like I was drowning in wedding admin. This master list divvies up the lists of jobs between myself, Ry, Carl and Jackie, and covers everything. If only I could get Ryan to look at it.

'*Pleeease*, Ry. We're getting married in less than eight weeks and there's still so much to do!'

Ryan pulls an apologetic face as he throws the last of his toast in his mouth.

'I can't,' he talks as he chews and then washes it down with a gulp of orange juice. 'I'm already late. I need to go to the gym before my staff meeting. Hey, I thought you were going to come?'

'I know, but I've been twice this week already and I just want to spend an hour before work doing some wedding admin. Eight weeks isn't long to get everything sorted you know, Ry!'

'It's too long for me!' Ryan says, dropping a quick, crumby kiss with top notes of peanut butter on my lips. 'I wish we were getting married tomorrow. Anyway, I thought this was meant to be a small, laid-back wedding!'

'It IS!' I reply, but must give a look of unbridled Bridezilla-ness that he laughs.

He brushes the crumbs from his stubble and glances at his

watch. 'Sorry, I've really got to go. Oh, and I'm gonna be late tonight, too. I'm doing some extra football coaching.'

'Really?' I put down the list and sit back on the sofa. 'Those kids are so lucky to have you, Ry.'

I stand up and kiss him gently on the lips and then nuzzle his neck. 'I just want you to look after yourself, OK? You're not invincible, even if you think you are.'

Sometimes, like now, standing in front of me in his Adidas tracksuit, I still see that 17-year-old I had a crush on all those years ago. But then I blink and I realize how much he's changed. He looks really tired at the moment, kind of gaunt and just older somehow. It's been a stressful few months at work and planning the wedding has been an added pressure. But I've tried to help by doing the wedding planning with Jackie. We are a great team. (I write the lists, she does all the things on them.) Still, it's tough doing it in such a short space of time – especially with one bridesmaid being in Australia and the other one going AWOL.

I think of Casey's estrangement and am hit by a wave of sadness. It happened shortly after I phoned her from New York to tell her the news of our engagement. I'd expected squeals of excitement, tears, laughter, that moment of friendship that will bond you forever when your childhood friend sees you being handed your happy-ever-after. For this reason, I'd phoned her first, before my parents, before Mia, before anyone.

'Case?' I had said excitedly when she answered on the third ring and I'd waved at Ryan to turn down the TV in our hotel room. We'd just come back from Central Park and he was perched on the end of the bed, engrossed in some basketball game. I'd ducked into the tiny, windowless bathroom, holding the phone to my ear and gazing at my left hand, stroking my beautiful antique ring. It had been Nanny Door's engagement ring. She gave this to Ryan when we got back together and Ryan decided to propose with it. After I'd accepted, he'd offered to buy me a different ring.

I'd looked into Ryan's bright blue eyes, so like his nan's, and I'd shaken my head as I'd told him that I didn't want a new ring, I wanted this one. It was special to Ryan and to his entire family and for that reason it was better than any ring we could ever buy. 'This ring will be a constant reminder of how lucky I am to be Mrs Cooper,' I'd said, and he'd kissed me again and again.

I'd squealed as Casey had greeted me on the phone. 'Case, I've got something wonderful to tell you!'

'You've bought the Ugg boots I asked for and they were even cheaper than I expected?' she says.

'Nooo, something way better.'

She gasps. 'You've bought me a pair of *Manolos* – Molly, you shouldn't have!'

'No, silly!' I laugh. 'Ryan just proposed!'

Silence.

I'd waited and waited and waited for the squeals to come, the cries of joy, the laughter. It's the scene from a million movies I've seen a hundred times over. I told myself Casey was just in shock. Understandably, after all, it wasn't that long ago I'd been crying myself to sleep on her couch. Her happiness would come, once she got over it.

But it didn't. All that came was the long beep of an ended call.

I'd stared at the receiver in my hand, wondering what the hell had just happened, where she'd gone. Had the long-distance call been cut off by accident? I'd waited for the phone to ring. It didn't. Then I'd redialled her number but her phone appeared to be switched off.

I'd gone back into the room then and told Ryan what had happened.

He hadn't looked away from the TV screen. 'Maybe her phone ran out of battery?' he'd offered distractedly.

'Maybe,' I'd replied, and I'd sunk onto the bed, feeling the cold hand of doubt clutching at my throat.

Two days later she called me back, told me it had just been a bad line and that when she'd tried to return my call she couldn't get the right number, the hotel put her through to the wrong room and she'd forgotten how to dial internationally to a British mobile. It was such a scatty Casey thing to do that I believed her. And I also believed her when she said that she was happy for me, so I excitedly told her we were planning on getting married in April, five months after the proposal and almost five years since our first *real* kiss, and in exactly the same place – that little beach cove he took me to in Ibiza. I asked her to be my bridesmaid.

I haven't heard from her since.

Ryan keeps telling me not to worry about it, that she'll come round. That she's just finding it hard that her best friend is getting married when she has barely had a serious boyfriend her entire life. But I can't help it. I miss her. I want her to be a part of this. I can't imagine doing this without her. But at the same time, I'm furious that she's acting like this. I thought she of all people would be happy that Ryan and I are back together. She saw what a mess I was without him. I miss her and resent her all at once.

It didn't help that whilst everyone else was over the moon about our news, only Jackie and Dave, in their typically upbeat Cooper way, supported us and believed we could plan it in six months. God, I love them for it.

''*Course* it can be done, darlin'!' Jackie had exclaimed. 'We just need to book you some wedding dress appointments, find a wedding planner in Ibiza to sort out the beach wedding and hire a venue for the reception – leave that with me, darlin'! The most important thing is your dress. Book some appointments at Harrods, Browns and Liberty. You can get off-the-hook designer dresses that can be altered to fit from all those places. Shall I get you appointments for this Saturday? Are you free? Of *course* you are, darlin'! What else could you be doing that is more important! Oh, this is going to be so exciting! Have you phoned your mum? She needs to come with us, of course, and Nanny Door wants to come, too ... What's that you say, Mum? Oh here, she wants a word ...'

'Molly, swee'dheart!' Nanny Door's scratchy voice had come on the line. 'How's that ring o' mine looking on your finger? My Arthur would be well chuffed. Now, about this dress. I thought maybe you should go for something like that Jordan wore to wed that luvvely Peter Andre. Ooh, I do love them. Did you see her eat them kangaroo balls on *I'm a Celebrity*? It were *classic*!' I hear Jackie grappling for the phone back.

'As you can see, darlin', Nanny Door's already got her opinions! And you can always be sure we'll tell you honestly what we think, that's what you need when you're choosing a wedding dress! So call your mum now and get her to meet us at Oxford Street tube this Saturday. We'll do Liberty first' – I hear her tapping on the computer – 'I see they have some wonderful Vera Wangs in stock, which would look just *gorgeous* on you, and money is no object. Obviously Dave and I will be paying for the wedding, I know your folks probably can't afford it ...'

At this point I interjected.

'No Jackie, really, Ryan and I have enough saved. We want to do it ourselves. Do it our way,' I add, forcibly, but it doesn't seem to register with her.

'Nonsense,' Jackie squeals, her tinkly laugh echoing down the phone. 'Why go small when you can go big?'

I'd pulled the phone away and gestured at Ryan who'd been marking GCSE PE coursework at the breakfast bar. 'Tell her, Ry,' I'd begged him. He'd grinned and taken the phone from me.

'Because we *want* to go small, Mum,' Ryan had said firmly. 'No! No arguments, of course you can help, we absolutely need your help with planning this thing – we've got six months and Molly is freaking out. But *no* taking over and absolutely no money is to pass hands. I mean it, Mum. Molly and I want this to be done our way.' He hands me back the phone and I smile gratefully at him.

'OK, darlin',' Jackie sighs, 'you just tell me what you want to do. My son has made it quite clear what he wants!' She sniffs dramatically. I try not to laugh.

'Jackie,' I say evenly, 'I'd *love* you to help me choose my dress. Could you book some appointments, like you said please?'

She'd gasped in delight. 'Oh, thank you, Molly darlin', you know that really means the world to me, especially with me never having a girl! You and Lyd are the daughters I never had!' And she'd burst into tears.

Ryan had kissed me on the forehead in thanks, and I'd sat down as Jackie started firing questions about shades of white, lengths, veils and tiaras at me until my head spun.

I have to admit we couldn't have planned this wedding without her. And doing it abroad, in our favourite place, Ibiza, was an inspired choice. It was Ryan's idea and as soon as he suggested it I could picture it all. Walking barefoot in the sand towards him; Mia, Lydia, and of course, Casey walking behind me in their beautiful bridesmaids' dresses. And it meant we cut the guest list in half immediately. None of my mum's family are coming – Mum told me they think we're heathens for not getting married in a church.

'What did you say?' I asked her when she fed me this bit of information about her uptight family.

'That I'm proud that my girl always does things her way, not how other people think she should do them,' she said brusquely.

'Including you?' I'd asked with a wry smile.

'Especially me,' she'd replied. 'You are your own woman, my dear, and that makes me proud.' It was the biggest compliment she'd ever given me. Then she'd added: 'Now Molly, what does one actually *wear* to a beach wedding?'

'Don't you worry,' I'd replied. 'Jackie will help you! You'll be in a pink frock and diamantéd up to the max by the time she's finished with you!'

*

'Are you sure you haven't just got a second to look at these?' I say desperately as Ryan heads for the door. 'It's really important . . .'

He turns and gives me a pained expression. 'babe, I love you, but how can favours be important if I don't even know what they *are*!'

'Typical man,' I mumble petulantly. 'Never thinking about the detail.'

He sighs and strides back over. 'Look, let's go through all this at the weekend, not when I'm trying to run out the door, OK Moll?'

I nod and swallow back a lump. 'I just don't want to feel our wedding is at the bottom of your list, you know?'

'You know I don't even do lists, Moll!' He kisses me on the nose and grins.

'The weekend,' he reiterates. 'We'll go over it all at the weekend.'

'I'm going on a work trip on Friday, remember?' I say dully. 'LA, cover shoot.'

'Most people would be well chuffed by that!' Ryan laughs, tickling my chin.

'Well *most* people aren't getting married in seven weeks,' I retort defensively.

He curls me into his arms and I melt into them, as I always do. 'Molly, I promise it will all be fine. We don't need favours or any of that other stuff. We just need me, you, and our vows. Nothing else matters.'

'And I can't help but smile. I know he's right, really I do. And I know I'm just feeling vulnerable because we're both so busy. Ryan keeps telling me not to worry. I just don't want us to make the same mistakes again, not spending enough time together, letting other things get in the way. I must've said this last part out loud because Ryan comes and gives me a quick cuddle. I close my eyes.

'Just think, Moll, in seven weeks we'll be married, then we can go on honeymoon. A month in New Zealand, remember? Just focus on that. It's going to be amazing. The beginning of our life together. But the bit before *is* going to be stressful. Now I'm sorry, babe,' he leans forward and kisses me on my forehead. 'But I've gotta go . . .'

And before I can kiss him back he dashes out the door.

The Missed You Kiss

Have you ever kissed someone and felt them slipping away from you even as you did it? Have you imagined the day when their lips are not yours to kiss any more? Have you ever closed your eyes and tried desperately to hold on to that kiss, that moment in your mind and in your heart so you can remember it forever? Maybe the kiss wasn't with your partner but maybe your child, a friend, or a parent?

These days I find myself throwing my arms around my mum and squeezing her so tightly, drinking in her familiar citrusy scent, feeling her soft, aged skin against mine, and wondering if she is doing the same; thinking about a time in the not too distant future, when she won't be able to hold me. Maybe she can still close her eyes and remember cradling me as a baby, or can conjure up my first kisses. Did she try and savour each of them, knowing that there might come a time when I might not be willing or – God forbid - able to give them any more? Did she love me so much that she was always scared of losing me? Did each kiss feel like I was one step closer to leaving her? Mum's always said that parenthood is one long kiss goodbye and, sometimes, I can't help feeling that's how I feel about life.

Every kiss, no matter how inconsequential – a quick kiss in greeting, a 'thank you' kiss or a 'see you soon' kiss is treated like it could be the last. It's like a permanent scar that I know will never heal.

'God, I've MISSED you,' I say, flinging my arms around my fiancé.

He plants a long kiss on my lips. 'Mmmm, how was your flight home?'

'All I could think about the entire time is that I'm going to be Mrs Cooper in six weeks' time!' I smile and he presses his lips to mine again so hard that they sting with pleasure and we kiss until my mouth aches. I come up for air first and open my eyes to see that we have an audience.

'Arghh!' I squeal, and smack Ryan on the back. He doesn't seem at all bothered by us snogging in full sight of Carl, Lydia, not-so-baby Beau, Gaz, Alex and Jake. 'I didn't know you guys were there!'

'Don't mind us, you two,' Carl grins. 'You just carry on! It's beautiful, just beautiful to see. Ain't love grand, eh Lyd?' And he throws her back and kisses her on the mouth as Beau wobbles around the room, clinging on to his Eeyore toy that Ryan and I bought him for Christmas.

'Is that all you got, Bro?' Ryan picks me up and cradles me in his arms, kissing me again and again as Carl throws Lyd over his shoulder.

'You boys,' Lyd, cries, trying to pull her miniscule skirt down. 'Always so competitive. Me and Molly are not footballs!'

'Coulda fooled me!' Carl says, approaching Lydia's chest with his fingers spread.

'Carl! Not in front of the baby!' she says as he makes a honking noise and then buries his head in her cleavage.

'Got any popcorn, Moll?' Gaz says, sitting back down with his arms on the sofa facing them.

I disentangle myself from Ryan's arms and then proceed to chase Beau around the room so I can cover him with kisses. He's honestly the most adorable boy on the planet. I can't believe he's eighteen months old already. I catch him at last and tickle him until he squeals with laughter, then look up and smile at everyone.

'How are you all doing, boys? Did you stop my fiancé from getting lonely?' I say, walking back and sliding my arm around Ryan, unable to be away from him for long so soon after getting home. He always insists on having friends to stay over whenever I have to go on a work trip. I no longer panic at the prospect of constant company but Ryan still hates being on his own. But that's never going to change.

'Oh yes, we had some lovely spoons in your double bed as he cried himself to sleep,' Carl nods, and I give him a big brotherly squeeze.

'Can you blame him?' I pull back and sigh, shaking my head as if the weight of being as wonderful as me is just too much to bear.

3.45 a.m.

BRIIIIIIING!!

I sit up in the dark, feeling completely disorientated and glance at the clock and then groan. Because of my jet lag I only got to sleep half an hour ago. I spent the rest of the time downloading pictures from our cover shoot that the photographer had sent me so I could look at them before work on Monday. Ryan, of course, hasn't been disturbed by the doorbell.

BRIIIIIINGGGGGGGG! The insistent noise proves that this isn't a drunken passer-by like we sometimes get, living on a main road. I heave myself out of bed, tempted to wake him, but he looks so blissful I don't see the point of waking both of us, unless it's some sort of major problem. He'll only panic and start looking for inanimate objects to bash an intruder with. Last time it happened I saw him brandishing a hairdryer. 'What were you going to do?' I'd said to him afterwards. 'Style them into submission?'

I go over to the intercom.

'Who is it?' I say sharply into the speaker.

'Molly? Can you c-come down . . . I step back from the speaker in shock as I instantly recognize the voice, even though I haven't heard it since Ryan and I got engaged. I quickly buzz her in, bolt across our lounge through our little hallway. I open our flat door and run down the stairs to meet her just as she steps through our front door. Casey looks at me dully. Her hair is all over the place, her eyes swollen and bruised, with tears and . . .

'Casey? What's wrong?' I pull her through the front door and into a hug. She feels so painfully small and thin and helpless in my arms. I can smell smoke in her hair, alcohol on her breath. I pull away from her and hold her at arm's-length. She tries to hide in my shoulder but then I notice that those bruises aren't just from tiredness. I glance down and take in the red rings around her arms, the marks on her throat.

'What the hell has happened to you, Casey?' I say, feeling the tears spring into my own eyes. She shrinks to the floor like a rag doll, her handbag strewn by her side and I am body-slammed by a vivid memory of her in a playground, her poor body lying helpless, defenceless. I bend down and lift her up so I'm cradling her in my arms. I don't know what has happened, I just need to get her upstairs. She opens her eyes and smiles weakly at me.

'I'm so glad you're here, Molly,' she whispers. 'I was so worried you wouldn't be . . . I don't want to be on my own . . .'

'You don't have to be, Casey. I'm going to look after you now.' I clear my throat and swipe my hand across my eyes. 'Come on honey, let's get you upstairs . . .'

We walk slowly up the stairs and into the flat.

'Ry?' I call loudly, the word catching in my throat, wanting his help, not sure how to handle the situation alone.

'No!' she says, shaking her head and looking at me with pleading eyes. 'Please don't get him. I don't want anyone else to see me.'

'But he'll know what to do, Case,' I answer gently, aware that I don't know what to do. Not at all. I bring Casey into our lounge and am at once acutely aware of how warm and inviting it is, how safe and secure and so far removed from wherever Casey has come from. I see her clock the cosy scene with one flicker of her dull, murky-coloured eyes, Ryan's discarded trainers and my Converse huddled together on the floor by the sofa, the open wedding file on the coffee table, the debris of a cosy night in for two. Suddenly I am all too aware how different my life is to hers.

I start to lead my best friend, who I haven't heard from for two months and who used to be closer to me than a sister, over to the couch slowly. How did this happen? Who did this to her? She winces in pain and clutches her ribs, and I'm trying not to cry at what I'm witnessing.

I hear Ryan stumbling down the stairs in the jeans he's hastily put on, brandishing a tennis racket as a weapon. My husband-to-be, sporty even in self-defence. He's rubbing his eyes blearily as he comes into the brightly lit room.

'What is it, Moll?' He looks shocked, then horrified when he sees her. He looks on as I lead Casey to the sofa. She looks at him and then he dashes over and skids to his knees in front of the sofa.

'What happened, Case?' He lifts her chin gently and she gazes at him, her bruised black and mauve eyes are soulless and empty. She buries her head in a cushion.

'Hey, Case,' he says kindly. 'We're going to look after you, but babe, whoever did this to you shouldn't be able to get away with it.' Her shoulders heave up and down, but her face stays buried. He pulls her hair back, kisses her on her cheek and strokes her head.

I sit down on the edge of the sofa and stroke Casey's hair, too. It is damp but warm, sweat mixed with a steady stream of tears, and – is that blood? Oh God.

'What happened Case? Can you tell me?' I ask gently, my voice wobbling with fear and shock.

She raises her head slightly off the sofa cushion and looks at me. Her face is the shade of newspaper carbon when it rubs off on your skin. Her hands are shaking uncontrollably. I notice there is dirt under her fingernails. I can see it through her pink varnish. I stroke her head and she lowers it again. Ryan pulls a blanket that's folded over the side of the couch and I pull it over her gently.

'I was l-l-leaving work ...' she hiccups. 'There was a group of them ... it had been a busy night at the club. Lots of people on the door pissed off that they couldn't come in. I finished early and had a few drinks to unwind after my shift. I was going home on my own ...' She trails off and I nod to encourage her to go on, and she does. 'They just came out of nowhere. The girls. They started p-punching and k-kicking me. I couldn't do anything ...' Casey talks quietly, stopping and starting, stumbling over the details, unable to recall the exact order of events. I look down at Casey in horror and clutch Ryan's hand as we stroke her hair, and Casey stumbles through her explanation of how they launched themselves at her on her walk home. They kicked and punched her in the face, called her a stupid slut and left her on the pavement outside her house. She'd been too petrified to go into her flat in case they came back so she crawled into her car and drove straight here. She said she recognized them. Southend is a small town.

I cradle her in my arms as she cries and I'm so fucking angry, not just with them, but with me. Why wasn't I there to protect her, like I've always been before? Back then, I didn't leave her side but now, when she needed me, I wasn't there. And I promised I always would be. Why have I been so consumed with myself and my life and this wedding that I've left her to fend for herself? Casey *can't* look after herself, I've always known that. She's not strong enough to live on her own, or to work in a club like that. I knew it but I didn't do anything to protect her.

What happened to BF's forever?

'I didn't mean to make this happen, Molly,' she sobbed, 'you've got to believe me, I know I'm stupid and irresponsible but I didn't mean to, I didn't mean to . . . I didn't, honestly . . .' She looks up at me imploringly '. . . and I didn't mean to not call you, and I'm sorry Molly, I'm s-so, so sorry . . .'

'Shhh, you don't have to be sorry for anything, Case, it's my fault, I'm the one to blame here, not you. I've neglected you. I should have been there, not just tonight . . .' I say as she burrows into my neck and cries and then I cry with her, for her and for us. For the naive kids that we were who thought that life would always go in the same direction for us.

'I've missed you, Moll,' she weeps.

'Shhh,' I repeat, and kiss her on her head, and I sit there stroking her hair for what feels like hours until she drifts off to sleep.

The Wish You Were Here Kiss

Why is it when you're about to wed there's this ridiculous tradition to spend a weekend away from your intended? I mean the whole point of getting married is that you want to be together forever. From this day forward.

In my lowest moments I have obsessed over the weekend of my hen do. Sometimes I lie in bed and I close my eyes and imagine that Ryan and I spent that weekend in Paris, or in Rome, or tucked up in a B&B on the coast together, or in a log cabin, lying in front of a roaring fire as the snow drifted outside the door, talking about the exciting future that lay before us. Sometimes we're even in Jackie and Dave's annexe in Leigh-on-Sea. Anywhere other than apart.

But then it's not long before my mum's words spoken on my wedding morning permeate my dreams. 'The only person your happy-ever-after is hinged on is you, Molly,' and I realize that nothing has been stolen from me, not really. How can I think about what I lost when I have gained so much? Instead of wishing he was here, I just need to be thankful that I am.

'Woohoo, this is fun!' squeals Lydia, lifting up two bottles and pouring the most gigantic amounts of tequila and vodka into her cocktail shaker, a tiny bit of orange juice, and then holds up a cranberry before dropping it in the drink. 'I'm going to call this one "Lyd's Loose Lips",' and she raises an eyebrow.

'You're all class, Lyd,' I giggle as I make the raspberry Martini just as the mixologist guy showed me, batting my eyelashes as I lift up my finished drink for his inspection.

'It's perfect,' he says with a movie-star smile.

'So are you,' sniggers Mia, and gestures pinching his arse as he turns his back on us. She gulps down her own Martini and slams the glass back on the bar.

'Hey, he's mine!' Lydia protests.

'I'll fight you for—' She bites her lip and glances at Casey, and I quickly grasp her hand and squeeze it. Some of her minor injuries have now healed but the emotional wounds of that night are still raw. 'Sorry,' Mia says, touching her bruised arm. 'I wasn't thinking.'

Casey looks up from her own non-alcoholic concoction and smiles wanly.

'Are you OK, Case?' I murmur, like I've been doing approximately every three minutes since my hen party began.

She nods and smiles at me – but without any of her usual sparkle. 'Fine, babes, happy to be here.'

I touch her arm. 'You know you don't have to be,' I say.

'I wouldn't miss it,' she says, her chin and nose pointed determinedly in the air.

I'm still amazed she's made it. She's been staying with Ryan and me ever since that night – God, was it a month ago now? It feels like yesterday. We only went back to her flat to pack up enough things to bring them to ours for the forseeable. She didn't want to go to her mum's, understandably. I'm not entirely sure that Toni would have been particularly bothered; she's got a new boyfriend at the moment. So Ry and I instantly offered her our couch. We've even exchanged it for a sofa bed to make it more comfortable for her.

There are squeals as Freya and Lisa both clink their cocktail glasses at the other end of the bar. We smile and do the same.

'To friends, your future and having FUN,' Casey says with effort, and I swallow back a tear at her bravery. Mia hugs us and I link my arms through both of theirs, feeling so happy to have them here. My best friends.

I still can't believe my hen do is finally here and in one week's time, I'll be Mrs Ryan Cooper. It doesn't seem possible, and yet it can't come quickly enough as far as I'm concerned. I kissed Ryan goodbye this morning. He and the boys are heading out to Ibiza early for his stag do.

I look at my two best friends either side of me and the other girls here – Lydia and the girls from work; I only invited a handful because I wanted the chance to spend quality time with everyone and not feel part of a circus. And more than anything, I didn't want to have a celebration that would make Casey feel awkward. Historically she hasn't coped well with other friends of mine, and although she and Mia have been fine(ish) for years, I'm sure that's only because Mia moved to Australia. I think as far as Casey has always been concerned, Mia couldn't ever threaten our closeness whilst she was living 10,000 miles away. Which is funny, because although Mia may live on the other side of the world, in many ways we've actually grown closer over the years. Perhaps it's because we understand each other's jobs, maybe it's because we don't demand much of each other, perhaps the distance stops us from having the petty ups and downs of most friendships, but Mia is my rock.

'OK ladies,' says the super-cute mixologist, 'are you ready for the next cock—'

'OH YES!' we chorus.

'. . . tail.' He finishes and we all fall about laughing. He rolls his eyes good-naturedly and throws his shaker into the air Tom Cruise-style, as we all ooh and aah and gasp with pleasure like we're at a fireworks display.

'Okaaay,' he drawls lazily, 'now I'm going to make someone a special cocktail designed just for them. A Moll . . . Flanger? Is that right?'

I scream and burst out laughing as Mia points and winks at me across the bar.

'And a virgin one for the pretty lady in the black dress,' he grins wolfishly at Casey, who has stuck to her decision to stop drinking since the night of the attack.

She lifts her glass and winks with the eye that isn't healing from the stitches (a heel cut the corner of it – she was lucky not to lose an eye). For a moment both eyes shut in transition and I realize that with no fake tan, her long black hair unstyled (she can't lift up her arms for long) and her olive skin sallow and still bruised from the attack, she looks ghostly, ethereal almost. 'I'm about as far from a virgin as anyone can get! Haaa!' she blurts out jokingly with what seems like a desperate attempt to get into the hen spirit. 'Besides, there's no chance of me getting any with this beat-up face!'

We all look at each other awkwardly as a ripple of discomfort works its way through the group. Lydia has assured her it's nothing that can't be covered with make-up on the big day. She is now determined to be chief bridesmaid at my wedding. I take Casey's hand and squeeze it again, trying to let her know that she doesn't have to do this, that we don't expect her to try and make crude jokes just because we're on a hen do. It's enough that she's here and she still wants to be there on my big day.

'Come on,' she says, 'you have to admit it's a bit funny! Laugh!'

And we obey her. If it's what she needs to feel like herself again, to claw back that confidence she once had, no matter what anyone thought, then I will laugh till my throat aches and my stomach hurts.

Casey begins to play up, dancing around, making jokes, and I know she's really making the effort for me. I want her to know that I love her and that I'd do anything for her. I might have neglected her a bit over the past few years but if I could have taken those kicks and punches for her, saved her from them like I did when we were teenagers, I would. I'll just have to make sure, as I swore to myself on the night she turned up on my doorstep, that I'm always there to take them from now on.

The morning after the night before, after we'd taken her to A&E, she and I and Ryan went for a walk along the Southbank. I think she hoped that the blustery gales coming in from the river would blow away the memory of the incident. But even as I told her how terrible I felt that she'd been alone and how I wished I'd been there to stop the girls, it occurred to me how horribly self-obsessed it was that in hearing her talk about that moment of horror, I'd been thinking about how it affected *me*. I told her that too, and then apologized profusely.

'Molly,' she'd said quietly, her brown eyes glassy with sadness that was reflected in the mulchy Thames beyond. 'You've done so much for me, you are the least selfish person I know. You both have,' she'd added. She smiled first at me then at Ryan and slipped her arms around us both, clearly still in pain, inside and out.

'You know you can stay with us as long as you need too, right?' I said as we'd walked across Waterloo Bridge, not asking Ryan first but knowing he'd agree.

'But, the wedding ... you don't want me ...' she'd begun, her fingers hovering over her poor face.

'Ah ah ah,' I'd stopped and interrupted her by popping my hand over her mouth, but she'd instinctively jolted back and I'd put it up to my own mouth in horror as I realized that this is what *they* must've done to her last night when she was screaming out in pain.

'Case, I'm sorry!' I'd sobbed then. I'd pulled her into my arms and we'd stood hugging on the bridge as Ryan had looked on. I desperately wished that a tornado would sweep us up and away, back to the past, before this had happened to her.

It's been a slow rehabilitation for her over the past five weeks. On day four she'd turned on the TV. On day ten she'd smiled at an old episode of *Friends*. On day thirteen she'd gone home to her mum's for a couple of days. She'd returned to us and told us that she'd quit her job – and the drink.

'I want to take control. I don't want to be fun-time Casey any more. I'm twenty-eight years old, babe. I need to grow up. I want to start making good decisions for me. And the first one is to stop drinking. Even if it's just for a while, to help me sort out my head. I'm trying to find a positive out of all this, Molly, please, will you help me?'

'Of course, I will,' I'd cried. 'I'll do anything you like, just tell me.'

'Thank you. I just hope I can repay you one day,' she'd said, adding whimsically, 'but your life is perfect. It always has been . . .'

A sad ghost of a smile had wafted over her face, illuminating her now-fragile features even more. 'You got your happy-ever-after,' she'd finished plaintively.

'I'm not sure such a thing exists,' I'd replied, feeling a momentary flash of my inner cynical Harry returning. 'After all,' I'd said, 'who ever really knows what's in their future?'

And she'd nodded sadly in agreement, and rested her head on my shoulder as she'd continued watching *Friends*.

Since then she'd agreed to be my bridesmaid and I'd shown her the dress I'd bought her from a designer sample sale when we weren't in contact, just in case she'd had some drastic change of heart. We never did discuss her reaction to my engagement. I knew she was jealous, and after what happened to her, it felt completely reasonable that she would resent the wedding. But strangely, it had done the opposite.

We bundle out of the Lab Bar in Soho, feeling deliciously relaxed. I have no idea what has been planned for the day. Mia has done it all.

'Where are we going now?' I ask, grasping the overnight bag I was instructed to pack.

'You'll see,' Mia smiles, stepping confidently into the street and hailing two black cabs, ushering me and Casey into one, and the rest of the girls into the other. She steps in after me and sits behind the driver.

'Knightsbridge please, mate.'

'Ma*iiii*te,' Casey and I echo Mia's affected Aussie accent and follow it with a burst of laughter.

'What?' she says innocently, taking out a Bobbi Brown compact and reapplying her lip gloss.

'You,' I say. 'No,' I look at Casey and we chorus in an Australian accent, 'Youiie! You're quite the Aussie these days; you've gone native, Mi.'

Mia raises an eyebrow. 'Do I look native to you?' she says imperiously, gesturing at her Havaianas, faded jeans and vest top.

'Yep,' I say cheerfully.

'Yeah, well, I'm on holiday.'

'You dress like this for work, too. I saw you,' I point out.

'Oh yeah, well, I LOIKE it. I *loike* not having to make a constant effort. I *loike* that I don't have to waste time blow-drying my hair to perfection or obsessing over what handbag I should be carrying. I still *loike* to dress up, but I'm too busy having fucking *fun* to worry about what I'm wearing. Even at work. Ooh, look, we're here!'

'Oh my GOD, this is AM.AZ.ING, Mia!?'

'Yep,' she'd grinned. 'And don't worry – I got it for free by doing a review for the magazine. Although you have to do one too for *Viva*. I figured your boss wouldn't mind!'

I look around our classy penthouse suite at The Berkeley hotel as we all burst through the door, chattering excitedly at the prospect of spending a night in the two-bedroom apartment that Mia has blagged. The room is an oasis of class and calm, white drapes fall from the windows, and everywhere is a sea of mushroom, taupe, beige and ecru – the exact opposite of what you'd expect on a hen night. I love it.

After we'd got dressed and had in-room manicures, Mia had taken us down to the cinema room at the hotel where we'd watched *Cocktail*. Then she'd played some messages she'd recorded from people who couldn't be here. There was one from Jo, my first ever picture editor, who now works with Mia in Sydney. Then my mum said a few stilted but sweet words from the comfort of her lace doily-topped chair; telling me to be good and to not get into any trouble because 'what will people think?'. Everyone had laughed at that, especially Case. Even Jackie popped up on screen in all her vivid-pink tracksuited glory, patting her hair and trying to check her reflection in the camera lens. 'Do I look alright, darlin'?' I could hear her ask Lydia, who was clearly behind the camera for this one. We were in hysterics by the end of Jackie's gloriously irreverent speech where she gave me first-night sex tips and offered me a box of her Ann Summers products. And then, just as our sides had stopped aching and we'd wiped away the last tears of mirth, darling Nanny Door had stood directly in front of the camera and screeched, 'Big Brother house, this is Nanny Door, do not swear, ha haaaa!' Then she'd cackled so much she'd nearly missed Jackie's throne she was trying to sit on. She'd composed herself, swatted Dave, who was trying to help her, out of the way and with her blue eyes twinkling with memory and love and wisdom, she'd smoothed down her hair, glanced momentarily off camera and said something that had made my throat ache and my heart swell and then dip, wishing that Ryan were here right now to see this.

'My only advice to you, Molly dear, is what I learned from the thirty-five wonderful years I spent with my Arthur – and the eighteen years I've spent without him. Savour every single moment, every word, every kiss.'

Then the video had gone fuzzy and the smiling face of my fiancé had appeared. This one had been Casey's doing, apparently.

'You were doing this when you kicked me out of the flat the other evening!' I'd exclaimed and hugged her. She'd just nodded.

'Hello, Harry,' Ryan said, his grin lighting up the entire screen. 'So this time next week you will be Mrs Molly Cooper, you'll have promised to love, honour and of course, the most important of all – obey me forever!'

'Never!' I yell, and we all laugh as Ryan rolls his eyes.

'Did you just shout "never"?' he asks into the camera. 'Well, don't you worry, I'm happy for you to promise never to obey me as long as you promise to never obey me as long as we both shall live.' He'd winked and grinned. 'I love you Molly Carter-almost-Cooper, have fun at your hen, don't let those girls lead you astray, and I'll see you next week, back in the place where it all began. I can't wait, babe!' Then he signed off with a kiss.

Ever since I'd seen him up on that screen I've missed him more than ever. I want to speak to him, but don't want the other girls to know. They've banned me from any contact, but now all I want is to let him know how much I love him. And so I activate the camera on my new phone, turn it to face me and I blow my kiss back at him and then attach it to my message:

I can't wait to be Mrs Cooper. Love you forever xxx

And I hit send.

The missed call flashing up on screen is from Mia. There's no voicemail but she's sent a text: *You're HOT! M x*

I smile as I deftly type my response: *Not as hot as you ... x*

Another text comes back immediately: *You will be. Soon!*

My phone rings almost seconds after I hit send.

'Mia!' I squeal as I begin walking down the stairs.

'Hel*loi*, darling,' I'm used to her Aussie inflections now. 'Can you believe today's the big day?!'

'I know!' I exclaim. I sit on the bottom step, smiling at the sound of my best friend's voice. 'I'm amazed you remembered!'

'Hey, I may be in an entirely different time zone but I do *sometimes* manage to recall major events in my best friend's life, you know!' she replies huffily.

'My birthday?' I tease.

'OK, maybe not *that*,' she concedes, 'but if you'd let me finish, I was *going* to add – especially when the major events involve me. And re your birthday, Molly, we're practically in our mid-thirties now and I thought we had an unspoken agreement to pretend *that* particularly depressing event doesn't happen any more ...'

'Fair enough,' I laugh.

'But this – this is more exciting than Christmas! It's going to be so brilliant Molly! Me and you back together again. Like when we were at uni. Do you remember those disgusting cocktails we concocted? What did we call them again? You know the ones that inexplicably tasted of fish.'

'Moll Flangers,' I reply, and we both crack up laughing.

'Just think, we can go out all the time!'

'I can't wait to see you,' she says more quietly. 'I've felt so bloody useless for so long.'

'You've helped more than you know.' Not for the first time I give thanks for my friends. I honestly don't know what I would have done without them. I just wish Casey . . . I stop myself before I start getting emotional again. *Pull yourself together, Molly,* I tell myself. *It's not like you'll be on your own . . .*

The Celebratory Kiss

Think about how often we kiss to celebrate the new: new job, new baby, new house, a newly married couple. So many kisses to revel in, so many 'new' things. But shouldn't every kiss be a celebration? Old or new, snatched or savoured. We should be throwing a party for every one.

I squint sleepily without opening my eyes, the custard-yellow sunlight is pouring through the curtains and spreading itself over our bed, covering us with its warmth.

'Morning!' murmurs Ryan. As ever, his naked body is curled around mine – even after nearly a year together we still sleep like we are locked in post-coital combat, with our limbs so inextricably tangled that I don't know where his end and mine begin. I turn my head and we kiss; a long, lazy affair that turns quickly into something more. I roll over towards him and we find our natural positions without word or conscious direction. Ryan's mouth tastes musty – a mixture of morning and lust – and I plunge into its warmth like a happy hippo in a muddy swamp, clinging onto his shoulders as we wallow in pleasure together. Afterwards, we emerge breathless and hot, throwing our sticky limbs across the entire bed as we pant, laughing with delight.

Ryan turns his head to look at me. 'Happy anniversary, babe,' he grins, and I roll up onto one shoulder, running my finger around the moles on his chest and wriggling in closer to him.

'But it's not our anniversary yet, Ry.'

'It's a year to the day of our real first kiss,' Ryan says, kissing my forehead and stroking my damp hair. 'Ibiza, remember?'

I look at the date display on the alarm clock and realize he's right. I shouldn't be surprised; Ryan has an uncanny ability to remember emotional events in great detail. He can recall our conversation in the café when we were teenagers in word-for-word detail, or what I was wearing when he saw me on the *Bembridge*. Ask him to remember to pick up some shopping, however, or to pay a gas bill, and he's floored.

'So how shall we celebrate?' I say, stroking his chest and burying my face in his neck.

'We just did, didn't we?' Ryan says, and I smack him playfully.

'OK,' he pulls himself up in bed, drawing me up with him. 'How about I take you out for dinner tonight after you finish work. My treat. I'll sort it out.'

'I know just the place we could try—' I say to Ryan, thinking about this new restaurant in London that I read about in *Time Out* but he interrupts me.

'Leave it to me, Moll. I said I'd arrange it.'

I stumble into the office and throw myself down at my desk.

Jo grins at me. 'What time do you call this, huh? Just because I'm leaving, it doesn't mean you can take liberties, you know!'

Jo is a really cool, straight-talking Australian. I look up to her; she's travelled the world, is married to her childhood sweetheart and is about to become Creative Director of *Shine*, the biggest-selling women's mag in Australia. I'm gutted she's moving back to Oz. What is it about that country? I've always wanted to go and yet everyone I know seems to end up there instead.

My computer starts up with a loud groan and I wave my hand at her dismissively and grin. 'File your complaint from Down Under, Jo. You only have one day left of being my boss!'

Jo laughs and taps at her watch. 'Half a day, you mean.'

'Ha ha.' My face drops as I open an email, sent ten minutes ago from the boss:

Molly, could you come to my office please? There's something I'd like to discuss with you. Christie

'OH my GOD! Really?' I gasp. 'You want me to be the new picture editor. Are you sure?'

Christie laughs and nods from behind her desk. I love Christie. Not only is she amazingly talented – she's won loads of awards since she launched *Viva* two years ago – but she's also really nice, which I've been told is pretty rare for an editor in this industry.

'You've done an amazing job in the last year, and Jo herself has said that she couldn't think of anyone better to fill her role. So what do you think?'

I stare at her.

What about being a photographer? Don't get sucked into the corporate machine!

'I-I thought you were interviewing loads of really experienced people?'

We said we'd never work in an office, this was meant to be temporary!

'We did,' Christie smiles. 'But none of the applicants were as good as you. You know the magazine inside out, you've been on cover shoots, Jo has said that you get on brilliantly with our crack team of photographers and have even made some new contacts of your own. You have a wonderful creative eye, great visual ideas and you are a great ambassador for the magazine.

I can feel myself blushing. I had no idea Christie thought so highly of me. And I have to admit, a promotion – and the pay rise that comes with it – would be handy right now. It might mean Ryan and I could start saving for a place of our own. I love our little pad at Jackie and Dave's, but it's basically an extension of his bedroom. Jackie even brings us breakfast in bed sometimes as she's got a key. I tune back into Christie.

'*Viva* is a fledgling magazine and I want my team to be young and hungry and passionate. And that's what we believe you are. So what do you say, can we officially announce your new position as picture editor to the rest of the team?'

Say no! Say no! This isn't what we want!

'Yes!' I exclaim.

No! What happened to pursuing our creative dreams?

A pay rise happened, that's what.

I'm waiting outside my office for Ryan to arrive. He said he'd meet me after work at the usual place at 7 p.m. but he's late. I've deliberately saved my amazing news to tell him over dinner. I can't wait to see his face.

I look around the bustling streets of Covent Garden at the hundreds of people floating along the sun-dappled street, like brightly coloured balloons that have been let out in celebration of this beautiful summer evening. I love London at this time of year. It's a constantly moving festival of colour that attacks the senses. I can totally understand why Dick Whittington thought the streets were paved with gold.

I'm making a mental list of reasons why it makes sense to move here and am already up to number eight just as my phone rings.

I smile as I answer. 'OK, Cooper, where are you? You'd better not be standing me up on our anniversary?'

'Hey, I'm here, where are you?'

'I'm here too!' I exclaim. I stand on my tiptoes and peer around, then put my hand up in the air. 'Wait, I'm waving, can you see me? I'm stood outside the office. Have you just come out of the tube?'

'Office? Tube? What are you talking about, Moll? I'm in Leigh! Don't tell me you're still at work!'

'What? But I thought you were taking me out for dinner? You said to meet at the usual place.'

'I meant The Crooked Billet, babe!' Ryan laughs, and my flight of fancy is well and truly grounded.

'Oh,' I say. '*That* usual place.'

'Don't worry, babe, if you hurry you'll still get here by 8.30. I'll get us some cockles from the cockle sheds an' I'll have a glass of wine waiting for you at our usual table outside. Make sure you don't miss the next train. Love you!'

We're sitting at our usual table, outside our usual pub, surrounded by the usual people, having our usual drinks and eating cockles from Osborne Bros from a small plate with a toothpick. The evening is warm, with the sea glistening in front of us and filled with the background noise of chat and laughter and music and clinking glasses of everyone enjoying the summer evening, apart from me.

Ryan throws his arm around me but I sit stiffly, unable to thaw my cold front, despite the warmth of the summer evening and Ryan's embrace.

'No fancy London restaurant could beat the fresh fish from round here!' Ryan says, with all the enthusiasm of a real foodie and a local lad. He glances sideways at me, but I am steadfastly looking away. 'I thought we could drive to Rossi's for ice cream after, just like we did on our first date, what do you reckon?' He kisses me again on my bare shoulder and I can't help but smile. That's such a sweet idea, now I feel bad for being so shallow. I still haven't told Ryan my news yet either as I've been too busy sulking. God, I can be such an idiot sometimes.

'Cheers, babe,' Ryan says, holding up his bottle of Becks. 'To the happiest year of my life!'

'So, Ry,' I wipe my mouth with my napkin and smile, 'I actually have some news!' I pause dramatically. 'You're now looking at *Viva*'s new picture editor!'

Ryan stops, his tooth pick lifted halfway to his mouth. 'Bloody hell, that's wicked! I'm so proud of you!' He leans over and kisses me on the lips.

He sits back in his chair and grins broadly at me. 'I'm so glad they can see how special you are, too.'

I swallow the urge to say that I wish he'd thought of somewhere more 'special' for our anniversary. And then it hits me, this *is* special. It's Ryan's special place. If he were Peter Pan he'd think of Leigh-on-Sea to make him fly, whereas I've always felt that it has clipped my wings. Right here, in the sun, by the sea, is where Ryan belongs. He comes bursting out of his bud when the sun is out. I look at him now, at how his skin has coloured into his usual tawny tan without him trying, and his already blond hair is now laced with threads of gold. His broad shoulders are relaxed, his body, unlike so many men's, looks really good in summer clothes. Shorts enhance his strong, muscular legs, his chest looks broader under a T-shirt. His body was made to be looked at. Which that gaggle of girls over there is proving.

Maybe I *could* learn to love it here as much as he does. I put my hand up at the passing bartender. 'Another glass of house white, please, and a Becks.'

And maybe sometimes it's best to just stick with what you know.

The Future's Bright Kiss

Ryan once told me kissing me for the first time felt exactly the same as doing a tandem skydive; it was as exhilarating as it was scary, risking his heart and throwing himself into the unknown with someone he barely knew. I understood that analogy exactly. Except for me, kissing Ryan felt like I was standing on a cliff-edge viewing platform; it wasn't scary, just beautiful seeing the world spread out below me and I knew that I could have it all with Ryan – he made me feel like I could touch the sky – but I also knew he'd never, ever let me fall.

A cheer erupts from our table in the corner of The Crooked Billet as Dave, Jackie and Nanny Door enter the warm, inviting pub. We've all been here for about an hour, chatting, enjoying the atmosphere and anticipation that New Year brings. Ryan is on top form as ever, telling the best jokes, buying bottles of champagne, making everyone feel like this is the only place to be in the world for New Year.

'Hello, my darlin's!' Jackie exclaims and comes over to kiss Ryan, Carl, Lydia and me in turn – and then makes her way round the rest of the gang. She is looking as youthful as ever in a pair of leather trousers and over-the-knee boots. I keep expecting her to slap her thigh and say, 'He's behind you!'

Casey, Alex, Gaz and Jake are all here too, and some of Ryan's friends from school. Even my mum and dad are here. I have no idea what they're going to make of Jackie and Dave in public (they're even bigger and more gregarious than in private). The Coopers are now at the bar, buying champagne for everyone in the pub and clearly preparing to have a brilliant time. They've met before – a few times. Because Jackie has insisted on having them over for Sunday lunch (thankfully Ryan cooked) but we've never managed to get them out like this together before. Ryan has coaxed them along as he always does, with charm and enthusiasm and *that grin*. I know Mum tried her hardest to disapprove of me moving in with my boyfriend but she's always had a soft spot for Ry. Most people do.

I smile as I watch my dad, smoothing over his comb-over with his hand thoughtfully, whilst chatting to Dave. Mum is sitting stiffly beside Dad, sipping on a bitter lemon and occasionally picking bits of invisible fluff off her tweed skirt. I wish she'd just relax.

Just at that moment I notice Jackie slide into the seat next to Mum and hand her a glass of champagne. Mum raises her hand in refusal before it flutters to the cameo brooch on her beige roll-neck jumper. Watching this strange meeting is as fascinating as watching a nature programme. In my head I am commentating like Richard Attenborough observing two creatures:

'The exquisite, rare butterfly flits over to the hanging chrysalis, as if daring it to emerge, showing it the possibilities of what it could be . . .'

'Come on now, Patricia – can I call you Trish?' I hear Jackie say coaxingly. 'Come on Trish, it's New Year's Eve! I insist that you have a little glass of champoo and relax!' She makes herself comfortable next to Mum and crosses her leather-clad legs. She looks amazing for her age. It's hard to believe my mum and her were born in the same year. They may as well be from different decades. Or centuries.

'Now, have I told you about this new thing I'm doing?' Jackie continues chattily. I see my mum shake her head in bemusement; gazing at Jackie her hand floats up to touch her short grey hair, a subtle, subconscious recognition of the difference between her practical cut and Jackie's high-maintenance, layered platinum bob. 'It's called an Ann Summers Party,' Jackie continues with a broad smile that reaches her heavily kohled eyes. Her lip gloss shimmers on her generous lips and I'm sure, if my mum were to look closely enough, she'd see her reflection in the shine. My mum mutters something in response and Jackie laughs.

'I know, Trish darlin'! It *is* a bit weird because I'm not called Ann at all, but apparently I can't call it the Jackie Cooper party!' She leans in and whispers, 'But of course, everyone round here does. They know that no one throws a soiree like JC! You have to come next week, I won't take no for an answer!'

From personal experience I know this to be true. I feel like telling Mum to just say yes and get it over with. JC will always wear you down in the end.

'They're getting on like a house on fire, aren't they! I knew they would,' Ryan murmurs into my ear.

'As long as it doesn't all come crashing down in flames,' I laugh, leaning back against him so his lips nuzzle my neck.

'It won't,' Ryan answers. 'They've already got one brilliant thing in common ...'

'What's that?' I say, looking over at the two diametrically opposed women on the other side of the table.

'Us!' Ryan grins and takes a long sip of champagne.

I turn and smile at my boyfriend, the eternal optimist.

I'm standing at the bar waiting to buy a round and taking photographs of the merry scene. I smile and chat with the friendly locals and feel half enveloped in the warm party atmosphere yet also a little bit removed, like a child's half-unwrapped and discarded Christmas present. My head is doing a filmic rewind of the past year that I have been living here in Leigh and I am seeing nights like this played over and over again. I guess that's what happens when you get everything you wished for.

But we didn't wish for this.

I shake my head. She always pops up and tries to spoil things when I'm happy. Everything is still so wonderful with Ryan and I'm getting to do amazing things at work. Life is good.

Life is predictable, you mean.

Yes, predictable, but good.

I smile at Dave as I pay for the drinks and glance back at the group of people who have become my life. I lift up my new camera again – Ryan bought it for me for Christmas – and I start taking photos of them all. Jackie is sitting on Dave's knee, one arm flung round him, the other is round Gaz, who appears to be serenading her. Casey has the full attention of pretty much every man there. Only Ryan is looking away. And that's because he's looking directly into my lens. At me. He smiles and beckons me over but I pull the camera up and keep on snapping, wanting to capture this scene because it represents everything about my life right now. Comfortable, warm, inviting, easy ...

Predictable.

I freeze, my finger hovering over the button, as it sinks in what those words actually *mean*.

I drop my camera back around my neck and turn again to the bar, feeling my heart pound and constrict with panic, like I'm having some sort of seizure. Suddenly, the noise, the warmth, it is all too suffocating. What am I doing here? Back in the little hometown I swore I'd never return to. Making Sunday lunches for his family and mine. I swore I'd be different. But I've got sucked in too.

'My missus just left me after saying I think about football more than her. I was gutted, I've been with her for five seasons!'

The pub erupts with laughter at Ryan's joke. 'Are you alright, babe, you seem a bit ... distracted.' Ryan curls his arm around my shoulder and I nuzzle in to him.

'I'm fine.' And that's my problem.

'Are you having fun?' he asks. I nod enthusiastically again.

'Fine and fun!' I say and Ryan laughs. I think he thinks I'm drunk. But I'm not. I'm sober as a judge.

We are playing pub games and are now on to 'Who am I?' and all have pieces of paper stuck to our foreheads. I've already guessed that I'm Annie Leibovitz; Ryan chose it for me and it's just made me realize that I am not her. Not anywhere near.

'Am I ... David Beckham?' Ryan guesses after one question and everyone applauds him.

We've spilled outside the pub like an overfilled champagne glass, bubbling with chatter and laughter, huddled in a pool around a picnic table to see in the New Year outside. It was Ryan's idea of course, any opportunity to be in the great outdoors. The cold air is biting my cheeks, the wind off the estuary burning through my layers of clothes. Outside, the black water waits, its mouth yawning hungrily as if it's waiting to swallow up this whole twee little fishing town, with its craft shops, picturesque pubs and fishing boats and cockle sheds and a history that goes right back to the Doomsday Book. A fact that suddenly feels very foreboding.

Ryan and I sit next to each other, his arm thrown territorially around me, squeezing warmth into my being. Scores of people have come over to chat to him, drawn as they are to our raucous group. Old acquaintances, parents from school, football team mates, sailing chums, colleagues; it feels like he knows every single person in this town. Suddenly I desperately want to be with just him for once. Just us. Alone.

Just then another arm is thrown around my shoulder and a head appears between us so I'm sure we appear like a mythical three-headed beast.

'My two fave-or-ite people in the whole entire *wooooorld*!' Casey calls, slurring and giggling as she kisses us both on the cheeks and then throws her head down and squeezes us together. 'I love you guys soooo much!'

'We love you too, Casey,' Ryan rasps. We joke that Casey's our adopted child, often crashing on our sofa after a shift at Players and staying there all day while we go to work. 'Now can you let us breathe? I want to actually live to see in 2003!'

Casey stops squeezing and we both exhale loudly and laugh. She pushes herself up using our shoulders as support and wipes her hand across her mouth. 'Shall we go clubbing after this? I can ge' us all into Players for freee. It'll be fuuuun! We haven't done it for ages an' ages. Me, you two, Alex, Carl and the rest of the boys!'

'Sounds good, Casey!' I glance at my watch. It's ten minutes to midnight and I know better than to say no to Casey when she's like this. I don't want to see in the New Year with a scene.

'Well, I can't stand here all night with you two lovebirds! I've gotta get myself a snog at midnight.' She stabs Ryan's chest with her finger and squints at him. 'I haven't decided which of your mates is going to be the lucky fella!'

'Is there anyone you *haven't* tried?' Ry grins.

Casey winks at me. 'You'd better hope so, Cooper, or I may have to come hunting for you. Then I can have the whole set. You boys can be like those Natwest piggy banks I used to collect when I was a kid.' She furrows her brow. 'Come to think of it, I only got two. I never was any good at keeping hold of money – or men! Ha, ha, ha!' And on that note of self-knowledge she staggers off to round up some other potential clubbers.

'You really want to go clubbing?' Ryan laughs, raising his eyebrow.

''Course not, I just didn't want to tell her that.'

'You're a wise lady, Molly.' He laughs and sighs happily. 'It's great being here with everyone, isn't it, babe?'

'Mmmhmm,' I say, taking a sip of my drink. My phone buzzes in front of me and I open the text. It's from Mia.

HAPPY NEW YEAR, BABE! How about you make 2003 the year of the kangaroo and come visit? Sydney needs you! X

My heart lifts, then immediately sinks as I think of Mia. I can't believe it's been over a year since I've seen her. She's having the time of her life in Australia, she's just been promoted to deputy editor at *Shine*. Suddenly I envy her the liberty of living on the other side of the world. She's free to make whatever decisions she likes, without anyone else's eyes on her. I can barely plump a cushion without Jackie popping over to comment. Everywhere I go I'm surrounded by people who know me, know my relationship and my everyday business. Sometimes it feels like I'm living in a zoo; Ryan is the majestic lion sitting on top of a fake hill, king of the small jungle he surveys, I'm the prowling lioness, pacing up and down in front of the staring public, waiting for an opportunity to ... escape or attack, no one, including me, knows which.

'Can we get away for a moment, Ryan?' I gasp.

'But it's nearly midni—'

'Please?' I beg, and Ryan stands up quickly. I think he notices the desperation in my expression.

'What is it, babe, are you alright?' We've stepped away a little from the crowds, towards the seafront. The sea thrashes tirelessly like a restless baby, the soothing stars hanging above it, like they're dangling from a mobile in the ink-black sky.

'Yes, no, kind of. Ryan, I need to tell you something ...'

'What, babe, what is it?' He has sensed the urgency in my voice and looks petrified. Ryan, for all his wonderful calm qualities, hates unexpected scenes. He panics. Imagines the worst. It's disconcerting, as if expecting something to strike a blow. And now I'm the one wielding the axe.

'It's nothing bad, Ryan, honestly I just, I just ...' God, I have no idea how to say this.

'I just need a break.'

'From me?' Ryan's face droops like wax on a melted candle, his normally sculptured features are suddenly long and drawn.

I grab his head and look deeply into his eyes. 'God, no! Not from you. I *love* you! I'm ridiculously happy with you ... it's just, I need a break from *here*. I feel like we're in a fishbowl. I need to get out, see the world, do something different.'

'But where?' He looks confused, like a toddler who has been told he's stolen a toy from a baby, when he was actually trying to give it to them.

I look at him in excitement as it occurs to me that I know exactly where we should go and what we should do. 'We should go to Australia, like we've always planned! I'm going to be twenty-four this year – twenty-four, Ry! My last year before I have to tick the dreaded 25–34 box! I want us to have fun, enjoy being young while we still can! We only have one chance to have no responsibility. I could take a six-week sabbatical this summer, when you're on summer holidays? We could do Australia, Thailand, just travel around. Just me and you together. I want to be with you always, Ryan, but I don't want it *always* to be this ...' I wave my hand across the panorama of the estuary, the twinkling lights of Leigh Old Town behind us shining like a searchlight through the fog and the tinkling laughter of our family and friends.

Ryan grabs my hands as the countdown begins behind us.

'10!'

'I don't want you to miss out on *anything*, Molly babe,' he says at last.

'9!'

'I'm happy as we are here but ...'

'8!'

'I want you to be happy too.'

'7!'

'I promised you the world and I want to give it to you ...'

'6!'

'Let's go wherever you want ...'

'5!'

'I'll do whatever you want Molly ...'

'4! 3!'

'New year, new life together, OK?'

'2!1!'

'Starting right now!'

I laugh through my tears as he leans in to me, the cheers erupting around like lava around us as he carries me away on his kiss. His lips are pressed powerfully to mine as if they're stamping their intention to change our life, sealing our decision to move away from here. We pull away and see everyone around us hugging and kissing. Casey glances over at us and raises her glass woozily, having pulled away from her chosen victim

And then, like air being sucked into a balloon, we're drawn into the centre of the pub where we all hold hands and start singing 'Auld Lang Syne'. I fight back tears as I take Ryan's and my mother's hands and I look around at the lovely, random mix of people that have become my family. And as we all start replacing words, unable to remember anything other than the 'For Auld Lang Syne' refrain, my mum trips tipsily on her sensible brown loafers into the middle of the group, still clinging on to my dad.

'I know the words!' she barks. And in her sharp mezzo-soprano voice she begins to sing:

> *'We two have run about the slopes and picked the daisies fine;*
> *But we've wandered many a weary foot, since auld lang syne.*
> *We two have paddled in the stream, from morning sun till*
>   *dine;*
> *But seas between us broad have roared since auld lang syne.*
> *And there's a hand my trusty friend! And give us a hand o'*
>   *thine!*
> *A right good-will draught, for auld lang syne.'*

I squeeze Ryan's hand as my mother sings and the fireworks explode in the sky above us, and I know that no matter where I am, I want to be with him forever.

Mia's phone call has given me a renewed sense of purpose. I can't be faffing around any longer. As well as finishing up here, there are a couple of final goodbyes I have to say. My phone rings again and I pick it up quickly.

'Molly!' Mum's voice is sharp but concerned.

'You OK, Mum?'

'Yes, but more importantly, are you?'

'I'm fine.' Pause. '*Honestly.*' I'm used to reassuring people I'm not about to fall to pieces. Clearly I have answered her satisfactorily.

'Good. How are you getting on?' She pauses. 'I hope you're not getting . . . distracted?'

'No!' I protest, lying through my teeth. 'I'm not a kid any more, Mum.'

'Hmm,' she says. I can hear the smile in her voice. 'You may be in your thirties, but I know you well enough to know you haven't changed that much, dear. Anyway, I just wanted to say we'll be there in half an hour or so to do the cleaning.'

'Great!' I reply, but she's gone. I shake my head.

I smile as I listen to Bob and his son, loudly and unabashedly singing along to One Direction on the radio. It instantly reminds me of Ryan. Him and his bloody boy bands, listening to them all the time used to drive me mad. But now? Hearing this music instantly lifts my mood. I smile and start singing along to the chorus as I head upstairs to check the bedroom. My stomach contracts into a tight knot as I see it looking so empty and desolate. I close my eyes, take a deep breath and imagine my shoulders being massaged into a state of utter relaxation, and I'm immediately calmed. I wander over to the fireplace and run my fingers along the mantelpiece. This is the one I painstakingly exposed after the previous owners had inexplicably built around it. It's dusty and bare, the fairylights all packed away, and the logs that I had twined them around are now out in the garden. I frown and stare as I spot something shimmering just behind the grate. I bend down slowly and pick up the shell, turning it over in my hand, feeling its edges and grooves. It is small and not particularly beautiful, but it was once the most precious thing to me in the whole wide world. I sit cross-legged on the floor and study it for a moment. The shell fits perfectly in the centre of my hand, its pale coral colour glinting a little in the sunlight that has just unexpectedly burst through the bay window, the lines on my palm carrying it like the waves that brought it to shore. Funny, I thought I'd packed it away years ago . . .

The Real First Kiss ...

... and the last.

'Look who I found,' I say, purposefully dripping water over Mia and Casey who appear to be asleep.

'Not Pizza Face from last night?' Casey opens one eye and then sits bolt upright. 'Oh hel—'

'*Lo* . . .' finishes Mia, as she peers out from under her sunhat and sits up slowly. 'Who's this . . .?'

'Ryan!' squeals Casey, and she jumps up and envelops him in a rather overzealous hug given she's naked from the waist up. She quickly whips her long black ponytail over her bare back like Angelina Jolie in *Tomb Raider.* I suppress a smile as Ryan glances at me with a panicked expression. It's nice to see Mr Confident suddenly lose his swagger.

'Fancy seeing you here!' she cries, putting her hands on her hips and posing like a *Playboy* model. 'Is Alex here too? Oh my GAWWD, I can't believe it! This is proper crazy! Half of Leigh is in I*beeefa*! So when did you come? When are you leaving? Where are you staying?' She throws questions at Ryan like frisbees, not pausing to let him answer.

I eye her up suspiciously as she continues to talk. I'm still not convinced that Casey didn't orchestrate this whole 'accidental meeting'. Although I do recall this holiday was my suggestion but perhaps she brainwashed me. I smile at the thought. Casey, capable of a clever, planned deception? Never.

'How you doing, Case?' Ryan coughs, averting his eyes from her body. 'I ain't seen you around for ages and now I seem to be seeing a lot of you . . .'

I pick up her discarded yellow bikini-top and thrust it at her as Ryan smiles gratefully at me.

'Yeah, well, your best mate dumped me, I ain't exactly felt like coming round your place for tea,' she says, as I thread it over her arms, and then she turns and brazenly asks him to do her up as Mia and I make WTF faces. I'm used to Casey's lack of decorum but this is ridiculous.

'No, you were too busy with your *next* boyfriend,' I interject. I don't want Ryan going back and giving his mate some big ego trip about how she's still in love with him. I know what blokes are like.

'How are you anyway, babe? I haven't seen you around Leigh much.'

Was she looking?

'I've been busy studying,' Ryan smiles.

'Oh, not another one,' she rolls her eyes good-humouredly. 'You're just too clever for your own good. Is *he* here?' Ryan and I look at each other warily. Presumably she means Alex. 'Does he know I'm here?' Casey asks, not even attempting to be blasé.

'Yep, he's here,' Ryan says uncertainly, his eyes flickering back to mine. 'We all are actually. My brother Carl, Gaz and a couple of other guys,' Ryan replies, shading his eyes from the sun so he can try to spot his mates further down the beach. 'They're all over there somewhere. They probably think I've abandoned 'em.'

'Or pulled,' I offer sweetly. 'Surely that's the most likely when one of you disappears. Don't you have a code for that sort of thing? Or a chart? No, wait, I've got it! Score cards. That's what most guys have in Ibiza, don't they?'

Ryan raises a thick eyebrow at me and shakes his head. 'You are way too cynical for your own good. HEY! LADS!' he cups his mouth with his hands and waves to them, which makes his stomach contract and curved dents like wishbones appear on his torso.

Mia, Casey and I can't help but giggle as we see the lads in the distance clock that their mate is with a group of girls. They scramble up off the sand really quickly, before trying to strut over as nonchalantly as they can. Unfortunately, in their haste to get to us before each other, they end up looking more like The Monkees.

'Alright Ryan, what have we got here?' Alex breaks away from the group, his long legs and pure determination making him get to us first. His sentence – and his broad smile – trails off as he takes in a grinning, scantily clad Casey who is pouting provocatively at them all. She squints at him into the sunlight and juts out her bikini-clad hip as she suggestively puts one hand on it.

'Hiya, Alex, I'm so glad you're here,' she says. I'm sure she doesn't intend to sound stalkerish but somehow she does. I notice Alex giving Ryan an alarmed look and Ryan quickly intervenes.

'Alrigh' lads,' he pipes up, gesturing them into the conversation, 'I just bumped into some old friends. Alex, obviously you already know Casey, but do you remember her best mate, Molly?' Alex grins at me and then punches Ryan on the shoulder.

'Ryan Shit Snog Cooper!' chorus the boys and they fall about laughing.

I see that Ryan's tanned face has turned an interesting shade of lobster. And it's not sunburn. I find it surprisingly sweet.

'I suppose that's usually Ryan's trick, eh – the hit-*on* and run?' I say drolly, and Alex laughs and throws his arm around Ryan's neck, before rubbing his knuckles on his head.

'She's got you there, mate,' he laughs, and Ryan and I join in. I glance up at Alex. He looks just as I remember, devilishly good-looking, if you like that sort of thing, which Casey clearly does. Gaz turns to Mia, who is sitting on her beach towel, sunhat tilted over one eye, make-up perfectly applied and looking for all the world like she's modelling for an upmarket beach catalogue.

'And what's your name?' Gaz asks chirpily, bouncing down on his knees so his brightly coloured board shorts are at her eye level.

She looks up imperiously under the rim of her hat and then looks away as if she just can't be bothered to answer. I can't *think* why men have called her 'aloof' before.

'It's Mia,' I answer for her, nudging her with my foot and giving her a 'be nice' face. Which is rich coming from me. I don't know why but I actually like these boys; they seem sweet.

'Mia LIKE-A!' Gaz says with a guffaw. Mia looks at me, looks at him, then rolls her eyes and rolls onto her front gracefully, resting her cheek on her hands, in the opposite direction. Gaz walks round to the other side and continues to bamboozle her with chatter.

Carl steps forward next and lifts his hand in a laid-back salute. 'I'm Carl, Ryan's bigger, better-looking, more successful brother.'

Ryan looks at me, looks at Carl, and then rugby tackles him into the sand. At which point, Carl, who is a foot taller and at least a stone heavier than Ryan, lifts him cleanly over his shoulder, runs down to the shore and throws him into the sea.

We all crack up laughing.

'Hey,' Carl grins when he returns with Ryan close behind. 'Where are you girls going tonight? Do you fancy all meeting up at a bar later?'

'Well, we've got plans for a quiet dinner actually . . .' I begin but I'm drowned out.

'We'd love to!' Casey pulls my ear to her mouth and whispers, 'We didn't come here to have quiet dinners!' and she raises her eyebrow suggestively.

'Mia?' I ask, not wanting to agree to anything on the girls' holi-day without everyone's consent.

She slowly looks at each of the boys in turn from under the rim of her hat, taking her time to slowly and unashamedly appraise them. Then she lies back down slowly. 'If we must.'

'Looks like I'm outvoted,' I laugh. Ryan smiles at me and as the sun beams down on us, suddenly it feels like all my summers have come at once.

It's the last night of our holiday and Casey, Mia and I are sitting in the Café del Mar, gazing contentedly across the beach at the horizon beyond. The sun is a ball of burning amber high up in the sky – we got here early and managed to get a table so we can enjoy the sun setting on our last day. We've had a brilliant week. Ryan and his mates are the only people we've hung around with since I bumped into him on my lilo. It's become our nightly ritual to meet up with them. And clearly bored of Spanish men, Casey soon turned her attentions to someone closer to home – Carl. He resisted for a while, but like most men, the offer of a no-strings night with a girl like Casey was just too hard to turn down. Not that she believed it was that. She even said we could end up being sisters-in-law.

'Wouldn't that be amazing, Molly?' She'd giggled one night in the hotel room after we'd spent the evening with them all. 'Imagine us married to the Cooper boys! We'd have the same surname – Casey Cooper does kind of have a ring to it, dontcha think?'

I didn't like to point out that Carl has avoided her all day and Ryan hadn't actually even made a move on me. I don't know why. I mean, it's not like there haven't been opportunities. I'm beginning to wonder if he's been playing me all week. Or if he's interested in someone else entirely. I make this point to Casey and she swivels her head towards me.

'Do you think? Well, I guess it's possible, I mean, Ibiza is full of pretty girls, but I presumed . . .' Her sentence tails off, I'm not sure if she's just lost interest in the subject, or she doesn't want to hurt my feelings.

'I can't believe it's our last night,' Mia says, lifting her margarita glass to her lips and taking a long sip. She looks beautiful in white jeans and a barely-there, bright-pink handkerchief top with little mirrored sequins sewn on that shows off her newly acquired belly-button piercing, which Casey convinced her to get done. After a rocky start, by approximately day three Mia and Casey had called a cease-fire on their snarking at each other and had bonded over their mutual desire for male attention. They were the wild girls and

I was the prude who cramped their style. I didn't mind. At least it meant they were getting on.

'Back to reality soon,' Casey sighs.

'Not for Mia,' I say enviously. 'She's about to jet across the world.'

Mia smiles at me. 'I've said you could always come with me.'

I think back regretfully to the grand plans we made whilst at uni. Our Life Lists. Our plans to travel the world together, to live in Sydney . . . but I realize it was just a pipe dream. When push comes to shove, I'm not the rebel who'll take a risk. When I told Mia that I wouldn't be coming, she was gutted. But it didn't change her mind about going as I suppose I'd hoped it would. I'm going to miss her beyond belief. I can't imagine living in London without her, but I know she's made the right decision. I'm just not sure if I have. Too late now though.

I smile sadly. 'You know I'd love to, but I've got the Holy Grail for a student with debts to pay off – an actual *job*! I'd be crazy to turn it down.'

'Yeah well,' Casey says defensively as if trying to compete with our circumstances. 'You can keep your fancy Australia travels, I don't reckon anywhere is better than Leigh-on-Sea anyway. I won't ever leave.'

And the sad thing is I know she won't, but not because she doesn't want to, because she's too scared. I'm just determined that the same doesn't happen to me.

I spot the boys walking towards us. Casey flaps manically at them and Mia raises a perfectly manicured hand. I take a sharp intake of breath as I see Ryan walking towards me. He's wearing a white shirt with the last couple of buttons left undone above his belt. The breeze lifts and parts the shirt slightly to reveal a hint of bronzed stomach. I gulp.

'Alright Princess,' Gaz says, giving Mia a wink as he slides into a seat next to her and plants a kiss on her neck. Mia rolls her eyes, but kisses him back anyway. They got togehter on the first night we went out. He looks around the table. 'You all look *blinding*.'

'Thanks Gaz,' I smile as I look at the rest of the guys, avoiding eye contact with Ryan as I know I'll blush, but he leans over anyway and I feel the hairs prickle on my neck as he comes closer.

'He's right, you really do,' he whispers. I don't want to tell him that I've taken extra special care over my appearance. My long, yellow silk sundress slides over my body perfectly, the delicate straps showing off my tanned shoulders, and my hair has turned golden in the sun. For the first time I feel beautiful and I know that's down to Ryan. The frisson between us has been building all week but neither one of us has made a move. There have been meaningful looks and hands brushing as we walk, but nothing else. I don't know if it's our past history stopping us, or circumstance, but it's like we're scared of what might happen if we do actually kiss again. It could either be amazing – or awful, and neither of us seems to be willing to take that chance. I don't know about him, but from the moment I met Ryan he got under my skin in a way I never thought possible. Seeing him here and spending the last week with him has only made it worse. He makes me feel sick with excitement and sick with uncertainty. A big part of me wants to run as far away as I can because I'm not ready to find him. I'm only just beginning my life plan. But at the same time I'm utterly paralysed by him. When I'm with him I can't imagine wanting anything other than him, forever.

When the sun finally disappears and the sky turns a deep purple, Ryan leans in towards me.

'Do you fancy going for a walk?' he whispers. Everyone else is still facing the horizon, drinking and chatting and enjoying the ambience. I smile and nod as he takes my hand under the table. Only Casey turns and spots us. She raises her eyebrow at me and

I cock my head and shrug, biting my lip and smiling to show my nerves and pleasure before turning our backs on them.

'I want to take you to this little place I found, a beach that isn't as hectic as here,' Ryan says, still holding my hand. 'It's about a fifteen-minute walk away, is that OK?'

I nod. At this point in time I feel like if he said it'd take fifteen days, I'd walk it with him.

'What a crazy week it's been, eh,' he laughs as we stroll comfortably alongside each other. Well, comfortably apart from the ringing in my ears, the pounding of my heart, the shaking of my hands and legs. Other than that, I'm completely relaxed in his presence. 'I still can't believe I bumped into you on that lilo.'

He turns to face me. I don't know what to say, all knowledge of words and speech seems to have disappeared. The balmy island air – and perhaps something else – wraps us in what feels like an impenetrable bubble of heat. We finally arrive at a tranquil little bay, nestled into the craggy cliffs that couldn't be more different to the bustling hubbub of Calo des Moro.

'Are we here?' I say, looking around in delight.

Ryan nods. 'This is called Cala Gracio,' he replies. 'It's one of a pair of bays that I found when I was windsurfing today. The other one's just round there.'

'What are you waiting for, slowcoach!' I duck under his arms and run across the beach towards the shoreline, squealing as he chases me. Just as I reach the edge of the glistening, moon-kissed water, I turn and he lifts me clean off my feet and into his arms and gazes up at me, his blue eyes fixed determinedly on mine. He slides me back down through his arms so my feet are back on solid ground, but I still feel like I am floating.

He bends down suddenly and picks something up. He opens my hand and places it in my palm.

'This is the first precious thing I'm going to give you,' Ryan says solemnly. 'I promise it won't be the last.'

I look at the beautifully fragile shell shimmering in my hand and close my fingers around it. Then he wraps his arms around me. He pulls away and I open my eyes. He strokes my cheek, his fingers softly tracing my jawline and he leads me along the shore of the bay, clambering over rocks together, our feet leaving footprints that glisten like diamonds until we get to a second, smaller bay. There's no one here.

'I'm going to kiss you now, Molly Carter,' he says. And as his soft, warm lips melt into mine, his tongue flickering gently like the waves that lap melodically at my feet, I feel like the world has stopped turning and that it is we who are swirling around and around, totally at one with each other and the sea that encompasses us. I feel like I am drowning but I'm not scared.

I'm sitting in the kitchen, silently turning the shell over and over in my hand. I look at it, then over at the TV that is still paused on the final frame of the DVD. I fold my hand around the shell, go into the lounge and eject the film from the player. I unplug it all so Bob can put it in the remaining box, marked 'Storage'. I go to put the DVD back in its box then take it into the kitchen, where my laptop still sits. I slide it in the hard drive. I know I should pack this away now, it's getting close to that time but I think I just need one more little fix. Then I'll be done. I'm about to press play when the doorbell rings and I jump guiltily. Mum. Gazing wildly around, I realize that the place is actually looking pretty sorted and it's with some relief that I head to the front door. Thirty-three and that woman can still make me feel thirteen. That's power.

A small, grinning, bright-eyed woman is beaming up at me.

'Nanny Door!' I exclaim joyously, and I throw my arms around her before helping her over the front step. 'What are you doing here? I was coming over to see you later. I wanted to have a last cup of tea at your place, for old times' sake.'

'Well, I thought *you* could make a brew for a change, doll!' Nanny smiles cheekily, slipping off her fur coat and matching hat. Her bright blue eyes are undiminished even though her body is shrinking and her hearing not quite as good as it used to be. 'Besides, I had something I wanted to bring you.'

I frown at her. 'Not another gift, Nanny, you've already given me something. I'm really looking forward to watching *Big Brother: The best bits* DVD on my laptop on the plane.'

'Ooh yeah, you'll have a right giggle at that,' she says, shuffling into the kitchen. I follow her and pop the kettle on as she sits at the Formica table.

'Oof, legs are bloody useless these days,' she says, rubbing her calf muscles.

'Well, if you will insist on wearing killer heels, Nanny,' I smile, glancing at her pink court shoes. 'Tamara Mellon has got nothing on you.'

'Tamara's Mellons?'

'No, Nanny,' I laugh. 'Tamara Mellon. She's like the brand ambassador for Jimmy Choo.'

'Jimmy Who?'

'Never mind!' I busy myself making the tea.

'Anyway, doll, as I was saying, I wanted to give you something. Lydia told me what you did earlier . . .'

I swing around quickly, suddenly horrified that I may have upset or offended her. 'Oh, Nanny Door, I hope you didn't mind too much? You know how precious that ring is to me, but giving it to Lydia felt like, well it felt the right thing to do.' I sit down next to her, putting the two cups of tea in front of us. I have lost count of how many I've drunk today.

She pats my hand, her eyes watering slightly. 'Molly, I understand, 'course I do. But I also know how hard that must have been for you. That's why I wanted to give this to you instead.' She pulls out a blue velvet box and slides it over the table towards me.

'What is it?'

'Open it and find out,' she smiles.

I open the box slowly. Inside is a silver St Christopher, slightly tarnished with age but otherwise in perfect condition. I look up at her quizzically, tears prickling my eyes already.

'It was given to me by my grandmother when I was a very little girl,' Nanny says. 'St Christopher is the patron saint of travel . . .' She pauses and grips my hand. 'I know you already have someone looking after you, well, two people actually . . . lucky girl.' I smile and swipe away a tear. 'But I wanted you to know that I'll always be thinking of you, OK, swee'dheart?' I nod, unable to speak. 'Now,' she continues, 'I'm an old bird so I have to think about these things rationally. I may not see you again in my lifetime, Molly dear. But if you keep this close by you'll know that I'll always be looking down on you, too.'

I can't speak so I throw my arms around her and sob. After everything that happened I struggled to maintain my relationship with most of his direct family. It was just too hard. Nanny Door was the one I couldn't bear to let go of. Our relationship is even stronger now, five years later, than it was then and this goodbye is the one I've really been dreading.

We're interrupted by Bob who pokes his head into the kitchen. 'We need to do in here next, luv, then we're all done, awight?'

Nanny Door pulls a raggedy tissue out of her bag and dabs my eyes and smiles at me reassuringly.

'Yes, of course, guys!' I say. 'Don't mind us!'

I look at Nanny Door, who is pulling herself to her feet. I stand up too and she slips her arm around me and squeezes me as we walk towards the front door. She pulls on her coat and looks up at me. 'Now, no more tears. We've had more than enough of those for one lifetime.' She smiles brightly and puts her hand on my cheek. 'You deserve endless happiness, dear Molly.' And with that, she shuffles out the door.

The After The Honeymoon Kiss

It was only after Ryan left that I realized how much of my life was inextricably linked to him. I'm not just talking about the pictures and possessions in our home, you know, the CD and DVD collections, but places too. Our local pub, The Crooked Billet and our favourite Thai restaurant on The Broadway all had signs that said 'us' when now it was only 'me'. Then there was 'our bench' on The Green where we'd shared many a kiss, Rossi's in Southend where we'd had our first date. Even Hadleigh Castle, the place that had soothed my troubled self as a teen, was no longer an option to comfort my broken heart. Then there were the friends we shared who no longer knew how to be a friend to just one of us. Our families. For a long time I clung to everything and everyone I possibly could – no matter how uncomfortable it made me or them. I'd cradle a glass of wine for hours at 'our table' in the pub ignoring the pitying glances thrown my way. When I wasn't round their house I'd phone Ryan's mum and wail about how much I still loved him, angrily thrashing out at her because he'd left me. I clung on to it all because I was so scared of what would be left if I let go. But gradually, with time, it became easier to pack away everything to do with Ryan in boxes marked 'the past'. And in the end there were only two things I couldn't let go of. Nanny Door and 'our film'. I know one day I'll have to say goodbye to them both. Just not yet. I'm not ready yet.

'*Viva* magazine,' I answer the phone robotically, zoning out as the PR on the other end of the line begins to talk. It's fair to say that I haven't been as . . . *focused* on my job since Ryan and I returned from our incredible honeymoon. I gaze at the photo that's taken pride of place on my desk since we came back six months ago. It's of Ryan and me lying on the Franz Josef glacier on New Zealand's South Island. We're wrapped up like Michelin men in our snow clothes, pink cheeks pressed against each other, our eyes glistening like the ancient ice formation we are lying on, having just explored the spectacular caves and pinnacles of the icefall terrain.

We expected that with all his climbing experience and general athletic tendencies, Ryan would show me up, but in fact he'd spent half the time on his arse. He was tired after all the skiing he'd done in Queenstown whilst I was lazing about in the spa, but it didn't stop me ribbing him. 'Is it possible to get a marriage refund?' I'd laughed, after he'd slid over in front of me for the seventh time. 'I thought I was marrying a young, fit, sporty man, not this uncoordinated shambles in front of me!'

'It's because I'm still hung-over after all that wine tasting you made me do the other day!' Ryan had spluttered, using my legs to pull himself up again on his snow spikes. 'I'm not used to it . . .'

'Excuses, excuses,' I'd said as I'd gone to help him up, but he'd pulled me down instead and we'd lain there, with our arms round each other laughing while I took one of our favourite holdy-out pictures.

Our honeymoon was the perfect balance of us both. It had all the exhilaration that Ryan required; we'd scaled glaciers, flown in helicopters and kayaked across lakes. We'd been on adrenaline-bursting hikes and seen spectacular lakes and national parks surrounded by vistas almost too beautiful to contemplate. We did a skydive in Wanaka, something that had never been on my Life List but Ryan told me it was no scarier than falling in love, you just had to surrender your trust to someone else and to the elements. He was right. I'm so glad I did it. He makes me do things I never dreamed I would.

But we'd also snuggled up in cosy, snow lodges where I could indulge myself in the spa, gone on wine-tasting trips where Ryan discovered that, actually, he did like wine after all (but only white) and whale-watched and stargazed to our hearts' content. We spent four blissful weeks travelling around the North and South Island together in a 4X4, sharing the driving and control of the iPod, his fingers tapping on the wheel as he played his current favourite pop tunes by Maroon 5 and Keane. Then I'd take the wheel, cruising through the beautiful landscape whilst listening to my favourite tunes; 'Wrist-slitters' Ryan calls them.

It had been wonderful, exhausting, but wonderful. Now it's back to reality. Both of us are working hard and it's taking its toll, especially on Ryan. For the last few months he's got up late and dragged his feet on his way out the door in the mornings – he can't even face going to the gym. He's put on weight around his stomach. We jokingly call it his 'marriage spread'.

'It's because you're so happy,' I tell him to cheer him up. 'And I love it – there's more for me to get my hands on!'

Last night he'd come in from school late and tired. He'd thrown his sports bag on the sofa and then himself, and hadn't even smiled when I told him I'd made pasta. Not that I could blame him. My version of 'made' wasn't the plate of fresh ravioli stuffed with split broad beans, mozzarella and hint of lemon that would have been lovingly prepared by Ryan. No, this was overcooked fusilli with a can of tuna and a jar of Dolmio. It was disgusting and even I'd chosen to focus on finishing my large glass of Sauvignon, rather than eat it. Ryan had left most of his too. He'd sighed and put his tray of uneaten food on the floor.

'Hey, something wrong with the room service, Cooper?' I'd said jokingly. 'Or are you just trying to lose weight?'

He'd glanced at me and smiled, but it was like someone had dimmed his 40-watt.

'Nah,' he'd sighed. 'Just another tough day at work.'

I'd rubbed his shoulders. 'Hey, you're putting too much pressure on yourself, Ry. You need to just switch off sometimes. I mean, most of these kids need better parents, not better football skills. There's only so much you can do.'

He flinches slightly, as if my words *and* touch are painful. He really is tense.

'You know I don't just teach them football, I'm trying to prepare them for life, make them see that there's more out there than they give themselves credit for. It's because they have such shit backgrounds that I can't switch off. I have to stop them from getting in trouble, inspire them to keep focused on their exams as much as their sport, but all the time I'm trying to balance fucking Ofsted reports and shitloads of paperwork that stop me from doing the bit about my job I really love.' He exhales slowly and closes his eyes as I continue to massage him. 'Then there's the inter-schools football league. The Year Nines and Tens need to get a load of extra practices in if we have a chance of making it through to the finals. They've never even made it through preliminary rounds before so I'm determined for them to see how far they can go.'

'Just be careful, Ry,' I say, finishing up the massage. 'I don't want you making yourself ill.'

'Hey, babe,' Ryan smiled weakly and squeezed my hand. 'I'm the fittest guy you know . . .' Then he'd picked up the remote control, flicking through the channels as quickly as ever as he heaved more coursework onto his lap. Even when he's relaxed he's still moving.

I touched him on the arm gently. 'Ryan, please. I can see you're knackered. Just stop, have a rest for a minute.' I sat back next to him and stroked his hair. He'd flinched and then relaxed, a smile fanning briefly over his face.

'Sorry, Moll, you're right,' and he'd put the papers on the floor and snuggled up for a cuddle, resting his head on my lap. Five minutes later he was snoring peacefully, leaving me to watch *Holby City* alone.

I sit up as an email pops up from Christie asking me to come into her office. I extricate myself from the conversation with the PR mid-pitch and stand up, realizing that I haven't thought of any cover lines yet and Christie probably wants to brainstorm with me before the official meeting in an hour. It's the bit I most dislike about my Associate Editor position. When I was Picture Director, I knew it was something I was really good at. Now it's all budgets, staffing problems, advertising meetings. With this promotion I've taken another step further away from photography. I mentally flick through the April features and the fashion and beauty sections as I walk towards her office, trying to come up with original ideas. A Spring Fling for main fashion? Rubbish. What about beauty . . . let's see, 'Take the passé out of pastel'? Argh.

I walk dejectedly, trying to pick up my feet and my enthusiasm for my job.

'Hi Molly,' Christie smiles and puts down her pen as soon as I walk into her office. I love how she does this, always giving you her full attention no matter what other urgent things she has going on. 'How are things? Are you happy with everything?' she presses.

'Errr . . . yes?' I lie, not sure what else I'm meant to say. I may have talked about jacking it in to Ry, but I don't actually want to be given the boot. I'm starting to panic now. Maybe I have misread the situation. My enthusiasm in my work has slipped recently, maybe she's noticed.

'Hmm.' She taps her pen on her desk and picks up her Pret

coffee. 'I've just been getting the sense that your new role isn't quite as good a fit as we'd hoped.'

'Well ...' I start fiddling with my fingers awkwardly, wondering how I can retrieve this. 'I admit there are bits I find challenging and ...'

'... boring?' Christie offers. She doesn't look annoyed, just interested. I decide to be honest.

I pull a face like a teenager being asked a difficult question in maths class. 'Not boring Christie, just not in my comfort zone.'

She nods. 'I thought so. That's why I've had an idea. She turns to face me. 'I'd like you to do a blog, a photographic blog,' she clarifies. 'I know you love photography, Molly, and I've seen some of your shots. You're stylish, creative and you know *Viva*'s readers better than most. I want people to want to look at your blog to find an interesting or thought-provoking or funny moment beautifully captured. There doesn't have to be any words – perhaps just a caption.' She is thinking on her feet now, waving her hands around like she does in meetings when ideas come to her. 'Or perhaps some might need more? I'll leave it up to you. But what do you think?'

I smile, feeling butterflies at the prospect of being paid to take interesting photos every day that hundreds – or even thousands – of people might see online.

I'm now exploding with excitement. 'Oh my God, Christie, that would be amazing! And I've already got lots of ideas that would transfer really well to something like this.' I dash out of her office and over to my desk, where my camera is languishing in the drawer.

I burst back into Christie's office and flick through the images digitally, showing her all the little moments I capture every single day. My focus is on people, it always has been, either alone or with friends, family, lovers, children. I love seeing the nuances of relationships framed in my camera, peeling back the façades and seeing the truth of the emotion through the viewfinder.

*

I walk out of the office into the dark evening, feeling a new thrill as my camera bangs against my chest, overawed by the possibilities of what I might be able to capture on my journey home. I rustle inside my handbag for my mobile and see that there is a missed call and two text messages from Ryan; one telling me he'll be late again, the other telling me that the boiler is broken. Not even this dispels my good mood. I text him back quickly when I feel a tap on my shoulder.

'Casey – hi!' I say in surprise, barely recognizing her in her chic work get-up. She looks more beautiful than ever these days. Her black hair has grown past her shoulders, is free of highlights and bad extensions and has the glossy shine of a hair ad. Her skin is pure Greek Glow, no tanning products – Casey says she can't afford them now she's an intern and besides, she prefers her new natural look. The fake nails and cheap, attention-seeking clothes have gone too, and in their place she's wearing a sleek, burgundy wrap dress and stacked court shoes with minimal gold jewellery. The only flaw in her appearance is the scar under her eye. But even that looks tragically beautiful, like a single teardrop falling from her lashes and a constant reminder to me of her vulnerability. I gawp at her for a moment before giving her a hug. 'You look amazing, Case. How's work?'

'Good – so good, Molly!' she says, her eyes shining brighter than I have seen them for months. She's getting her life back on track. She has barely been home to Essex, let alone the club, since the attack happened. She said to us that it felt like the town had turned on her that night as much as those girls did, and that London is the only place she wants to be now. So we sat down one night, shortly after we got back from honeymoon and brainstormed ideas of what she could do. I made a list of all her strengths – you can solve everything with a list – and then we went online and she did a career personality test. There were several options that fitted her personality type – but the one that stood out the most was Public Relations.

I'd slammed my hand on our coffee table and made the scented candle flicker and the wine jump in my glass. 'That's PERFECT, Case, I have loads of contacts in the PR world; I know I can get you in somewhere!'

'You think?' Casey had said, her old smile coming back and lighting up her face. 'For real? That would be awesome, Molly!' And then she'd thrown her arms around both Ryan and I and squeezed us till we could barely breathe.

Weirdly, she hadn't seemed quite as enthusiastic after I'd listed all the companies I wanted her to email and gave her the task of doing her CV. In the end I'd composed the email for her. And managed to fudge her CV so that her extensive skill-set that I'd listed hid her lack of experience.

A week later she'd been offered a two-month placement at a well-known fashion and lifestyle PR firm called Myriad Communications.

'I'm seriously loving it, I mean I really honestly think that this could be a job that I could actually do, no not a job – a *career*. An actual career, Molly! And I think I could do it really well! I mean, if they actually give me a job that is, which they might not, but oh my God, could you imagine if they did? It would be totes amazing.'

'Brilliant, Case, I'm so happy for you,' I say linking her arm as we walk down Long Acre.

'Well, it's thanks to you, Moll,' she says, 'it was your idea and your contacts that got me the work experience at Myriad. Honestly, what would I do without you?' she jokes. 'First you let me stay at your flat, then you set me up with a new career.' She'd smiled. 'The only thing left to do on the list is find me a husband.'

'I'll lend you mine, if you like,' I laugh.

Casey gasps dramatically, her chic dark nails covering her carefully glossed lips. 'Why, what's he *done*?'

'Oh, nothing, just not bothered to call the plumber when our boiler broke this morning! Usual wifely moans.' I smile to show her that I'm joking really. 'If he'd just write a list like I keep telling him to, you know?'

'Nope,' Casey replies cheerfully. '*I've* never had a boyfriend last longer than a couple of months, remember? *I* can barely get them to have breakfast with me, let alone cook my dinner and look at my plumbing – no pun intended. To be honest, I think you should count yourself lucky, Moll. Most girls would do anything to have a husband like Ryan – including me.'

'You're right. Now, let me just try and find an emergency plumber so we don't freeze in the flat tonight ...'

I quickly phone one, agree to the hideous call-out charge and hourly rate, and then send a quick text to Ryan:

Boiler all sorted x.

Team work. That's what it's all about.

I link Casey's arm again companionably and we head for home.

The Kiss And Run

If I could choose where to kiss Ryan now I would make us run back, back to where he wanted to be instead of where I was forever reaching for. We would run back, not stopping for breath until we got there. To the place that always made him happy. The place we should have stayed. And when I kissed him I'd never have stopped. Maybe then none of this would have happened.

'Awww, Moll, do you really have to go?' Ryan tugs at my sleeve and my heartstrings as he leans in the doorframe of our lounge, wearing nothing but a pair of Diesel jeans and clutching a glass of fresh goji berry juice (his latest health fad). He watches me check my Things I Need for the Airport List, empty my hand luggage to make sure I have them all, and then check my separate Work Trip List, rifling through my suitcases to ensure everything is there. I check my handbag for my passport for the seventy-seventh time and glance up to see his lips protruding in a petulant pout, his new spiky hair making him look leaner, more chiselled and tougher than usual. God, I wish we had time for a last little goodbye. Three weeks is a long time without him. Perhaps it is the strain of work over the past few months showing in his face, or maybe it's because he's hurtling towards his thirtieth birthday, but Ryan no longer has that softness around his cheeks and general air of everlasting youth. His eyes have dark trenches which makes him look more rugged. And even hotter than ever. Maybe I could call the airline and tell them to hold the plane on the runway while I indulge in some pre-flight entertainment.

They do say that men age better than women, but as I glance in our hallway mirror I'm not too disappointed with how I've shaped up either. I know I look pretty good in my 'airport outfit' of skinny indigo jeans, vintage black cowboy boots, a slim-fitting, white T-shirt, big Louis Vuitton scarf (a press perk) and these cool 1980s Ray-Ban Wayfarers I picked up in Camden. I've perfected my make-up: pink blush, clear lip gloss and minimal mascara. My hair has found its best style after I had it cut into a sharp bob with a fringe when we got back from honeymoon. I was done with being 'long-haired bride'. I lift my handbag up on my shoulder and pull my camera over my neck so it rests on my scarf. It has pretty much permanently lived around my neck since I started the blog on the relaunched Vivamag.co.uk. I still can't believe what a success it's been. I've even been featured as a 'blogger about town' in one of the weekend supplements. It's been completely bizarre, but wonderful. It has meant Ryan and I have got to do some amazing things together as well as apart, with press trips thrown at me by PRs who want me to take cool, interesting pictures and then credit their hotels or resorts. We've stayed in a luxury Bedouin tent in Marrakesh as part of my 'Market Life' series. The pictures I took of the amazingly colourful markets that we spent a happy weekend meandering around worked brilliantly juxtaposed alongside the London shots. Like the one I took of foodies selling at Borough Market and the characters selling blooms at the bustling, vibrant Columbia Road flower market. We've stayed in gorgeous boutique hotels in Venice, San Francisco and Prague because I had an idea to do a series of photos capturing couples kissing on famous bridges. One of my favourites was a blog called 'High on Love' which featured a series of rooftop scenes which gave me a chance to shoot London in all its glory, from lots of amazing viewpoints. Ryan and I got to take a private pod in the London Eye which was incredible. I set up the camera on my tripod and took a portrait of us, with our backs to the camera, looking down at the sparkling, moonlit London skyline. It was utterly magical.

I feel like the luckiest girl in the world now that Ryan and I are living the life I always wanted us to. Of course, we can't do everything in tandem. And I'm about to jet off to New York for three weeks too, as the editor of *Viva* New York has invited me to do a series of blogs based over there, featuring as a photo spread in their April issue. Christie thought it would be great exposure for the blog and guarantee us even more unique visitors – which so far seems to translate into more readers for the magazine. Things couldn't be going better. Obviously it's not ideal having to leave Ryan for three weeks but he can't be away from school for that length of time.

'I just don't understand why you have to go for so long,' he says, rubbing his hand over his chest.

I sigh and put my bag down and twine one arm around his waist, putting the other on his chest, just over his moles. He tucks his head into my neck and I kiss his hair. It tastes of the great outdoors, and pomade.

'I promise it will fly by,' I say softly now, as much to myself as to him.

'Don't leave me with her,' he looks at me pleadingly. 'She'll do my head in.'

Casey is currently spread-eagled on the sofa, eating toast and watching a recorded episode of *Heroes* – a show both she and Ryan love – in our lounge, which has become her makeshift bedroom.

'You'll be so busy with mock exams that you'll barely miss me.'

Ryan smiles and his eyes flicker over to the TV.

'Hey, over here, Cooper!' I say, and pull his chin back so his blue eyes meet mine. He looks tired. I kiss him long and hard on the lips, flicking my tongue in gently for good measure. He pulls away as we hear the beep of my account car outside.

'I've got to go, Ry,' I say, stepping closer because I don't want to leave him. He kisses me again, but this time I pull away. 'Be good!' I say and I blow him a kiss, pick up my bags and run out of the door. 'I'll ring you from JFK!' I call over my shoulder as I slam the door behind me, run across to the car with my camera beating against my chest like a second heartbeat.

'Heathrow please!' I say brightly and as the cabbie pulls out onto Kingsland Road. I immediately clamber around in my hand luggage, pulling out my book, my flight details, hairbrush, iPod, mobile, until I finally pull my passport out. It is only then that I remember to look out the back window at my flat and I see the distant shadow of Ryan's face with one hand raised and I wave furiously. But I don't know if he can see me any more.

I quickly text him. Only capital letters and hundreds of kisses will do.

I LOVE YOU SO MUCH xxxxxxxxxxxxxxxxxxxxxxxxxxxxxxx

Eight hours later, after airport queues and immigration kerfuffle, I step out of JFK and into the longest taxi queue I've ever seen. I pull out my phone and ring Ryan. There is no response from our landline or his mobile. I move my fingers quickly over my BlackBerry:

Arrived safely. Call me when you get this M x

Once my message has sent I quickly use my thumb to scroll back through my old messages, smiling as I see one from Casey. I glimpse at it before continuing my search for the SoHo apartment the US division of Brooks Publishing have rented for me:

Have fun!!!!!! And don't worry about anything here!!!!! C xxxxxx

It occurs to me that a few months ago this message would have filled me with a sense of dread. The old Casey was a loose cannon; if I hadn't heard from her in a few days, I'd always have to phone her, like I was her mum, checking up on her. And even if I did hear from her, every message saying 'don't worry' made me do the exact opposite. But Casey is a new woman, strong, in control, mature, enjoying her newfound career with a renewed purpose and confidence that I have never seen in her before. My friend has come through something bad and come out stronger and better than ever and that makes me so happy.

I shuffle forward in the taxi queue and it occurs to me that 2006 might just have been the year that finally, everything came good for us all and 2007 will be even better. I resolve to thoroughly enjoy this experience in New York. Doing this blog has made me start looking at the world – and my world – in a new way, and I realize that I'm finally ready for the next adventure. Perhaps the biggest one of my life.

Ryan and I have done everything I ever dreamt of: we moved to London (tick), bought a flat (tick), got married (tick), we've travelled to amazing places (tick), I've lived with my best friend (tick), I've flown all over the world for work (tick), and have even started taking photographs for a living (tick). For once, teenage Molly is quiet as a mouse.

In fact, she has been quiet ever since Ryan and I got back together. Maybe it's because Ryan is a different guy to the one I first went out with and I'm a different girl. Before we got married, we had a long talk about how to make the relationship work. Neither of us wanted to risk heartbreak for a second time so we had to be sure we were doing the right thing. I even wrote a list of questions for us both to answer, like a Mr-and-Mrs test. There were sections on marriage, children, travel, home and work – with questions to answer in each. Ryan knew me well enough to see why I wanted to do it. And it was no different to us going through my Life List all those years ago. It was just an updated version – one for both of us to be sure that our heads and hearts were in the same place – about everything.

And it was a brilliant way for us to answer all our 'Big Life Questions'. In the home section we had to say where we'd like to live in the long term. Ryan put Leigh and I put London, so we talked it through and Ryan said he was happy to live in London for the foreseeable future – and to make more effort to embrace the lifestyle (so no going back home every weekend). But he said he'd definitely want to move back there before our first child went to school. I didn't even have to think about it before saying yes. That gave us at least five more years in London and by then I knew I'd be ready to move back.

Ever since we got back together it feels like we've finally met in the middle, become a team shooting at the same goal instead of in opposite directions. And now, I realize that the next goal is a family. I'm twenty-eight years old, happily married, fulfilled by my career and I'm ready. My life has finally caught up with my age and I can't wait to tell him that I'm there. I'm exactly where he is. I want to start trying for a baby.

I look up and thank whoever is up there for giving me so much. I don't think it's possible for a girl to be any happier.

The What-If Kiss

There's a brief moment before surrendering entirely to a kiss where you make that semi-conscious decision to just let go. But what if, one day, in that exact moment, you realize that you can't let go? Instead, you're desperately clinging on to it. That's how I feel now. I'm clinging on to this kiss for dear life.

'What do you mean he's been "weird" since you got back?'

It is Saturday evening and I'm lying on my bed, talking to Mia on the phone. Ryan is out at one of his teacher friend's birthdays.

'I dunno, Mia. He's snappy and doesn't want to be at home, which isn't like him at all.' I slip the phone and hold it between my ear and shoulder as I upload new photos that I took last night, a close-up black-and-white shot of a father's hand grasping his daughter's. My 50 mm lens has picked up every line in his hand and the soft smoothness of hers. In the picture his hand is pulling forward, as if he's leading in life, showing her the way. It's part of my 'Alternative Valentine's' blog, celebrating love other than that between a couple. I've taken pictures of girlfriends chatting over coffee in Covent Garden, their faces alight with laughter. One of my favourites is of two old women hobbling arm in arm along Southend Pier. I caught them just as one of them threw her head back in laughter.

I focus back on my conversation with Mia. 'It's like he can't bear to be alone with me.'

'Or *not* alone with you . . .' Mia says pointedly.

'What do you mean?' I stop going through the photos.

'I mean *Casey*,' she expostulates, obviously desperate to get on to this subject. 'How long has she been staying with you now? Nine or ten months? I mean, it's not exactly conducive to a new marriage, is it, having your best mate as a lodger? Especially someone as needy as her. Maybe he's just fed up of—'

'Me?' I say mournfully.

'No, you drongo, Casey!'

I laugh, but it's half-hearted. 'Mia, you're so Aussie, next time I see you I'm expecting you to have an eighties Kylie perm, Dame Edna specs and be wearing Steve Irwin khakis!'

'Have you been spying on me?' she laughs. 'Look, I'm just saying that I think it's great that you've helped Casey get back on her feet, but I think it's time you focused on you and your husband. You need some space, just the two of you. I honestly reckon that's why he's being weird.'

'I don't know,' I say quietly, thinking about the last few times we've been together since I got back from New York. How he hasn't been able to look me in the eye. How he's been unusually quiet, made excuses to not spend time alone with me, even though I've been away for nearly a month. I was so excited about coming home and telling him that I was ready to start trying for a baby with him. But there hasn't been a moment to do it. Let alone DO it. Mia's right, Casey has been here every single evening, practically glued to my side. It actually feels like she missed me more than Ryan did.

I start trying to count the number of times that Ryan and I have been alone since I got back two weeks ago and, apart from in bed, I find I can count them both on one finger. Casey was even here on Valentine's night. I asked Ry if we could go out to dinner but he said he didn't want to make her feel uncomfortable, so we all went to the cinema. Even my welcome home wasn't as I imagined. He wasn't waiting at the airport, as I'd secretly hoped, and as I'd walked through Arrivals I felt nostalgic for the time he surprised me when I got back from Australia. It all feels so long ago. Fair enough, we're an old married couple now so he doesn't have to make as much effort. But still, we've not been married a year. Has all the romance really gone already?

'Hmm,' Mia says. 'Well, babe, it's all a mystery to me I'm afraid. You know I like my men how I like my coffee ...'

'Wait, don't tell me!' I say. 'Gone first thing in the morning?'

'Exactly,' she replies. 'You're quick off the mark. New York was obviously good for you.'

'Yeah, but bad for my marriage.' There is a crash and I turn and wave at Casey who has sauntered into the kitchen in her PJs . . . *my* PJs. My favourite blue-and-white striped ones that Ryan says make me look like the little boy in *The Snowman*. I know Casey and I have always shared everything, but I draw the line at my favourite pyjamas. Is nothing sacred? She goes to the fridge, pulls out the orange juice and drinks it straight from the carton. Suddenly, everything feels like a massive liberty. Casey has been living here, rent-free, for months. She's never offered to pay and I never asked before because of her work situation, and everything else, but now she's got a job as a PR assistant (thanks to me) and she *still* she hasn't offered any sort of contribution.

Ryan has mentioned this to me before in the past, but I've always been incredibly defensive of her. Now, I just feel annoyed that she is standing in front of me, wearing my PJs (which she looks better than me in – like some model wearing men's pyjamas) and she is brazenly drinking the juice – no, hang on, *finishing* the juice that *Ryan and I* paid for. I watch as she walks over to the bin and chucks it in. She misses but doesn't bother to pick it up. Then she sits up on the counter and mouths, 'Who is it?' and points at the phone.

'It's Mia,' I say out loud.

'What?' Mia replies at the end of the line.

'Oh, Casey's here,' I say. 'I was just telling her it's you.'

'Hey Mi-Mi!' Casey calls, crossing her tanned legs and waving at the phone, as if Mia can see her. 'What's going on "Down Under"?' she calls. 'And I don't mean your sex life!'

Mia tuts in response. 'Tell her *Mia* says, "Why are you still there?"'

'I can't say that,' I reply.

'Do it,' she commands.

'Mia says, why are you still here?' I say to Casey, and she laughs – as thick-skinned as ever – then slides off the counter and grabs the phone.

'Because Molly and Ry would be bored out of their brains

without me! I'm like their very own marriage aid!' She hands me back the phone and kisses me on the cheek, then sidles out of the kitchen.

'Has she gone?' Mia mutters.

'Yep,' I say, feeling the unrecognizable wave of annoyance subside. I know I vowed to always be there for her, but this is ridiculous. Mia's right, I need to leverage my own life; focus on my husband who's working too hard, and on our future. I don't want to start trying for a baby, with her in the house. Having Casey here *is* like having a newborn baby. 'I think it's time I had a chat with Casey,' I say out loud.

'Whoooo,' she whistles. 'Good luck with that!'

I walk back into the lounge where Casey is sprawled over the sofa. Her things are spread everywhere too, even more than Ryan's are – and she knows how much that winds me up. Every single surface seems to have a bit of Casey on it. She looks up as I walk in and obviously catches a glimpse of my disgruntled expression. She sits up quickly, pulling the duvet with her to make a space for me on the sofa. *My* sofa. She pats it.

'Here, babes, sit down and tell me all about it. I heard you saying to Mia that you and Ry are having problems. I mean, I've noticed things have been a bit weird with you guys for a little while but I haven't wanted to say anything.' She pulls her face into an innocent grimace. 'It's none of my business ... but you know I'm here to listen. And I'll probably understand better than anyone, especially Mia. I mean, she doesn't know Ryan like I do, or know *you* like I do, come to think of it. I mean, we've been best friends since we were thirteen! We're, like, soul sisters, aren't we!'

I look at Casey, sitting snuggled under the duvet, her dark hair pulled off her face with a hairband, *my* hairband, looking as needy and helpless as ever, and I feel a pang of guilt. She's only just started getting back on her feet. How could I expect her to pay rent when she's probably barely had one wage packet yet? And she lives like this because it's how she was brought up. No one taught her any different. Her mum was too busy chasing men to mother her. I glance on the floor and spot a bunch of shopping bags – Topshop and Zara. I bristle – how can she buy this when she's not paying us rent – but then I remember that she mentioned she needed new clothes for her new job. Although she's been borrowing loads of mine. I remind myself to ask her to show them to me – and try to get her a couple of freebies from work, just like I've done with some of her beauty products. I know she'd do the same for me, if the situation was reversed.

'So come on,' she says, slipping her hand into mine, 'tell me all about it.'

And suddenly I do want to share it all with her. Just like we used to. I want her to look after *me* for a change, to remind me of why Ryan loves me and only me. Tell me that we're the couple she looks up to, aspires to be part of. That we're stronger than ever. She's right, she does know us better than anyone.

'I don't know, Case,' I sigh, leaning my head back against the sofa. 'It's just that Ryan seems to be really distant since I got back from New York. It's like he's a different bloke. Something is bothering him, something big, I know it. I just don't know what.'

'Ooh, do you think he's had an affair or something?' she says glibly, like we're talking about someone we don't know. I forget that Casey's relationship barometer is permanently set to the lowest expectation level.

'Um, no, no. Why? Is there something I should know?' I laugh edgily. I'm joking, kind of. Well, I thought I was. But suddenly she's planted a seed of doubt.

Could he have cheated on me? I realize as I think it now that it's always been a fear, lying dormant at the back of my brain. That one day he will do as I have done. An eye for an eye and all that.

'God, NO!' Casey exclaims with a laugh. I don't join her. 'Not Ry, he'd never do that to you ... would he? I mean, I know *you* did in the past and some men might feel the need to, you know, get back at you because of their ego. But that's never been Ryan. I mean, he totally doesn't have an ego!'

Suddenly, my teen voice is back, and louder than ever.

Of COURSE he does, and his ego has told him that it's time to make things even! Tit for tat, and all that . . .

Shut up, I think, *shut up, shut up!* Stupid teenage insecurities always coming back to haunt me when I think I'm over them. Ry wouldn't do that. He's not just a typical lad. He's more, so much more.

I swallow, sickness and uncertainty suddenly suffocating me. I was away for nearly a month. That is a long time in any relationship, let alone in the first year of marriage. Were we so busy trying to repair past mistakes that we didn't make sure there weren't any more to come in the future?

Casey is still talking and I tune back into her, hoping that she can dispel my fears.

'. . . but all that's water under the bridge anyway,' she says, 'why would he do anything now? I mean if he was going to cheat I'm sure he would have done it ages ago. Although . . .' She bites her lip and her eyes darken.

'Although . . . what? *What,* Casey?' I say urgently. Suddenly it feels like Casey has all the answers to our relationship. She has seen more of us individually over the past few months than we have seen of each other. And she's just spent a month with my husband when I was across the Atlantic. Maybe she picked up on some sign that I wasn't here to see. Looks like I'm lucky to have her here after all.

'Just . . .' She shakes her head. 'Oh, it's probably nothing. Yes, in fact I'm sure it is. Honestly, Molly, don't listen to me, you know I never think before I speak. I honestly don't think there's anything to it at all . . .'

I don't want to know but I need to get it over with, like ripping a plaster off instead of teasing it gently. Come on, Casey, now isn't the time to stop talking. Keep talking. *Keep talking.*

'To what, Casey? To *what?*' I say, gripping her fingers so tightly that her skin turns pale.

Casey exhales and looks at me uncertainly. 'It's just, well, there was a night ... not long after you left, I remember it because I was here all evening, just hanging out. It had been a really busy week and it was the very first episode of *Benidorm* – it was so funny because there was this bit where they were singing karaoke at Neptune's and—'

For once I have run out of patience with Casey's incessant talking without saying anything. 'I don't *care* what was happening in some TV show, Casey, please, just get to the point and tell me what Ryan was doing.'

'I dunno,' she murmurs, not quite looking me in the eye. 'I dunno because he didn't come home. All night.'

I put my hand up to my mouth. Tears threaten to spring into my eyes but I swallow, and tighten my jaw, focusing hard on keeping them in. I just nod and then I stand up and walk slowly to my bedroom.

He. Didn't. Come. Home.

Suddenly I wish I'd left the plaster alone.

I'm lying in bed, staring at the ceiling, when he comes in. He looks crumpled and I roll over onto my side, facing the door, and sigh to let him know I'm awake. I'm hoping he will speak but he doesn't say anything, he just deposits his clothes on the floor and climbs into bed, curling into a ball, facing me, instead of our usual spoons position. I don't snuggle over to him like I usually would. I can't move. I'm paralysed with my knowledge. It's as if this new information in my brain has shut down the part that controls movement.

The silence lies heavily in the space between us, like an extra body in the bed (has there been an extra body in this bed?). Ryan is so unlike himself at the moment that he's positively a stranger to me.

He smells of alcohol, his new buzz cut has hardened his features again, sinking his eyes into black pits and turning his sexy laughter lines into streaks of stress. I want to stroke his hair, I want to stroke it so badly, but my brain can't make my arm do it. All I can manage is lifting my hand and resting it on his head, as if I'm blessing him or forgiving him, like the priest used to do during confession.

Say ten Hail Marys and two Our Fathers for not coming home while your wife was away.

My fears gnaw away at me. Suddenly I see our baby, the one that I've spent the last few weeks imagining, disappear in a puff of smoke.

'Molly,' he whispers, and he tilts his lips up to mine and pulls his body closer to me. He begins to kiss me passionately in a way that I've wanted him to do for weeks, but he has always been too tired, or stressed or just not interested.

I'm amazed and repelled that my body responds instinctively, still too in tune with Ryan to be able to do anything else.

He moans and as he kisses me he presses his body against mine and I let out an involuntarily moan too. We're still looking at each other, like we're trying to work out what each other is thinking. We used to know. I suddenly think of the song, the song from Ry's favourite film, *Top Gun*. The one about not closing your eyes any more when you kiss. He stares at me and I gulp and focus hard on kissing Ryan the best I can, making it as desirable a kiss as I can muster, like I'm playing at being sexy. I flick my tongue and scrape my teeth along his lip and brush mine against his jaw and I breathe heavily, and all the time I feel like a fraud. The tears are stinging my eyes, the shame is flooding my body because I can't help but wonder if the last lips to have touched Ryan's were not mine. I pull back slightly. What if this kiss he's instigating now isn't borne of want or need, but guilt?

I kiss his neck, his chest, anywhere but his lips.

He cannot see my tears fall in the darkness. I squeeze my eyes shut and focus. Maybe making love will make it all better. Just as I have convinced myself that this will heal us, Ryan's kisses become lighter and lighter. Then he brushes my cheek gently, rolls over and leaves me lying here, awake and alone, wondering what if . . . what if . . . what if . . . until I think I might go mad.

It's official: he *has* lost that loving feeling. Or, worse, he's found it elsewhere.

3.17 p.m.

I'm sitting eating a doughnut in the lounge, my laptop with the DVD inside is beside me. I know I shouldn't – Mum will be here any minute – but I'm not sure I can stop myself. I'm about to press play when I notice a new email in my inbox and open it.

> Hi Molly,
> Hope you're well. Just to confirm that your exhibition will definitely be transferring from London to a gallery in Sydney at the beginning of next month. We have also had offers from New York and Milan. You've also been asked to speak at another fundraising dinner at the end of the week. Would you be willing to do this? I know it doesn't give you long to settle in. Could you let me know and I will reply to them asap.
> Good luck with everything.
> Speak soon.
> Jane

I fire off a quick response without even thinking.

> Jane, re: dinner, I'd be honoured to. And thank you, for everything. I'm completely overwhelmed by the response. Would like to talk soon about future projects/fundraising ideas. All is good here. Have left everything till the last moment as ever but I'm not stressing, it'll all get done!
> Molly x

I press send and close my email. I hover the little arrow over the Shut Down icon in the corner of the screen, but instead find my

finger moving the mouse and pressing play on the DVD icon. I turn
the shell over in my hand.

Just one more time then I can put it away. For good.

Bob pops his head into the lounge where I'm still sitting with my
laptop, drowning my sorrows by stuffing the last of my doughnut
into my mouth. I mute the film and smile weakly at him. Seeing
Nanny Door again and watching this has really thrown me. But then
I think of what she said about finding happiness and the guilt fades.

'We're all done here now, luv!' he says. 'Just one more box for
storage, which I'll take out to the van on my way out.'

'Thnnk yow,' I reply, still with a mouthful of doughnut. He
smiles at me, a cheery, eye-winking smile that warms the cockles
of my heart.

He lifts his hand in a wave, his copy of *The Sun* rolled up under
one arm. 'What time's your flight then?'

'Not until tonight. There's just a couple of things I have to do
first . . .'

'Well, we'll leave you to it, luv.'

I glance at the DVD that is silently playing on my laptop. It is
near the end but I press stop anyway, I know that the time has
come.

'Sorry, Bob, is that last box sealed up? I've just got one more
thing to pop in.'

We walk out into the hallway and he rips off the masking tape
that he's carefully sealed it with.

'It's something I want to keep, but I don't need to keep *with*
me any more . . .' I mutter more to myself than to him as I slip the
thin DVD box inside.

Bob takes the masking tape out of his pocket and deftly swipes it
around the box, before lifting it carefully up onto his shoulder, like
a coffin – I think fleetingly – and then I discard that unwelcome
thought and he carries it away.

The Tell Me It's Not True Kiss

Have you ever tried to erase something with a kiss? Expunge
an experience, minimize a mistake, a memory, a moment with
your mouth? Have you ever squeezed your eyes shut and hoped
that your lips had the power to eliminate bad news, to eclipse the
entire world that has just come crashing down around you? Have
you ever wished, not upon a star, but upon a kiss?

I have. I just wish I could tell you that what I wished for came
true.

I need to tell u something. I'm in Leigh. Please come now. I'll pick u up. R x

I'm at work when I get the text message from him. It is the one I've been waiting for with dread. But it is almost a relief to get it. Soon I will know why he's been leaving the house and going in the opposite direction to school for the past few days. Who the person is that keeps calling his mobile, causing him to leave the room to answer it. Why he can't seem to bear to be in the same room with me. I know it is bad news, but nothing can be worse than not knowing. The not knowing is killing me.

I pop into Christie's office and tell her I've got a doctor's appointment and won't be in for the rest of the afternoon before heading back to my desk to shut down my computer. I reply quickly and simply as I pick up my bag:

OK. Leaving now x

I sit on the train with my face pressed against the cool window, thinking about the revelation Ryan is about to tell me. I'm prepared for the worst. But it occurs to me there might be an even worse scenario than I'm imagining. Not just a kiss, or a one-night stand, he could be *in love*. He could have gone back to an old girlfriend. Maybe that's why he's in Leigh ... Who was that girl he was dating before me? The one I met on the *Bembridge*. What was her name? Stacey. Or perhaps it's someone I know, but not that well, like one of Lydia's perky girlfriends maybe? I can't stop my brain from hurtling at a million miles an hour, the thoughts rushing through my head like the landscape around me, ever changing and yet still the same endlessly depressing view. The sky is as dark with foreboding as my thoughts. I'll be one of those young women with a marriage and a divorce under her belt before she's thirty. I'll be a laughing stock forever; an example of the failure of modern love. Maybe Mum was right. I should never have chosen passionate, undying love over the practical kind.

I shake my head, berating myself for becoming as naive about men as I used to warn Casey about being. It's a cruel kind of irony that my marriage is on the cusp of collapse and everywhere I look I am reminded of my big day. The girl over there, ensconced in a copy of *Brides* magazine, diamond ring sparkling. Her face is alight with love and possibility, her ring still sparkles with promise, not sullied by the everyday toils that make it glitter that little bit less every day. I glance at my left hand now, at Nanny Door's ring, with the pretty cluster of diamonds and the simple platinum band that it rests on. Until now, I liked that it wasn't perfect, that it had seen life, survived an entire 50-year marriage with all its ups and downs; like Ryan and me, it had been through the mill. I liked that it didn't shout 'new' because Ry and I weren't new. We've been together a long time, grown together, grown *up* together and this ring represented that perfectly. I remember shyly showing it to Nanny Door, just after Ry and I had got back from New York. She had held my hand gently and stroked her arthritic fingers over the diamonds with her eyes closed, as if the precious stones held the love story of her life. When she opened her eyes again she had pulled me close. Nanny Door is not known for being softly spoken but this time I'd had to bend down a little to hear what she was saying.

'The Cooper men have always been regular heart-throbs, doll, but they also choose their women well.' She stared at me knowingly with her delphinium-blue eyes that drifted in and out of focus, as if she had one foot in the past and one in the present. 'When Arthur and I were dating, I remember feeling like I wasn't good enough for him – he was so devastatingly handsome, just like Ry – but as soon as that ring was on my finger I knew that it didn't matter how I looked, what I felt, or what people thought, I was more than enough for him.' She'd patted me gently on the hand. 'This ring will bring you so much happiness and you deserve it. I know how much my boy loves you, Molly, and he's chosen well. You are a strong, beautiful, caring, insightful woman. A true Cooper. Now you just have to believe it.'

I'd hugged her and cried, feeling like she had seen me from the inside out, just like Ryan had done on our very first teenage date many years before. I didn't have to pretend any more. But now, as I twist the band between my fingers, I worry that this ring, the ring I have always loved so much, isn't perfect. It has the scratches and wear of a marriage before; a marriage – no, a life, that ended too soon. Maybe it has never sparkled as brightly as the girl's over there and I wonder, was our marriage tarnished before it had even begun?

I just can't bear not knowing any more. I don't want to deal with this on my own. But I have to. No one else will understand. I stop as I realize that there is someone; there's always been someone who completely understands me, perhaps even more than Ryan.

I pull my phone out of my bag and quickly text Casey:

Ryan wants to talk to me. On way to Leigh now. Feel sick. M x

I want her to tell me not to worry, that it'll all be OK. I get a text back instantly:

Oh Molly I am so sorry xxx

My heart plummets like a rock being kicked off a cliff. She knows this is the end too. She can see it hurtling down the tracks, just like I can. My phone beeps again. It's another message from her:

Please forgive me?

I furrow my brow and look out the window at the bleak identikit houses we are now passing. *Forgive her?* For what? For telling me? Or for something else? Why is she making this about her when it has nothing to do with her? Typical Casey. Unless she knows more . . .

My hands shaking, I quickly scroll through my address book and press call. She picks up immediately and starts crying.

'Casey,' my voice is hard, cold. 'Your text. What does it mean?'

Casey sobs. I don't say anything. I just wait until she can compose herself and string a sentence together.

'Oh, Molly, I'm sorry, I just saw . . . your . . . text . . . and . . . I know Ryan's going to tell you but I need you to know h-how-how it happened. It wasn't my fault. I pr-promise—'

'What happened?' I interrupt. I need fast answers. I need to know what the hell is going on. 'Are you saying you know that something happened?'

'Y-ye-yess,' she sobs.

I pause as a terrible thought occurs to me for the very first time. Worse than the possible worst-case scenario I could've ever imagined. 'Between *you*?'

'It wasn't my fault, Molly!' She splutters. 'I promise, it wasn't! You have to believe me. You just have to!'

I press my lips into a hard line and stare out of the window. The train is just pulling out of Benfleet, we are minutes away from my stop. I'm stopping this now. I want this conversation, this friendship to screech to a halt.

'I don't know what to believe any more, Casey.' And I put the phone down.

Ryan is waiting in his dad's car at the station. I stare at it for a moment. He's sitting in the Mercedes, in the driving seat, his arm stretched over the passenger seat, head turned and looking out the window. I can see his face in his rear-view mirror. Looking at his profile like this reminds me of when we used to drive up near Hadleigh Castle when we were dating, and just sit there, talking and kissing. But his expression is sad, scared ... guilty?

Emboldened by a surge of energy and the desire to shock him, like I've just been, I run over to the car, throw open his door and start pummelling him with my hands.

'You bastard, you shitty fucking bastard! How could you? How could you? How COULD you?'

He slides out of the car and catches me as I fall to my knees, clutching my chest and moaning with pain, like I've been shot in the heart.

'Molly? What the ... Molly!' he hoicks me up under my arms and holds me in front of him like a rag doll, his blue eyes flitting between mine. They are glistening, like when the sun catches a wave and I recall how looking at him has always felt like being instantly transported to a summer day. Not now though. Right now I'm in the middle of a storm.

'Molly? What's going on?'

'You tell me, you fucking ... fucker!' I pummel my fists furiously against him, crying harder with every strike.

Ryan holds my wrists. 'Hey! Molly, what is all this? Honestly, I don't know what you're on about!'

'Casey!' I cry. 'I'm talking about you and Casey!' I see a flash of acknowledgement in his eyes then, but there's no guilt, just relief.

'Oh *that* ...' he sighs wearily and drops my hands. He sits back in the car, leaning his head back against the rest as if he can't quite hold it up on his own. I know how he feels. I grip onto the car for support, knowing that my legs aren't able to do their work alone right now.

'It was nothing, Molly babe, honestly,' he says flatly. 'Nothing I didn't expect anyway. I told her she was out of order. End of.'

'You're saying she ... ? Not you ...? And you didn't ...?' He nods to all three of my unfinished sentences. The next one I finish: 'Why should I believe you, Ryan?' I murmur.

He looks at me, his eyes watery with tears. 'Because you know it's true.'

And I do. I think of my vows. *I do.* And I know that he's telling the truth. She has flirted with every single one of his friends and my friend's boyfriends, she's slept with men who have girlfriends, wives even. She has always been completely indiscriminate in her romantic choices. And deep down, I guess I've always known that Casey was in love with Ryan. I've known it since that holiday in Ibiza. Maybe even before. I saw the way she looked at him. But I never thought, I never thought, she would ever do this to me ...

I lean my whole body against the car door, clinging on to it for support. I look at Ryan, my saviour, the one who has always kept me afloat. 'So you really didn't come on to her, then?' I say quietly, knowing even as the words leave my mouth that he wouldn't. Not ever.

'No! Of course not! I would never ...' He reaches up to take my hand and smiles weakly as he rubs his thumb over my engagement and wedding rings. 'You're the only girl for me, Molly, you always have been ... and ... always will be ...' He turns away and rubs his forehead and I see his shoulders are shaking. He's crying.

I feel so stupid. And so confused. I know there's something more. I run round to the passenger seat and get in the car. 'What is it? Tell me.' I'm crying now. 'I don't want to lose you, Ry ... I'll do anything. When I was in New York I realized that I want what *you* want. I'm ready. I want to move here, buy a house, have kids. I've done everything I ever dreamed of doing and I don't want anything to take me away from you any more. Being with you is more important than anything else. I love you so much, Ry. Please we can work through whatever it is that's happened, whatever it is you've done. I know we can. I-I love you so much.'

I'm sobbing now because somehow it feels like I'm losing him all over again and I can't bear it.

Ry lifts his hand up to my chin and smiles. 'I know you love me, Moll, you silly cow.' I put my hand over his and stroke it. We sit there for a moment staring into each other's eyes. There's something different about him but I don't know what it is.

'Then what is it, Ry?' I whisper urgently. 'What's wrong? Why have you been so distant since I got back? Why have you brought me here? I've been so scared, not knowing what's going on is killing me. Please just tell me. We'll work through it, whatever it is.' I cling on to him and squeeze his hands. He looks down at them clasped together, joined so tightly that it's impossible to tell which hand belongs to who. Then he looks up and the years have fallen away and suddenly he looks just like the teenager I fell in love with. He takes a deep breath, his voice is soft but laboured. He can't look at me. He looks at our hands, at his wedding ring glinting at us, shining brighter than the sun.

'Listen Moll, while you were away I went to stay with Mum and Dad for a night, and Mum noticed this mole. On my back. It looked a bit weird and she got me to go to the doctor. I told him about feeling constantly tired and thinking I had flu because my glands were up . . .' He looks at me and I gaze at him silently. 'I didn't tell you because I didn't want to spoil your trip and have you worrying over something that was probably nothing.' Probably. I hate that word. He speaks again but this time his voice is quiet and it cracks. 'I mean, I thought I'd just have the mole removed and that would be it. Plenty of people have cancerous moles, right?' He squeezes my hands and then smiles brightly. 'They removed it and said something about swollen lymph glands which might involve an operation, and the tests they did said that it was stage three. But then they said they wanted me to have a CT scan today. Which I'm sure will show it's all fine.' I blink at him.

'Wh-hwat are you saying, Ry?' I whisper.

'I'm sure they've got it all, the cancer was just in that mole, but I've got an appointment today to get the results of the scan and see about the lymph glands. I'm not scared or anything.' He lifts up his shoulders and then they slump again as if he hasn't got the energy to pretend.

Cancer.

I want to speak but I can't. I can't speak because I can't breathe. I shake my head, trying to dislodge the word from my head.

One word.

Cancer. Cancer. Cancer.

I put my hands over my ears to drown out the word. It is roaring its name like it's the Gruffalo in our nephew Beau's favourite book.

I gaze at him pleadingly, and then disbelievingly, and then defiantly.

'No,' I say quietly, then louder. 'I don't believe it. NO!' I grasp his hands again, entwine my fingers in his, and I close my eyes and I lift them to my lips and kiss them all over, kissing each finger, each knuckle, every last inch. I open my eyes and rest my cheek against our cold hands. Ryan kisses my head.

'Babe,' he says, 'it's going to be alright. I promise you, I'm going to be alright.'

And I nod to show I believe him. I'm a Cooper now which means I am an optimist. We are optimists. The mouse *can* defeat the Gruffalo.

The First Last Kiss

Why did no one warn me that every kiss is a countdown to goodbye? It's only now that I'm treating them like they're the most precious things on earth that I realize that each one is like a grain of sand slipping through my fingers and I can't hold on to them no matter how hard I try. How do I stop the sands of time?

How can I make a kiss last for a lifetime?

Half an hour later we're standing outside the private hospital in silence, clutching the strong takeaway tea and flapjacks that Ryan stopped off to buy before we came here. We're early and waiting till the last possible minute to go in for the appointment where we'll be given the results of his CT scan. Neither of us wants to sit in the waiting room so we informed the receptionist we're here and then came back outside, into the fresh air.

I can't speak yet. The words 'skin cancer' and 'malignant melanoma' and 'Stage 3' are pounding my brain like feet relentlessly running on a treadmill. I'm clinging on to Ryan with my spare hand like my life depends on it.

Between the train-station car park and here, we have talked about it all, with me storing the information he gives me like a squirrel hoarding nuts for winter. The more I know the less my imagination can work overtime.

I'm struggling with the knowledge that Ryan and his parents have known about this for weeks. I'm his wife, I should have been told. Instead, I was in New York, selfishly living out my dreams whilst my husband was living a nightmare. I close my eyes and try to rewind to the meeting where Christie asked if I wanted to go to *Viva*'s New York office for a month.

No, I want to shout, not for the first time today.

NO.

I take a sip of tea and try to eat the flapjack that Ryan bought me. But it gets stuck in my throat. I have no saliva, no moisture left in my body; I'm sure I have cried it all out. Which is lucky, because I do not intend to do any more crying. I am going to be positive. I throw the flapjack in the bin we are standing next to.

'Hey! That's a waste,' Ryan says. 'I'd have eaten it.' Always thinking about his stomach.

'I don't want a fat husband,' I say shrilly, in a voice that doesn't sound like my own.

'Had you noticed the mole had changed before?' I then ask quietly.

He nods. 'A year or so ago, I think. I honestly don't know. I didn't think anything was wrong, it just looked a bit ... misshapen, bigger maybe, but I didn't think anything of it.'

'Why didn't you tell me?' I demand. '*I'd* have told you to get it checked.'

The words come out as a squeak, a whine, a *self-obsessed* whine. Ryan just laughs (how can he laugh? How can we ever laugh again?). He puts his tea down, ruffles my hair affectionately, and winds his arms around me.

'I just didn't think there was anything to it,' he says gently. 'And then when I thought it might have grown, we were always so busy with work and going here and there, and I just didn't have time to get it checked.' His fist tightens into a ball and he presses it against his forehead and closes his eyes. Then he opens them and smiles at me. 'It's fine though. It'll all be fine! The docs removed it after the CT scan.'

'But why didn't you tell me when your mum noticed it?'

'Because I didn't want to worry you over nothing, Moll, you were in New York and I had the ... mal-ignant mel-an-oma removed ...' He pauses. The words fall clumsily out of his mouth, '... almost immediately. Within a week! And yes, my blood test results show my red-blood count is up, but I feel fine! Fit as ever!'

He doesn't look at me when he says this, and I know that this isn't true. He hasn't been feeling himself for months. He's been tired and listless, exhausted just walking up the stairs to our flat, but he thought it was just work taking its toll. Or his age. He is nearly thirty ...

Only nearly thirty.

This shouldn't be happening. Not to him! He's a PE teacher! He juices every day! He's run marathons! He's scaled cliffs! Dived out of planes!

He's used a sunbed for years.

Her voice is quiet, discreet, reverential, but completely unwelcome as ever.

Get out Get out Get out! I hate your cynical, negative thoughts that are as cancerous as the cancer itself.

I cling on to his hand and he looks up and smiles brightly. 'I'm sure the CT scan result today will show they've got it all.'

'That's why I didn't tell you,' he continues, 'because it could have been nothing . . . it could *still* be nothing.'

'Stage three cancer isn't nothing,' I reply. The word 'cancer' is hostile in my mouth.

'It will be when I've finished with it.' Ryan mimes drop-kicking a ball into the far distance, puts his hand up to his ear as if waiting for the sound of it landing, then brushes his hands together and cups my face. 'Look at me, I'm as fit as you like! There is no way some stupid little mole has had any other effect on this finely tuned machine!' He jumps back, waves his hand at his body, flexes his muscles and poses, body-builder style. Then he grins and jogs on the spot. 'You're going to have to put up with being married to me for many years to come, Moll, so don't you start thinking there's any other way out . . .'

'Don't joke about it, Ryan, please, I can't . . .'

I'm crying and I hate myself for doing this but I'm not ready to joke. I won't be until I hear the doctors tell us that he has beaten this.

No, that *we* have beaten it.

'Hey,' he swipes away my tears with his thumb. 'Molly, stop.' He grips my wrists gently and makes me look at him. 'Hey, listen to me. *I know* that these results are going to show that everything is alright. At worst, a couple of bouts of chemo, some radiotherapy maybe to make sure, and I'll be right as rain!'

I look at my husband, so positive and upbeat, so strong and sweet, protecting me for as long as possible because he didn't want to worry me. I don't know much about cancer and the details I do know come from reading the real-life features in our magazine, but I know stage four is bad, so stage three must mean there's a chance? Maybe if it was isolated to that mole, it can be beaten? In fact, now I come to think of it, I'm sure we once featured a girl who had skin cancer, had the mole removed, had chemo, and had been clear of it for five years. Was it stage three? Probably! So that just goes to show it could definitely be curable! Almost certainly in fact! Cancer isn't a death sentence any more. And there's so much they can do. Really, we shouldn't be at all worried. I'll look into alternative medicines as well as whatever treatment the doctors decide to do. I'll write a list. I've heard of cases where people have beaten cancer purely with diet alone. Obviously I'll need to learn to cook first. But I could learn reflexology. Do a course in it or something? Or go to Holland & Barrett and get lots of essential oils. I'll get some books on it from Amazon as soon as we get home. Maybe *I'll* be the one to cure his cancer, not the doctors. He won't even need treatment, probably. I'm all he needs now. And maybe one other person ...

'Good,' I smile as I take his hand. 'Because we haven't got time for cancer if we're going to start trying for a baby ...'

His face breaks out into the biggest smile I have ever seen. His skin rumples around his eyes with lines stretching out towards his temples like arrows shooting from a bow.

He grabs my hands and pulls me into a hug. 'You're ready, you're really, honestly ready?' he whispers into my ear. 'You're not just saying it because of the ... cancer?'

I pull back and stare at him intently. I need him to know this isn't a knee-jerk reaction.

'Ry, I've been trying to tell you this since I got back from New

York. Being out there made me realize that I'm ready for the next stage of our life. I'm more than ready! More than anything I want to be a mum.'

He grins then, and I feel a spark of hope. Someday we will look back and realize it was a narrow escape, a second chance, no, a third chance. We've overcome obstacles before, we'll do it again.

'So let's go in now and let them tell us the good news, OK?'

Ryan doesn't answer. He just nods and swallows so his Adam's apple bobs up and down in his throat like a buoy. I hold out my hand to him and I smile, bigger and wider and brighter than I have ever smiled before. I can feel the positivity flooding my body like the sunlight that is now filtering through the clouds. It's all going to be alright. I know it. I just know it.

We're sitting in silence outside the consultant's office, steadfastly watching the clock. But the digits are barely moving. We've only been here five minutes but it feels like five hours. Time has slowed almost to a standstill. I'm hoping this is a sign that we have time. Lots of it. Because suddenly I feel like I've wasted so much.

I look up and everything goes into slow motion as the door opens and there he is. I'm sure there is a head, attached to a body, in some clothes. Perhaps there is a white coat. I don't notice because all I can see is his smile. A gentle, coaxing, encouraging smile.

This is A Very Good Sign. I am certain of this. His floating mouth reminds me of the Cheshire Cat's and I watch transfixed as it morphs into an 'oooh' as he speaks.

'Mr Coo-ooooh-ooo-per,' he yawns.

Why has everything gone so weird? I feel like I have taken hallucinogenic drugs or something . . .

'Molly?' I look at Ryan but he is yawning too, his face taking on Edvard Munch-like qualities as he curves and twists and then . . . everything goes black.

We are sitting in the consultant's office and I'm sipping more strong, sweet tea as Ryan holds me. I fainted apparently. How embarrassing. A nurse is smiling kindly at me, the consultant is sitting behind his desk.

'I'm so sorry,' I mumble, to no one in particular.

'Don't worry,' the doctor replies. I'm relieved to see that there's now a face attached to the mouth and a body attached to his head. 'You chose the best place to faint. Plenty of people here to help!' The nurse smiles in acknowledgement of his weak joke. The doctor – Dr George Harper, his badge says – isn't smiling any more. His face is serious, kindly, considerate. *Benign*, I think. Then I mentally chastise myself. Why has that word appeared in my brain to torment me?

'So Mr and Mrs Cooper,' Dr Harper says. A giggle erupts out of my mouth and he glances at me like I might just hit the floor again.

'She always laughs when she's nervous,' Ryan explains with a smile, and the doctor nods patiently.

'It's because it makes us sound so old! But we're not!' I blurt out. Ryan squeezes my hand. 'We're so young . . .' I whisper.

It occurs to me that I would love to see Ryan with grey hair. Grey and old and lined and wrinkled, I want to see that desperately. I can feel my chest tightening, my breath shortening and the tears coming back. I blink furiously.

Ryan squeezes my hand again, and I smile at him weakly.

'So,' the consultant says, 'we have the results of your CT scan and . . .'

Pause.

There's no noise in the room, not a single breath, not a whisper from the trees outside, only the wall clock can be heard.

'It's not good news, I'm afraid.'

Tick.

I gasp as I take a breath.

'What do you mean exactly?' Ryan says. His voice is a whisper. He's squeezing my hand.

Tick .

Clinging on for dear life.

Tick .

'This is not stage three as we suspected; the scan has shown it's stage four. As well as the presence of melanoma in your lymph glands, the metastatic cancer has spread,' the consultant says gravely. He folds his hands on his desk. I glance at the picture on his desk. A wife, two kids. Boy and girl. 'And the melanoma cancer cells have formed a metastatic tumour that has caused an intravasation ...' Furrowed brows all round. 'By that I mean that the cancer has spread through the walls of your lung and liver ...'

I think of Ryan panting after a short jog, of his swollen stomach that no amount of sit-ups could shift. He thought it was age. The dreaded 3-0. The beginning of middle-age spread. I'd joked it was 'marriage spread'. We'd joked about it.

We'd. Joked. About. It.

Ryan is clutching me now, pulling me closer as we grasp for each other as the consultant continues to speak, the words and phrases coming out of his mouth that are another language to us. Then he nods at the nurse and she picks up the baton in the bad-news relay, talking in simpler terms that we can understand. We can try chemo, they can offer pain relief.

Relief, not cure, I note. She'll put us in touch with a local Macmillan nurse ... treatment plan ... surgery to remove the lymph glands, chemo if we want to go that route ... to win time ... ensure we have lots of support.

'How much time?' Ryan says, his voice sounding like an old LP that's been put on the wrong speed.

The nurse gently replies that there's no estimate on time, he could have months ahead, a year. The doctor says that he can see that this is hard to take in. Then comes the apology.

'I'm so sorry ...'

And then the retreat.

They'll leave us alone for a few minutes. So we can take it in . . . but I'm not listening any more. I am looking only at my husband. I'm thinking only of my husband, my incredible, handsome, active, fit young husband.

My dying husband.

And then the door shuts and Ryan's lips meet mine in a sequence of stumbling movements that reminds me of our first kiss; it literally transports me back to that moment in The Grand, when Ryan tried to find my lips so indelicately. Now we do the same, clutching as we gasp for breath between our tears, and we kiss as if we are drowning and it occurs to me that this is actually a world away from our first kiss.

This kiss, right now, begins the countdown to our last. It is our first last kiss. And as that thought occurs to me, I kiss Ryan with every ounce of love for him I have ever had, a love that at times has been too big for me to cope with, a love beyond my years. And, now it seems, beyond his. As his body begins to shake and the tsunami of tears comes, I cradle his head to my lap and I stroke his golden hair, and I whisper that I'm going to make every kiss, every touch, every moment last a lifetime. I'll savour every single kiss from now until the . . . not the end, until forever.

Mum and Dad arrive just as the van's leaving. I'm glad to have them here. They flank me closely as we watch it pull out of the driveway and down the road.

'Are you OK, dear?' Mum says, one hand on my shoulder, the other on my arm. 'This must be so hard for you.'

I nod. 'It is, Mum, but I also know that van is just full of sentimental crutches that I don't need any more because the memories, well, they're all here, aren't they?' I tap my head. I look at them both and they smile and nod.

I know I sound like I'm just saying it, but if there's one thing that Ryan's cancer has taught me it's that it's the memories that stay with us forever, not the stuff that's attached to them. I used to think that taking photographs would make me see things better, freeze the moment, remember it forever. But I realize that the only way to do that is to *live* in the moment, not behind a lens. We don't actually *need* pictures or endless videos or keepsakes or engagement rings to recall these special moments, because they'll always be there. Even if they fade a little over time, one day the sun will shine in the sky on a particular morning in a particular way, or we'll discover a long-lost item, a shell, perhaps, or a card will arrive in the post . . . and it'll all come flooding back. And the memories will be good, and we'll know that we are blessed to have them. And then we'll feel lucky to have been given the chance to make more . . .

'I'd better get started on the house,' Mum says, throwing a look at Dad that says 'Let's give her a moment'. Dad nods and is about to follow her inside, when he turns around and puts his arms around me and kisses me on the head as if he is blessing me.

'You just keep putting photos up here in the album, OK, Molly? I know you have so many more wonderful ones to come.'

I nod. Wanting to say all the things I didn't say to him for so long. Finally I settle for four words.

'I love you, Dad,' and he smiles and walks inside.

I pull out my mobile, feeling a sudden urge to call him. I just pray that he answers.

'Hey,' I say softly as he picks up on the first ring. 'I'm all done here,' I say. 'Are you ready? Because I'm coming to get—'

'I love it when you act all bossy,' he laughs.

A flash of a memory, quickly replaced, but not without a mental nod of acknowledgement.

'You'd better get used to it,' I laugh, tucking the phone under my ear as I put my coat on and lift my bag onto my shoulder. 'I'm not about to change.' I tilt the two suitcases that are sitting next to me into a pulling position. 'I'll be at the hospital in half an hour, OK?'

The Constable Kiss

'The heart is a museum, filled with the exhibits of a lifetime's loves.' Diane Ackerman

Isn't that a lovely quote? I came across it recently and it made me think about my relationships; not just with Ryan but my friends and family too. I imagined them all carefully curated in my heart. Ryan is on display as reportage-style photographs, a never-ending series of him running, jumping, kicking, diving, sailing, laughing, winking, reaching, staring, grinning, kissing.

Casey is pop art – eye-catchingly beautiful, vivid and of the moment. Mum is there in various guises; as a sculpture, painstakingly chiselled and poised, and also as a portrait. One of those stilted nineteenth-century ones where you can just see a glimmer of a smile in the starchy get-up. Dad is an Edward Hopper, you know, 'Man seated in front of a desk in a light-flooded window gazing musingly at a wall with a painting on it'. It is how I always picture him.

I used to wonder what it was he was looking for and recently, on one of Ryan's bad days (and by proxy, one of mine) I asked him. He lowered his glasses and looked at me with his soft hazel eyes. Then he took my hand and said: 'The truth, Molly dear. I'm looking for the truth.' I'd looked at him questioningly, not really understanding what he meant. He'd taken his glasses off and placed them on his laptop. 'It's so easy to lose our faith whilst we're caught in the cogs of the endless grind of real life. But there are three places the truth can always be found: In God ...' he'd glanced at me, acknowledging that this has never meant much to me, and I'm finding it even harder now, '... in love and in art.' He'd rested his elbows on his desk and pressed his fingers together. 'Whenever I am wondering why I am being tested and I can't get the answers from the first two, I seem to find them in the last. It makes me look at life as a bigger picture and then everything seems to make sense.'

If I'm honest, it is the first thing that anyone has said that has made sense to me since Ryan was diagnosed with terminal cancer. Without realizing he was doing it my dad gave me an answer to a question I didn't even know I was asking.

Up until that moment I honestly thought I'd lost faith in 'forever', but now I know that both love and art can last forever because they have the power to transcend everything – time, age and indeed, life itself.

And what better way to capture one than with the other?

It's the day of our first official date. I'm sitting in his dad's Mercedes and all I know is that Ryan is taking me to his favourite place in the world.

'Australia?' I joked when he phoned me the day after our kiss in Covent Garden.

'Maybe next year,' he'd laughed, and my heart had soared with pleasure. Next year? He thinks we'll be together next year?

'I'm thinking somewhere a little closer to home for now. Are you free this Saturday?'

'I might be,' I'd said noncommittally, cradling my work phone between my shoulder and neck.

'Well, babe,' he'd laughed down the line and I felt a glow of warmth at his words. For some reason, the way he said 'babe' sounded sexy, not patronizing. I'm officially a babe now! Molly Carter: teen outcast, now officially a babe! 'If you *can* spare some time to hang out, meet me outside Leigh train station at eleven. I'll pick you up straight after footie training.' My heart had sunk a little when he'd suggested going out in Leigh.

'I hope you'll have a shower first!' I'd noticed that his Essex twang was more defined on the phone, he sounded almost cockney. 'I promise it'll be worth it,' he'd added, as if reading my thoughts.

I step up and tentatively clamber over the stile, trying to keep as much dignity as I possibly can, which is tricky given that I mistakenly allowed Freya to dress me for this date. She instantly confiscated my Converse and presented me with a pair of kitten heels. I should've listened to my instincts telling me that anything with the name of an animal is not appropriate attire. Leopard skin, rabbit fur, pussycat bow, kitten heel. I'm furious with myself for wanting to look like the kind of girl he usually dates. I wanted to be as far from my teen self as possible. I thought we'd be going to some restaurant for lunch. Instead we're going for a picnic up here, in my favourite place. Which turns out is his favourite place, too. Before Casey came along, to free me from my social leprosy, Hadleigh Castle *was* my best friend. As a tortured teenager it was the place I came to unburden my soul, to let out my frustrations and to find peace. I'd come here after school, when I couldn't face going home, and sometimes I'd come here when I couldn't face being at school. Those years from eleven to thirteen, before I met Casey, were pretty dark. I just didn't feel like I fitted in anywhere. My personality traits as stated in my school reports were always: tidy, quiet, disciplined, good. But inside I wasn't any of those things. I was crying out to be different. But no one heard. I wasn't aware that my parents wanted more children, but I was painfully aware that I was the only one, and with that came the responsibility to be perfect. I didn't allow myself to make mistakes, be silly, reckless, careless. Have fun. I was bullied for being the stuck-up girl with the stupid plaits who worked tirelessly, read endlessly and skulked around school with a camera. At home I was under the intense scrutiny of my mum who paid so much attention to me to make sure I met her exacting standards that everything else – including my dad – seemed to disappear. I wanted so badly to hide away. Maybe that's why I always retreated behind a lens. Or came up here to Hadleigh Castle. It was the only place I felt happy and free. I don't know what I'd have done if Casey hadn't come along. She helped give me the courage to find myself, or at least the self I aspired to be from watching those endless 80s films with her. I didn't realize that was a fake version of me, too. At least now I've finally found myself. It only took twenty-two years.

'I hope this is worth it,' I say, as we gaze at the hill that leads towards the ruin. 'I know you said this view is to die for, but surely that's only if the walk doesn't kill me first? Remember, I'm not as fit as you.'

'I dunno, you look pretty fit to me!' Ryan says, and I'm startled out of my reverie by him cupping my bum as I straddle the stile.

'Hey, keep your hands to yourself, Cooper! No groping until after you've fed me lunch.'

'Now there's an incentive to get up that hill!' Ryan says, and he leaps over the stile and starts running ahead, despite carrying a heavy hamper. I start running but stagger to a halt with a stitch after a few metres, clutching my side and panting. Ryan comes back and shakes his head at me despairingly as he slides his arm around me.

'You need to get fit, Molly.'

'Hey,' I pant, bending over my knees and holding my side. 'I thought this was meant to be a date, not an assault course. Besides, if you run everywhere all the time you never get a chance to just pause and take in the view. Life isn't all about the destination, Ryan, it's about appreciating the journey.'

He tilts his head thoughtfully as if taking in my words, and I stand up and lift up my camera from where it is dangling around my neck. It's new – I bought it as a 'congratulations on my new job' gift to myself.

I pause from my snapping; I can feel Ryan staring at me. He's bouncing up and down on his feet, clearly unable to keep still.

'What?' I exclaim. 'Stop bloody jigging about, you're making me nervous!'

He holds his hands up and freezes in position. 'OK, OK, you win, we'll go much slower,' he says. 'I don't want to wear you out. Well, at least not like this.' And he winks and grins in a way that makes me glow with warmth and burn with heat. I don't know what it is, maybe it's the vivid, sun-soaked memories of our holiday in Ibiza, but being with Ryan makes me feel like I've swallowed sunshine.

I lift up my camera and scour our surroundings through the viewfinder. I start snapping, adjusting the lens and focus to try and catch the beauty of the panorama before me.

I'm so focused that I don't realize that Ryan has gone. I look around, suddenly panicked that I have upset him somehow by becoming so ensconced. I can't see him anywhere, but then I look down at the ground and laugh. There's a breadcrumb. And another. He obviously didn't want to interrupt me, and so he's left me a trail leading to our lunch. Smiling, I put my lens cap on and walk up the hill, suddenly feeling the urge to ignore the photographic opportunities surrounding me and to run, run to Ryan and not look back.

I reach the top of the hill and see Ryan standing there, facing out towards the Thames Estuary, framed by the ruins of the two towers. I quickly lift up my camera. Through it, he is a modern-day Adonis silhouetted in the historical footprint of the thirteenth-century castle. I carry on snapping, my throat feels raspy, like the earth's gravel has infiltrated the air and my lungs. I feel like I'm here, but not here. Present in this moment, but looking at it from above.

I look down to change the film. A whisper, then, just behind my left ear, a hand stroking my hair off my face and neck, a breath on my throat and over my lips that is as delicate as Constable's brushstrokes. Then a kiss, as delicious as the last and as tantalizing as the next. I yield to it and here, on this hill, our lips meet again. This time with no audience, no fanfare. No one but me, Ryan and the elements.

We are lying on a blanket, the debris of our picnic surrounds us: an empty bottle of Chardonnay and a beautiful home-made feast that Jamie Oliver would have been proud of. The sun is going down in a riot of glorious colour on our first date. Ryan turns his face and looks at me.

'So how was it for you?'

'The date, the view or the picnic?' I reply with a smile.

'All of it.'

'Are you looking for a score?'

'If you're offering!' He stares mischievously at me.

I slap him. 'Cheeky!'

'So come on, what's my score then?

I stare deep into his eyes. 'It was perfect. A perfect ten.'

A smile hovers over his lips that are as inviting as a thick duvet on a cold winter's night.

'Good.' He turns his face back up to the sky and we're both silent for a moment.

''Course, we haven't even had dessert yet,' he murmurs.

I gulp as his fingers brush against mine. 'What do you suggest?'

He rolls over and looks at me, his lips inches from mine. 'Something big.'

I blush.

'Something big and mouth-watering . . .'

'Something big, mouth-watering and creamy . . .' he grins, swoops up our picnic blanket and lunch debris, and chucks it into his rucksack. Then he grabs my hand, pulls me up and we run down the hill.

'Ice cream? You were talking about ICE CREAM?'

We're standing outside Rossi's on Southend Pier.

Ryan grins and opens the door. 'Yup! Why, what did you think I was offering?'

I ruffle my hair over my face so my flushed cheeks are hidden by it and walk in.

'So what's your flavour?' Ryan says, looking at the immense display of flavours.

'Black cherry,' I reply quickly. 'Because it's sweet and sour. What about you?'

'Tutti frutti because . . . just because.'

'So,' he says, leaning his lips into my ear. 'Shall we try putting them together? See if the combination works?'

I nod, mainly because: a) I have lost the ability to speak and b) I'm busy wondering if he's talking about ice cream or us.

We sit with our glass dish of ice cream between us, spooning the combination of flavours into our mouths (and it is perfect) as we chat easily.

I say easily, but the only thing that isn't easy about this conversation is the number of people I recognize in here. It feels like we're being watched and I say as much to Ryan.

He laughs and puts a menu up in front of us. I look at him.

'Are you ashamed of me, Cooper?' I say, putting on my best Sandy voice as I prepare to bastardize a quote from *Grease*. 'What ever happened to the Ryan Cooper I met at the beach?' All I need is the white cardi and yellow dress. And pumps. I *knew* I shouldn't have worn these heels.

'Huh?' he says, his expression blank. 'We didn't meet on the beach!' He drops the menu back onto the table and I laugh and then make my face deadly serious.

'You're a fake and a phoney and I wish I never laid eyes on you!'

Ryan looks startled. 'Eh? What have I done?'

I start laughing as I realize he thinks I'm serious. '*Grease*! It's a quote from *Grease*, the movie, Ryan!'

He shakes his head, his face blank. 'Nope. Never seen it.'

'What?' I reply. 'How can you never have seen *Grease*? It's a coming-of-age classic! Boy meets girl on holiday, they fall in love but when they get home they realize they've got nothing in common.'

'What year was it made?'

'Huh?'

'If it was before 1977 I wouldn't have seen it.'

I furrow my brow. 'Er, *why*?'

He grins. 'I don't watch or listen to anything that came out before I was born.'

I shake my head in disbelief. 'And again, *why*?'

He scoops up a massive spoonful of ice cream and pops it into his mouth.

'Because I'm all about the present, babe. No looking back.' And he flashes that grin again.

You Can Kiss This Goodbye Kiss

It is my experience that some friendships can flourish in the face of adversity but others bend and then break with the strain, like a tree in a thunderstorm. The roots remain there under the earth, a reminder of what once stood so tall but is no longer a visible part of the landscape of your life. In some ways it's sad because the tree no longer brings you daily joy with its strength, permanence and beauty. But then again, nor can it cast a shadow.

I can't tell you how hard it is when the person you love tells you they want you to leave. I didn't *want* to leave Ryan, not for a second. After we left the hospital we went for a walk down on the pier. Ryan said he wanted to get ice cream at Rossi's, so we did. We ordered a big multi-coloured mountain of our two favourite flavours. I'd once pointed out that my flavour was too bitter and his was too sweet but together they were perfect. A bittersweet thought now. The ice cream is slowly melting as we look at it and each other. Not crying, not talking, just holding hands across the table and watching it all melt away.

We didn't even need to speak about what we were going to do next. We knew we were both psyching ourselves up to go back to Jackie and Dave's. And when we finally did, it became clear that the best thing I could do was go home the following morning to give them some time alone with their son, and to pack some clothes so we could stay there for a few days. Jackie wasn't going to let Ryan leave so I had to leave him behind. Even if it wasn't the right thing for me.

I unlock our front door and walk through it, feeling like years have passed since I was last here. Was it really only yesterday morning that I watched Ryan leave in the wrong direction for work? I sink against the door, my feelings overwhelm my body and it feels like I am being carried on a tidal wave of grief. I stumble into the flat. Everything is exactly as we left it, the debris of a life together. Ryan's clothes are spread all around the place, breakfast dishes and an empty glass of home-made smoothie, the thick berry-red residue stuck to the glass. All discarded on the coffee table where he hurriedly had them in front of the news before leaving for work. Except it wasn't for work. And over there, on the windowsill, my mug of tea left, half-drunk because I was too busy spying on him and wondering what if . . .

I hear a noise approaching from the spare bedroom and then a plaintive call.

'Molly, is that you?'

Of course, Casey. I'd forgotten all about her, I'd deleted her from my mind like an unflattering digital photograph. I don't answer, I just pull our overnight bag out of the hallway cupboard and start throwing Ryan's discarded and dirty clothes in. I don't care what I pack. I just want to get some stuff and get out.

I feel her presence behind me, waiting for me to speak. But I don't. I can't. I can't tell her because Ryan doesn't want anyone to know, not yet.

'So I take it you're not speaking to me . . . right?' she says petulantly. 'Well, that's a bit *immature*. I thought you'd at least give me a chance to *explain* . . .' She starts to cry, a self-pitying whimper that instantly winds me up. I turn around and answer her curtly. I don't have time for these dramatics. Not now. Not any more.

'As far as I'm concerned, there's nothing for you to explain,' I say quietly. 'Ryan told me what happened. I get it. End of story.'

I want her to just accept that I am not going to talk about this further. She'll get over it, and so will I. But not right now.

'Oh, and you're just going to mug off my explanation then, huh? I bet you didn't mug off Ryan . . .'

'Don't, Casey,' I say dangerously quietly as I turn around and look at her.

She has thrown her hands on her hips and jutted them out in one direction, like a tween with attitude.

'Oh, well, if *you're* not in the mood. Because it's all about *you*, innit it, Molly? Huh?'

'No, Casey, it *isn't* about me.' I snap. I realize I am sounding like I'm correcting her language. I'm not, although she does always sound more Essex when she's emotional. Just like Ryan. *Ryan*. I swallow, close my eyes, breathe. Open them. All actions I have to concentrate fully on. 'You don't understand anything, so just leave it, OK?' And I turn my back on her again. 'I don't want to talk about it right now, I can't . . .'

'Well I do, OK, Molly? I want you to listen to me for once!' She pulls my arm and I swing around to see her brown eyes glittering at me with pent-up fury.

'Yeah, I came on to Ryan, and I'm sorry, but yeah, he rejected me, OK? It was just a stupid moment but oh, I for*got* – the mighty Molly never has stupid moments!' She pauses but just to draw breath. 'I'm SORRY, OK?' She shouts her apology, which is a curious method when trying to get someone's forgiveness, but I let it pass. Then she moves quickly into tears. It's like watching a toddler flitting between tantrums. She sniffs dramatically. 'I'm sorry that I was too scared to tell you the truth, Molly, because I *knew* you wouldn't understand. You could *never* understand how it feels to be me. I-I just wanted a little of what you had, I wanted it so much. I know I'm stupid, but that's me, ain't it, Molly? I've always been your stupid friend that you have to make excuses for. It was wrong. I know that now.' She is sobbing.

'Casey, I don't have time for this.' I push gently past her and into our bedroom. I start throwing clothes into the bag; his and mine, tangled together. She follows me in and slams the door shut behind her.

'You don't have *time*, Molly?' she screams, now in full tantrum. 'You don't have *time* because you're too busy living your perfect life to see just how perfect it actually IS. I mean . . .' this comes out as a high-pitched squeak, '*most* girls would be happy to have someone like Ryan. *I'd* have been happy to have someone like Ryan. I wouldn't have risked a relationship like that! I'd have stayed in Leigh, made him happy, I wouldn't have expected more, more, more, all the time! But you've always wanted more haven't you, Molly? Always thought you deserved better, even though you always had it ALL. You whinged about your parents, even though I'd have killed for mine to still be together, whinged about your glamorous job and then, *then* you whinged about Ryan!' I slump over the bag momentarily, her words disabling me because they're true. She shakes her head and her dark hair swings out around her face as she starts to cry again. 'But Ryan didn't want me.' She flops on to the floor. 'It's always been you. Right from that very first moment on The Broadway when I was trying so hard to get his attention but all he saw was you. And then again in Ibiza. I thought he'd come for me. I'd spent months, Molly, *months* while you were off swanning around at your fancy fucking uni, trying to get him to notice me. I even told him I was going to Ibiza in the vain hope that he might come. Not for you, for *me*. But as soon as he saw you, that was it. Game over. That's when I decided I'd try and settle for his brother. But even *he* didn't want me.'

I swing the bag over my shoulder and then I open the bedroom door and walk out. I'm barely hearing anything any more, even though Casey is still talking. Why is she still talking?

'I followed you, you know, on that last night, I saw you kiss. I would have done anything to switch places with you then, and I'd do anything to switch places with you now.'

I turn and look at her, one hand on the front door handle, the other is clasped around the the bag. I look at my best friend who suddenly doesn't know anything about me any more. She's a million miles away from me, even though she is right here in the same room.

'No, you wouldn't, Casey, you really, really wouldn't.' I open the door. 'I've got to go now and I'm afraid you can't be here when we get back.'

'What are you saying, Molly?' she half-yells, half-cries. 'Are you saying that's it? Fifteen years of friendship over just because of one stupid mistake? I said sorry! I said I'M SORRY!'

I close the door.

The PDA Kiss

Think of the most romantic PDAs in film history and you'll
probably think of these classic kisses: The 'Golly, Moses'
kiss between Katharine Hepburn and James Stewart in A
Philadelphia Story; Ingrid and Humphrey's 'Kiss me as if it
were the last time' in Casablanca; the infamous 'water's edge'
kiss between Burt Lancaster and Deborah Kerr in From Here
to Eternity; Clark Gable and Vivien Leigh's epic kiss in front of
a flame-orange sky in Gone With the Wind; the kiss in the rain
between Audrey and George in Breakfast at Tiffany's; and not
forgetting Ally MacGraw's 'I care' kiss with Ryan O'Neal in Love
Story. All beautiful, touching, romantic, heartfelt, passionate –
and not a tongue in sight.

They sure knew how to kiss back then, didn't they?

In my job, I've been sent thousands of pap shots from picture
agencies, always containing a batch of pictures of celebs tongue-
thrashing in a club, or at a PA. I've witnessed pictures of Paris
Hilton with lips (and legs) locked around various men (and
women), Pink and Carey sucking face, Britney doing whatever
with whoever. No wonder it put me off PDAs for so long.

But recent events have lead me to realize that I want to
celebrate love in all its glory. PDAs don't have to be vulgar and
uncomfortable viewing. Because at their best these intimate
declarations of affection are beautiful; a snapshot of someone
else's love that makes the world feel brighter and better
somehow. That's how I feel about them, anyway.

I hope you feel the same.

Things to do!!!

1. ~~Get tickets to a cup final match? (UEFA CUP querter finals in Glasgow – done!!!!!)~~
2. VIP tickets to a Take That reunion gig (spoken to their PR. Said is definite possibility. Plus backstage pass!!!)
3. See the national surfing championships (Newquay? Or abroad maybe????!! Talk to Susie, the travel & lifestyle ed)
4. Get bespoke suit made? Savile Row? He's always wanted one – could wear it to his 30th party??
5. Meet David Beckham?!?! (Talk to DB's football academy about the work Ryan has done with the kids in Hackney?)
6. Something with Jamie Oliver? (Or just go to dinner at Fifteen maybe?!)
7. Create bespoke ice-cream flavour?!!
8. Go to a film premiere – a romantic comedy maybe?? (Ask Cara)
9. Go back to New Yor—

The tube jolts to a stop and my pen scrawls across the page in a big, thick angry line. I tut and try to finish writing my list. *Go back to New York.*

All around me people have been pressed against each other like the climax of some sort of fully clothed bacchanalian orgy, and now they jostle to get off and I watch as the carriage refills and I go back to studying my to-do list. The most important to-do list I've ever written.

It's his Bucket List, you see . . . no, it's his *Fuck it* List.

Fuck it, Cancer! You're not taking him until this list is complete! And maybe by then you'll have forgotten him and won't take him at all.

I waggle my pen quickly between my teeth. I need more things on here.

More things, more things, more things.

More things means more time.

Fill the page, Molly. What about go to a Grand Prix? Or drive at Silverstone? Ryan would LOVE to do that! I scribble it down in excitement. What else, what else? What else can my husband do before he dies?

I look up with a sudden overwhelming urge to tell everyone around me that my husband is dying. He's Dying. It's cancer. Skin cancer. He's twenty-nine.

It would be a Chinese whisper that spreads through the carriage like the disease has spread. That way perhaps it would infect everyone else's life, not just mine. No, not infect, that isn't very nice. I mean *af*fect. I want it to affect everybody. Move them, mark them, shake them like the tube is shaking on the rails right now.

I want their lives to be shaking on the rails like mine is.

And Ryan's, *obviously* Ryan's. I know this isn't all about me, but sometimes, it feels like it is. Is it wrong of me to say that? I mean, in some ways, and yes, I know this sounds awful but I can't help it, in some ways I'm jealous of him. Ryan's pain is going to come to an end. Mine isn't. Mine won't.

The two people standing in front of me part momentarily and I see a man in a suit opposite, absent-mindedly turning the pages of his newspaper. Suddenly I hate him. I hate that he is OK and my husband isn't. I hate that he can casually read a newspaper when I can only concentrate on this list. I haven't read a book, or newspaper, or magazine article in weeks. I can't. Not even the ones in our magazine. I pretend to, but I can't take anything in.

It's like my brain is overflowing with information. Since Ryan was diagnosed I feel like I have to remember *everything*. Not just about him, us, the day-to-day of life, but the entire six years of our relationship.

I'm busy trying to commit to memory every moment as it happens, every single glance, word, joke, tear, kiss – as well as all the ones that have been before. I'm saving them in a folder marked 'After' in the desktop of my brain. And then there are all the things I have to do on a daily basis, for me, for him, for work, but mostly for him. Thank God, I've always been good at writing lists. I need them more than ever now.

Not that Ryan seems to be very happy with them. He shakes his head when I pull out another piece of paper filled with my neat writing and pin it up around the flat.

'Is this what my life is going to be reduced to?' he'd said angrily, ripping the list of medication I'd pinned up just a few days after his diagnosis. 'A series of fucking lists? Why don't the doctors make some lists of how to actually *make* me better rather than just trying to make me *feel* better. These ain't going to stop me dying, are they? Well? Are they?'

We'd both been warned by the doctors and support nurses to expect this reaction but still, it was hard, seeing him so unlike himself, oscillating between fury one minute and utter depression the next. It didn't last long though, a week maximum, and then he seemed to gradually get back to himself. It was almost like he'd needed to get it out of his system, like some big emotional purging. He still doesn't like the lists though. But I need them. Sometimes it feels like they're the only things helping me hold it all together. There's a list of his medication, the anti-sickness drugs for after his chemo that he has at our local hospital. (Ryan refused his parents' offer for private care and an instant move back to Leigh. He said he wanted to stay at home in London with me.) There's also various painkillers and aperients for his constipation. There's another list of all his appointments; his chemo treatment plan (there was no question about him wanting to try it. He told the doctor he was going for the miracle. He was going to be the statistic that beat the odds. I hated seeing the doctor's blank expression.). Then there's Ry's school timetable (he's determined to keep working as much as possible, for as long as possible) so I know exactly where he is at any moment, just in case, and a list of emergency numbers for me to call if I need help; his GP, Crossroads – the carer support organization that Charlie advised me to contact as I don't have any family really close. Charlie is our Macmillan nurse and he's been so wonderful, such a great support. I honestly don't know what we would have done without him. And thank God I can talk to him. No one else seems able to deal with me these days, apart from my parents. But Charlie is the perfect confidante. He listens and advises and organizes and supports. He acts as a go-between with Ryan and I, he makes us laugh and relax. He makes Ryan feel like a young man, not a cancer-stricken young man. He talks to him about football and bands, the news, teaching, life. But I know Ryan also asks him things that he won't ever discuss with me. Like how much time is left. And me? I talk to Charlie to find out just how the hell I'm meant to deal with Ryan's illness – as well as being my husband's carer. It's a role I haven't trained or prepared for. I don't know what I'm doing, or if what I'm doing is right. And I don't know what's going to come next. That's what scares me the most, actually. What Comes Next. Charlie is helping me prepare me for that. That day in the not too distant future when I'll have to sign a Do Not Resuscitate form. He gives me eventualities, options, tells me things to consider. He is compassionate but he tells it how it is, too. Something that not many people I know want to do any more.

Take the list of people to call to tell them that Ryan has cancer. Ryan doesn't want to do it and I did ask Jackie but she refused to do it as well.

'Why worry them about nothing?' she'd trilled cheerfully, music pounding down the telephone line from behind her. She said she was doing Davina McCall's workout DVD. 'Just trying to keep fit, Molly babes!' as if she can get fit for the both of them. I understand; this is her list. 'We'll just invite them to the party when he's got the all clear!'

Then there's my daily to-do lists for home, all the normal domestic stuff: paying bills, food shopping, jobs to do around the flat. There's a list of numbers for odd-job men who can help me when Ryan can't. There's also a list of local estate agents as I need to start getting valuations for the flat. We haven't really spoken much about the next stage because Ryan is determined to stay in our flat for as long as possible. It's been so hard for me knowing that just isn't possible. I was so desperate that I asked Charlie out for a drink to talk about everything. I just felt the need to pour out my troubles like I would with a friend. It's painful that Ryan won't talk about the future. It makes me so scared feeling like I'm going to be dealing with all this on my own, right till the end. And then I feel horribly selfish. I mean, of course I'm going to look after my husband, I wouldn't have it any other way, but Ryan isn't thinking of how much worse it's going to get. So I took Charlie to our local bar and talked about Ryan's stubbornness to plan for the future. He listened like he always does and gave me some great advice. At which point I, embarrassingly and very publically, kissed him on the cheek. People probably thought we were on a date or something, but I just wanted to say thanks for being such a great support. It didn't bother Charlie, he handled this scared, grateful woman with his normal, easy charm. Neither Ryan nor I would know what to do without him. Anyway, on his next visit Charlie did try to gently point out to Ry that living in a second-floor flat might prove 'difficult' in the near future and laid out some options, but Ryan didn't want to hear them.

I know that a move back to Leigh is not far away. Ideally, I'd like us to try and move there before it's too late ... Somewhere where he can see the sea and be near his friends and family. I wish we could go now. I wish I could give up work and dedicate *my* life to the rest of his. But he won't consider it yet. He says he wants life to go on as normal and he wants life to be as normal as possible for me. But he doesn't seem to realize how hard it is. My life has stopped already. I might be going through the motions of normality, but really, my life is on permanent pause as I try to prepare myself for the next few months of caring for my dying husband.

I can't concentrate on anything else, I can't go out and have fun, get drunk, lose myself in my work, listen to a song without bawling my eyes out. I can't sit on a train without hating everyone else for not having Ryan's cancer. I can't stop hating myself for not noticing that mole sooner.

And I also can't stop thinking about all the things I've done wrong over the course of our relationship.

That is the longest list and the most depressing of all, and the one that's constantly in my head. The list of my fuck-ups. It's the list that berates me for running away from Ryan that night in The Grand, and on the *Bembridge*. It chastises me for doubting our relationship. It mentally beats me up for every moan and gripe I've ever had with him. For not stopping him going on all those bloody sunbeds. For letting him slather himself with baby oil on holiday instead of factor-30. It shouts at me for every argument we had, every kiss of apology that I stubbornly turned away from and every graze of his lips that I took for granted.

And then of course, there's that other kiss. The one that broke us up. That's the one festering away in my memory, infecting all the others. And I hate it. I hate it because it debilitates me. It causes me to sob in the night when I think of Ryan dying and him ever doubting for a millisecond how much I've always loved him. Then I hate myself for crying and I have to take myself off to our lounge so he doesn't hear me, but I know he does because the next morning he always tells me that it's OK, that everything is OK, and that he is so lucky to have me. That he's always felt lucky to have me.

So no matter what Ryan or anyone else thinks, I can't actually do anything to forget any of this. But still, every night he asks me if there's a bar I could go to, or some press launch I could drink champagne at – as if that might make me forget for a moment.

He also asks if I've spoken to Casey, and I tell him I have, but I know he doesn't believe me.

'Don't let what happened ruin nearly fifteen years of friendship, Molly, it's not worth it,' he said the other night, when we were curled up on our couch, watching back-to-back DVDs and picking over some snacks after he'd come out of hospital from his third – and as it turned out – his last bout of chemo. The doctor told us that there was no point continuing. It is now in his bowels too. I knew Ryan wanted to add, 'Life's too short', but thankfully, he didn't. Instead he said, 'Casey just made a silly mistake.'

I'd nodded, but ignored him all the same. I didn't want to talk about her, not any more and especially not now. Strangely, this post-chemo time has become something to look forward to. It's been an opportunity for us to slow down time, slow down life. I'm not at work and no one bothers us. When he's in hospital for the day, on a drip after the chemo injection, we just hang out, chatting for hours, reading magazines and making each other laugh. I've started taking along photo albums for us to look through as we'll always have a giggle at ourselves. Afterwards we always go home, get lots of little snacks (Ryan doesn't have enough of an appetite to do anything other than pick at things) and we re-watch our favourite movies, just like we used to do when we were first dating.

Life feels normal, for a while.

But the cancer is a silent partner in our relationship, sprawled confidently on the couch between us, just like Casey used to be. In many ways we have replaced one poisonous disease with another. Because the way I see it, Casey tried to kill our relationship, and that's why I can't forgive her. Or forgive myself for letting her infiltrate her way between us. For ignoring her, like Ryan ignored his mole.

All I want to do now is close off the rest of the world and look after my husband. Although according to him, I'm not *allowed* to look after him. It's why we're still living in our flat in London instead of moving home, like Jackie and Dave want him to. It's why he's still teaching, well, part-time anyway. I want him to stop but he says being around the kids makes him feel better. And he can still shout and train them on the pitch, even if he can't run any more. He says he's a bit like Tom Cruise in *Born on the Fourth of July*, but without the wheelchair (yet) and less hair.

So the lists, but mostly *this* list – Ryan's Fuck It list – has become my life. It feels like the only positive list I have. And it gives me a reason to go to work. I know I couldn't organize a fraction of the things without my colleagues. He doesn't know I've written it, but it's my way of getting the most out of the last few months . . . out of his last summ— out of his *life* as we possibly can. I want him to feel like he's achieved everything he's ever wanted, I want to pack in everything we possibly can, make him feel like he hasn't missed out on a thing.

'Hey! Molly! I've got something for you!' Cara comes over to my desk with a weird smile painted on her face. I look up from Ryan's list and I study her face, her teeth-baring, eye-squinting, frozen smile.

Everyone seems to be sporting these for me ever since I told them that my husband is dying. The reactions from people I know are extreme; they're either black-and-white woeful or technicolour cheerful. Is that really what life and death comes down to? Those two theatrical masks?

It's like they're worried that if they don't act upbeat I will fall apart in front of them, and if they think I'm going to fall apart they want to be properly prepared to join me in my misery. Most of my friends don't know how to talk to me. Some of them *aren't* talking to me, OK ... I mean, I'm not talking to *them*.

Mia phoned me immediately. She just cried. I've never heard her cry before. It was most odd.

My mum and dad told me they were praying for him. I hadn't thought about doing that, so I'm glad they are. It's strangely comforting.

Jackie, well, Jackie doesn't believe it's happening. She's what the counsellors call 'in denial' and what I call 'unhinged'. She won't even utter the word 'cancer' and she calls his chemo 'the saviour'. She doesn't seem to understand that it isn't curative, it is just to prolong his life for as long as possible.

Dave is perpetually quiet and sober. Neither are words I'd have ever used to describe him before.

Carl won't talk about it, and all Lydia will talk about is holidays; where we're going next, the ones we've had before. It's like she's gone into Extreme Hairdresser mode. It's her way of not speaking, in that she's saying nothing at all.

No one seems to be dealing with this disease in any sort of help-ful way, but at least it means I can just put all my focus on Ryan. I feel very alone though. Already.

Then there are the people I don't know. I've told them, too. Funnily enough they don't know what to say either. Like the guy from the call centre who was trying to sell me life insurance and was understandably thrown off script when I burst into tears and told him that my husband has cancer. Oh, and the man from the newsagents at the tube station who asked if I wanted a free bar of Dairy Milk with my magazine and I said no, I'd just like my husband to not have terminal cancer. I don't mean to tell them, it just kind of comes out. It's like it's always there, on the tip of my tongue, in my mouth, my throat, behind my eyes, under my nostrils, beneath my fingernails, on my skin, between my toes, under my scalp.

I'm living and breathing the cancer, and Ryan is dying from it.

'Hi, Cara!' I smile and sit back on my chair. I spin around and then smile again. Her smile is still frozen in place, her eyes dart from side to side like she's looking for an escape route. 'Ahh, what can I ahh . . . do you for?'

I frown. God, I sound like my dad. It's the kind of thing he blurts out awkwardly. Cara swallows, looks around awkwardly and then the cartoon smile returns.

'I just wanted to let you know I've got you guys tickets for tomorrow! Can you go?'

'YES!!!' I do an air punch then pick up my pen and draw a thick straight line through 'Go to film premiere'. 'Thanks, Cara! That's brilliant!' I stand up to give her a hug and then glance down at my computer screen. It's open at my blog page, and on it is a photo that I've just uploaded. It's me and Ryan kissing on the top of the Franz Josef glacier in New Zealand.

The sun is just rising behind us, shrouding us in light so we look almost metaphysical. Ever since Ryan's diagnosis I've been posting pictures of us. Mainly because I don't seem to feel much like taking photos right now. I give them all a little heading; this one is 'The Kiss at the top of the World', and sometimes I write more. A memory of ours, a moment or a thought about love that I want to share. I want it to be out there in the ethos, so that when Ryan is gone, I'm not the only one left with them. They feel like my own little messages in a bottle. I don't know who's going to receive them, or what they're going to think, but it helps me somehow.

'I'm sure there's more I can help you with, too!' Cara says brightly. 'And I spoke to Susie and she's sure she can sort the surfing championships, and the press passes for the Take That gig is a definite!'

I feel my heart flutter with appreciation and . . . is that panic?

So many things to cross off The List! That means I need to think of more things to do.

'Thanks, Cara,' I say gratefully. 'Ryan is going to be so thrilled! We went to the UEFA cup quarter-finals at the weekend, too!'

'Wow!' Cara exclaims overzealously. 'I bet he absolutely loved it!'

I think back to that afternoon. We'd sat in a corporate box, glass of champagne in our hands, a rug over our knees, watching Seville play Tottenham Hotspur. I kept glancing at Ryan in excitement and squeezing his hand, and he'd turn and smile at me, but then I'd see him look away and down, into the crowds, and it would disappear like a cloud passing over the sun.

'Are you enjoying yourself?' I'd asked in excitement.

'Oh yes, Molly,' he'd said politely. 'It's well good! A dream come true! I can't believe you organized all this!' But there was something in his voice that told me this wasn't the whole truth.

'Well, you know me, friends in high places and all that!' Everyone knows about The List – except Ryan. It's quite overwhelming how much my colleagues want to help me and how much they're willing to put themselves out. Christie couldn't have been more supportive.

'I can sign you off if you like, Molly,' she said gently, 'at full pay. Whatever you need ... however long you need, you just let me know.'

I'd shaken my head vehemently. 'No thanks, Christie, I need to be here. I've got so much to do! Such a long list! And Ryan wants things to be normal. He's at school most days. I just need the days off after he has the chemo, if that's OK?'

'Of course, whatever you need ...' she'd paused. 'This photo of you and Ryan is beautiful.' I'd looked up and seen that her computer was open at my blog; it was the one of Ryan and I kissing in a photobooth in Lakeside.

'That was just after he asked me to move in with him,' I'd said, tears burning behind my eyes. 'God, we look so young! What *are* we wearing?' I'd laughed, then snorted so that a bubble of snot came out of my nose. I'd wiped it away quickly, embarrassed to be doing this in front of Christie. She'd quickly clicked the window shut.

We're standing in a heaving Leicester Square, the crowds are pouring into it like mixture into a cake tin, the drip, drip, drip, of the crowd trying to spread as close to the edge of the red carpet as possible. I'm clutching our embossed tickets. I feel horribly overdressed in my metallic dress, giant chandelier earrings and silver high heels. Ryan looks like he wishes he was at home on the sofa. Dressing up just felt like the thing we should do but no other non-celebrity has made this much effort. We look like we think we're the stars of the film. It's excruciatingly embarrassing.

'Shall we just get this over with?' Ryan says, his voice reedy with nerves and exhaustion. We stare at the stretch of red carpet before us that felt incredibly exciting in our heads, but now looks petrifying. It's like we're being forced to walk the plank.

'No,' I say determinedly with a big smile. 'Let's just wait a bit longer.' I'm not going to show him I'm scared. We need to get as much out of this as possible, and that means waiting to ensure we get to stand near some superstar celebrities.

'Molleee, come on,' Ryan says through gritted teeth. 'I'm shitting myself here.'

'You Essex boys,' I chastise, 'all mouth and no trousers.' I grab his hand. 'Come on, there's nothing to be scared of!'

'Right now, cancer seems less frightening than this red carpet,' Ryan replies, uncharacteristically quietly. This is the most subdued I've ever seen him but I know how he feels.

'Look,' I whisper, 'we're only doing this once and we're going to do it properly, OK? Now, just do what I say.'

'Ooh, OK, Little Miss Bossy,' Ryan says. I look at him and wink, trying not to show how upset I get when I look at him. I glance back quickly and see a long, sleek black car has arrived. Then I see a leg emerge, a short, suit-clad leg, with a body attached to a smile. And another Cheshire Cat smile, like Dr Harper's. But this is bigger, beamier. It is one of the most recognizable smiles in the world.

'It'ssss him,' I hiss. 'Tom Cruissssssse.' Ryan's head swivels, trying to catch a glimpse of his all-time favourite film idol.

'Don't look now!' I say. 'Play it cool. Do what I do, OK? Wait, wait ... And GO!' I start walking, slowly, deliberately down the red carpet, waving at the crowds, clinging on to Ryan's hand. He squeezes it and looks at me, his eyes bulging out of his head as if to say, 'What the hell are you doing?' But also because they do that these days because his face is so sunken. He's lost so much weight since the last bout of chemo – and his hair loss doesn't help. Not that he isn't still jaw-droppingly handsome, of course. He's still gorgeous to me, just in a more ... ethereal way. But I know to others he's horrifying. His skin is sallow; the yellowy-grey of a streetlamp glowing in the fog. His head is bare and there are lesions over it. His clothes, which fitted just a week ago, hang off his body, even his teeth appear too big for his mouth.

'Walk slowly,' I hiss. 'Re-ea-all-yyy sloooow-leeey.'

'Why?' Ryan hisses back at me. 'Everyone's looking at us ...'

'That's the point, Ry,' I say. 'We, my friend, are going to get papped next to Tom Cruise!'

'Are you *crazy*?' he says, pulling my arm taut to try to stop me. 'Everyone can tell we're nobodies. And have you seen his security team? They're massive!'

I stop in my tracks, right in the middle of the red carpet, turn and grip him by the arms. I realize that I can feel his bones. 'You, Ryan Cooper, are not *nobody*, you never have been a *nobody* and you never will be a nobody, *do you hear me*?'

People are looking. A couple of photographers are holding their cameras away from their faces and looking at us quizzically. 'You are *not* a nobody, OK, Cooper?' I repeat firmly, doing my best not to cry.

Ryan glances back at the crowds behind us, at the photographers who are now ignoring us because actual celebrities are walking past ('Kelly! Kelly Brook! Over here! Nice dress, darlin'! Oh, and Fearne!!! Fearne Cotton! Can we get a picture? Gis a smile, Geri, come on, darlin'!') I wipe my hand across my nose and put my clutch bag under my arm, and then I see Ryan turn back round to face me and he's grinning and his eyes are bright, and then he grabs me, pulls me towards him, tilts me backwards and kisses me for such a long time that I can't breathe. Flashlights pop and I close my eyes, not just to savour this kiss, just like I promised myself I would, but because I am blinded by the flashes. ('Who are those two? Were they in *Big Brother*? Oh yeah, I knew I recognized them! What are their names! Gissa another kiss, wontcha?')

And Ryan pulls back from my lips and looks into my eyes, a little twinkle forming in them like stars coming out when the sun is still up in the sky.

'That oughta do the trick huh, Moll?' he says, and I start laughing. And then he raises me back up and we kiss and hug. But suddenly Ryan goes stiff and slowly turns his head as someone pats him on the shoulder.

'Hey, loving your PDA, dude! It's almost as good as mine!' And Tom grins, his face looming towards us as he murmurs quietly and then sweeps on by with his minders, leaving only the memory of his words and his smile as Ryan and I look at each other. Both sets of our eyes are now bulging out of our heads and we burst out laughing.

In the cinema we take our seats and I slip my hand – which is still shaking after our close encounter with Tom Cruise – into Ryan's, and settle back to enjoy the film. But five minutes in he leans over and whispers, 'Can we go home, Molly? I don't think . . . I don't think I'm feeling very good.'

That night I put him to bed and I lie there until his breathing becomes heavy and regular. I lie there holding him for as long as possible, willing sleep to come for me, too. But I can't. I slip out of bed and I go to the lounge, crying more the further away I get from Ryan. I'm crying because I know what I'm doing isn't stopping anything. We are doing all these amazing things we've always dreamed of, but it's not enough. I sit on the sofa and it is then that I see a piece of paper that is propped up on the coffee table by the flamingo. The bloody flamingo. He's found it then. My list. The Fuck It List. He must have seen it before we went out tonight.

I reach out to take my list to see if he's added anything to it. I glance down the page in confusion, and disbelief. The heading and every single thing on it has been crossed off.

Underneath he's written a new list:

Ryan's To Be List
I want to be with you

I want to be with my family and friends

I don't want to be mollycoddled!!!!

I want to be able to live life as normally as possible with you

I don't want you to be constantly beating yourself up or feeling guilty for things you can't change and that I wouldn't even want to change

I want to be able to take time to look back on my life, not try to cram in any more.

I want you to be able to see what I feel: that I'm a man completely fulfilled. I have everything I ever wanted, Molly, and I don't regret anything. Not a thing

And then, this:

I don't want to DO any more, Molly, I just want to be

I bite my lip as I read his list, nodding and sobbing as I take in what he is trying to tell me. I've just been blindly forging ahead, trying to do things that will make me feel better about Ryan dying, not him. Because I'm not ready for him to die. He may be, but I'm not. I don't know how I'm going to live without him.

His handwriting blurs before my eyes and I start seeing double, then I realize that it's the writing from the other side of the thin A4 notepaper showing through. I don't remember writing anything on that side. I turn it over and that is when I begin to really sob, because on it Ryan has written another list. One just for me. I read each line slowly, trying to commit each one to memory, stroking his scrawly, spiky, handwriting with my fingers.

Molly's To Be List

I want you to be happy!

I want you to be positive!

I want you to be able to look back without any regrets!

I want you to be able to let go of the past and live in the moment!

I want you to be a photographer. You are brilliant at it. Why have you stopped taking photos? I may have cancer but you still have your eyes, and your hands, and most importantly, your vision

I want you to be loved. Whoever loves you next, will love you forever. Because it will be impossible not to. Believe me, I know. And if I were still here I'd shake his hand, because I know how lucky he is

I want you to be a mum. You will be properly awesome

at it. And no, Moll, I don't regret us not having children. It would kill me (ho ho!) to know I was leaving them behind. I am glad it was just me and you, Moll, do you hear me? I mean it

I want you to be proud of the woman you are and to know that I was so proud to be loved by you. You made my life complete, that's why I don't care about not getting old. We had it all so young, didn't we? I had it all so young. And what man could ask for more?

I finally have a list of stuff that actually matters. The only list that will ever matter to me again. I kiss the piece of paper, brushing my lips over his handwriting, trying to inhale his words and sentiment, to swallow the love that he's written this list with. This here, is Ryan, a man who has never wanted anything more than what's he's got, who's lived a full life by living simply. He has always had his priorities right, not just now, when facing death, but his whole life. He's never chased ridiculous dreams or put emphasis on anything other than being a good friend, son, brother, boyfriend, teacher and husband. I've learned so much from him but he is still teaching me. And I know he'll be teaching me for a long time to come.

I put the piece of paper down on the coffee table and go into the kitchen and switch on the kettle, I know sleep is not coming for me tonight. As I lean against the wall, looking around our flat, our home, I start constructing something in my head. Words, then sentences, then a paragraph.

I carry my tea out to the lounge, get my laptop and tap into my blog account. My fingers hover over the keys as I sit and stare at the blank screen, unused to pouring my feelings into anything other than a photo. Then I open the folder on my laptop marked 'Wedding' and flick through all the photos on there until I come to the one I want. It is of Ryan and me, standing under the canopy of sunset-red, orange and yellow wild flowers that I'd chosen, the sun was about to dip into the sea behind us and we stood, me in white, him in pale blue, like we're the eye of a fire. Our heads are tilted towards each other, smiling lips pressed against each other, hands clasped to each other's cheeks, sharing our first kiss as man and wife.

I stare at it for a moment and then I write. I pause and underline it.

The 'Til Death Do Us Part Kiss

For a girl who never thought she believed in marriage, once I came around to the idea I wondered what the hell had held me back for so long. All this time I'd been afraid of the permanence of the institution, the finality, the absolution.

One person for the rest of your life.

Now I know that this isn't always possible.

I look at the wedding photo again, take a sip of my tea and then continue typing, the words flooding out of my fingers.

Because after finally finding my 'happy ever after' I have recently found out that my gorgeous, athletic, funny, kind, caring, fitness- and football-fanatic husband, has terminal cancer. He's nearly 30 and I'm 28. We've known each other since we were teenagers; we had our first kiss when I was 15 and he was 17 in a bar called The Grand (it was disastrous); we had our second (incredible) kiss in our early twenties, after bumping into each other on holiday in Ibiza (I think he stalked me, he still denies this!). We moved in together when all our friends were having one-night stands, but then split up temporarily, only to realize that we belonged together. We got engaged in New York, in Central Park, by the Imagine Memorial in Strawberry Fields on 23rd November 2005 (my 26th birthday). It was an utterly magical moment. Then we got married, in Ibiza on 22nd April 2006, and it was completely out of this world. I feel like I have loved him for forever, and because of that, I foolishly thought we still had forever.

Since his diagnosis I've been consumed by the need to make every single moment count, to try and make what is left of Ryan's life worthwhile. I've even written a to-do list, a way of making sure Ryan has done everything he's ever dreamed of. My colleagues have kindly helped me to arrange some incredible experiences for Ryan, which we've been slowly working our way through, but I've just found a list that he has written for me. Not a To Do List, but a To Be List. He's pointed out that there is nothing that he would do differently, that his life has been full because of the choices he has made, the incredible friends he has, his amazing family who he has always been enviably close to, his teaching job which he loves. His students are like his own kids; he nurtures them, gives them unequivocal time, patience and understanding when no one else has. He's never desired more than he has. He's always been happy, sometimes annoyingly so (have you ever tried arguing with someone who is smiling? It's infuriating!) And that all he wants from now on is to be with those he loves. To be, not do.

His mum, Jackie, always jokes that he was born smiling. Now he jokes that he will die smiling too. You've got to laugh, I guess. And we do, but sometimes I find it really hard.

I have spent hours wishing that I could find a way to hold on to Ryan forever, and right now, it feels like this blog is it. For the past few months you've shared my view of life and love through a camera lens; on my trip to New York, my walks to work, all the places Ryan and I have been. Since he was diagnosed I've been putting up some photos of Ryan and me.

I guess it's because I want other people to share the greatest love I have ever, will ever, know. I wish I could have captured every single kiss that Ryan and I have shared and post them here so you could see how much I have had by having Ryan, and who I have become by being with him. I wish that all of you would go and kiss your loved ones right now and savour it – and savour every one that follows it. Because when you know that those kisses are finite, that each one you share is bringing you closer to goodbye, you'll wonder why you wasted so many. So please, for me, take Ryan's life advice, stop doing and start being. Be kind to each other, be grateful for each other, be true to each other. Don't throw away your kisses, not a single one. The future isn't promised to any of us, so kiss till you can't kiss any more, on the street, in front of everyone! Kiss as if each one were the last. And then save them to your memory so you can cherish them forever. Just like I'm doing.

Molly xx

The Uncontrollable Kiss

Have you ever given yourself to a kiss so completely, so indisputably, that you felt like you surrendered some of yourself and replaced it with a part of them? It happened when I came back from Ibiza. With that kiss, Ryan triggered my metamorphosis into a butterfly. Socially, physically and psychologically. He'd breathed new life into me, caressed my soul with his lips. And I couldn't go back into my cocoon. Not now, not with him, not ever.

REW 30/07/01 18.00 p.m.>

'God, that felt like the longest Monday ever,' Jo sighs as a group of us huddle into the lift just after 6 p.m. 'I hate press week. No matter how organized we are, it always ends up being totally stressful. I need a drink. Anyone going to join me?'

I glance at my watch – all I really want to do is get settled into my new flat, pour a glass of wine and unpack some boxes.

'Oh, come on,' badgers Jo, as the lift doors open into the yawning reception of Brooks Inc, *Viva*'s publishing company. 'I want to hear more about this holiday romance . . .'

I ignore her. I really don't want to talk about Ryan any more. I'm pretty sure I won't hear from him again. Once a player . . .

The revolving doors spit us out one by one and into Long Acre, the main thoroughfare into Covent Garden that's absolutely heaving on this balmy July evening. We stand chatting for a couple of minutes, trying to work out which bar to go to, finally settling on The Langley, which is just round the corner.

'MOLLY!' I hear a distant shout and turn around quickly, unsure where it came from and if it was directed at me. The early evening sunshine bounces off the glass of the store windows, blinding me temporarily, and we are suddenly swallowed up by hordes of people who are swarming out of the tube station. All I can see is a mass of heads.

'Did you just hear that or am I going mad?' I ask Jo.

'I heard it,' she affirms.

'MOLLY!' I swivel around again and this time I see the biggest bouquet of flowers crossing the road, causing the crowds to part and cars to magically screech to a halt. Even black cabs. The person who appears to have a bouquet of flowers in place of a head is dodging across the road and shouting like it's a matter of life of death.

'Sorry, excuse me ... I've just got to ... MOLLY!'

I hear the girls gasp and my jaw drops open as Ryan appears before me, grinning widely and panting. Little beads of perspiration have formed on his tanned brow, his arms, totally exposed in a blue T-shirt with a red hooded puffa warmer over the top are pumped with exertion, and his blue eyes are shimmering like the sea we swam in together in Ibiza.

'Ryan? What on earth are you doing here? You're meant to still be in Ibiza!' I say, holding my hand over my eyes to shade them from the still-bright sun. I can't believe he's standing here before me like a mirage, bathed in the soft yellow late-evening light. He looks almost angelic with this aura of light around him.

He looks at the group of magazine girls gathered around me, who are all visibly swooning, and he holds out the flowers to me.

'I just couldn't get through another day without seeing you,' he says. 'I cut my holiday short and caught the next flight home, shortly after you.'

I stare at him in shock, studying his face for signs of this being a joke. I look around to see if I can see Alex, or Carl, or any of the other lads with him.

I fold my arms – mainly to cover up the fact that it feels like my heart is pounding out of my chest.

'Are you being serious, Cooper?' I say, raising my eyebrow at him, just like Casey taught me.

'I'm deadly serious,' his beautiful mouth is set in a determined line. I look at him for a moment, then down at the ground, unable to take this in. I see his hand reach for mine and I acquiesce to his touch. I feel like a magnetic force is drawing us together. I'm beginning to think it has been for years.

'I have been in love with you since the moment I first saw you, Molly Carter,' Ryan says. 'Now can we stop pretending that this isn't meant to be?'

He steps towards me and despite the crowds, despite the fact that I am standing in front of my new workplace with my new colleagues, and despite the fact I don't do PDAs, I throw myself uncontrollably into his arms, unable to resist him a moment longer. I gaze deeply into his eyes as our lips meet again and I see his unguarded expression, the love and vulnerability in place of the fake machismo. And just as that has vanished, so does my last thread of doubt about him. Ryan Cooper is my destiny. I know that more than I've known anything in my life. As our arms entwine around each other and we continue to kiss, I hear the sound of my colleagues cheering and I break away from him, embarrassed suddenly. But he pulls me back close to him and then we begin to laugh, our bodies shuddering together, foreheads touching bashfully as we realize that Jo has been taking pictures of us.

She shrugs, lifting up her camera. 'Soz, it just felt like a classic Kodak moment!'

'One more for luck?' Ryan smiles as he leans in.

And for the first time in my life, I really do feel like the luckiest girl in the world.

The Long Distance Kiss

It was Blanche DuBois (well, Tennessee Williams actually) who said, 'I have always depended on the kindness of strangers.' I realize now that I don't think I've ever really let myself depend on anyone other than Ryan. But I need to now. I need my friends and my family, but I also need this. You. All of you. I draw strength and support from the messages on this blog every single day. I've been overwhelmed by them all. And I want you to know, that no matter the distance these kind wishes and prayers have travelled over, they have all been accepted with heartfelt, untold thanks. They mean more than you could ever know.

My work phone rings, an urgent, persistent drilling sound that disturbs any creative thought I have left in my brain. I can't think straight at the best of times, let alone when I am interrupted every five minutes and am battling with Mika's perpetually perky album, *Life in Cartoon Motion*, pumping out on the stereo in stark contrast to my own dark inner monologue.

How is Ryan? Should I call him? Has he taken his meds? What shall I make him for tea tonight? I'm in the middle of trying to quickly think of a tag line for next week's issue, a part of my job I hate, so whilst this call could be seen as a welcome distraction it is also stopping me from doing practical stuff, like looking at rental properties for Ryan and me in Leigh-on-Sea.

Because I know it is nearly that time.

'Yes?' I snap, picking up the phone and answering in a non-approved *Viva* style and not caring in the slightest. I am immune to rules or criticism these days. It is really odd. I can't seem to do any wrong, no matter how hard I try.

'Moll-eeee,' trills Jackie down the phone. 'How's my gorgeous daughter-in-law?'

I think of my brave, sweet, patient husband, and how much he adores his mum, and I try to channel some of his goodness and force myself not to just answer 'Busy' and put the phone down.

Be nice, be nice, I chant in my head. And then: *This is as hard for her as it is for you, remember.*

'I'm good, I'm really good, thanks!' I cheep in a weird, high-pitched Alvin Chipmunk voice that I always find myself adopting when I'm conversing with her these days. I can't tell her what I'm really feeling; that I'm scared, petrified of every single day, of what it might bring for Ryan. That I am waiting for Death's scythe to strike, watching for every sign, any new symptom. I wish I had the luxury of her denial, but she got served both our portions.

'So Molly, darlin', I'm calling because I've just read in the newspaper that apparently red wine can beat cancer! Can you believe it? That's as good an incentive as any for Ry to enjoy a drink, isn't it? Heee hee heee!'

'Haaaa!' I squeak automatically in response.

Jackie's voice disturbs my thoughts – again. 'I thought you should perhaps stop off and get some for Ryan on the way home, darlin'! It's probably the most enjoyable medicine he'll ever have! Dave says *he* knew it was the cure all along, that's why he drinks it so much. Heee heeeeeee!'

So if the cancer doesn't kill him, liver failure probably will.

Be nice, Molly.

Nor do I point out that the antioxidants in red wine are thought to prevent cancer, not beat it. Or remind her that Ryan hates red wine and always has. Or that he can't actually drink too much with all his medication. I want to say all this but I don't. I want her to have to deal with everything I am learning on a daily basis. I want Ryan to tell his mum to face up to the fact he's dying. I want him to see that I need some help. I don't want to pretend that everything's alright. I want to go home. I want my mum and dad. Or Ryan's. I want them to take responsibility, stop singing la la la with their hands over their ears.

Because la la la, I just can't get cancer out of my head la la la.

Go away Kylie!

Is this the legacy you're leaving me Ryan? A lifetime of shit pop music in my head?

'Molly? Are you still there, darlin'?'

'Yes Jackie, I'm still here.'

I don't dismiss her because I know that she needs to do this, she needs to think that there's still a chance. And I envy her that positivity, I do. But she hasn't had to listen to Charlie talk about 'the future'. She hasn't been with Ryan when he's tried to go to the shops to get a pint of milk and we've had to come back in an ambulance because he's had a seizure. I am just Cooper enough to know that his mum deserves to cling on to whatever hope she can. I am just Cooper enough to listen and to do whatever I can to make this easier for her – even if it makes it harder for me. I've learned that much from being with Ryan and being part of his family.

Since his diagnosis I have, on behalf of Jackie, served Ryan endless amounts of:

1. Curry (Jackie: 'It enhances the effectiveness of chemo, Molly darlin'! And apparently, it helps stimulate the death of cancer cells!')

2. Garlic ('It says here, Molly, that it enhances the immune function! That's got to be good, right, darlin'?')

3. Leafy greens ('They're an antioxidant, you know!')

4. Sprouts ('Ditto, darlin'!')

5. And grains ('It does something or other with the levels of glucose and insulin!')

I've obeyed, mainly because part of me hopes that she's right.

So for this reason I squeak, 'Thanks Jackie, I'll try that! Perhaps we'll have curry, sprouts and a bottle of red tonight!'

'Why don't you come over for a Chinese, Molly, you and Ryan? We'll have such fun, darlin'!' Jackie squeals. 'It's always such FUN when all us Coopers get together ... all the family ... Come on, Molly darlin'! Why don't the both of you hop on the train and come down!'

I want to say that Ryan isn't capable of hopping anywhere. He can just about walk these days. Charlie is organizing a wheelchair for us, for the days when Ryan is too exhausted to walk – which are getting more frequent. But that doesn't solve the issue with the stairs. I've asked him to talk to Ryan about it again, because he won't listen to me. He seems to think he'll feel better tomorrow. Whereas I dread tomorrow. His frailty is the thing that's been hardest to get used to out of all of this. The hair loss was easy – although I didn't anticipate him losing his eyelashes, eyebrows and his hair 'down there' too. He calls himself Gollum now. 'So what does that make me?' I laughed when he first said it. 'A hobbit?' Anyway, he started losing it a couple of weeks after starting the chemo, so little bald patches appeared in the mornings, a little layer of hair left on his pillow. Ryan asked me to shave his head Grade 1 all over. I decided to have some fun first so I grabbed my camera and started doing different crazy hairstyles, stripes all over his head, then a grid, then a Mohawk, then a ladder, taking a photo of each one for posterity – and for our enjoyment – until there wasn't a strand of hair left.

'It's just like David Beckham, circa 2001,' I'd pointed out after studying it for a second.

'Here, let me just do this as a finishing touch . . .' I shaved a little diagonal line across one of his eyebrows and with a flourish held up a hand mirror in front of Ryan. He seemed really happy with it. Then he said thoughtfully:

'Moll, how many hours do you think I have wasted of my life doing my hair?'

He fell silent for ages and I actually thought he was trying to count up the hours, in the same way that I've been trying to count up our kisses. I've even tried to work out a formula.

After furrowing his (shaved) brow for several minutes, he shook his head sadly. 'I should've shaved it off years ago.' A few days later the lesions started appearing.

'Did you hear me, Molly?' Jackie's sharp voice permeates my thoughts. 'I said, why don't you come down!'

'We're coming at the weekend, remember, Jackie?' I chirp

brightly, 'And guess what! I'm looking at rental properties right now, so maybe we'll be moving back sooner than you think!' I mistakenly think this will please her.

'To *rent*,' she sniffs. 'Are you *trying* to offend me, Molly darlin'?'

'What? No, I just—'

'Why would you *rent*? Why don't you and Ry come and stay here, in your old home? It's his HOME.'

'We would but Ryan doesn't want . . .' I was going to say that Ryan doesn't want to die in their home, but a) she doesn't let me finish, and b) I realized halfway through that this is not a Jackie-friendly sentence.

Her voice raises several octaves. She is trying to sound all tinkly and bright. She just sounds scarily unbalanced. 'If you are about to say that my son doesn't want to come home, *darlin'*, then I will put the phone down on you. My son should be here. At home. With his famileee . . .'

I am his family.

I hear her sobbing, it is the first time I've heard her cry. There is the muffled sound of the handset being passed and Dave comes on the line. I barely recognize his voice, it seems so long since I heard him speak.

'Molly,' it is a low rumble, like distant thunder down the phoneline. 'I'm sorry, Jackie is a bit upset. Don't be offended, she's just . . . finding this hard. We all are . . .'

'I know, and I want us to come back to Leigh, Dave, I do, I need help but Ryan is determined . . .' I am crying now. 'I need some help . . .' I put down the phone when I realize he already has. I look up but everyone is studiously working, heads down. Looking anywhere but at me.

Sometimes I think people worry that what I'm going through might be catching. That if they hear too much, or speak to me too much, then something terrible will befall their loved ones. And part of me wonders if they're right.

'Molly? Could you come into my office for a moment please'
Christie has popped her head out and is gesturing to me to come
in.

'Hi,' I say, and Christie gestures to the chair opposite.

'How's Ryan?' she asks. It is always the first question anyone
ever asks me these days. I appreciate their concern but I'm never
really sure how to answer.

'Oh, you know,' I smile at Christie and decide to give her my
pre-prepared, jokey, upbeat version of the truth. 'Still perpetually
stubborn, incredibly vain and annoyingly football-obsessed, but
pretty good, all things considered . . . the doctors say he is doing
very well.'

Except for the nausea and the breathlessness and the headaches
and the incontinence and the nightmares and the pain, I refrain
from adding. I have learned the hard way that people don't actually
want the truth, just some marshmallow-covered version of it. Some
(Jackie) don't want even that.

'Oh, that's GOOD!' Christie beams, like she has just heard,
'He's cured'. 'Listen, Molly, I've brought you in here because I
want to talk to you about your blog. There's a post on there that
has come to my attention . . .'

My mind flits to the latest image of Ryan and me currently at
the top of my blog page with the title 'The PDA Kiss', and then
underneath is the photo of us kissing on the red carpet in front of
Tom Cruise. Underneath I'd typed 'Next stop . . . Oprah's couch!'
I'd shown it to Ryan as well and he'd found it hilarious.

'Well, that's my fifteen minutes of fame ticked off the list,' he'd
joked. 'What with this *and* Take That reforming, I can die a happy
man now!'

I'm getting used to his jokes.

'It's actually the reaction to your blog that I wanted to talk
to you about,' Christie continues. 'Not just to the most recent
post, but to all of them. I'm not sure if you've noticed how many

comments you've been getting since you started posting pictures of you and Ryan kissing?'

I shrug bashfully. I have noticed, and I have found them incredibly moving. There have been so many overwhelmingly kind and uplifting words written by people I've never met. Messages from people writing to share their own stories of cancer, advice from women – and men – who have been, or are, in my position, and from people telling me how much they enjoy seeing the photos I post and who feel moved by our love story.

Ryan knows what I've done but I don't think he's looked at the blog. His only concern is how he looks in the pictures.

'Just don't post any of me in dodgy outfits, Moll, I want to be remembered as a stylish man, not a fashion victim,' he said last night.

'But you ARE a fashion victim and always have been!' I'd laughed, pulling up the duvet and whispering as his eyes began to close, 'Remember those dungarees?' He is sleeping increasingly more these days due to the morphine he's now taking. Our bedroom is also becoming his office, couch, cinema and library. Some days he doesn't have the strength to get out of bed. For anything. It is a strange thing to see a room that was once a place of sex and sleep turn into somewhere so clinical. Beside our bed is a bucket and fresh towels; a jug of water with his dosette box (which I'd never heard of but which Charlie told me to buy to put all his pills in) is on his bedside table. It is full of his pills, labelled from Monday–Sunday and Breakfast/Lunch/Tea and Supper, and it helps us both to remember exactly what he needs to take and when. It also puts my mind at rest that he's taken them when I'm not with him. I've bought incontinence sheets for the little accidents that seem to be happening more and more. And we now have a bed pan for the same reason, if he's in too much pain to get up in the middle of the night.

'Ohhaaarrr,' he'd yawned, closing his eyes and ignoring me. 'I'm

so tired, this cancer is very draining, you know . . .' And then he'd
weakly pulled me down into a cuddle and pretended to go to sleep
with me locked in his arms so I couldn't get out. Not that he was
strong enough to contain me, mind you. His arms have lost all their
muscle tone. I can barely touch him without him wincing, and I
spend most of my time applying soothing emollients and bio oils
to help ease the discomfort.

This blog has become my therapy, my self-medication and my
way of celebrating our love. I don't want Ryan to be in any doubt
of how much I loved him. Love him. Present tense. Not past. Not
yet. Not ever.

Christie reaches across her desk and touches my hand, I realize
I'm crying. Again.

'Molly, I have honestly never seen such a passionate reaction
to a blog before. I've had emails from readers wanting to hear
more from you, wanting to give you advice or for you to talk
to them. They've been emailing our web email address with
messages and pictures of them kissing their partners, some have
been from women in the same position as you, some are saying
that what you wrote on your blog really resonated with them.
Look . . .'

Christie clicks open a folder that is full of emails – all with headings that simply say 'Molly and Ryan' or more specific headings
like 'Making every kiss count . . .'

I'm sitting with my hand over my mouth, trying to stop yet
more sobs. My shoulders are shaking, there are hundreds – and they
keep coming. I glance up and see another email in bold. I recognize
the name. It's the editor of our sister magazine in New York. The
heading says 'A Central Park Kiss' and has the date 23/11/2005.

'Can you open that one please, Christie?' I say quietly. Christie
glances at me and then back at the email. She clicks on the attachment and suddenly an image of two people kissing in the middle
of Central Park, standing on the Imagine mosaic, appears.

'Oh my God – it's Ryan and me, when he proposed!' I gasp. 'But how ... who ...?'

'*Viva* in New York linked your blog to their site when you went out there,' Christie says, 'and it looks like they've never taken it down.' She reads the email from Anna, the editor. 'She says that she's had a massive response from their website. They are all enraptured by you and Ryan, by your beautiful blog post and pictures of you and Ryan.' Christie thinks for a moment.

'I wonder if you'd like to post this photo and then put a call out on the site for anyone else who may recognize you and Ryan? I mean it could be to your friends or family, people you used to know. They might have old pictures of you that you and Ryan have never seen.'

I am still staring at the computer screen, utterly entranced by the picture of Ryan and me at our happiest. I lean over Christie's desk and read the message underneath. It says:

I was visiting Strawberry Fields in Central Park a couple of years ago and witnessed one of the sweetest, funniest, most beautiful and heartfelt proposals. It stayed with me and when I realized it was the same couple from this blog, I had to send this picture. I hope Molly can add it to her collection of kisses and cherish it forever.

Wishing them both lots of love,

Sandra

I sink back into the seat opposite Christie. I can't quite take it in. *This* is a way to keep him with me forever. By collecting these photos and putting them on my blog, Ryan and I could live on forever. In art and in love, just like my dad taught me.

The Can't Complain, Won't Complain Kiss

Forget that old movie line, you know the one: 'Love means never having to say you're sorry.'(Love Story, in case you're wondering.) Well, in my love story, cancer means never being able to say you're annoyed . . .

I walk into our lounge, step over Ryan's shoes that are spread-eagled in front of the door like a naughty pet, pick up his socks that have been discarded by the coffee table, and lift his sports bag that has vomited its contents – including his medication – all over the couch. I lay out his next dose of pills on the coffee table, get a glass of water, tidy up all his books and papers into a neat pile, pop them back in his bag and then walk to the front door and hang it over the coat hooks that I put up soon after we moved in because I couldn't cope with Ryan's various coats by the front door, over the sofa, on the bed, in the bathroom. Then I think about how I'm going to have to start packing all this up soon. We've rented out our flat and in a matter of weeks we'll be leaving our home behind. It makes me feel breathless with sadness, but I can't let it. I have too much to do. I'm desperate to write it all down to stop me from going crazy with the stress of it all, but, Ryan made his point and I am learning to live my life in the moment, dealing with things as they happen rather than treating everything as a perfunctory exercise to get through, things to tick off on my endless lists.

I look around at our flat that is bursting at the seams with our life; the collections of ephemera that Ryan won't throw away: endless Shrimpers football programmes, cinema stubs, gig tickets, piles of receipts from nights out from years gone by – including, amazingly, our very first teen date when we went for coffee which I was amazed to see (funnily enough I stopped complaining about them all when he showed me that). The shelves full of his old boy band CDs sitting uncomfortably next to my music collection. I shake my head as I think of Jeff Buckley squeezed between Boyzone and the Backstreet Boys, and suddenly I can't bear to think of him without them.

Anyway, there's no way we'll be moving anywhere big enough for our stuff. I know our little house by the sea isn't going to happen now. His bad days are becoming increasingly bad; if he isn't in pain physically, then he is struggling mentally. He still tries to pretend, but when he can't get out of bed, or he is sick or has a raging temperature (from a lung infection, according to his GP), he can't disguise how hard it is. We seem to be finding new lesions on his body daily and he has lost so much weight he jokes he looks more like a goalpost than a sports teacher. Jackie is desperate for us to move back, and as much as Ryan protests, I know that he has been staying in London for me, not him. He wants my life to continue so it won't be such a shock after he's gone, but I know I won't be able to face coming back here.

I walk back into the lounge just as Ryan is shuffling out of the kitchen. He's still in his tracksuit but it's hanging off his almost unrecognizable body. And yet to me, he is beautiful. He smiles and focuses on raising his cup of tea, which he holds in one hand, and a small child-sized plate of sausage and mash in the other. He watches as I take in the mess around me, smiling like a rebellious child. I don't say a word. I just walk up and kiss him.

'Good day?' I ask flippantly, going into the kitchen to pick up my plate.

'Yep,' Ryan calls. 'Brilliant! I managed half the day,' he says proudly. 'And I watched the Year Sevens thrash Dalston Comp. at basketball!'

'It wasn't too much for you?' I say, worriedly, walking out of the kitchen with the tea that Ryan has made. He's still trying to cook every day – even if he doesn't feel like eating it. He says he finds it therapeutic. And he also says he has a good incentive as the alternative is eating *my* food.

'No, babe,' Ryan rolls his eyes affectionately at me as he sits down on the sofa. He puts his cup of tea down on the coffee table and rests his plate on his lap as he flicks on *Eastenders* and pushes his sausage and mash around the plate. I can tell that he doesn't want it now. He does this a lot; have a craving for something, make the effort to cook it and then not be able to eat it. 'You know I'd tell you if it was,' he says, pushing his plate away and lying back on the sofa.

No you bloody wouldn't, I think but don't say. Instead I just pick up a coaster and slip it under his tea, then go and sit next to him. I stroke his head. Ryan flicks to another channel. *Hollyoaks* is on. It makes me think of Casey. We watch it for approximately five seconds and then he flicks again. I bite my lip, and then a bit of sausage. He asks for his cup of tea, I help him up into a sitting position, he takes a sip and I go to put it back, but he won't let me. He grimaces as he shuffles forward and puts it back down on the table, but not on the coaster. My eyes flicker to it, to the ring that I can already imagine marking the table, and then back at my plate, a sea of mash and beans and meat that is suddenly making me feel sick. He flicks to *Friends* on E4, laughs and flicks over again. I take another mouthful but can't seem to swallow it, so I get up and scrape my dinner into the bin in the kitchen and start filling the dishwasher with dirty plates, bowls and saucepans that have been there since this morning. I take a deep breath and close my eyes. I'll feel better when it's tidy. Ryan won't even know how wound up I am. I'll make sure of it.

No one warns you that once you know your partner is dying of cancer you'll never want to shout, criticize or nag again. Since he was diagnosed I haven't as much as raised my voice in annoyance. I am a veritable saint on the outside. But sometimes, inside, I feel like I'm going to explode. I'm doing my best, but when he does things that he knows wind me up, like leaving the loo seat up, or missing the laundry basket by 5 centimetres, I want to revert to my default-nagging setting ('Just put your socks in it Ry! It's not hard!'). That sounds horrible, doesn't it, but it's not that I mind that he's doing it, of course I understand that it's as much as he can do to take his own clothes off, or get to the toilet some days. I just miss shouting at him. This relationship of compliance we now have is not natural. We've had to quickly take on these new roles, act in a way with each other that we're not used to and it feels . . . fake. I'm not a natural nurse and Ryan isn't any better as a patient. He's a man, for a start, and he's a sporty, athletic man who has never taken a sick day in his life. He hates taking tablets, being a slave to the medicine and the morphine, the seizures that now come out of the blue and that mean he can't go anywhere on his own any more. No more school (Charlie took him to the Year Seven match today as a treat as I had to work). He hates all the appointments and the only person he'll really properly open up to is Charlie. Sometimes I think he is the only person who truly knows what Ryan is feeling. Even more than me. Yet again, we have another person in our relationship. But this time, Charlie is a welcome addition. I need him as much as Ryan does.

The other day he came round when Ryan was asleep and we just sat and chatted for ages. About everything. How I was feeling, how Ryan was doing. And I asked him the thing that I've wanted to ask for ages, but not had the courage to.

'Charlie,' I said, handing him his cup of tea across the breakfast bar. He glanced up, tilting his head in that instant 'I'm listening' position he does. 'I know you must get asked this all the time, and I know I'm not meant to and I don't want you to think I'm in denial or anything but . . .'

'You want to know how long,' Charlie had said, taking a sip of his tea. He put it down on the counter and linked his fingers. A childhood rhyme had instantly popped into my head:

Here's the church and here's the steeple, open the door and see all the people.

Then an image of a funeral flashed into my mind and I began to cry.

'Hey, listen, Molly,' he says, reaching out and taking my hand.

'I can't foresee the future and I don't want to give you bad news or false hope, but I will say that you need to think about the next stage very soon. Living in this flat is too much for him, and caring for him on your own is too much for you ...'

Ryan comes into the kitchen and leaves his plate on the breakfast bar, unscraped, and then goes back into the lounge. I take a deep breath. I hear him laughing at something and I want to scream. *How can you laugh? How can you laugh at anything?* But I don't. I just roll my shoulders back several times, massage my neck with my hand, and pour myself a large glass of wine. Then I walk back into the lounge and sit down, snuggling up to him silently as Ryan puts on *A Question of Sport*, which he knows I hate. I don't say anything though. I mean, I'm not going to tell a dying man that he can't watch his favourite TV programme, am I? In fact, I'm now questioning all the times I ever moaned about it in the first place. I mean, what kind of shitty wife have I been? Moaning and nagging and ...

I swipe away a tear and take a sip of wine, but Ryan nudges me just as I do and then laughs as a bit dribbles down my silk shirt.

'Shit!' I exclaim, putting my glass down (on a coaster) and going into the kitchen to get some kitchen roll. I'll have to get it dry-cleaned. It's a Reiss top and I spent a ridiculous amount of money on it. An amount of money which now seems horribly indulgent. I should've stuck to black. I should be hanging out at home, looking after Ryan, wearing sloppy clothes, or a nurse's outfit to make him laugh. Not this stupid office attire. I stop dabbing. What does it matter if it's ruined anyway? What does anything matter any more? I cling on to the kitchen counter and let my tears fall into my wine. I hear Ryan come into the kitchen.

'Moll-eee,' he says softly. I lift my head up and smile through my tears without turning round.

'It's all right!' I say, as I start to dab furiously again. 'It'll come out! And it doesn't really matter anyway! I never liked the stupid top much!'

'Moll-eee,' he says again. I turn around and smile brightly at him. 'Why won't you shout at me?' he says disconsolately.

'Because I don't want to!' I say cheerfully, refraining from adding the word 'darling'. I am not a mum.

I will never be a mum.

I will never be a mum to our children.

'But I'm being annoying, Molly.'

'No, you're not!'

'I am. I know you want to write a list. You're desperate to write a list. Here, let me do it for you.' I watch silently as he walks across to our kitchen drawer and pulls out a notepad.

List of Annoying Things Ryan Does

he writes at the top and underlines it.

Then he taps the pen against his poor, shorn head and reads aloud as he's writing, his voice getting more strained with every word he scribbles. He is wired, angry and frustrated. I'm not sure if it's with me, or the situation. Whatever it is, I hate seeing him like this.

'Annoying thing Number One: doesn't use a coaster for hot drinks. Or cold. Even though they're on the coffee table right in front of him!'

He looks up. 'There is a mug of hot tea on the coffee table out there. Fact. You did not tell me off. Another fact.' He looks back down.

'Annoying thing Number Two: channel-hops constantly.'

He looks up. '*Hollyoaks, Friends* . . .' he pauses, '*A Question of Sport* . . . You *hate* that programme. You didn't tell me off.

'Number Three . . .' He gestures at the floor. 'Shoes and socks left all over the—'

'Ryan, stop.' I say. 'Those things don't matter ...'

Ryan throws his pen down on the counter and looks at me. 'But they do matter, they do! They matter because you're not being normal. I need you to be normal, Molly, please. Tell me off, shout and scream when it's necessary. Be a bitch, just for me, please!' He wanders over and tries to weave his arms around me but I push him away furiously.

'But I don't want you to remember me as a bitch, Ry, don't you see? I hate that I used to moan about all those stupid things when none of them matter. They don't fucking matter, OK?' I shout, snot is pouring out of my nose, spittle flying out of my mouth. I am gesturing wildly with my arms. 'I don't care if you sit watching football for the rest of your life, Ry, I wish you would! I want you to do whatever makes you happy. I don't want to shout or moan. I want you to remember me as a sweet, loving wife ...' I sink to the floor weeping. 'I don't want to be a moaning bitch, Ry, I'm so sorry if I have been ... I'm so sorry ...'

Ryan kneels down and grasps my hands, clasping my neck and pulling my head forward so our foreheads touch. 'But don't you see I just want the girl I married? The girl who ain't afraid to speak her mind, who always knew how to keep me on my toes and put me in my place. I love that you stopped me obsessing about myself. From the moment we met you showed me that I wasn't perfect, that my life wasn't perfect, that I could do more, be more, explore more. My life has been so much better because of you! You made my life perfect as soon as you showed me that *I* wasn't. No one had done that before. It's one of the many reasons I fell in love with you, Molly. So don't stop now, don't ever stop. I need you to keep on fighting with me to give me the strength to keep on fighting. Do you see, Molly? It's you that is making me keep on fighting ...' And he begins to cry.

We sit huddled, crying in the kitchen as *A Question of Sport* blares in the background until I say, 'Will you turn that shit off?' and Ryan laughs and kisses me on my head.

The Ghost Of Kisses Past Kiss

'We cannot change our past. We cannot change the fact that people act in a certain way. We cannot change the inevitable. The only thing we can do is play on the one thing we have, and that is our attitude. I am convinced that life is 10% what happens to me and 90% how I react to it.'

A writer called Charles R. Swindoll wrote this. I like it. It sums up some stuff I've been thinking about recently. I can't change Ryan's diagnosis but I can control my approach to it. So, from now on I'm going to be positive, positive, positive ...

It is late on Saturday afternoon and I'm pottering around in our kitchen, making a nice, healthy casserole for Ryan's tea and preparing his medication.

'Hey, Doc,' Ryan calls sleepily from the couch where he is stretched out, watching the football results. He calls me Doc because since getting rid of my lists I have somehow memorized every single medication – both prescription and the natural ones – by name and dosage. I am a walking prescription pad. 'Come here, will you?' he croaks.

I resist the urge to run to him because I know how much it winds up Ryan. He says it makes him feel like he's emitting his dying breath, when actually, all he wants is a pee. I lift the lid on the casserole dish, pull a big spoon down from a hook where they hang behind our cooker. I stir it, taste it, make a face and throw in some more seasoning. Not that I think it's going to help. No matter how much Ryan tries to teach me (he says he's making it his mission so I don't starve to death after he's gone) I'm never going to be any good at this.

As I look around our kitchen I'm suddenly knocked sideways by a memory of Ryan and me moving all our stuff in here. The units are lined with gadgets and gizmos that Ryan has bought over the years: the pasta maker, blender, an ice-cream maker, fondue set, even a Kitchen Aid. And the juicer. Fat lot of good that thing did. There's more stuff than space. Even the things that could go in drawers, like the set of chefs knives I bought him one Christmas, are all on display on a metallic strip along the wall. And Ryan insisted on hanging the pots and pans over the breakfast bar, despite my protestations that I kept banging my head on them.

'If you had your way you'd have a microwave and two forks,

and that would be it,' Ryan had grinned. 'And you'd probably store your shoes in the oven and your make-up in the fridge.'

I'm suddenly struck in the stomach by an image of me in the future. I rest my head against the cool kitchen tiles and take a deep breath. I don't think I will ever be able to come into this kitchen again when he's gone. There is just too much of him in here. They say the kitchen is the heart of the home, well, surely that's only if there's someone there who can make the heart beat.

I wander into the lounge and over to the sofa. 'I reckon I'm going to catch forty winks,' Ryan sighs, looking up at me then smiling and closing his eyes. 'How about you call one of the girls from work and see if they fancy a night out? You could do with it. I'll be fine here.'

'No thanks,' I murmur, trying not to get annoyed at yet another veiled attempt by him to make me have a social life. 'There's loads of good telly on and I want to do some work.'

Ryan's eyes flicker open and he tries to pull himself up. 'I really think you should go out. It's been ages since you had fun.'

'I do have fun, with you . . .' I say tightly.

Ryan raises his eyebrow comically at me. 'Oh yeah, because hanging out with a cancer patient is a right barrel of laughs. You must *really* love wiping my arse on a Saturday night and changing the sheets because I've shat myself again.' He's trying to make light of it but I know it devastates Ryan when he doesn't get to the toilet in time. And it's happening more often. 'Come on, Moll,' he says, planting on a bright smile, 'you need a break now and then. It's important, you know, for after . . .'

I stand up hastily and turn away from him so he doesn't see my tears, but I know he can hear them in my voice. I don't want to think about after. I just want to appreciate him being here *now*.

'And that's exactly why I don't need a break,' I snap. I face him again. 'I'm here because it's the only place I want to be, Ry, and you can try and tell me to go out and have fun, and if that will make you so much happier I will pretend to, but you need to know that I will be miserable. I will hate being away from you, I'll hate being out in some bar or club or at the cinema when all I want is to be here with you.' I turn away and put my hand over my mouth to stifle the sobs that I know are imminent. I take three deep breaths and turn back again, pleading with him to understand. 'I know what you're doing, Ryan, I know, but I can't be away from you. Please don't make me . . .'

'OK, OK, shhh,' Ryan says, gesturing at me to come back to him as I properly start to cry. I sit next to him and rest my head lightly on his chest, and he strokes my hair softly. 'You can stay, of course you can.' Pause. 'But can you do me a massive favour, pleeeease?'

I close my eyes to savour his touch. 'Of course, anything!'

'Order me in a pizza?' I lift my head up and he grins. For the fleeting moment it makes its appearance it's like the old days. 'Sorry, Moll, but I've got to be honest, I just can't face eating another one of your "casseroles". I've got this real urge for a Domino's and I would've sneaked one in if I'd convinced you to go out, but no such luck. I should have listened to your mum. What was it she called you? "Molly Molly Quite Controlling"?'

'Contrary,' I laugh at his deliberate mistake and he wipes away my tears.

'Sounds right. I've never got you to do anything I say so far, Moll, I dunno what made me think you might start now . . .'

'Too right, Cooper!' I kiss him on the lips and narrow my eyes as if considering his request. 'OK, seeing as you've got cancer and everything, pizza it is!'

Ryan raises his hands to the ceiling in mock prayer. 'Thank you, God, I knew there'd be an upside to this disease!'

I laugh, but only to cover up the lump that is still in my throat.

Five minutes later and with the pizza all ordered, I walk back into the room with a glass of wine for me and a Becks for him. He's not allowed to drink a lot, but he likes to have an occasional beer, it makes him feel normal.

Ryan is asleep, still exhausted after the treatment. I stand watching him for a moment, counting his breaths as his chest rises up and down, up and down, hypnotically. I'm counting because I am scared they might stop. I know sleeping means Ryan isn't in any pain but a part of me hates it because I am always scared he's not going to wake up. But at the same time I love having some time to myself. I'm still with him but I like that while he's dozing I can just be his wife, not his nurse.

I take a sip of wine, New Zealand Sauvignon Blanc. Every time I do I'm transported back to our honeymoon. I tell myself that's why I'm drinking at least two glasses a night, every night (one for me, one for him). It is a comfort, not a crutch. As is my blog. Although I do find myself looking at it an awful lot, I can't help it. Reading all the comments is so uplifting, more helpful than talking to my actual friends and family somehow.

I open my laptop and click open my email, gazing at an inbox that's full of new messages from people I don't know but who are sharing this journey with me. Strangers who feel as familiar to me as my own friends because they're so supportive and willing to open up about their own experiences of love and loss.

I open an email titled 'Remember this?' and smile as I realize it's from Jo, my old picture editor when I first started at *Viva*, who weirdly, now works with Mia. We've stayed in touch over the years and I saw her when I went out to stay with Mia.

Dear Moll,

How are you? How's Ryan? Silly questions I know, but it's hard not to open with those ... I hope he's doing OK and that you're getting lots of support. I can't imagine what you must be going through. I, well, I just wish I could help somehow. I'm sure you hear that a lot.

Anyway, life here is good. Mia talks about you all the time. I know she wishes she were closer, so she could help you more.

I just wanted to say that I've been following your blog and I realized that I'm pretty sure I have those pictures I took of you and Ryan, do you remember? Back when you first officially started at Viva and he turned up outside work with that bunch of flowers? It was so romantic, you guys couldn't keep your hands off each other! Anyway, I thought maybe they'd make a nice addition to your blog. Another kiss to add to your collection . . .

Take care Moll, thinking of you heaps

Jo xx

I open the jpegs that Jo has attached, desperate to see new images of my husband and of me in happier times. There are four consecutive ones, taken seconds after each other. I squeal with delight as each image fills my screen. Ryan is wearing the bloody ridiculous red body warmer he used to live in – even in hot weather – and you can see by my expression that he has just floored me with his kiss in the middle of Covent Garden. In the first picture I look shocked and mildly horrified as his lips approach, then disbelieving, then comes the acquiescence, then the pure, unadulterated enjoyment. 'Proper pashing' I seem to recall that's how Jo had described it at the time, and now I can see what she meant. I save the pictures to my desktop and open up my work blog programme.

I write 'The Surrendered Kiss' at the top of the post and then attach all four pictures. My fingers hover over the keyboard to post it, but suddenly I find them moving, almost without me thinking about it.

The Surrendered Kiss

You may not believe this (and frankly, nor will Tom Cruise) but before I got together with Ryan I was the girl who hated public displays of affection, or indeed any displays of any sort.

Even as a child I was never the girl to hold hands or link arms with my best friend round the school playground. I'd never spontaneously pull my mum into a quick hug and whisper, 'I love you', before I went to sleep. A stilted kiss and a 'me too' was all I was willing to give – to anyone. And then came Ryan, with his unaffected, unashamed, puppy-dog affection. I remember being astonished at how he wore his heart on his sleeve for everyone to see. He wasn't ashamed to kiss his best mate on the cheek, or hug his dad in the middle of the street, or tell his mum he loves her in front of his mates, or kiss me in front of my new colleagues – and the whole of Covent Garden.

As you can probably tell, I've been doing a lot of looking back recently. Cancer does that to you, you know. It makes you examine everything; it's like having an emotional CT scan of your life at the same time as the physical one that your loved one is having. Anyway, now I wonder what I'd been so scared of and I realize that I didn't want anyone else to look at me and think that they knew how I felt. I didn't want them to be a witness to my emotions. The less people saw, the less they could hurt me. But in doing so it meant I never really let anyone in. I kept everyone – even my best friend – at arm's-length, always keeping my counsel when it came to my real emotions and feelings (apart from in my typically angsty teenage diary).

But Ryan changed that. And I'm glad he's changed me because in letting him in, I realized that he was what I was looking for all along. Somewhere warm, inviting, a place where I felt instantly comfortable. He was the home I'd been looking for my whole life. Somewhere that embraced me without expectation. He opened his heart to me and in doing so, opened the door to my heart.

Because of him I let his wonderful family in, and my own family who I'd shut down from a long time before. I became closer to my friends and I have grown to adore his. And now I'm glad because I need everyone to know how I feel now. I am scared, no, I'm fucking petrified, every single day, of what horrors it may bring. I am also desperately sad (but trying so hard not to seem so!) and I'm achingly lonely. Ryan is still with me, but I know that really I am in this thing alone. He's only here for the short haul and I need to know how to live when he's gone. And honestly, I'm not sure I can. So right now I need to be able to cry to my best friends, to have my mum soothe me with kind words and cuddles, I need to tell my colleagues when I feel shit, when I am in pieces because my husband is dying of cancer. Yes, dying. I need to say that. Over and over sometimes so that it feels real. I need to cry uncontrollably and laugh hysterically whenever I want to, in whatever situation and at whatever time. I need to be able to do this and for people to understand and not judge me for letting my feelings out – no matter how they come and how ugly they are, because living with someone with terminal cancer is ugly. It can't be covered with frosted icing and sprinkles. It can't be dressed up in a LBD and a pair of heels and dragged out for a night on the town. It can't be glossed over with a smile. It needs to cry in a room and be comforted. It needs for people not to be scared when it looks them in the eye. It needs to not feel like it should wear a mask in order to protect everyone – including the cancer itself. It needs to go public.

But the irony is, now that I need these public displays of affection, no one seems able to give them to me. I feel like I'm

being punished for my approach pre-Ryan. Because everyone
is so fucking controlled around me. Can I use the F word here,
Ed? Sorry if not. It just seems the only appropriate one to use.
It feels appropriate to be inappropriate, if you like. Because
every word that is spoken to me, every facial expression that
my friends and family expose me to, or conversation they know
I'll hear, is sharply regulated. It's like when I edit photos from
a shoot, to only show the best possible picture. The only people
who don't do this are Ryan's doctors, and Ryan. And actually,
come to think of it, probably not even him.

Because I have no idea how much Ryan is controlling in all
of this. I'm sure he hides the worst from me, even though we
swore on the day that he was diagnosed that we'd be honest
with each other. But the truth is, we love each other too much
to be completely honest. So we laugh and joke, and we pretend
everything is OK, in order to make it better for other person.
But we know that, ultimately, we can't take away each other's
pain because we're travelling in different directions. Going on
different journeys. He is facing no future and I am ... facing a
future without him.

Which would you pick?

I know, tough call, right? No, don't put your mask on because I
asked you a tough question. I know that's what my friends and
my colleagues and my family are trying to do. They are trying
to control the amount of pain that I see in them because I have
enough of my own to deal with. And I know they're also trying
to protect themselves from seeing too much of the pain that I am
in. Their masks are on – and so is mine.

But you know what I wish? I wish that at some point we could
all just let go, just let go of everything, scream, shout, cry, laugh,
fucking swear (sorry Ed. Again.), weep and wail uncontrollably

in front of each other, like I know we all want to. What's the famous quote? 'Love is the price we pay for grief'? Well then, let's love uncontrollably and then grieve uncontrollably. Right now, I don't think I can do anything less.

M x

The I Think I Love You Kiss

Something I can't help but wonder in these cancer-stricken days is, what was I so afraid of? Why did I worry that I'd met Ryan too young? Because now, when I look back, it's clear to me that I fell in love with Ryan long before our first kiss, long before I said it or perhaps even thought it. Now I feel like I was born loving him which means meeting him could never have happened early enough.

I'm cuddled up with Ryan on my second-hand sofa, in my draughty, badly furnished flat on Holloway Road. Ever since meeting his parents two weeks ago, Ryan has been getting on the train from Leigh into Fenchurch Street and coming to meet me from work every night after he finishes teaching at school. We go for a drink, or a meal, or sometimes we just hang out together at my place.

Right from the moment we kissed I had this awfully, wonderfully, terrifyingly liberating feeling that I could fall in love with Ryan. I know, right? This from the girl who always said she didn't believe in it. I've never told a boyfriend I love him or been with anyone who would say it to me.

I smile blissfully and close my eyes as I breathe in his comforting scent and wonder how I could have resisted him for so long. It, like him, is a riot of contradictions: it's sexy but safe; he smells of home but also of adventure, of sport; sunshine and rain; the past and the future. It – he – is utterly intoxicating.

When we're not together, we exchange text messages at work, he phones me at lunchtime to tell me what he's been up to and I get updates of his whereabouts on his journey into London to meet me. He tells me what he's reading, watching, doing, seeing. And I want to know it all. For the first time in my life I want to know every single thing about him, and – somewhat scarily for me – I want him to know everything about me.

The other night Ryan and I were curled up on my sofa with our limbs entwined, 'Like the tentacles of a giant love monster,' Ryan had said, and stroked his finger down my arm. I bristled, like I always knew I would if a guy used the L word – but it was with excitement. We'd been seeing each other for three weeks and I knew we were on the cusp of Saying It.

I turned my face from where it was resting on his chest and unbuttoned his shirt, slipping my hand underneath to expose his chest. I studied his torso appraisingly for a moment, trying to memorize each patch of skin, each freckle or blemish, I felt like I wanted to know every single slope, every bump and crevice of his body.

I'd traced my finger over the assortment of three different moles that lay just under his left nipple. 'These look like Revels,' I'd solemnly announced, and Ryan had lifted his head off the couch and burst out laughing.

'Molly Carter, how do you always manage to see things that no one else ever would?'

I'd grinned and brushed the apex of my fingertip over his nipple. 'This is the nutty one.' Then I'd traced my finger down to a little mole directly underneath, that looked like a disc. 'Right here is a Minstrel, and here', I'd pointed at a small, pale-brown nugget that sat up proudly further down his chest, 'is one of those little toffee surprises.'

Ryan took my hand and guided it down until my hand hovered over his groin.

'Now let me introduce you to the king of confectionary,' he'd said, his voice husky, not with humour but with longing.

I couldn't help it. I burst out laughing and slid off the sofa and onto the floor, holding my stomach as Ryan pelted me with cushions. Then he tickled me and we rolled around together until he pinned me down and kissed me softly, deeply and with such intensity that I knew I couldn't hold out a moment longer.

We waited until we could wait no more, until our kisses were so urgent, our skin so desperate to connect that we peeled each other's clothes off like oranges, layer after infuriating layer, panting and grabbing, grasping and grappling, until we lay down naked next to each other on the sofa. I wanted him so desperately. I kissed him hard and deep, my tongue exploring the deep recesses of his warm, welcoming mouth. I grasped his buttocks, begging him to enter me. But he just lay gently on top of me, covering me with warmth, his strong forearms either side of my face taking the weight of his body, his fingers slowly combing through my hair. He gazed at me for what felt like hours, his eyes a mirrored prism of blue, a sexy, crooked smile hovering over his lips that hinted at lust and experience and confidence and patience and ... and ... something else, something not quite distinguishable. Love? I didn't know for sure because I hadn't ever seen it before. I didn't want to think it, but it's what I felt. I felt it in his gaze and in the way that he rolled onto his side, his eyes never leaving mine as he rested his head on his arm and let his fingers travel from my scalp down my neck and shoulders and then across the contours of my body, infuriatingly slowly, like they were branding me, until I groaned with frustration and desperation.

'What are you doing?' I'd mumbled, wanting to feel him on me, in me.

'I'm tracing my name on your body, so you remember this always,' he'd murmured, and then he'd covered my shoulder and neck with dancing kisses as his fingers started dancing elsewhere.

'Please, I can't take it any more.' I'd buried my face in his neck. 'I want you,' I'd groaned.

'You've got me,' he'd replied softly, 'you've really got me, Molly Carter.'

And as he entered me I did the thing that every modern girl is taught not to do as soon as she is taught about sex. But the words had risen up into my mouth, along with my heart and I said it. *It*.

'I think I love you, Ryan.'

He hadn't paused, hadn't missed a beat, he'd just smiled and lowered his forehead to mine as his body reached every single part of me.

'Well, that's good because I *know* I love you, Molly Carter. And he kissed me again with such sweet tenderness that in that moment and in every moment since, I gave in. I gave in to him, to love, to my destiny.

The SOS Kiss

There's this song on Ryan's current favourite album by Take That (obviously!) called 'Reach Out'. It's been on the radio loads recently, literally every time I turn it on I hear it. Sometimes I feel like someone is trying to tell me something. You see, I'm not good at asking for help, I never have been. I'm too proud, but when I hear the lyrics about how we all grieve in different ways and that it's only love that pulls us through, it pulls me out of my insular world I've created here with Ryan, where in between 'working' (to be honest these days I just go in to show my face, then come straight home again) I'm his full-time carer. I make him comfortable, pick up his drugs, change his sheets, take him out in his wheelchair. And hearing it reminds me that this isn't all about him and me. I'm not the only person hurting. And that by asking for help, I might also be helping other people too – not just Ryan, because he and I aren't the only people needing support right now. It doesn't all revolve around us. So this is my SOS. Not just a cry for help, but a cry to help ...

'Hi, Moll,' the boys say collectively. Their voices are hushed and they look pale and anguished. If Essex were to be able to prove the existence of vampires in their county I'm pretty sure this is what they'd look like. They're still more sunrise than *Twilight*, but it is instantly clear to me that they are not in any way dealing well with the fact that Ryan is deteriorating fast.

'What's up? You all look like death warmed up,' I quip. Their horrified looks at each other tell me they are not ready for these kinds of jokes. I'd better prepare them. Ryan isn't likely to hold back, no matter how they're feeling. 'Sorry. It's what we do around here to deal with it. Joke, I mean. Ryan likes it. He's still the same old Ryan, you know, despite it all.'

'All' being the fact that at his last blood test we were told that the cancer has spread even further. He'd been suffering from increasingly bad headaches, sometimes so bad they made him vomit, and then he woke up with blurred vision in one eye and we both knew what it meant. When the oncologist confirmed what we'd already guessed, Ryan simply said that meant he now had a five-a-side team: skin, spine, bowels, lungs and brain.

Carl stares at me and then looks away. I want to hug him but I am afraid he will crumble. Then I hug him anyway. I'm sick of ignoring what my intuition tells me to do. It's why I called the Haven Hospice in Leigh yesterday. I want to be sure that when Ryan gives me the nod, as we agreed, that they're ready to receive him. I know it'll be soon. I can see by the way Ryan looks at the flat, and at me. Like he's trying to take it all in. Memorize it. Carl clings on to me like a toddler on to his mum. I squeeze him and then pat him on the back, trying to instil some courage into him. He looks up at me bleakly and then drops his head like it is just too heavy to lift. I take his hand and then usher the rest of the boys in, chatting as much as I possibly can to put them at ease whilst thinking no wonder Ry and I like being on our own. This is *really* hard work.

'Come in, boys! Ryan will be so glad you're here! Ahh, you've bought beer? Thank you!' I am talking in exclamation marks and I don't know how to stop. 'Yep, go on up, he's up there waiting for you! Oh, he's good thanks! Watching football as always! I always know it's Saturday as I officially become a football widow—' I realize my mistake as soon as the words come out of my mouth and Carl's hand goes limp in mine.

The rest of the boys freeze in mid-disrobing of their jackets. Ryan just won't deal well with this weird, subdued atmosphere. I'm going to have to warn him. Or knock some sense into them before they go in.

'I'm sorry boys, but you really need to try and be upbeat. I know it's hard, but Ryan won't let you be miserable around him. Just tell him all your news, treat him like you always would and don't freak out if he makes bad jokes, it's just his way of coping.'

No one answers for a moment. None of them seems able to look at me. Then Carl looks up.

'No, it isn't,' he says slowly. 'He just can't tell good ones. Never could.' A flicker of a smile flashes across his weary, sunken face. I touch him on the arm. He seems so much smaller than usual; like a child-size version of himself. No more Carl the beefy builder. Now he's Carl the kid in the wetsuit grinning next to his little brother, but with the added knowledge that one day he'll have to go to the beach on his own.

'That's it, Carl,' I smile. 'I knew you could do it. Now, in you go.' They all look at each other, take a deep breath and sweep in, all chattering at the tops of their voices. I nod and lean against the wall for a moment's support, and then follow them.

I'm in the kitchen, getting bottles of beer, pouring tortilla chips into bowls and cutting lime wedges. I'm enjoying hearing the banter and laughter from the lounge as they all watch the football together.

I turn around, holding the bowls of tortillas and dips and see Carl standing in the kitchen, he's crying silently, big fat tears falling down his cheeks and onto his T-shirt. I put the bowls down hurriedly and open my arms, and he sobs into my shoulder. 'My brother,' he keeps saying, 'my baby brother.' Then he sniffs and wipes his eyes and pulls a packet of Kodak photos out of his back pocket.

'I just want to say Molly, thank you for doing what you're doing for him. You're his world and we all know how hard . . .' he pauses as his voice cracks '. . . how hard this is on you.' He hands me the envelope. 'Me and the boys, and Mum and Dad, we've gone through all our photos and wanted you to have these . . . for your blog. We are all reading it. Mum especially. It's a beautiful thing, Molly babe, it really is.'

'Thank you,' I whisper, and I wipe my hands on a tea towel and open the envelope. Inside are dozens of photos of Ryan and me kissing: on holiday with the Coopers in Portugal, on nights out in Southend, at Carl and Lydia's wedding, at our wedding, on various birthdays, New Year's Eves and Christmases. It is all here. Practically our entire relationship in photos. Some of them I've never even seen before.

I take Carl in my arms and I let him cry for his little brother, for himself, for his mum and dad and his son, and for me. I pull away to wipe his eyes and a photo drops onto the floor between us.

'Where did you get this?' I gasp as I kneel down on the kitchen floor to pick it up. It is Ryan and me, as teenagers, at The Grand. He's all pouty lips and floppy hair, like a young River Phoenix and I . . . look quite pretty actually. That long slip dress and T-shirt combo was really cute and I'd hidden my terrible self-cut hair by scraping it back into a bun. Funny how ugly I always felt. Now I can almost see what Ryan saw in me. Carl smiles as he looks at it. 'We were trying to catch his big moment on camera. Shame it didn't go quite to plan though, he was well embarrassed when he saw his shitty snogging technique caught on camera,' Carl laughs and sniffs simultaneously, swiping his face with one hand quickly and rubbing his thumb and forefinger under his eyes.

I nod through my tears as I look at the photo. The look of horror on my face as Ryan enthusiastically covers me with his entire mouth and attempts to suck my face.

'I reckon he practised on his arm for months before he tried that on anyone again. I remember him telling me he was determined to make it up to you one day. Give you a kiss to remember . . .'

'Well, he definitely did that,' I say quietly.

'Molly!' Ry's voice is raspy and I jump, my heart thumping with the panic I feel every time he calls. Or doesn't call. Carl puts his arm around me and I pick up the chips and dips and walk back into the lounge, where Ryan is surrounded by his mates, empty beer bottles and his favourite sport blaring away on the TV.

'You OK?' I smile.

'I will be when you come over here,' he says.

I sit on the floor in front of him and he strokes my hair. I tilt my head up and smile.

'Happy?' I murmur.

He nods and I take a mental photo of his expression, the way his eyes are lit up, his contented smile. I pick up a tortilla chip and pop it in his mouth and turn round to watch as a striker attempts to shoot a goal.

'OFFSIDE, Ref! Come on, are you BLIND?!' I yell at the TV and the entire room shudders into silence. 'What?' I gaze around at the awestruck room, who all look like they have been paused, some with bottles of beer halfway to their mouths, Ryan is mid-crunch of his tortilla chip. 'You think a girl can't pick up the offside rule after six years with a football-fanatic PE teacher?'

*

Ryan is in bed and I'm just finishing tidying up after the boys' afternoon visit turned into a takeaway-curry-and-movie night. Once they'd relaxed I could see they enjoyed being here. And Ryan had loved it.

I put away the last of the dishes and turn off the lights. As I walk towards our bedroom I realize that I can hear him crying. I slip into the room, crawl onto the bed and gather him up in my arms. I stroke my hands down his poor, ailing body, softly and methodically until his breathing slows, and then I lie next to him, my body lightly touching his. And we lie here just crying and cuddling until Ryan whispers that he wants to make love to me. I nod my admission, petrified of hurting him but desperate to feel him one more time. Maybe one last time . . .

It was the worst and best moment since his diagnosis. I hated seeing him so scared and at first we were both like nervous new lovers; there were lots of 'Is this OK?', 'It doesn't hurt, does it?' and tentative caresses. I ran my hands over his body, lightly touching every part of him, my fingers stroking his excision scars and the toffee-Revel mole on his chest. It felt like I was reading a Braille version of him. A frail version of him. Afterwards, as we cried ourselves to a kind of climax, we just lay in each other's arms, our breath melting into each other's, bodies rising and falling together, hands clasped tightly, feet tangled together like wool. It was maybe an hour before we spoke. And when we did, we talked about *everything*. The moment we first met, how we felt about each other when we were teenagers, our terrible first kiss, Ryan's proposal, our incredible wedding day, our meeting on the *Bembridge* when I was back from uni, our honeymoon, our first holiday to Ibiza . . .

'Molly,' he mumbles, closing his eyes, 'I think it's time to go home. I want to go home now.' Ryan weaves his fingers through mine and sighs as he falls into a slumber.

'Whatever you say,' I whisper, squeezing his hand gently.

After he goes to sleep I slip out of bed and into the lounge.

Shivering in my stripy pyjamas, despite the warmth of the night, I email my letter to Christie, which I've had drafted for weeks, telling her that I won't be in the office for the foreseeable future and that as of now I'll be starting my extended leave of absence.

After I send it I notice a new email in my inbox.

It's from Casey. I look at it for a moment, unsure whether I want to deal with whatever is inside.

I furrow my brow as I read the subject head. It says 'The Real First Kiss' and I can see that there is a jpeg attached.

Dear Molly,

I know you don't want to hear from me but I had to get in contact so I could give you this photograph. I took it on our last night in Ibiza; I followed you and Ryan when you went for your moonlit stroll. I've never shown you it before because I was so ashamed of myself. I convinced myself I wasn't spying, just 'looking out for you'. And I had my camera with me anyway to take pictures of our last night. I was so jealous Molly . . . but I don't want this email to be about me and my fuck-ups, I just want you to have this for your blog. It is the kiss you should always remember, your real first kiss. It looked so perfect from where I was standing. I guess that was the problem . . .

I'm so sorry, Molly, not just for what I have done but for what you're going through now. I hate not seeing you, but I'll always be here for you. I am here for you, if you ever need me.

C xxx

I read it without blinking, save the photo attachment to my desktop, and then log on to my blog and I start to type.

The Real First Kiss ...
and The Last

I wasn't going to post a picture today. Not because I have run out of kisses – far from it. But I do feel it is time to stop the relentless PDAs. I'm sure there's only so many photos of Ry and me slobbering all over each other that you guys can take!

But then, today, I was given the most wonderful selection of pictures of Ry and I from the people that we love. This one in particular meant the most as it is our first real kiss. I thought we were having a private moment, but it turns out someone else witnessed it. She saw the moment my life changed forever – and she desperately wanted hers to as well.

And I don't blame her, not any more. Life's too short, right?

This blog has been an incredible support to me during the worst time of my life. You have all become my friends and your kind comments and words of advice have truly made me stronger and able to deal with each day as it came. But now I feel like Ryan and I only have today. There's no more time to look back. I want to focus all my energy on the here and now. I hope you understand.

Molly x

I close down my computer and then I pick up the phone to Ryan's parents so I can tell them Ryan's coming home. We're coming home.

The Keep On Moving Kiss

I promised Ry no more lists, and myself no more blog (I just
don't have the emotional strength) but Charlie said if writing
stuff down was helping, I should continue doing it for myself.
And I do find I need to mark these moments with Ry somehow.
So my camera is still my constant companion and now, so is my
laptop.

Next time they come they are ready for us. I open the front door to a doorway full of grinning boys, looking utterly ridiculous but grinning widely anyway.

'What d'you reckon, Moll?' Carl smiles, gesturing at himself and then the guys. They are all wearing dungarees, are topless underneath and have one strap undone and hanging down in true Take That 'Do What U Like' video-style (minus the jelly). Gaz is still wearing his pork-pie hat, but the rest are wearing baseball caps facing backwards.

'What the hell have you come as?' I snigger.

'Take *Flat*, your Essex boy-band-style removal service!'

I put my hand over my mouth and call up the stairs. 'Ry, wait till you see this!'

They bundle through the door and bound up the stairs to where Ryan is. Laughing, I follow them up just as they start doing a choreographed dance in front of him and finish with a flourish by lifting him up on the couch.

I watch him chuckling and feel thankful again for our brilliant friends. I know he's been in equal parts looking forward to and dreading this day. He's ready to move – we both are, we haven't been out of this flat in days, and I know Ryan dreams of lying in a garden, or seeing the sea and being near his family. But he has also been dreading it, not just because we're saying goodbye to our home, but because he hasn't been able to do anything to help. In retrospect, we should have done this weeks ago, the drive is going to be hard for him, being up for any length of time is impossible for him now, but at least he's looking forward to going home. Jackie and Dave are beside themselves; they've bought top-of-the-range wheelchairs and stairlifts and all sorts to make him as comfortable as possible. As much as it's been hard for me looking after him on my own, I think it's been harder for them not being able to help.

I look around at our flat that is still bursting at the seams with our life, despite me packing what feels like a hundred boxes.

'So where do you want us to start, boss?' Alex says, as they lower Ry back down.

I open my mouth to answer them but Ryan interrupts me.

'Hey, how do you know they weren't talking to me?' he protests sulkily. 'I could totally be the boss.'

Everyone bursts out laughing. 'Yeah right, Ry, like you've *ever* been the boss of her!' Carl ruffles Ry's head.

'I've got cancer, you know,' Ry pouts. 'You're all meant to be constantly stroking my ego and telling me I'm brilliant.'

I lean down. 'You're handsome and brilliant and you have *always* been the boss of me,' I say.

'Oh, do you really mean it, Molly?' he says with dramatic effusiveness.

'Nope.' I wink and I kiss his hands and then clap mine officiously and turn around. 'Now boys, are you going to get to work or what? We've got a move to get underway. Can you start with the boxes in the bedroom please? The ones marked "S" are for storage and the ones marked "J&D" are for Jackie and Dave's. They need to go in the little van with Ryan and me. There aren't many but can you make sure the bedding is all laid over the top please? I want us to be able to make up Ry's bed as soon as we get to their house. And make sure the box in the bathroom marked "Meds" comes with us too. There's a "J&D" marked on it, too, but it needs to go in the car last so I know where it is. Then can you ... uh ...'

My voice trails off as I realize that my mind has gone blank. I think about the list of things I've memorized in my head. Shit, this is no time for my brain to freeze. What was I going to say next? Shit shit shit. I rub my forehead and resist the urge to scream in frustration. Then I feel Ryan squeeze my hand. I turn around and he is holding up a piece of paper in front of me. I look at him quizzically.

'What's this?' I ask, and Ryan flaps it as if to say, go on take it.

I look at the heading that has been written and underlined shakily and the painstakingly considered subheads and notes. I know this would have taken a lot of effort and that he did this because he didn't want to be useless, he didn't want this entire move to be on my shoulders alone. Because of this, I am fighting back tears before I even read what he has written down.

Ryan's 1st EVER list of things to do that will stop Molly from having a mental breakdown on moving day

I look back at him and he smiles sheepishly and shrugs. 'You know Moll, sometimes only writing a list will do. You should try it sometime . . .' He winks cheekily and I bend down and kiss him on the lips then hand the list back to him.

'I reckon it's time you did the bossing around, Mr Teacher. Just read out what you want me to do first.'

And as I wait for his instruction, totally reliant on my husband for the first time in months, I realize that we've both had to re-learn our relationship now that cancer is there between us.

Suddenly I spot that Ryan is clutching the pink flamingo light, which I thought I'd put in a box marked 'Storage', but had secretly marked 'Bin' in my head.

'Ry,' I say warningly, and he looks around the room, whistling innocently. Except he can't whistle. He just makes a hollow, squeaky sound. 'What are you doing with that? You'd better not be messing with my system.'

'I want to take it,' Ryan says, as if that is answer enough.

'Oh come on, Ry, you know we don't have room for junk like that . . .' I go to grab it but he sticks it under his sweatshirt.

'It's not junk,' Ryan says fervently.

I laugh. 'It's a pink bit of plastic! A hideous piece of pink plastic.'

He shakes his head. 'No, Molly, it's not.' He pauses and takes a deep breath, looking up at me. His eyelids are naked, the eyelashes long gone with his hair. He blinks and I see a single tear leave his right eye and trickle down his cheek.

'This flamingo, it's everything I love about our relationship . . .'

I go to protest indignantly but stop. This is no time for jokes. Finally there is no time for jokes. 'This flamingo is you, my awkward Molly, trying so hard to stand out all the time, often pulled in two directions, between what you think you should want and what you actually want. Standing on one bloody leg all the time!' He laughs and I smile in recognition of this observation. He holds it in front of his face so he and the flamingo are staring at each other. 'And it's me, a social bird that lives in colonies and needs others to survive! Don't we, mate?' Ryan makes the flamingo nod and I giggle. Ry turns to me and grins effusively. 'Oh and hey, they eat shrimp Molly, that's why they're pink! Did you know that? Shrimps, Moll! Like the Shrimpers!' His eyes are glistening. If anyone were listening to him now they'd think he was mad. But I get it. Finally I get it. He holds the flamingo out to me and I tentatively take it. 'And they're bred in Ibiza,' he says quietly. 'I saw some fly away that first night I kissed you. This flamingo is the only thing I want to keep because it reminds me of us.'

'Well, then,' I say, choking back a tear, 'the bloody flamingo stays.' And I pop it in my handbag for safe keeping, so its head sticks out the top ridiculously. Then I look back at Ryan, at my teenage love, my husband. We've come such a long way together. And that's what scares me. It means there isn't much further to go.

Two hours later, we're all packed up. Ryan is sitting in an armchair as the boys, iPod blaring, gather round him and lift him up, carrying him down the stairs, all singing along loudly and tunelessly to *Shine* by Take That.

*

That evening, with Ryan comfortably asleep in his newly converted downstairs bedroom after a monumental amount of fussing from Jackie, I'm sitting on the sofa in their house feeling strangely detached. Like I'm here in body but not in spirit. I sink into the sofa and close my eyes as the waves of exhaustion overwhelm my body. I realize I haven't eaten all day. The boys stopped for a McDonald's on the way home, but I just wanted to get Ryan here. Back to his home.

I open my eyes as I feel a presence next to me and Dave is looking down at me. He puts a plate of cheese toasties and a steaming cup of tea on the table in front of me. Then he lays a soft, sheepskin blanket over my legs and kisses me on the head and turns on the TV, sitting in his leather chair in the corner of the room clutching his own mug of tea. *Gavin and Stacey* is on and he chuckles softly at something Smithy says.

And all I can think is, I'm home.

I walk out into my small overgrown garden that so badly needs some tender loving care. I want to say my goodbyes to it properly. I've never been the green-fingered type. Most living things seem to wilt under my watch, but one thing I planted seems to thrive year after year. It's standing tall and pink through the desperately neglected flowerbeds, waving at me in the breeze as if to remind me not to leave it behind.

'I can't believe I nearly forgot the bloody flamingo!' I roll my eyes heavenward and shake my head, overwhelmed by the urge to laugh. I bend down, groaning a little at the exertion, and it looks at me disconcertingly knowingly and for a moment I can see Ryan doing the same.

'Yes, I *know* I have to get fit,' I say to it. 'But I've got an excuse ... I have!' I think of the Jammie Dodger addiction. OK, not *that* much of an excuse.

Oh *great*. If I was making a list (which I'm not) of signs of the onset of madness I could add talking to a pink plastic flamingo.

And who knew this pink beacon of freakishness would be the only thing left standing of my worldly possessions, lording it over every other memory from the past twenty-odd years of my life. I smile because it feels like some kind of sick joke. Which it probably is.

'Come on, you,' I say, tucking it under my arm. 'I've got just the home for you ...'

Mum and Dad help me pack the luggage, a very disgruntled Harry and Sally in their cat box and the flamingo into the car. Our goodbye is short, not without emotion, but we hold it together in true Carter style. Mainly because we know it won't be long till we see each other again.

Ten minutes later I pull up outside. I walk up the path nerv-ously, just like I did the first time all those years ago. I knock on the door and wait for her to answer. I see her silhouette in the glass and I inhale sharply before she opens it. I suddenly realize that I haven't felt able to exhale in her presence for the past five years.

'Molly,' she says quietly, and then stares at me without saying any more. I stand awkwardly on the step for a moment, clutching the flamingo for dear life. She looks so old. So unlike the woman I first met all those years ago. She is no longer perfectly turned out like she used to be. The lurid pink lips and nails are still there, as is the blown-out hair and bright, fashionable clothes, but the most striking thing about her is her coat of grief. It's there for everyone to see, no matter what else she's wearing. It's in the deep lines on her face, her watery blue eyes, it's there in her subdued smile and her anxiously wringing hands. The abundant jewellery has been replaced by a simple gold locket that I know contains a picture of her two sons.

Unlike me, she is thin – too thin. She has shrunk in stature, size and confidence. Her voice is quieter and her gestures more restrained. Her blonde hair is now the heavy grey of a January day. It matches the clouds in her eyes.

She studies me for a moment in the unflinching way that she always has done, penetrating right through me as she looks up and down, pausing deliberately on my swollen stomach before looking up and into my eyes. I feel self-conscious suddenly, like my preg-nant belly is flaunting the fact that I have somehow – despite it all – moved on. I fight the urge to look away. Sometimes I can see him so clearly in her face I can't bear to look. How hard must it be for her to look in the mirror? Perhaps she doesn't. I know I didn't for a long time. What must it be like for her?

'I wasn't sure you'd come,' she says at last.

'Nor was I,' I reply honestly. It's strange when I think that for weeks I couldn't leave this house. I could barely get out of bed. I became the patient, someone for Jackie to nurse and look after, and I enjoyed it. We both did, I think. But then, slowly, really, really slowly, I craved space and I moved back home, to my home, to my mum and dad, finally moving into my little house two years after Ryan died.

'I couldn't leave without saying goodbye,' I say simply.

She nods briskly and turns her back on me. 'Come in,' she says. I follow, ever the dutiful daughter-in-law. 'Cup of tea?' she offers over her shoulder.

'Please,' I reply, automatically remembering how this quickly became the only thing we were comfortable doing together. We must have drunk gallons of tea in each other's company in those early weeks. The act of making and drinking it disguised the awkwardness of our new relationship; that of grieving mother and widow.

We tried to unite, we really did. We kept trying because it didn't make any sense for Jackie and me to turn away from one another when we needed each other the most. I mean, she was my surrogate mother, a woman so warm and loving and unencumbered by the awkwardness of my own, that when I first met her I remember joking to Ryan that I fell in love with her. As a wife I wanted to be the most important woman in Ryan's life. But, understandably, as his mother, so did Jackie. It became a silent battle between us – one so subtle and nuanced that Ryan didn't even realize what was happening. Nor did we. We put down our swords when he was diagnosed with cancer and nursed him together. We thought we'd be able to share our pain, help each other through it, but at times we just seemed to make it worse for each other. Jackie resented me for taking Ryan away from her. I resented her for never really letting him go. We both wanted him, but afterwards, what we were left with was each other. And it wasn't good enough.

Now I look at this woman, this *mother*, and I am filled with shame. She gave birth to my husband, she carried him and she will carry her grief for the rest of her life. I want to hug her, to say I'm sorry and that I miss her. But I know it will be no comfort. It's not me she wants. She'd swap a million hugs from me for just one more with her son.

As I walk through the hall to the kitchen I force myself to face what I couldn't for so long. That he is here. He was always here. I remember going back to our London flat after he died to collect all our stuff, wondering why I couldn't feel him there. I wanted to be flooded with memories of our life together. I lay in bed begging him to make me feel like he was still with me. But he didn't come. Even when I bought the little Victorian semi – the house by the sea he'd always dreamed of coming back to – and filled it with our stuff, he wasn't there. But being by the sea in Leigh felt right. It was the place we'd fallen in love – and the place he'd *always* loved. Because I realized that this town was his first love as much as I was.

Now here, here in this glorious house with sea views, on an expensive street in a desirable seaside town, in the house his dad built, in the place he grew up, here is where I see him. My Ryan. He smiles at me from every wall and mantelpiece, the kitchen dresser, the table where he'd spend hours marking, the annual school photographs all the way up the stairs. He's there on the sofa in the lounge, where we hung out together as newlyweds, and where he lay for those few weeks before Charlie advised us it was time to go to the hospice. He's in the garden, where he used to play football with his brother before cancer struck – and after, where he'd sit when he wanted to breathe the fresh sea air that he loved so much. He called it his special medicine. 'Better than any amount of chemo they've given me, Molly.' He'd smile and he'd hold my hand tightly, tilt his head back, close his eyes and breathe in and out, in and out. And I did what I always did – I counted each one. I wished I could count on forever but I knew that, just like our kisses, as the number of his breaths increased, so the number we had left decreased.

I walk into the kitchen, still clutching the flamingo, and there she is. Jackie's back is to me and she is filling our mugs with boiling water. I know she's crying because I can see her shoulders shaking. I walk over to her and put my arm around her. Her body is taut.

'I'm so sorry, Jackie', I say.

'I still miss him so much, Molly,' and she folds into my arms, sobbing, like a baby.

'I know, I know,' I whisper. 'I wish I could make it better and I feel so guilty, Jackie. For not being a comfort to you. For still being here, for reminding you ...'

'Don't!' She grabs my arm so tightly it hurts. 'Don't ever feel that, darlin'! Ryan would be so ... bleeding ... furious if he heard you say that. And as for this ...' she presses her hand softly against my stomach, '... I *am* happy for you, darlin'. You'll be such a wonderful mother. It is the best thing in the world.' She pauses and looks at me. 'Do you have a picture?' she says quietly. I nod and pull my purse out of my bag uncertainly, open it and carefully remove the grainy black-and-white scan of my baby that I took down from my wall earlier.

She takes it and I'm mortified when she sobs again. 'He would have made a wonderful dad,' she wails, and I clutch her hands.

'Don't Jackie ... I don't want this to cause you any more pain.' I take the scan, hug her, and moments pass, and a lot of other things pass. We're holding each other but we're both letting go at the same time. 'Jackie,' I say at last, 'there's something I think you should have.'

Her brow wrinkles as I hand her the flamingo, and she holds it and looks up at me and smiles, but she also looks confused and hurt.

'But I gave this to you, darlin', it's yours. Yours and Ryan's ...'

I put my hand over hers before she can hand it back. And we both clutch that ugly pink plastic light, and with my hand still over hers, I begin to speak.

'I want you to have this, Jackie, because Ryan once told me that it was his most beloved possession. He wanted it with him at the end. And this is his end. Here, with you. So you see, the flamingo has to stay with him. I thought perhaps you could put it in the garden, where we buried his ashes, it's where they both belong . . .'

Jackie nods and for a moment I see a glimmer of the woman I met over a decade ago. And as I put my arms around her one final time, I feel not just hers around me – but his too, and he's wrapping me up, telling me it's OK. That it's OK for me to go.

The Take That Kiss

Ryan says that one of his greatest 'wins' didn't come on the
football pitch, but the other week when we were watching MTV
and I finally conceded defeat and admitted that Take That have
always been the soundtrack to our love story. Those five boys
have been with us all along. They even split up, just like us ('Love
Don't Live Here Any More') and came back together, stronger
than ever! ('Back For Good')

'GOD, Ryan Cooper is SUCH a prat,' I say, lazily sticking two fingers up at the group of lads who have just walked past us on The Broadway, as they throw lewd remarks in our direction. I turn my back on them and ignore the shouts of 'Fridgey, fridgey FRIDGIIIIID', that they're now throwing in my direction. How mature. All that money their parents are paying on private school has made them so eloquent and erudite that they're practically modern-day Shakespeares. NOT.

'I think he's WELL hot,' Casey says, hitching her navy skirt a little higher and playing with her school tie as she peers around me and grins lasciviously at them.

'Look at his legs – only he could make school sports shorts look sexy. *Literally everyone* in school thinks he's fit.'

'Not me,' I sniff. 'Just because he's OK-looking, is doing his A levels, has got a Golf GTI and is good at sport, everyone treats him like he's Leigh-on-Sea's very own Brad Pitt. He's just so . . . so . . .' I am struggling to find an appropriate put-down '. . . *Essex*.'

Casey arches one dark, pencilled eyebrow at me. I know she's been trying to perfect this expression for years and I have to give her credit, it has just the right amount of nonchalance and know-ingness to make her look cool.

Casey and I are BFFs because we're not your typical Essex Girls. We don't conform to the usual stereotypes. She made me realize that I did fit in. With her. And that's made life pretty good, actually. We're soul sisters, we do everything together. She's my support system, my partner in crime, my confidante. We laugh, cry and dream together. I protect her and she entertains me. We are inseparable. Life would be *unthinkable* without her.

Just then a low, smooth gust of a voice with a familiar sharp

Essex breeze drifts past my neck, causing the hairs to stand up on end.

Oh God, Ryan's staring at me.

Ryan tilts his head and looks at me appraisingly. 'You're Westcliff girls, right?' he says with an interested smile.

'Wow, how did you know *that*?' Casey says enthusiastically as she puts her hands on her hips and pushes out her tits.

I look at her incredulously. We're wearing the school uniform for God's sake. I roll my eyes and somehow catch Ryan Cooper looking at me with an infuriatingly sexy smirk.

'Molly Carter, ain't it?' he says.

OK, *now* I'm kind of impressed. I have never spoken to the guy and have no idea how he knows my name. I mean, everyone knows Ryan Cooper, he's practically a celebrity in these parts. And everyone knows Casey, thanks to her working at her mum's caff. But me? I'm not sure why a Year Ten Westcliff girl would be on *his* radar.

'I've seen you down at the Yacht Club? With your mum and dad?'

Oh great. All the teenagers in Leigh-on-Sea go to the Yacht Club, but mainly to hang out on the top deck of the *Bembridge* and snog. Not have dinner with their parents. Worse, their *God Squad teacher* parents. Garghh.

Casey stifles a giggle and I prod her in the ribs. Hard.

'Your mum was my form tutor last year!'

Brilliant. I picture my feet as a Hanna Barbera-style cartoon drill and will them to rotate me into the ground.

'That's nice,' I mutter, stubbing out my cigarette with my biker boot.

He leans forward and my breath catches in my throat at his proximity to my lips. 'Don't worry, she didn't give away any deep, dark secrets.'

'That's because we don't have any,' I shoot back, looking up at him defiantly. 'Not when we've given ourselves to *Jesus*,' I add with a sarcastic flourish.

Ryan looks at me longer than is entirely necessary and I momentarily lose myself in his gaze. His irises are like ever-changing ice-blue glaciers and suddenly I feel like a lone explorer who is in perilous danger.

'I find that hard to believe,' he murmurs. His lips are pure Johnny Depp; pillowy clouds on the perfect horizon that is his face. I glance at Casey, she's leaning back against a wall, a look of unbridled astonishment on her face. She's bent one bare leg up against it and Alex is lighting her cigarette for her whilst looking over at us. I look back at Ryan. He is smiling disarmingly at me.

Suddenly I feel very exposed. Like he knows exactly what I'm thinking.

'I know what you're thinking,' he murmurs, and grazes my arm with his hand so a volt of longing shoots up my body.

Kiss me.

Shit, stop it. Focus Molly, for God's sake.

'I didn't shout those things at you just then, you know,' he whispers urgently, glancing at Alex who is being pawed by Casey who has, in the seconds that I've looked away, hitched her skirt up to an even more alarming Julia Roberts in *Pretty Woman* height. It is her current favourite film and I've had to physically restrain her several times from buying wet-look thigh-high boots from a dodgy shop in Southend. I resist the urge to reach across and tug her skirt down for her. Girls like us need to use our wit and our wiles to attract men. Failing that, we need to wait for our transformation moment. Which could be *years* away.

'I had a go at them for shouting at you,' Ryan continues. 'I know they're my mates an' all but they can be idiots sometimes.'

I shrug as if to say, *like I care*, and fold my arms as I gaze at him unflinchingly. I can't help but notice how his eyes have now darkened to a glorious shade of dark-wash denim.

'So,' he says, leaning in towards me, 'do I get a reward for defending a damsel in distress? I reckon a kiss is the going rate, yeah?'

'Er, who said I was in distress?'

He parts his curtains and his plump, pouty lips. 'C'mon, babe, gimme a little something to work with here, won'tcha? I've wanted to talk to you for a while,' he says softly. 'I've seen you around town and, you just stand out, you know?'

Stand out. Hmm, that's one way of saying, 'You're a freak'.

A nice way of saying it.

I look down at my biker boots, scuffing the toes against the ground, and I pull my army-surplus jumper sleeves over my fingers as he stares into my eyes and grins. I open my mouth and close it again.

Shit, my wit has totally disappeared.

'Well, er, I'll take that as a compliment, I guess,' I mumble. 'But I'm not sure the same can be said about you ...'

I can't believe I'm talking to *Ryan Cooper* like this. Mr Pin-Up Popular not being gushed over by a girl for a change. 'What I mean is,' I clarify, examining my fingernails for added dramatic indifference, 'you're just another Leigh-on-Sea lemming.' I point back to his group of mates who are standing in a circle, admiring their Nike Airs, their identikit boy band-esque haircuts flopping in their faces.

'But Molly,' he protests, shaking his head at me so that I find myself hypnotized. 'I'm not like them,' he says firmly.

'HAAA!' I guffaw helplessly. He looks affronted as he steps back from me, thrusting his hands deep into his Adidas shorts pockets.

'Why is that funny?' he says defensively, shifting from one Nike-clad foot to the other and biting his lip till it turns as red as a cherry Tunes throat lozenge.

I shrug dismissively. 'Because you and your mates *are* all the same. You wear the same clothes, hang out at the same places, like the same music, fancy the same girls, smoke the same brand of cigarettes—'

'I don't smoke,' he interrupts. There is a pause as he eyes me meaningfully. '*Or* fancy the same girls.'

For the first time in my life I'm speechless. Is Ryan Cooper coming on to me?

'C'mon, Molly,' he drawls. 'Don't make me beg in front of me mates, it'll ruin my cred! What do you need me to do? Serenade you or something?'

I fold my arms and raise my eyebrow expectantly, knowing that he wouldn't dare. He wouldn't make a fool of himself like that for me.

'Oh well,' he says, 'I did warn you . . .' He clears his throat and launches into the chorus of 'Sure' by Take That, complete with the classic side-step-and-click dance move.

Casey is looking on in astonishment but Alex distracts her by putting his hand on her arse. I fold my arms and watch Ryan's performance, praying that I'm not blushing, my mouth twitching as I try desperately not to smile.

'Well?' Ryan pants as he grins at me at the end of the chorus.

I don't know what is happening here, or why, but I know enough about the kind of boy he is, and the kind of girl I am, that this can only be a dare. And I'm not getting sucked in. No way.

I think for a millisecond then know exactly what I'm going to do. I clear my throat and launch into the chorus of 'Loser' by Beck. I reckon that'll shut him up. The part of the song I sing seems interminably long but once I finish moshing in front of him, I look up and he's just standing there grinning at me (that grin is *infuriating*!).

Then he leans forward and whispers, 'Molly Carter, you're a challenge. And I warn you, I don't give up on challenges easily.' And he turns and he walks away, taps Alex on the shoulder and heads off down The Broadway towards Cliff Parade, without looking back.

'OHMYGODDD!' Casey bounces over and squeals in my

ear, apparently oblivious to my anger. 'Can you believe what just happened? Did you see me and Alex? Oh my GOD, he's just GORGEOUS. It totally felt like I was in a movie. I'm sure he was about to kiss me, Molly! That was the best moment of my life EVER!'

I zone Casey out as we head towards my house, trying not to think about Ryan sodding Cooper for another second.

Or how badly I wanted him to kiss me.

The Eternal Kiss

They say you can't change people, well I don't believe it. I am not the same person I was when I met Ryan (thank God!) and I'm not the same since he died either. I am better. I am better because I loved him and was loved by him. He taught me to be the very best person I could be.

Ryan left a mark on me that nothing can erase, no matter who or what comes after. I imagine this mark like an imprint of his lips on mine, a whisper of a lost love that reminds me that I am and always will be loved. No matter what.

In that sense, once again, Ryan has done, without trying, what I spent the months of his illness desperately trying to do. He has given me a kiss that will last forever.

The marquee billows merrily on The Green in front of Cliff Parade; a big, showy splash of white against the pure blue backdrop of sky and sea.

'It's perfect,' Ryan says, and I bend down over his wheelchair and kiss him softly on his bare head, tucking his blanket over his suit trousers that are flapping around his legs like a stilt walker's. It had been touch and go whether he'd be well enough to make it today. Ryan even said while we were all gathered around his bed the other day, that if he wasn't well enough, at least the marquee wouldn't go to waste – his 30th birthday party could turn into a wake instead. None of us laughed – and nor did he. I think he's finally realized that the joke has worn thin.

The staff at Haven's hospice, where he moved to three weeks ago, told us to be prepared that he wouldn't see the week out, but then Charlie said that last week too – and the month before when we were in London and he had to ask me to sign the Do Not Attempt to Resuscitate form. He's not officially our Macmillan nurse any more since we moved back here, but he's kept in touch and even came to see Ryan yesterday, which was so nice of him. And I know Ryan appreciated it; I could literally see him fighting back tears, his eyes looked brighter, and his face took on that determined expression I always saw when he was on the football pitch. The doctors were all amazed but I think they have learned never to underestimate Ryan Cooper. Charlie said he's a winner off the pitch as well as on.

The staff have been completely wonderful with him and Ryan is much happier since we moved there. We only managed two weeks at Jackie and Dave's, not because they didn't do a great job of looking after us, they did. But Ryan was deteriorating fast and it was all a bit too intense; Jackie and I were both vying to be top nurse. I knew I should be the bigger person and let his mum look after him, but looking after Ryan has become so much a part of who I am and our relationship, it was hard to let go, no matter how much I wanted to. So there were a few awkward battling-over-boiling-vegetables moments (that he refused to eat anyway, getting his dad to go out for McDonald's instead) and running to get his meds first from the bathroom. We realized how ridiculous we were being when we were fighting over them in front of the sink. We both simultaneously looked at the mirror, at our harried, desperate faces that were contorted into comically determined expressions, and we both burst into laughter – and then tears and had a big hug. At that point we started taking it in turns.

It was Ryan's choice to come here though, three weeks ago. He's resisted this route for so long, but once we knew the cancer had spread to his brain he suddenly became frightened and he said he wanted to be in the best possible position for what he called 'the penalty shoot out'. This is his way of referring to the end because each morning was another chance at staying in the match. Coming up to the hospice has given him his space and his dignity back – and his appetite.

'No offence, Moll,' he said. 'But the food here is like a hotel compared to yours and mum's cooking!' I didn't tell him it's also partly to do with the dexamethasone steroids he's on now (they make him crave sweet food). And I don't underestimate this remarkable place and the wonderful care they are giving him. The staff are fantastic, it's an incredible place, at a beautiful location with gorgeous sea views. Him being here means I can just be his wife, not his nurse. Even Jackie seems more laid-back, quieter and more tranquil since he's been here. I think she has finally accepted and dealt with what is happening. And we are a team now: she, Dave, Nanny Door, Carl, Lydia and me. Not a team of carers, A Family Team: 'Cooper United' Ryan calls us. We laugh together with Ryan, when we're playing board games in his room, or watching movies or playing video games, then we cry together when we're grabbing a coffee, or going home to get an hour's kip. Not that I leave Ryan often. They let me sleep here with him, on a bed they've made up next to his. We fall asleep holding hands every night, just like we've always done.

And as for this party, I always knew he would make it. Ryan has never missed a party in his life and he wasn't about to start now. He was never going to let cancer ruin his chance of going out on top. He's decided to have it here, on The Green on Cliff Parade, because he loves the view and because he wanted anyone who knows him to feel welcome to wander in. I know most of the town will turn up for this afternoon event (Ryan is too tired in the evenings), not just because of the free bar – as Ryan quipped to me earlier – but because they all want to celebrate with him in style. Every time I go into a shop to buy a newspaper, or grab a coffee and his favourite carrot cake, I'm asked about him. I overhear conversations in coffee shops, old students talking about Mr Cooper, who hush when they see me come in. I feel like the whole town is holding its breath and I just hope we can all try to forget, just for a few hours, and give him the party of his life. Literally.

'Are you ready?' I say, and he looks up and nods, taking a deep inhale from his oxygen cylinder – something he needs around the clock now. The excitement is evident in his eyes. His wheelchair has been adorned in yellow Southend United coloured streamers and balloons by Charlie and Carl. It's the perfect colour for my Ry, sunny and bright. He said it matched his new, jaundiced skin tone and round head (the steroids have caused something called 'cushionoid', which is an altered, rounded face shape). I always said looking at him makes me feel like the sun is perpetually out. Now he says that he looks just like it.

'Let's go then,' I say, and I start wheeling him towards the entrance of the marquee, which is harder than it looks in pink

4-inch heels and my film premiere Bacofoil dress. Ryan insisted that the dress code should be 'Essex Excess' and judging by the amount of leopard print, hot pink, feathers and white I can see – people have utterly embraced the theme – by wearing their everyday clothes.

As we approach the entrance, Ryan looks up at me cheekily.

'It's rare you've ever had to roll me *in* to a party, eh Moll?' he says.

I put my hand on his shoulder. 'The amount of champagne I'm planning on drinking I'll be expecting you to roll *me* out,' I reply. 'So make sure you save some room on that wheelchair for me.' And I kiss him on the head.

I go to push him in but Ryan puts his hands on the wheels to stop them and looks up at me. 'Thanks for doing all this, babe.'

'Your mum did most of it, Ry,' I reply modestly, 'you know she loves a project to get her teeth into. This birthday party is going to be bigger and blingier than our wedding!'

'I didn't mean the party,' he says quietly. And then he grins up at me and I'm hit by a wave of love for my brave husband. 'Come on then, what are we waiting for?' he says. I swallow, smile and start pushing him inside.

The crowd hushes as we appear in the doorway. As I expected, the town and its mother, daughter, father and brother have turned out for Ryan. There seems to be at least 300 people cramped into this beautiful marquee, like exotic butterflies in an enclosure. Ryan slides a hand over his shoulder and I take it and squeeze it just as he raises the other and waves.

'Get on with it, bro,' Carl heckles, 'you ain't the Queen!'

The crowd reacts by cheering, three big 'hip hip hoorays!' that are fuelled by the moment and emotion and which seem to carry my husband into his party as if he's on a crest of a wave.

I smile as Jackie comes over and I let her wheel him off and show him what she's done. He glances back and smiles at me to let me know that he's still with me really. The marquee is filled with beautiful, bright-pink flowers (in her eyes there is no other colour). The big family photos from their house have been printed and hung all around, the tables on the edge of the dance floor have a picture of Ryan from every year of his life from the day he was born. There are hundreds of helium balloons in the shape of the number 30 bouncing around the place. Kids are running around, caterers are laying out a buffet banquet fit for a king, and the bar is bustling as the barmen try to pour champagne faster than people can drink it – and discovering this is physically not possible. We're in Essex after all.

I smile and nod as I take it all in. Jackie has done an incredible job. I have already told myself that this is her day, her moment to show off her son and she deserves to enjoy it, so I am going to step back.

I smile as my mum and dad come over and stand either side of me, clutching their glasses of champagne as they gaze out at the party. I love that they have tried to follow Ryan's dress code. Mum is wearing her pink cardi from the wedding. I can't help but wonder if she has replaced the sequinned words 'Mother of the bride' to 'Mother of the widow-to-be', but then check myself and also mentally curse Ryan for my inability to stop making inappropriate death jokes. The cardigan is buttoned up over a (racy for her) fuschia knee-length dress. She is even wearing a pair of little white heels. Dad is wearing a zipped-up anorak with a pair of jeans (I have never seen him in denim. Ever) and some white trainers, like so many of the local lads do. He's even combed his comb-over forward so it covers his brow. But he still looks more like a trainspotter than an Essex boy, bless him.

'Mum, Dad, you look great. Properly Essex!' I say with a smile.

'Nonsense, Molly,' Mum retorts. 'We look like the Queen and Prince Philip going to a *The Only Way Is Essex*-themed party thrown by Prince Harry!'

I laugh then, and they slip their arms around me. I feel like they're flanking me to give me strength. My mum kisses my shoulder, a light peck but it is enough. My dad rocks on his heels a little and stares up at the draped roof as if it is a piece of beautiful architecture. It feels nice, my little family unit. I realize that we fit, the three of us. Despite my attempts to be different, to see more, do more, I am more their daughter now than I've ever been. And I am proud of it.

We stand there in our easy silence, watching the party from the outer edge, as we Carters do. Ryan keeps looking for me, making a connection to me with a wink or a wave or a smile, and I keep my radar on full alert to know where he is at any given time, who he's talking to and what he's doing. I smile fleetingly as I remember the early days of our relationship when I was so insecure that I used to do that in order to check for predatory girls who might be after my boyfriend. Now I long for those days. I'd put up with Angelina Jolie flirting with him rather than have the hand that we've been dealt.

Lydia bounds over with Beau, who is dressed in a white suit and has shades and a spiky hairdo. He looks like a mini version of Carl on his wedding day. It's so cute. Lyd kisses Mum and Dad, who squeeze her tightly, and then they slip off to get a drink from the bar and have a sit down. Lyd rests her hand over her pregnant tummy and exhales. 'Bloody 'ell, my feet are killing me,' she moans.

Then she omits a little cry as she puts her pink manicured hand over her mouth. 'Oh Molly, I'm sorry, I wasn't thinking.' Her eyes fill with tears and she flaps her hand in front of her face as Beau runs circles around me shouting, '*Neeeyow*'. 'I'm sorry,' she says, as the tears stream down her face, 'it's the bleedin' hormones.'

'It's OK, Lyd,' I glance over at Ryan who is holding court in the middle of the dance floor. 'Honestly, it's OK.'

'You're incredible, Molly,' she says tearfully. 'I wish I was half the woman you are. I don't know how I'd deal with what you've had to . . .' I see her look over at Carl, who has his arm flung around his brother and is in the middle of doing some double-act joke, just like they always have done. I know she is imagining Carl in Ryan's wheelchair. Just as all the wives and girlfriends are doing here. 'I just don't think I could cope.'

'Yes you could, Lyd,' I reply with a smile. 'Us Coopers are made of strong stuff you know.'

She looks up at me and nods, smiling through a veil of tears. 'You know Carl and I are always here for you, don't you? Whenever . . . you know . . . you need us, we will always be there, OK?' She grasps my hand and squeezes it. 'I see you as my sister, Molly, and I always will.'

I don't have the words to tell her that I have always wanted a sister, so I just nod.

She gently redirects Beau so he zooms off in a different direction and we both stand in companionable silence as we watch our husbands from afar. I remember how as a teenager, and even as his girlfriend, I was so in awe of Ryan's confidence and ability to talk to anyone, to command attention without seeming to do anything at all. He's gliding around the room in his wheelchair now, taking time to talk to every single person, making them feel like they are the only person in the room he wants to be with before he waves someone over to join them, then moves seamlessly on to a different group. I know he's determined to talk to everyone and it makes my heart hurt to think why. It also makes me feel like I've lost him already. I'm so used to it being just him and me.

'Molly,' Lyd whispers, and she nods towards the entrance of the marquee. 'I think there's someone here to see you, babes.'

I look over and see a vision in sunset orange standing uncertainly, looking like the awkward teen that I seemed to know better than I knew myself all those years ago. Her eyes flit uncertainly around the room, at the people who are now dancing, at Ryan's parents who are doing a great job of putting on 'The Cooper Show' by the bar, and then at Lydia and me.

We stand there for a moment, just staring at each other. And it feels like there is so much distance between us; no, not distance, time. I know that we are both rewinding back, back to our school days, to that first time she slipped into the seat next to me and we became BFFs, to the years spent practically living at each other's houses, our nights spent lying awake dreaming of what our future held for us. That blinkered determination of youth that nothing, no one, not *anyone*, no man, friend or job would ever, *ever* come between us. Then I glance across the room and I see Ryan looking at me. He smiles and nods and I know then that he asked her to come today. I know that he has done this for me.

And at that point I walk forward. I walk slowly and deliberately towards her and as I get close I can see that she is crying.

I stand in front of her, wondering what the hell I'm supposed to say, if anything at all. I can't hug her or say anything to make her feel better. I don't have the words and I'm not sure there is anything to be said. I see Ryan over by the DJ and just at that moment I know exactly what to do. I hear the opening intro to the song and I kick my heels off, then I slip my arm through hers and we walk towards the dance floor with Casey hopping on one leg as she takes off one of her heels and then the other. And then we walk into the centre and we begin to bounce, jumping up and down with our arms in the air to 'Electric Dreams', not taking our eyes off each other as we sing our own lyrics that we wrote a lifetime ago.

And that's when the party really begins.

I am outside, clasping my champagne glass, watching the sunset over the water and enjoying listening to the party within when Carl rushes out.

'There you are, Moll, I need you in here now!'

'What?' I gasp, flinging my glass to the ground and going to run inside but Carl grabs my arm.

'Don't worry! Sorry, Ryan's fine. You just need to come inside – come on. Bring your glass ...'

We walk back into the marquee and I see Ryan standing with a laptop in front of a projector screen, holding a microphone. I glance at Carl and he nods and pushes me forward as Ryan begins to speak.

'I just wanted to say thanks to everyone for coming to this party today. It's been brilliant – and I really want to thank my amazing mum, the unstoppable Jackie Cooper, for putting on such a brilliant bash. She is one in a million and is the best mum in the world.' Everyone claps in agreement and Jackie squeals and covers her face with her hands as Dave hugs her.

'Obviously, I've loved this party being all about me – I'm an Essex boy so being the centre of attention is something that's never been a problem.' A ripple of laughter and Ryan takes a deep breath. 'But I can't let you all stumble drunkenly home' – another swell of mirth – 'without drawing some attention to my beautiful wife.'

I bow my head as everyone turns and looks at me. Really looks at me for the first time in a long time. 'You probably know that Moll and I have been together since we were practically teenagers. And if I'd had my way—'

'And a better kissing technique!' heckles Carl.

'Yeah, thanks for that, bro,' Ryan calls back. 'Anyway, as I was saying, if I'd had *my* way, she would have been my girl as soon as she'd been legal.' Another swell of laughter rises in the room. 'Sorry for being crude, John, Pat!' Dad nods and puts his hand up as if to say 'That's OK, son' and Mum wags her finger at him, a flush of embarrassment rising up her neck. 'But I just want everyone to know that this girl, this amazing woman, took my heart and soul with her first kiss. She's taught me so much about love, life, culture – although she still hasn't convinced me that The Beatles are better than Take That, John!' My dad laughs and raises his hand as Ryan takes mine. 'She's also taught me a different way to see the world, and showed me what a beautiful place it is. On our first date she told me, "Life isn't about the destination, it's about appreciating the journey." I look at him, astonished. How does he remember this stuff? 'And I can't leave here . . .' He pauses and looks at me and I know that he doesn't mean this party. '. . . I can't leave here without showing her just how much I've loved taking the journey with her.'

He nods at Carl who presses play and an image of the famous sculpture *The Kiss* and the words 'What's in a kiss?' appears on the screen underneath.

Then the strains of Take That's 'Greatest Day' comes out of the speakers as a photo of Ryan and me with our first kiss at The Grand fills the screen. The next shot is of Gustav Klimt's painting, then *Lady and the Tramp*'s doggie lips meeting over a bowl of spaghetti, which cuts to the photo of Ryan and me from a night out at Ugo's on The Broadway, jokingly recreating the pose from the film.

I laugh through my tears as I marvel at how Ryan has put on film a complete, beautiful, big-screen version of what I began with my blog but couldn't finish. He has included every single photo I collected and mixed our kisses in with other more famous ones, so in one frame we appear alongside Audrey Hepburn and George Peppard in *Breakfast at Tiffany's*, and in the next we are in split-screen, kissing on the red carpet alongside a picture of Tom Cruise kissing Katie Holmes.

As the video plays out this beautiful, lovingly crafted, clever, funny, embodiment of our entire relationship, Ryan lifts up his lips to me and we kiss, softly, sweetly, and it feels like transferring a piece of each of our souls to the other. He moves his lips away from me and nods at the screen and I look up to see the last shot, a freeze-frame of Ryan Cooper, my Ry, on a beach, on our honeymoon staring straight at my camera and blowing me a kiss.

I can hear the sobs behind us, quiet, controlled tears of our friends and family who have been in mourning for the past five months and who know that this party is Ryan's way of saying goodbye.

'This is for you,' Ryan murmurs to me, and I turn my back on the crowd as I look at him, at my beautiful husband, the love of my life, and then the rest of the room, the people, the town, our past, it all melts away. I sink into his lap, the arms of his wheelchair supporting my weight as I lie across him, so that it is like he is carrying me over the threshold. I wish he could carry me over the threshold to wherever he is going. I am crying, my arms weave around his neck, clinging to him, clinging on to him for dear life. Our dear life.

'I know you collected them all for me, Moll, and I love you more than ever for it, but you know, I already had every kiss. Every single one. Up here.' He taps his head. 'I saved them all.' He pulls me down towards him. 'And I need you to know that I wouldn't change a moment of what we've shared. Every up, every down, they've made us who we are.' He takes the disk out of the DVD player and hands it to me, but I can't move my hands from his neck so he places it in my lap.

'Watch it when I'm gone, not just to remember me, but so you always remember how unexpected, how magical, how life-changing love is. Do you promise you'll do that?' He stares at me and I nod. He brushes his thumb under my eyes, taking my tears with it and then drags it over my lips. I kiss it and close my eyes. 'And when love finds you again,' he says, 'which I know it will, I don't want you to watch this any more, OK? I want you to be ready to start a whole new collection of kisses.' I tuck my head in the crook of his neck and fresh tears trickle down it like a waterfall.

Out of nowhere, I am aware that Carl has come and he has

pushed us into the middle of the dance floor and is slowly pushing us in a circle so it feels like we're waltzing. I lift my head and look deep into my husband's, my Ryan's, deep-sea eyes, drowning in this moment with him. 'I've been happier than I could ever have imagined because you loved me, Molly,' he smiles.

And right there, in front of our friends, our family and the entire town, we have our final and best PDA. I know it's a kiss that no one – especially me – will ever forget.

I drive out of Leigh-on-Sea fully expecting to cry. When I moved back here after Ryan died, five years ago I needed to be where the essence of Ryan still was, to be near his family, his friends, his, no, *our* beloved hometown. The little neglected house I bought was just like the one we'd dreamed of bringing up a family in, and so I put the same love and care into nurturing it as I would have done our children, spending the first few months tenderly bringing it back to life in a way I couldn't do with my husband. The cats were my only company – but I was so glad of them. Ryan had bought them as a gift for me when he went into the hospice.

'Do you want me to turn into crazy Cat Lady?' I'd joked when the little balls of fluff had tumbled out of the box and onto my lap.

'No, Moll,' he'd smiled, taking my hand. I'd stroked his fingers, trying not to disturb any of the tubes. 'Harry and Sally are gonna make sure that you never forget that love can be found in the most unexpected places.'

Right, as always.

Ryan may never have lived in the little house I've just left behind, but for the first couple of years it felt as much his as mine. I couldn't pack away his stuff (not even the bloody flamingo) so I lined my new nest in the same way he would have done, with lots and lots of memories. I needed them next to me simply because he couldn't be.

And when I walked out of my front door I still felt him around me in the familiarity of being in the place where we'd grown up and fallen in love. I liked the fact that practically everyone I passed knew Ryan or at least knew of him. They'd smile at me, or sometimes stop and talk, and for that moment I felt like he was still here, that by being here I was keeping him alive for a little bit longer. In many ways, this little town kept *me* alive, too.

During the first year I'd leave the house at dusk every day – no matter the weather – and walk down to his favourite bench that was on the sea-view path, tucked just below The Green where he'd had his 30th birthday party a week before he died. I'd watch the violet clouds drift by, along with the boats, and I'd listen to the caw – or as Ryan had once pointed out – the 'cor' of the seagulls as they flew overhead ('They're Essex Seagulls!' he'd said). That was our time to talk. I'd tell Ryan all about my day, what I'd been doing to the house, the floors I'd stripped, polished and varnished, the colours I'd chosen for the walls, the 1950s kitchen table I'd found at an auction. I'd tell him about the conversations I'd had with Nanny Door, how his mum was coping, and I'd ask him advice on how I could cope with her better. I'd tell him about the grief support group I was going to, and about Casey's latest escapades. I'd talk about Beau and Gemma, and how Carl was doing, I'd tell him about The Shrimpers' latest footie results, where they were in the league and who they were playing next. I'd tell him I missed him, and that even though I still didn't think I could live without him, I was doing my best.

But even though that was the place I talked to him the most, the truth was Ryan wasn't there, he was all around me. I found comfort in the fact that his footprints were indelibly marked on the pebble beach and on The Broadway, on every street corner in fact. He was there in the schoolchildren's faces that passed me on their way home and who would never forget cool Mr Cooper. It comforts me to know that Ryan's legacy lives on in all those he taught both here and in Hackney. Who knows what they might achieve in their lives because of him? The pubs had his finger-prints moulded on their pint glasses. His footballing prowess was clearly marked on the local pitch. The sea breeze had his spirit. And, of course, his parents' house has his ashes. It was what he wanted and I understood. He said he didn't want me to feel tied to a place just because he was there. He wanted me to be free to travel the world if I wanted to. But he knew his parents would live in their house forever.

But it was hard living here too. It felt like everyone had unachievable expectations of me. Widows are meant to be old, to wear black, to be poised when it counts and to sob at expected moments, like at the funeral. But the one thing I remember about Ryan's funeral is that I didn't cry. Not one little bit. I just gazed at the casket, blaming Ryan for my lack of crying action.

'Hey, Cooper,' I said in my head. '*Look no tears. Just like you made me promise – now everyone is looking at me like I'm some unfeeling bitch. You happy now?*'

'*Ah, but Molly, you're* my *unfeeling bitch,*' I'd heard him say, which made me laugh. Which was also inappropriate behaviour at a funeral apparently.

I cried every day, *other* than the day of his funeral, for that entire first year. And I watched his film every day, too. Often more than once. And the same during the second year. On each of those 730 days I would be struck with a memory that made me weep with the pain of losing Ryan. And not just on the 'difficult' days, you know, birthdays, anniversaries, Sundays. Every single day and at any given time. In the toilet, on the train, in my bed, in the supermarket, into my cereal bowl, in a bar . . . there was no warning of when it would happen. It just did.

But the day we cremated him? I promised him that I would wear the brightest colour I could (my old yellow sundress I wore the night he kissed me in Ibiza – not just because it was his favourite, but because it's the Shrimpers' colour) and a smile. I wore bold red lipstick because I knew Ryan would like it (even if my mother didn't). And also because it meant I wouldn't have to kiss any distant relatives. (Or close ones, to be honest.) I could just wave my face in their general direction, without making actual contact. Because I didn't want to kiss anyone. His lips were the last that mine had touched; if I closed my eyes I could still feel his mouth on mine on that last day as he finally slipped away, and I wanted it to stay that way forever.

So on that bright September day in 2007, I stood in my citrus bright sundress, with my shoulders back and my head high, and I smiled. I smiled as I stared at the stained-glass window that was directly above his casket, imagining how I would photograph the way that the protracted sunlight shone through it, the colours glittering like jewels as they danced across the box where his body lay. I smiled through my eulogy and when his brother and the boys carried in Ryan's coffin to Take That's 'Rule the World' – just as Ryan had requested. I didn't even let my chin wobble. I just gripped my hands together and I smiled. I was like some sort of smiling machine. Then I smiled as I met all the hundreds of mourners. I smiled though my face ached and my heart hurt. And then I smiled some more. I said hello to everyone but all the time I was saying goodbye.

So yes, I said the hardest goodbye five years ago. But today, today is about saying hello.

I arrive at Southend Hospital at 4.45 p.m., just as I'd promised. And he's there waiting just as he'd promised, looking more like George Clooney than ever. I pull up in front of the reception and his serious, shadowed, night-shift face evaporates into a smile.

I smile back as I open the passenger door and he leans in, his arm resting on the door.

'G'day, Sheila,' he drawls, exaggerating his native Australian accent for effect.

'Taxi to Stansted for Doctor Prince?' I say in a broad Essex accent and pretend to chew on some gum as he slides in and kisses me.

'How are you doing?' he says gently, stroking my cheek. 'You haven't been doing too much, have you?' Chris gazes at me in concern and his hands weave their way from my waist to my front and he bends down suddenly so his face hovers over my bulging six-month bump. I smile as I rub my hands over it, marvelling at the glorious convex shape, the hard little mounds that hint at little feet, or elbows, or knees, the constant nudges – and the new weight – that never lets me forget just what I'm carrying.

'What's that you say, Minnie?' he says. We call her that, because Chris thinks she'll be a mini-me. He puts his ear to my tummy, listening and nodding intently. 'I should be looking after your mum? Oh, don't worry, I plan to do just that. For the rest of her life.' I think of the St Christopher Nanny Door gave me and that is tucked away safely in my handbag and I smile. Chris kisses my tummy and then the wedding ring that hangs on a chain around my neck because it will no longer fit on my swollen, pregnant fingers, and then my lips.

And I smile because I know he will look after me, but I also know that even though we're flying to Sydney today to start our new life together, he accepted that emergency shift when they called him up last night because he's a surgeon first and my husband second, and I'm completely cool with that.

I glance at Chris as I weave through the hospital car park, towards the exit. Lovely, calm, patient, strong, intense Chris, the 'prince' who came into my life three years after I lost Ryan, who cemented everything I'd learned from being with (and then losing) Ryan, and who made me realize that there is love after death. People often ask me if they think it was a psychological decision to marry a doctor after losing Ryan. I mean, he saves lives for a living and doctors aren't supposed to ever get ill themselves, are they? But to this I simply tell them that the only psychological decision I made the day I met him was to go out and get drunk in a bar. I wasn't looking for love, I think it came looking for me. Either that, or it was sent ...

It was eighteen months ago and I'd just found out that my collection of photographs called 'The Eternal Kiss' had been offered exhibition space at Gallery@Oxo. These were the photos I'd taken of young couples who had contacted me through my blog and who were living with a cancer diagnosis – and who wanted to make every kiss count. The messages had flooded in after I'd posted my final message and photo of Ryan and I, and I'd asked Christie if my blog could be continued by readers who were dealing with or had lost a partner to cancer. She had understood completely when I also said I wouldn't be returning to work after Ryan died. I couldn't face it. And besides, I had quickly decided that I was going to do what I'd promised Ryan.

I was going *to be*: happy, fulfilled and optimistic. I couldn't imagine falling in love again and I couldn't imagine going back to work either, so I started by picking up my camera and taking photographs again. It was on the first anniversary of Ryan's death that I had the idea. I wanted to thank Macmillan Cancer Support and the Haven Hospice in Leigh-on-Sea for everything they'd done. I started taking portraits for anyone who contacted me, either through the blog, or through the hospice. I didn't do it for money, or for my career, I did it because I wanted to give them a little of what Ryan had given me: a kiss that would last forever.

The photos were simple. There were no fancy settings, no beautiful backdrops, just these terminally ill cancer patients kissing and being kissed, just them and their love shining through the lens. I realized that this was what I have always loved about photography; everything we can't find the words to say, it snaps. Everything we feel, it frames.

The exhibition was shown in conjunction with Macmillan Cancer Support and the Haven Hospice – and so far has raised lots of awareness and money. After London, it travelled around the country. I still can't believe how successful it's been, with national and international press picking up on it – and now international exhibitions, too. It is a wonderful feeling to be finally doing some good, making sense of, not just my life, but Ryan's too. I honestly believe that it helped to heal my heart and gave me the confidence to do what I've always dreamed. And then I met Chris.

I pull over in the car park as I hear my phone by his feet. He grapples for it amongst the passports and tickets and the tinfoil-wrapped ginger biscuits I carry with me at all times. Minnie likes them.

'It's your BFF,' Chris says, handing my phone to me.

'Hey, Case,' I answer as I put it to my ear. 'How are you doing?'

'Still hung-over from your farewell party last night, trying to pretend you're not leaving as well as working out how long it'll take us to save up enough money to fly to Australia on his crappy nurse's and my PR's wage.' I hear her sniff. 'I'm not sure who is crying more about you both going to Oz, me or Rob.' I hear her pull away from the phone as a familiar voice chastises her, and I press speakerphone so Chris can be privy to the conversation between our two friends.

'I'm not crying! Do not let Chris think I'm crying . . .' Rob calls gruffly. Rob and Chris met at Southend Hospital and when Chris and I had been together a few months, we orchestrated a meeting between Casey and Rob by inviting her to a fundraising ball. Just as we'd predicted, they'd clicked and ended up getting married a month after us. Mia and I were bridesmaids. I think of the photo I have in my purse of that happy day and smile. He is a lovely bloke, a trainee nurse and a bit younger than us, well, eight years actually – but they are so happy. I mean, who says you can't fall in love in your early twenties? Not me . . .

'He so *is* crying,' Casey mutters. 'Listen Moll,' she says tearfully, 'I just wanted to say I love you, I miss you already, and I am *well jel* that Mia has stolen you away from me, and if you don't come back when that little bubba is born so I can dress her up in lots of super blingtastic Essex-style baby clothes I will have to just do something drastic and . . . have a baby of my own!' I laugh as her voice goes all muffled. 'Of *course*, I'm joking! I've already got one baby to look after . . .'

'Whoops,' she laughs when she comes back on the line, and I squeal as I hear Rob shout, 'Can we start practising now, Case?'

Ahhh, young love, I think fondly. Chris and I have moved on a bit further from that first flush of carefree passion. It's just who we are together. We *are* more serious, more grown-up. And I like that. No, I *love* it.

'Case, of course we will come back soon. *And* we can Skype all the time, remember?'

'OK, but I don't really get that Skype stuff, Rob will have to set it up,' she sighs. I chuckle. So much for feminism. 'Now just go will you, Molly? But don't say goodbye or I'll bawl, OK? Say . . . I know, say . . . see you tomorrow instead . . . too late, I'm bawling. Oh no, I'm going to look a right mess . . .'

'See you tomorrow, Casey,' I say but she's gone.

The sun is just starting to dip in the sky as I pull onto the motorway, tinting the clouds with a pale pastel-pink hue, the exact colour of the gorgeous little outfits that we've been given for our baby girl at our farewell party. True to form, my mum and dad gave us books. 'For the journey that you're about to embark on,' Mum had smiled as she'd handed the present to me.

I'd furrowed my brow at this. 'But we have lots of travel guides already, and Chris is Sydney born and bred so we don't nee—'

'These books aren't for *that* journey, dear,' she'd laughed as I ripped it open. In the precisely wrapped parcel was every baby-rearing manual you could imagine, downloaded onto a Kindle. 'Easier to travel with,' she'd explained proudly.

'*Finally*, a bit of technology you approve of!' I'd laughed, giving her and Dad a hug.

'Well, these are for you to read until your dad and I arrive in Sydney.'

Her hand had fluttered up to her throat, and then hovered under her eyes where she'd dabbed them with a handkerchief. 'We'll be on that plane as soon as she's born, and we will stay as long as you need us, won't we John?'

Mum and Dad finally took the plunge a few years ago and retired.

Dad had nodded. 'Ahhh . . . of course! Or at least, until we decide it's time to continue our own journey!' He'd popped his arm around Mum. 'Patricia and I have already planned our trip to New Zealand after our extended holiday with you. And then we're going to go to America. First to New York, and then your mother has agreed we'll go to Connecticut and see the original Constable painting of Hadleigh Castle that's on display in the Yale Center of British Art!'

'It's his way of bringing home with him on our travels,' Mum had said, and had gone to give Dad an affectionate tap on the wrist, but then had kissed him gently on the lips instead.

I turn on the radio and smile as I put my foot down and cruise along the motorway towards Stansted airport. The sky stretches out in front of me and through my windscreen I distractedly watch two aeroplanes soaring up and across the sky. Chris has dropped off to sleep beside me and I feel a tingle down my spine as my current favourite song, 'Paradise' by Coldplay, comes on the radio. The first time I heard it I felt like it was written for me, well, written for the girl I once was. I *did* expect the world, I *did* dream of paradise, and life *did* get heavy. I listen to the song, swallowing back the tears as Chris Martin's distinctive voice soars out of the speakers. And in my mind, so does another.

We did it then, she says. *We found happiness, after all.* Against all the odds

We did, I reply silently in my head, looking at Chris, and then looking up.

From now on, it's about looking upwards and onwards, just like both the men in my life have taught me to do: Ryan is the love I grew up with, and Chris is the love I'll grow old with. Up and on . . .

As that thought enters my head, I look up at the sky and watch the same two aeroplanes crossing paths, one ascending heavenward, the other cruising straight across, both leaving a white trail that crosses the other, like a kiss in the sky.

THE END. AND A NEW BEGINNING

Acknowledgements

Writing this book has taught me so much, not least to appreciate everyone in your life and to try and make every single kiss count. So here goes.

An eternally appreciative kiss to my fabulous friend of 18 years, Nick Smithers, who turned up one cold January morning when I was close to breaking point and stayed for the next three weeks to support me whilst I tore my hair (and my heart) out writing the final chapters of this book. He became my first reader, my early editor and my saviour. Nick, you know this book would not be what it is without your incredible input and your absolute certainty in me when my confidence was failing. Without you I'd never have seen the Light at the End of the Tunnel so thank you for being my ... wait for it ... 'Starlight Express'! And thanks too, to your wonderful mum, Freda Smithers, for bringing her district nursing wisdom to my manuscript and for putting me in contact with Rupert Deveraux who gave me such great insight into his job as a Macmillan Nurse, as well as the plight of both cancer patient and carer.

Big thanks to Macmillan.org.uk for their invaluable help and to the WAY foundation (www.wayfoundation.org.uk) an organisation that supports young widowed men and women as they adjust to life after loss. A special thank you to the members of that foundation who so generously shared their stories of losing a partner with me. I'm in awe of your strength and spirit.

Enormously thankful kisses to my amazing family and friends for putting up with my stress and tears for a year. If you notice that I hug you all a little tighter these days, now you know why. A special mention too to my fellow author and new friend Paige Toon for the weekly playdates/writing pow wows that have become the highlight of my week since moving to Cambridge. Here's to many more happy years of hanging out to come! Thanks too to Rachel Bishop for looking after my kids so wonderfully while I was writing this book and putting up with me coming downstairs all the time for essential tear-drenched cuddle fixes with them!

Big kisses to Juliet Sear for throwing open her home (not to mention her incredible cake shop, Fancy Nancy) in Leigh on Sea to me while I was researching and then writing the final chapters of the book, and for the brilliant and hilarious tour of the area you gave me with your sister and my great Uni chum, Nancy Maddocks. You guys helped make the book come alive in my head before I'd written a word.

Especially thankful kisses to my mind-blowingly incredible agent Lizzy Kremer and my amazing editor Maxine Hitchcock for believing I could write such a big story and then encouraging me to go even bigger. Oh, and then for extending my deadline when I realised, actually, I *couldn't* write it in that particular timeframe (babies, moving house and writing books really don't mix, do they?!) Your creative contributions were invaluable and I feel so blessed to work with you both, not to mention your wonderful teams at David Higham and Simon & Schuster.

And finally; endless kisses to my husband Ben and my beautiful children, Barnaby and Cecily, for never ceasing to inspire and encourage me and for making me laugh more and love more than I ever thought possible. You are my world.

Kiss Stories written by you

The Goodbye Kiss

We had shared many kisses.

The pecks on the cheek at the end of every walk home from school.

The raucously giggly drunken ones in the twilight of another girls' night out.

The supportive kisses of condolence at the news of a break up.

The congratulatory kisses at the news of new jobs, babies, engagement and a wedding.

The untold thank-you kisses for birthday, Christmas and 'no specific reason other than loving your best mate' presents.

So many kisses over such a long period of time, you take them all for granted.

But then there was the goodbye kiss. At the hospital. The one and only kiss she couldn't return.

It's that kiss that I shall never forget.

– Dawn Burnett

December 18th 1999. I was sitting at a bar in Soho. It was our work Christmas do and a large, obnoxious media mogul was boring me senseless with talk of himself and his enormous wealth. My apathy was apparent so he said something hurtful. I picked up my bag and ran out of the bar. Halfway down the street I heard someone call my name. It was Toby. The new guy at work. He grabbed my shoulder, turned me around and, to my horror, saw me in floods of tears. I can't remember what either of us said. Only the kiss. We were on the corner of Shaftesbury Avenue and Greek Street and I swear everything stopped. That kiss was amazing. That kiss changed my life.

– Emily Hynd

He was my best friend. We were accustomed to lazing about, listening to music in one of our bedrooms, but we'd found ourselves in a student club – and we didn't like it. We pushed our way through the crowd until we were free, ran a few paces further, and flopped down on the nearest seat, laughing. Without realising it, we had clasped hands in the foray. When we noticed, we looked at each other but we didn't let go and I let the words I'd silently practised spill out.

"Have you ever wondered what it would be like to kiss me?"

"Yes." No hesitation.

"Would you like to find out?"

"Yes."

We kissed. And it was wonderful.

– Lorna Murphy

Back in 1997, on an afternoon following a trip to Paris where my wife accepted my marriage proposal (second time lucky, don't think she believed I was serious the first time I popped the question), we went to the cinema in Oxford to see *Jerry Maguire*. There's a scene about halfway through when Tom Cruise plants a touching kiss on the top of Renee Zellweger's head at the breakfast table the morning after they've spent their first night together. Immediately before that scene happened I did the very same thing to my wife in the cinema (ie. planted a kiss on the top of her head – we didn't bring a breakfast table or any cereal into the cinema with us.) so you can imagine my surprise when the same thing happened on screen. Not quite sure what the word for it is (serendipity, perhaps?) but it certainly felt like fate was smiling down on us that day.

Anyway, we've recently celebrated our 13th wedding anniversary and I always reflect on that moment each time I see the film and smile fondly to myself.

– Andrew White

In February 2011 I attended a festival outside of London, it's a niche music event with a capacity of about 5,000. The event is held at Butlins in Minehead and attendees stay in the adjoining chalets. I was sharing a chalet with my best gal pal. Her boyfriend was arriving on the Saturday and was sharing a chalet with a stranger. That stranger turned out to be an incredible boy from Brooklyn and he and I hit it off immediately. We spent the entire weekend together and could barely stop kissing. Unfortunately Tuesday came around too soon and he had to fly back to New York. We stayed in contact via email until I met someone else in London and the contact fizzled out. In his last email he told me that the stars would realign someday and we would meet again.

Recently, I broke up with that person I had met in London. My friends persuaded me to book last minute tickets to a festival in Croatia. Against my better judgment I booked the trip. It was the first year of the festival, a 5000-capacity event set in Pula. It was the most beautiful place I have ever seen. On the first night the venue, an abandoned fort, was crowded with beautiful revellers. There were about 5 stages and people running everywhere. Early on the first night my friends and I began exploring the fort, and climbed down into the moat. As I stood there, looking around and taking everything in I turned back to find my friends and was face to face with my Brooklyn boy. Stunned, we embraced tightly, not wanting to let go. Pulling back to look at each other's faces, neither of us speaking, we leaned in and kissed each other repeatedly, only stopping to laugh and gaze at each other in amazement.

We spent the entire weekend together and now I'm planning my next trip to NY. I won't let him slip away again!! Under the stars in Croatia, it's certainly a kiss I'll never forget.

– Laura Hally

It's a beautiful sunny April afternoon in St. Mark's Square, Venice and I'm with Chris. He suggests we have our photo taken together and gives our camera to a passing tourist to take it. As she takes the picture he kisses me and asks me to marry him! Of course I said yes! We used the photo for our wedding invitation stamps and celebrate our 10th wedding anniversary this December.

– Cristina Bergman-Dye

A kiss I will never forget was with my first love. We had met at college, and gone to universities close to each other so we could still see each other at weekends. He was my world. My first week at uni was so hard, I had never missed anyone so much in my life. However, as with many first loves, we were young, we met new people and had experiences with them. Well, you know woman's intuition where you bascially know things won't work out . . . I had that towards the end of our first year.

I knew he had fallen out of love with me. And when he said he was driving mid week up to see me, I knew what was coming. He arrived and he said I could choose between having a break and splitting up. I chose split up – why drag out the pain longer, only to have him tell me later what I already knew was coming?

He wouldn't stay the night when I asked him to. I was distraught. And with my tear-stained face and big puffy eyes, he told me for the first time I was beautiful. I had to ask him for that one last kiss, I was still so in love with him and I needed to savour it just that one last time. We kissed and I just never wanted it to end. There was no overwhelming passion to it, just a sad acceptance that we knew we were going to part ways. But it was that moment I just wanted him to say, hang on, I still love you so much and I've made a terrible mistake. I thought, please, just take me back into your arms and let's be the way we were . . .

But he didn't, and my heart ached for months after.

– Vanessa Lee

on Sloane Street. Then I might sit in a little pavement café, like Bar Italia in Soho and have an espresso whilst I flick through my day's photos before going home. I call Ryan for a chat and then go out for tapas with the girls from work, or, if Casey's down, we head out to a cocktail bar and then a club. I miss Ryan, but I love this time too. It's a day in my week where I feel most like me.

Sometimes I am skewed by guilt that twists me over hot coals of doubt as I think about how I promised Ryan when we moved to London that I'd go back every weekend. But I can't. I find it too stifling. And one of us should be making the most of what London offers at weekends, right? And I only promised to go back because I thought once he was here he'd change. But it's like he's on a bungee umbilical cord and it keeps pinging him back to Leigh-on-Sea. Whenever I complain he reels off his 'Family comes first' speech to me.

And besides, absence makes the heart grow fonder. Everyone says so.

The truth is Ryan and I have realized we like doing different things. And that's OK. We still have plenty of things in common. Like ... our *history* for one and, well, you know, like ... Well, just plenty of other things.

I shake my head, wanting to focus on my weekend with Casey. 'We're going to *have fun!*' she squeals.

'I know!' I exclaim, clapping my hands excitedly. 'Why don't we go to Camden, have a mooch around, have a drink, then come back here and get ready to go out later! I'm so excited about having a Saturday night out! It's been way too long!'

'Sounds good,' Casey says, lying down on the sofa languorously. 'Just let me get over my hangover first. I was out late last night with the girls and came straight here.'

'Really?' I say, feeling a pang of unexpected jealousy. I guess that explains the outfit.

She leans across to the coffee table to pick up a glass of water I left there and slumps back, spilling some over the floor. I quickly get up and go to the kitchen to get a cloth, wiping round her feet whilst she lifts them up like a teenager. I suddenly have an image of my mum doing the same and I throw the cloth down on the floor in disgust.

Two hours later and Casey and I are wandering around Camden.

'No wonder you like it here,' Casey giggles, pointing at a stall that's selling fringed, mirrored sequin bags.

'Hey,' I say, picking a bag up and throwing it over my shoulder. 'I'll have you know these are the height of fashion these days! Kate Moss has got one just like that!'

'Only ten years too late for you then, babe,' Casey giggles. 'Didn't you have one when you were fourteen?'

'I can't help being ahead of my *time* darling,' I say faux pompously, and we burst into laughter. It's lovely spending time with Casey, but ever since Ry and I moved to London, and we see each other less, we're only really comfortable when we're talking about the past, drawing on shared memories of our childhood when the bond between us was so strong that we couldn't imagine anyone or anything ever coming between us. But the truth is, life has come between us. OK, I admit, my relationship with Ryan has contributed to that. I need to make more effort to spend quality time with Casey. But it's weird; I sometimes find myself feeling nervous about spending time with her. Like I may bore her, or that we will run out of things to say. Our lives have been so different for so long that it's hard to make more memories, maybe that's why we rely so heavily on the past, using it to fill the moments now when it becomes glaringly obvious that we just don't know each other as well as we used to. And in truth, half the time I can't keep up with her. If she's not working late, she's out partying. The girl keeps vampire hours and doesn't seem to need any sort of rest. I'm not going to pretend I don't get worried about her sometimes. But I feel like I have to worry about Casey, because no one else will.